TEMPEST
A story of last
ON RIVER
50 years of India
SILENT

Sandeep Khanna

olive turtle

NIYOGI
BOOKS

Published by
NIYOGI BOOKS
Block D, Building No. 77,
Okhla Industrial Area, Phase-I,
New Delhi-110 020, INDIA
Tel: 011-26818960, +91 7428978881
Email: niyogibooks@gmail.com
Website: www.niyogibooksindia.com

Editor: Shirsha Ghosh
Design: Nadeem Ahmed
Cover design: Ahlawat Gunjan

ISBN: 978-81-19626-23-6
Publication: 2025

Printed at Niyogi Offset Pvt. Ltd., New Delhi, India

To

those stars which

didn't become the sun

Contents

Preface

Tempest on River Silent is a story of India as I have seen it since the 1970s till present day. Overlaid on this factual story of India is a fictional account of a few imaginary characters, some of whom are portrayed as my friends. The third thread of the book is the spiritual lessons that I draw from the socio-economic changes in India and the tumultuous journey of my 'friends'. Perhaps the word 'spiritual' is too big for me to use, it would be more appropriate to describe them as lessons of life which I have tried to unravel alongside the growth of a nation and the life stories of my 'friends'. The three threads hang off each other and I narrate the book in first person. Thus, the book is both a story of India and a story from India's last 50 years.

Two characters—amongst several I have created in this book—hold the narrative together. These two 'study' with me at school and university, and then go onto their respective professional and personal lives with the backdrop of a modernizing India. I have sketched several day-to-day incidents of college, social and professional lives from India of the 1970s through the five decades, which I hope will resonate with the readers. However, telling a story over a long time span has meant that there are many fictional characters I have had to create in addition to the main and supporting protagonists. In order to make it easier for the readers, I have divided *Tempest on River Silent* into 4 parts and at the end of the book, provided a list of the 'main characters' without giving the story away.

Part I has come out more descriptive while Parts II, III and IV are more conversational and dialogue oriented. Also, the beauty and colours and ironies of India emerge in all their splendour as the two central characters, the main protagonist Devavratt and the supporting protagonist Eklavya, meet and embark on their respective journeys which I have covered in Parts II, III and IV of the book.

In order to put the narrative in perspective, I have made reference to factual historical, political and social events as well as ancient texts. I have used information on the internet for fact-checking as well as getting the dates right. I am thankful to these sources of immense information and knowledge. It will be clear to the readers as to the real-life thinkers, poets, sportspersons, statesmen and other achievers who have inspired the main protagonist in this book; I am too small to even thank these great personalities who would have inspired millions of people around the world and shall continue to do so.

I realise that my love for cricket might not be shared by all readers in same measure. I have accordingly restricted reference to the riveting game, though in two of the early chapters I have described a couple of school cricket matches mainly to build the character of the main protagonist.

All the characters, institutions, organisations and incidents in *Tempest on River Silent* are imaginary and bear no resemblance to any person, living or dead, or to any actual institution or organisation. Resemblance to any person or institution or organisation is purely coincidental and unintentional. This applies to people, institutions and incidents I have ascribed to myself as well, as the narrator in the book. If this story makes the readers nostalgic or reflective and brings a smile to your face, I would consider my few years' effort in writing this book well worth it! If the story as I have told inspires even one person, even though it's not necessarily my intention to do so, I shall feel immensely fulfilled.

Part I

Devavratt Pratap Rajvansh

In the March of 2015, work engagements took me to London. The central government in India had changed in May 2014 and a new government had been voted in with clear majority on the back of hope and promise of economic growth. The management consultancy firm I had joined a few years prior, focused on new market entries, was beginning to receive propositions of interest.

It was always exciting for me to travel to London. You could spend a lifetime there and not exhaust its sights and sounds. I had lived there in the late-1990s on a cross-posting when I worked at a multinational company. I had since travelled there on work and holidays half a dozen times. Images of England endured: waking up to the sound of cock-a-doodle-doo, the freshness of the mornings, the walk to tube station, traffic actually stopping to allow pedestrians walking across the zebra crossing, the cafes on the high street smelling of freshly brewed coffee, and smartly turned-out office goers who would avoid eye contact in the tubes and trains. In the late '90s, commuters would be immersed in newspapers and books, while now a decade and a half later, it was smartphones which ensured that eye contact was avoided and personal space maintained.

When the sun shines in England, gods of all religions must want to live there. When the sun doesn't shine, it is still a delightful place for mortals. The walk from Leicester Square to Big Ben past Trafalgar Square, the bursting of youthful energy at Covent Garden on the weekends, the lush green parks of London—Holland Park, Hyde Park, Green Park, St James' Park—beautifully manicured with colourful flowers and thick trees; the scores of west end theatres running musicals and plays, some for half a century; and Lord's, the home of cricket in the heart of the city. But London could be very lonely for those without partners or families. It was essential to be in love in London, else the branded stores on Oxford Street and High Street Kensington and the tranquil parks that dotted the entire city would lie waste. The black cabs, the London eye, the South Bank, the night clubs, the museums at South Kensington, the barbecue parties during summer, the fairy lights on trees and buildings during Christmas, the coal-lit fires in the living room, the very occasional snowfall, scones and strawberry jam with a cup of tea, the plumber visits to the central London flats, Sainsbury's and Tesco, and the motorways M4 and M1 which took city dwellers into the picture-postcard countryside. I looked forward to my visit to London in the March of 2015 for another reason as well. Devavratt had relocated there in the previous year.

I had known Devavratt Pratap Rajvansh since 1975 when we first met in class V in The Ashwath Public School on Max Mueller Marg in New Delhi. Amidst the crowd at the Heathrow Airport, I spotted the tall and not-anymore-so-lean figure of my friend. Still in his forties, he seemed to have aged more every time I met him. His hairline was mostly grey now and the lines on his face had become noticeable. His eyes were sunken though I could see them light up when he saw me. We hugged and quickly walked out to the mini cab Dev had hired.

'Welcome Sandeep,' he smiled gently and put his arm around me again, 'Good flight?'

'Flew the Dreamliner for the first time. You are looking nice Dev, despite all this grey.'

We rested our eyes on each other for a few seconds. Dev took one of my bags and enquired about well-being of my family, as we walked towards the mini cab he had hired. As we pulled out of Heathrow, and found our way on to the A4 towards Chiswick where Dev had rented an apartment, the radio of the mini cab was announcing the next day's weather as 'miserable' since rain was forecast. I couldn't help thinking how we used to enjoy the rain as children growing up in Delhi.

Rain is the finest celebration of nature in the torrid tropics. The leaves and grasses become young with life, branches of trees sway in majestic abandon, bare-bodied kids splash mischievously in puddles of water and release paper boats in them and people seeking shelter here and there smile at those temporarily sharing the same roof. The mountains in rain always seem to reveal the secret of life better than they do in other months, and the moon appears that much cleaner after a crisp night drizzle. The months of rain called the monsoons in India are a period of naughtiness and romance. Adolescent girls in villages to and fro on swings, poets get more prolific and a boy-girl association turns to love. The sound of rain on a subsistence farmer's broken roof in central India is as sweet as the music of *shehnai* on his daughter's wedding. The smell of rain-soaked earth is a fragrance bottled on our planet and sold in the heavens.

It was raining on the 15th of July, 1975, when I saw Devavratt Rajvansh for the first time. He had tentatively walked into our classroom, lean and reasonably tall for our age, with sunken eyes. He had seemed to be agonisingly sober. Now in the mini cab on A4, he said, 'Wish Eklavya could have come too.'

'I asked him, he is busy fleecing gullible clients.'

Dev laughed.

Dev and I had met Eklavya Malhotra during University and had become close friends over the years. As ever, Dev would always address everyone by their full given name. I was Sandy to most of my friends, not for Dev. Eklavya was Luv for all his friends, not for Dev.

Just before we turned off the A4 towards Chiswick I was reminded of Dev's old home where he used to live 10 years ago when posted in England. He had moved to India in between for a few years and was now back in London. I pointed to my right, 'Old home, right?'

'Yes, Grove Park,' replied Dev.

I remembered staying in that beautiful plush house on Staveley Road with a large ornamental back garden with benches and garden lights shining through the hedges. The spacious living room with two gas lit fireplaces and mantelpieces on which Dev would keep the many souvenirs he bought during his international travels

We turned left, past the Chiswick green and arrived at the private entrance of the complex of flats. 'It's a little one-bedroom flat,' said Dev self-effacingly.

We all live by comparison; our situations are relative to our past or aspired present. The Earth, our home, is not even tiny in comparison to the vast nothingness of the Universe. The eight billion inhabitants of this tiny planet are like little ants on a grain of sugar! A single sweep of time and the strivings and egos of us all can blow up in smoke and ash. It's just energy: here, there, everywhere, in different forms. Yet the fallible mortal human species always feels its intelligence distinguishes itself from other forms of energy. The intelligent human species frequently tries to annihilate each other! The greed of our species comes packaged in clever forms and is justified with cunning theories. None of the other species in our tiny home have similar convincing powers. We also possess that transcendental curious emotion of love which we convey in the hope of a good return. And for the management of aggression, greed and love our species has two exceptional systems: one appealing to the moral instinct called religion, while the other to the baser instinct called laws of land.

Land or nations, like organised religions, despite their obvious and vital inevitability, are divisive at mankind level. The human species is ceaselessly creating boundaries. However, as for its co-inhabitants on Earth, the dawn followed by dusk and reappearance of dawn is the only validated truth. Eight billion human beings, coming and going, is just a little puff in the great cosmos. Their intelligence—of construction and conquest, invention and destruction, love and deceit, friendship and greed, kindness and jealousy, possessiveness and procreation, conflict and negotiation—ever evolving but always stopping short of the final question of our origin and destination. In between all this harmonious chaos are numerous stories. One such story is Devavratt; another shorter, though amusing, tale is Eklavya. And the two lands where most of the stories of these friends of mine played out are India and England.

Urban India in the late 1970s and '80s was trying to break away from its conservative past and socialist present.

Dance parties and pizzas at fast food joints filled the leisure time of boys and girls in Wrangler and Levi's jeans. Men with noticeable bellies and women with noticeable hips would reserve their Saturday evenings for devouring butter chicken with *naan* in neat restaurants with white tablecloths in Delhi. Very few people anymore requested a radio transistor or Wrigley's of their kith travelling overseas, and more than one telephone was invariably found in small cul-de-sacs of big neighbourhoods.

The images of India I carry from the late 1970s and '80s encompass the introduction of colour television in early '80s; innovative sales promotion techniques such as Ramon Bonus Stamps and printed lucky numbers on the inside of a Campa-Cola cap indicating India's potential for marketing competitiveness; local detergent brand Nirma posing competition to transnational Surf, and Reliance showing the small investor the way to a new asset class—the stock market. Cigarette advertisements with the caption 'You only live once, live in style' started appearing on the back cover of magazines and any interesting TV programme would be preceded with the commercial of mummy making noodles for her kids in two minutes! Employment markets were beginning to acknowledge professions other than engineering, law and medicine with quasi-respect. Business schools began growing and MBA posed competition to IAS. Liberalisation became an old word with a new meaning. Mahatma Gandhi was not forgotten but was no longer the only idol, and Harivansh Rai Bachchan was better known as the father of one of India's greatest actors rather than one of the greatest Hindi poets of his time. Those below twenty-five years of age would cheer American singers like Michael Jackson and Bruce Springsteen. Those of any age were beginning to understand cricket, Sunil Gavaskar and Kapil Dev were faces even grandmothers would recognize. 'Sexy' and 'fuck' were the two commonly used words to describe a variety of feelings, objects and activities. The finer aspects of human living had not perished, but amongst the young and modern concepts of nationalism, honesty and relationship, were being redefined. Relationships between unmarried men and women were hesitatingly gaining acceptance but was always suspected to involve some form of physical intimacy if not wanton sex. Honesty was slowly becoming synonymous with a deprived existence, and a film star who used to act in patriotic movies was no longer the general favourite.

Devavratt, Eklavya and I lived through this era, influencing it indeed ever so minimally, and being influenced by it in different ways.

Dev paid 25 pounds to the cab driver as I stretched my limbs and looked around at the neat complex where Dev had rented an apartment since relocating back to London in the August of 2014.

The Ashwath Public School

What a night must the 15th of August, 1947 have been. My generation would never know the mass of emotion. What we learnt later in our conscious years was that on the eve of Independence, India's first Prime Minister delivered a stirring speech—'at the stroke of the midnight hour'—and that India got partitioned losing a third of her land leading to mass migration of people and a mayhem that was so gruesome and tragic that it remains a painful scar on the conscience on a fifth of humanity to this day. Upon Independence, India adopted *Satyamev Jayate* as the national motto. May truth ever prevail! India was relatively poor then, but not dishonest. We were taught always to speak the truth. She was also so diverse that some described India as 'an idea' where such diversity was imperatively attempting to co-exist. It is this diversity that forms the backdrop for several crucial policy decisions made by India's leaders. It was thus decided that the Union of India shall be a federation of states, so states will have powers to legislate on certain subjects but the Union Government had to be strong since there was such diversity in the 562 princely states, which the leaders had managed to unify, that a weak centre would fail to curb the 'fissiparous tendencies' extant in the country. It was also decided that India, that is Bharat, wanted peaceful and friendly relations with both the American block capitalist countries and the Soviet bloc communist countries and hence chose a policy of non-alignment as the guiding principle of her foreign policy. Logically, therefore, the economic development model adopted was a mixture of the free market private sector businesses existing along with the socialist type state run, state funded public sector businesses. It was called a mixed economy.

The approach to education also reflected this diversity. The *gurukul* system of education—where a student would stay with a guru to learn language and scriptures, sciences and philosophy, sport and morality—had been replaced even before Independence by modern school system that focused mainly on mental, and to a lesser extent physical, aspect of education, with emotional and spiritual teaching left to the respective families of students to impart. Post-Independence, newly-founded education boards came to dominate the scene. Various forms of schools—state-funded government schools, Kendriya Vidyalaya and privately-run public schools were affiliated to one or the other such boards.

Urban middle and upper classes always sought privately-run public schools for their children, where the medium of education was English and the fee was high. The Ashwath Public School was one such example. It was located on Max Mueller Marg in the heart of New Delhi, what is sometimes called Lutyens' Delhi. The British architect Edwin Lutyens designed New Delhi in the 1930s and the areas surrounding Max Mueller Marg are still the most well-designed parts of the city. A walk in the nearby Lodhi Gardens or shopping at the adjacent Khan Market are always refreshing.

I was in class V, section E of The Ashwath Public School, when on a rainy 15th July 1975, a few days after the new academic year started, I first saw Devavratt Rajvansh. He was thin and reasonably tall, and looked as though he never smiled.

On his first day in TAPS our class teacher suggested that Devavratt share the desk with K.K. Ramkumar. In our school we always sat two to a desk and for most of us, the desk partner was of immense importance. My parents had told me to associate with 'good' children in the hope that their intelligence would rub off on me. Giving due consideration to Devavratt's first day in a new school, our gentle class teacher asked him circumspectly if he would attempt answering a question.

'Yes Teacher,' he said.

The immediate advice he received from the upright Ramkumar was, 'Here we address the teacher as Miss.' It didn't matter if she was a much-married lady! Devavratt was transferring from a primary Christian school where they used to address the teachers as 'Teacher'. Going from 'Teacher' to 'Miss' was the first quick cultural adjustment that the 10-year-old Devavratt had to make.

Ramkumar was one of the most intelligent students in our class who usually stood second or third in the exams, yet given that he had good general knowledge and also participated in sports, he was often regarded as the brightest in section E. He was of slender build and very short in stature and was referred to by all north Indian boys as Ramu; of course, as was his wont, Dev was the only non-south Indian student who called him by his full given name. Dev turned out to be a good student himself, though not a brilliant one, and very well behaved. He had straight thick black hair, a long prominent nose and wheatish complexion. His eyes were large and clear, black-brown but sunken and somewhat sad.

Fear is the great enemy of intelligence. Intelligence is original, it thinks for itself and observes that cessation of thought is where it begins. The fear of hunger, anxiety for money, fretfulness for shelter, horror of seclusion, trepidation of tomorrow, terror of disgrace are daggers that cripple intelligence. 'Think with your mind, not from your heart' is what fear preaches in different cloaks. Humanity fears death. That death which in its worldly impact is devastating, yet in its spiritual force is beautiful. Scores of dependencies are lost with death, and ironically the starkest lessons of life are learnt in the crematorium without the use of words. The shrivelled flower disappears from the garden into the same soil where it germinates from, it reappears in season again. That debt of earth each man and woman has to repay. Intelligence is fearless, but the intelligent species fears death in its many forms. It worships the unknown for delaying repayment of the debt. Purity scares it and the innocence of the heart is held enslaved to the crookedness of the mind. Death is the loveliest turn in the caravan of life, which the convoy makes not of its own volition.

Devavratt's parents had died in an accident when he was five years old. He had since lived with his uncle and aunt. They had brought him up along with their own son. The uncle was a government officer who had transferred from Jaipur to Delhi. Devavratt's cousin, couple of years junior to us, was also admitted to TAPS. I met Devavratt's aunt and uncle only when we were in senior school. They stayed in a government flat at a place called Bapa Nagar in Lutyens' Delhi and Devavratt would cycle down to school.

I used to sit behind Ramkumar and Devavratt at that time and my desk partner was Sanjeev Agnihotri. And behind us sat mischief unadulterated! It was Tarun Mehra who in later school years was to describe himself as 'beast-cum-barbarian'. Sanjeev was Sanju to us, and Tarun's pet name was Goldie. North Indian pet names circumscribe the place: uncomplicated thought, unfussy actions executed with a sense of subtle craftiness and nonchalance!

A sight I recurrently saw while growing up, particularly north of the Vindhyas, was three men standing at the local *paanwallah* shop with a cigarette held in their fingers, scratching their crotch, extending a limp hand to greet their acquaintance and withdrawing it even before it could be clasped, and declaring the most shocking bogus fact about high politics, films or cricket with absolute certainty. The unfussy popular pet names being called out from one terrace to another and in bustling markets like Bobby, Bittoo, Neetu, Lucky, Raju, Goldie, Babloo, Anu, Sweety, Tinku, Punnu, Binny, Sonu, Sunny—chances are exceedingly high that one of those three men at the local *paanwallah* would have one of these pet names. Proud owners of auto-rickshaws and trucks often dedicate their vehicles to such names as well, presumably their kinfolk. Thus, the posteriors of thousands of autos and trucks plying in north India implore the vehicle behind to 'Horn Please', wish them 'Ok Tata', and kindly inform that the eminent driver in front of them is driving an automobile that is 'Bobby *thei* Neetu *thei* Sweety *di gaddi*'!

***

The layout of The Ashwath Public School was simple and elegant. The entry of the school was into an open space meant for school bus parking. Next there was the dark and light green-coloured senior school building housing classes VI to XII, each year divided into five sections A-E-I-O-U. The entire school was also divided into five houses—Himalaya, Rocky, Andes, Alps and Atlas; a student's house never changed throughout their school time even as they moved up the classes. The senior school building opened out into a large ground meant for sports and morning assembly. This ground had basketball and volleyball courts, barracks for sculpture and music, and a little canteen that specialised in bread *pakora*s and *chola bhatura*. Adjacent to the canteen was a small cricket ground and just beyond that the junior school building. In that small cricket ground many a long and happy day were spent by us either playing, walking or simply contemplating the time which lay ahead. Behind the junior school building were a few teacher's quarters and a large villa which was the principal's residence.

In every great kingdom and in successful modern nation states, art and culture has found its due. Literature and poetry, music and painting and dance forms build a nation's character, they foster the soul and essence of its people, they paradigm its culture. Likewise, the values enshrined in a nation's constitution, a country's national song, its national emblem and what its founding fathers stood for, its national sport and national anthem all go into forming the DNA of its people. It is another discussion why after decades of Independence and despite the foundations of India established on such lofty ideals the country found itself in the throes of corruption and conflict for several years, sometime before and soon after the turn of the century, *Satyamev Jayate* notwithstanding.

India's national anthem *Jana Gana Mana* was first sung way back in 1911 in a session of the Indian National Congress. In 1950 it was adopted as India's national anthem by the Constituent Assembly. A complete rendition of the national anthem takes 52 seconds, and every morning in TAPS began with the entire assembly of teachers and students singing *Jana Gana Mana*. Dr Oberoi, the lean principal with a towering personality, would stand ever so upright on the stage with his head held high as he would sing the national anthem. Even the reticent Devavratt would sing *Jana Gana Mana* loud and clear, though with his eyes half closed. The coarse voice of the 'beast-cum-barbarian' Goldie would always stand out in the morning assembly. Occasionally, he would be out of line with the rest of the school, and while we would have all finished singing, Goldie's lone voice would be concluding with, '*Jaya jaya jaya, jaya hei*'.

A few minutes every morning in the assembly were spent with the principal and other teachers announcing special achievements of the school and its students. The assembly would applaud the winner of the essay contest or the girl who stood second in national swimming competition; we would clap for the team winning the Bournvita Quiz Contest or for the emerging school cricketer who had scored a century against a visiting international team in a warm-up game. The scorching sun on summer mornings would usually tire us after a few minutes and when the applause was feeble the teacher announcing would implore us to 'give them a big hand'. Sanju would not clap at such times, instead he would raise his 'big' hand skywards with all his five fingers wide open. He would be 'giving them a big hand'! The good looking and plump Sanju was bright but naughty. He would go on to becoming the leader of the prank pack in our class, with Goldie the trump card in it.

Not Yet Teenagers

The little lady who comes to work in middle-and upper-class homes in India, who we refer to as maid servant, used to work for Rs. 100 a month in late-1970s. Today it is Rs. 3000 a month. She runs from home to home, brooming floors and cleaning dirty utensils, doing physical work, occasionally enduring insult during her labour. She brings up her two children with the hard-earned money. The simple food that she cooks for her children and feeds them, that act of maternal care if one of transcendent spirituality. Parents whose career is too important for them to give time to their child and those rare parents who abandon their child are much poorer than the little lady who comes to work in our homes, and who we refer to as maidservant.

My childhood was never deprived of parental time. Both my parents were teachers in the Delhi University and had a very accommodating work schedule. In the late-1960s they constructed a house in Nehru Enclave in south Delhi. The land and construction cost were just over Rs. 60,000. In 2010, I had taken about 10 of my work associates for dinner and drinks to the famous Bukhara restaurant in Delhi: the bill was Rs. 60,000! My parents perhaps never had too much money but it was adequate for a decent lifestyle. My father used to ride a motorcycle in the late-1960s. One day after dropping my mother at her college, he sustained a fracture when the bike fell on his legs. After recovering, he purchased a second-hand Standard Herald car and would say that, 'Four wheels are always safer than two'. Later, he bought a second-hand Ambassador and later still, a Fiat.

Every day some neighbour or the other would be in and out of our home; every week we would visit my maternal grandfather in Andrews Ganj; once a month there would be a dinner at home for relatives or family friends; once in two months we would go out to a nice restaurant in South Delhi; once in three months we would go to see a movie at a cinema; once in six months we would visit the family temple in Chhipiwara in old Delhi; once a year there would be a picnic in Buddha Jayanti Park or Suraj Kund; and once in two years we would take a four-five-day vacation to a nearby hill station. None of us knew the meaning of the word 'lonely'. Living in family is one of the greatest societal norms evolved by mankind, whose value is fully appreciated only by those who have known and then lost its warmth.

Every morning at 7, my younger brother and I, dressed in navy blue shorts and white shirt with black shoes and a bag full of books on our back, would leave home for our school bus that stopped 200 metres from home. After picking the children from our stop, it would drive and pick up school children from Kalkaji, Chittaranjan Park, Greater Kailash II, Panchsheel, Defence Colony and finally reach school at Max Mueller Marg just before 8 am.

We were in grade VI in 1976. On the first day of the new school year, our class teacher changed desk partners. She made me come forward and sit with Ramkumar, and asked Devavratt to go back and sit with Sanju. Goldie was still behind us but a bit further back where he had been paired with a new joinee, Manohar Pal Billa. Billa was from a family of wrestlers, though he was himself uninterested in sport of any kind. Known to be a mathematics prodigy, Billa had a squeaky voice. He was very short like Ramu but was exceptionally strongly built and shaking hands with him was a metacarpal-crushing experience even in those young days.

I adjusted with Ramkumar easily. He was studious, upright and not talkative. He had his boyhood convictions and idiosyncrasies. He would sign his name with not just a line under scribing it but an arrow, when asked he told me it meant that Ramkumar shall always move forward in life! We would all share our tiffins that we brought from home in those days. My mother usually gave me tomato sandwiches or three *paranthas* with *bhindi*. Ramu's tiffin was the most delicious and contained *dosas* or *idlis* which in the north India of 1970s was pure delicacy. However, his habit was that he would share one out of the four *dosas* or *idlis* he was carrying in the tiffin, never more! His general knowledge was marvellous and he was so genuinely well-mannered that teachers cited him as an example to wayward students. I used to struggle with mathematics in secondary school. Despite lessons on morality from my paternal grandmother, I found myself seeking Ramu's 'help' during maths class tests. Ramu would oblige when he was in a good mood by showing me some of the answers, but never more than three answers. I would occasionally try and get around his 'three answers only' rule by requesting him to show me more answers on that particular day and 'adjust' it in the next test by showing me fewer answers! To this day he has not allowed me to forget a sentence I made in an English language lesson. We would be asked to make sentences using some slightly complex words in order to improve our vocabulary. The word that stumped me was 'predilection'. My sentence was: 'When I did not know the meaning of the word predilection, I asked my teacher'. My sentence received a cross mark from our English teacher and a lifelong chuckle from Ramu.

Sanju and I were beginning to be recognized as bright sort of lads, Devavratt was seen as hard-working but enigmatically reticent. We all managed to come in top 10 during class exams. Sanju's congenial antics endeared him to the class and made him the informal leader of the mischief gang, with Goldie the ace prankster of this pack.

Our Geography teacher at that time was Mr Murari Lal Bhola; he was of frail built and sported a pencil moustache. His elder brother Bihari Lal Bhola, who was rather different from him in built and looks was also a teacher in TAPS for senior classes. One day in year VI while Murari Lal Bhola was partly teaching and partly roaming in and out of class he heard ruckus from that side of the classroom where we were sitting. For some reason his eyes fell on Dev and he was on him like an eagle and registered two slaps on either cheek. Mild clarifications followed from the boys sitting around Dev including Ramu and myself, and stronger protests from the girls. It was Goldie creating the bloody racket! On realising his mistake Mr Bhola apologized to Dev and 'took back the slaps' by placing his hands gently on Dev's cheeks and then taking them away in a direction opposite to the one in which they had a few minutes back savagely travelled! Dev's eyes were misty.

In those days whenever a student had their birthday, they would carry a small bag of toffees or sweets, which were distributed to the class with the teacher's permission. Usually, two Parle orange sweets or Kismi toffees would be given to each child in class. But on the best friend's desk a handful would be placed with an impish smile. In 1976, however, in addition to the sweets distribution in class, I invited a few of my school-friends home as my parents wanted to celebrate my 11th birthday with some fanfare. Amongst the birthday presents I received was a small cricket bat on which was printed 'Kashmir Willow'. I lived with the belief that Kashmir Willow was a great batsman for many months! Till one day for our recess time cricket matches with a tennis ball I carried my Kashmir Willow bat to school. It was here in the course of boys' chat that Dev mentioned that Kashmir willow meant wood from Kashmir, and that no one with that name had ever lifted a cricket bat!

It was sometime after this incident, perhaps when we were in year VII or VIII, that I noticed that the very low profile and excruciatingly sober Devavratt was somewhat different on the cricket ground. He would step forward in those tennis ball class cricket matches, in fact, almost taking control. On the field, his eyes seemed to brighten up. His stride was more purposeful. Once while deciding who would captain our section E in an inter-class cricket match, the decision was locked between Goldie and Dev. The tough and wiry Goldie was a terrific cricket player who staked his claim to captaincy, and while the reticent and lean Dev didn't make that claim, it was clear to those of us who were going to be in the team that he would make a better captain. So, we decided to have a small contest between Goldie and Dev to establish who would captain our section. Both bowled an over to each other, both got each other out once and both hit a few sparkling shots. This quarter of an hour of action didn't establish much but it did make Goldie acknowledge that Dev was as good, if not better than him. Given Dev's good understanding of cricket we unanimously decided that he would be our class captain for cricket games.

Time would roll on, yet time was so still in childhood. The school day would be followed by return journey home by the school bus. My brother and I would walk back home from our bus stop as the blistering sun would be beating down during summer months. Summer afternoons in Delhi sang a poignant folk song, the streets would be largely empty and earth looked parched. Yet in that poignancy was simplicity which I yearn for till today. Our lunch would be followed by homework and then the relatively cooler evening would take us out to play with neighbourhood kids in those open untamed fields that surrounded our house in those days. Just about every game was played, though cricket was the clear favourite. Lemon water or Rooh Afza would be ready when we got back home. Occasionally, my brother or I would be sent to the nearby corner store to buy a loaf of sliced bread—sometimes we were instructed to buy just half a loaf. In those days, the grocer would use a blunt knife to cut a loaf of bread in exact half. If the division was not exact, he would take one slice from the bigger half and place it on the smaller one to make them equal halves. Then he would put a piece of paper torn from a newspaper on top of the half he was selling and secure it with a rubber band. Back home, we would watch the black-and-white TV for a while before dinner, and post dinner, pack the school bag for the next day.

'Who were we' and 'where had we come from' were questions I would fascinate myself with every summer night as I would lie on my camp cot with a white bed sheet awaiting sleep, on the terrace of our house in Delhi, watching mystified, the vast open sky. For several years in the 1970s and also in the early '80s during summers, we slept on the terrace in the open. I would usually carry a transistor radio and listen to either the cricket commentary broadcast from West Indies or England, or entertain myself with old melodies from Hindi films, or delight myself with exciting sponsored programmes like *Inspector Eagle* or *Modi Ke Matwale Rahi* to help me slowly fall asleep.

As I would lie with Lata Mangeshkar's divine voice softly emanating from the transistor or Suresh Suraiya's vivid description of Gavaskar's 'meticulous and methodical' forward defensive shot, I would gaze at the sky. There would be complete and infinite emptiness; there was timeless silence and there was beauty. There was the beauty of the moon which seemed so close that I would almost feel its touch on my face, there was the beauty of the clouds which would obscure the moon momentarily and then reveal it again, there was the beauty of the late solitary bird flying back to her loved ones, there was the beauty of the seven stars whose formation never changed though their position did. I would feel insignificant, just another speck of nature. I never got answers to my questions but in that vast nothingness, I realised that sometimes the answer precedes the question: the emptiness seemed to be the truth.

Delhi and its surroundings have since got industrialised. Sleeping on the terrace now belongs to the age of gramophone and black-and-white TV. Black soot starts settling down as dusk approaches and the summer nights have to be combated with an air-conditioner. Those of us who have never slept out in the open will find it difficult to appreciate just how rejuvenating it was to become ensconced in the cool summer nights and wake up with the first rays of the morning sun.

My paternal grandmother was a fine storyteller. I recall a story from the *Mahabharata* which she used to narrate about the devoted wife Savitri and her husband Satyavan. They used to lead a simple and contented life in the forest, with

Satyavan's parents. Satyavan's father was blind and used to be a king before losing everything and was living in exile in the forest. Satyavan was predicted to die exactly one year after his marriage! On the pre-destined day, Savitri accompanied Satyavan to the forest where he collapsed, his head in the lap of the devout Savitri. As she sat with the corpse of Satyavan, the Lord of Death, Yamaraj, appeared to extract the soul of Satyavan and carry it on its celestial journey. Savitri, pious and determined and articulate, stopped him. The conversation that followed between them impressed Yamaraj so much that he granted three boons to Savitri, with the exception of Satyavan's life. Savitri's first wish was restoration of her father-in-law's sight and kingdom, her second wish was a hundred sons for her father and her third wish also seemed to be commonplace for that time—she desired a hundred children for herself and Satyavan. Yamaraj nonchalantly granted the same. Savitri had trapped Yamaraj! 'If you take away the life of my husband, how will I mother a hundred children?' Yamaraj had to restore Satyavan's life to honour his commitment and the couple lived happily ever after.

'What was the connection between existence of the life of a husband and childbirth?' I questioned my grandmother but didn't get a satisfactory answer, only a suppressed smile. I would have been 12 then. I asked my parents the same question and didn't get a satisfactory answer from them either. It was not until I was 14 and one of my school friends explained the meaning of the word 'fuck' to me that wisdom finally dawned. Sanju always seemed to know all about these interesting subjects like sex, masturbation, the male and female anatomy and blue movies. Ramu, for all his simplicity and rectitude, never seemed astonished at these revelations. Goldie would let out a roaring laugh at the mere mention of this topic and eventually twist the discussion towards his own body, which he mentioned he was modelling on that of Sean Connery. Dev's seriousness made him off-limits in those early days for this type of discussion.

Adolescence

It was only after I read Bertrand Russel's essay titled 'The Long Childhood' that I started thinking about the few years journey I had had till then. The human childhood is indeed a very long one. Year after year, school exams would arrive, we would successfully take them, friends and neighbours would come to congratulate, and we would then enthusiastically welcome the summer vacations. Big plans for summer break would be made and invariably we would end up doing something not planned for; as the vacation neared its end, we would get busy buying books for the next class and parents would help us cover the books neatly and paste a label with our names on it. A new class would start, new subjects would be taught, Dussehra and Diwali would come and go, a new year would come, a birthday get celebrated, some new friends would be made; some would get transferred and lost forever. A new cricket series would start and then end. A few new clothes would be made, a new white good would enter the home. A few bean seeds would be planted in the lawn to confirm the previous school lesson on germination. A few new facts about life would unfold and the pencil line on the wall measuring our height would climb up a few inches.

A few astonishing events would take place in the country and the world. It would keep everyone engrossed for a while and ensure that socialising got a prop. In the early-1970s it was the Indo-Pak war and the blackouts, Gavaskar's sensational debut in West Indies and our learning the game of cricket, the crippling oil price hike in 1973, Nixon's Watergate scandal, Mohammad Ali's world heavyweight title and imposition of Emergency in India in 1975. Mao Tse-Tung's death, Nadia Comaneci's perfect 10 in Olympics gymnastics and ouster of Bhutto in Pakistan, the death of Elvis Presley in 1977 and the Indian general election when during election result time we got to see films all day on TV! The first test-tube baby arrived in 1978, the Soviets invaded Afghanistan the next year, the Iran-Iraq war and boycott of the Moscow Olympics in 1980. Then another Indian general election happened as the government had fallen and a few more days of many popular films on TV. Sadat's assassination and the wedding of Diana and Charles in 1981, and then seemingly the long childhood was over and I realised that there was birth and death and in between a few years to live.

This long childhood craves for maturity, absence of examinations, late nights, the urge to see adult movies and the desire to make money and indulge with it. When all this does actually happen, it happens so gradually sometimes painfully, that the pleasure of 'not being a child subjected to examinations' is seldom realised. Maturity, ironically always craves for innocence and carefree childhood, but that carefree childhood is known never to return. Tragic is the day when a child realises that he or she is mortal. The world loses yet another innocent and spontaneous creature.

I would be quite nervous on the first day of every new academic year. Having got used to the 'help' I was getting from Ramkumar, especially in maths tests, but more generally overall, I wanted to remain his desk partner. I felt secure with him around. The little I noticed of Dev at that time suggested that he was indifferent to whom he was sitting with. But then he seemed to go through most movements in school with detachment. I stayed Ramu's desk partner in years VII and VIII as well. His temperament even in those boisterous days was usually calm. Yet a few incidents which happened at that time, when the world was so young and innocent, revealed human flashes to an otherwise saintly demeanour! Those incidents have been recounted several times, usually in Ramu's home in Chirag Enclave in South Delhi. In one of those recess-time cricket matches that we were playing near the school compound's wall, Ramu hit the ball outside the school compound boundary. Now, that according to our rules was 'out'! I approached Ramu with well-meant, but ill-timed advice. I told him he ought to have rolled his wrists on the bat to keep the ball down. An agitated Ramkumar got even more infuriated and before I realised, he picked up his right leg and registered a spanking kick on my bottom. Whenever we discuss this incident with common friends and Ramu's cousins, I tell them how it's paining till today! Whenever Ramu and I have an argument over anything nowadays, he tells me that it's time for another kick!

For the final exams of year VIII, it was announced that a different seating arrangement would be organised, and during the final exams, a class VIII student would sit with class VII student. This was done to prevent any cheating and it meant that I had to work really hard for Maths in order to get through with decent grades. The tall Abhishek Goel as usual stood first, Ramkumar stood second, two bright girls in our class, Shweta and Ira, stood third and fourth but there was a new name in the top five—it was Devavratt. I stayed in top ten, as did Sanju, though his rank had come down a couple of places.

The year X examinations were not conducted by the school but at an all-India level by the Central Board of Secondary Education. They were called the Board Exams or simply Boards. The syllabus included not just the topics we had to cover in the academic year X but also in the academic year IX. This meant that a race for Boards began in year IX itself. A good year X result implied that we could choose our preferred electives in years XI and XII. Year XII was another Board Exam; it was the senior most school class and year XII Boards results determined which college at the University we would get admission into. It was the most important result in our lives!

I was as always nervous on day one of year IX and desperately wanting to get to class as soon as possible and sit with Ramu. As soon as I entered the class my heart sank. Lo and behold, the short and slender Ramkumar was sitting on the first desk with the tall, bespectacled Abhishek Goel! The top two students had seemingly colluded! They presumably wanted day to day academic discussion and help from each other so as to excel at the Boards. I looked at Ramu with embittered and sulky eyes who suggested with a wave of his hand that I needed to find another desk partner. It was second evidence that Ramu was not entirely a 'saint', for the bottom was still sore! My world was collapsing. As I walked down the aisle, I found Dev seated alone on one of the front rows. I checked with him if I could be his desk partner; he smiled and with his hand, welcomed me on the chair adjacent to his. I was relieved. Dev had stood fifth in the previous final exams; my parents had told me to associate with 'good' students and he was as good as I could get, given that the apple-loving Abhishek and *dosa*-carrying Ramkumar had formed a formidable team.

Poetic justice was delivered next day when our class teacher observed that the two best students were seated next to each other. The teachers tried to always team up a bright student with a less intelligent one. Ramkumar was asked to vacate his vantage position and made to sit with Sarabjit Singh who usually brought up the rear in academics. Of course, where the academically-brilliant and the commonplace ended up in life is story for latter part of this narration. Poetic justice was also delivered to Abhishek whose new desk partner was the now adolescent, very short but very beefy, hand-crushing Billa!

Billa and Goldie had been desk partners for nearly three years before being split up. They had started out as foes but soon became friends. During their initial association, they had challenged each other on who was stronger. Goldie suggested they run around the cricket ground till one of them gets exhausted! He was a bundle of energy even in those early secondary school years while Billa was disinterested in sports or outdoor physical activity of any kind, his family background notwithstanding. He declined the challenge and Goldie claimed victory. Billa however urged him, '*Aao panjja khelein*'—'let's arm-wrestle'. After three minutes of locking their hands, with elbows on the desk, their faces turning beetroot red, Billa brought down Goldie's forearm! Neither accepted conclusive defeat, but both became fast friends!

If Goldie's mischief was instinctive and untamed, Billa's was almost innocent. He never knew how funny his own antics and diction were. Billa would pronounce love as '*lowve*' such that it rhymed with 'stove', and refer to 'a lady' in the plural as '*ladiss*'. He would address me as '*Sh*andy' and refer to Abhishek as '*Appil* Goel' due to his fondness for apples. It was only many, many years later that I appreciated that Billa's first language was not English; however, in those school days, inward-looking as we were, his diction caused hilarity. While Goldie was an average student, his interest in and knowledge of India's national movement was astonishing. It was Goldie who first told me why midnight of 15th August, 1947 was chosen as the time for Indian independence. 'After Mountbatten announced 15th August as date for independence at a press meeting, several astrologers wrote to him saying any country taking birth that day would have to go through a long period of hardship and strife,' said Goldie to me, 'He could not change the announced date, but to give respect to view of astrologers, he made it midnight!' Goldie's desire was to join the Air Force and become a fighter pilot.

Billa's academic interest was unique. He barely passed in most subjects but, always got nearly full marks in mathematics. Billa wanted to become a mathematician! Adolescence had a wild impact on Billa. His penis became his favourite topic of conversation. Every day he would tell a few of us such bizarre tales of his penis that Sanju once remarked that our knowledge of Billa's penis was better than our understanding of medieval history or Charles Dickens stories or trigonometry. While nothing around the world is known by more different and popular names than the male penis, Sanju had coined his own name for a man's best friend—he called it *mann-mauji*. The English equivalent would be somewhere between 'fun-loving' and 'whimsical'. A mere reference of *mann-mauji* would send both Billa and Goldie into hysteria of laughter. Around this time, Goldie's association with Sanju got closer. Sanju became the undisputed ring leader with the attention-grabbing Goldie the super member of the prank pack. Often, Sanju would convert his handkerchief into the shape of a *mann-mauji* using paper and rubber bands. Goldie would then hang this from the fan and gaze at the girls in the class to observe their reaction. Based on their reaction the prank pack would decide which girl nursed what feelings about taboo topics. Occasionally, Goldie or Sanju would fling the *mann-mauji* made from handkerchief, paper and rubber band up towards the fan. The blades of the fan would powerfully hurl it to some corner of the classroom, and often it would hit a student or land near him or her. Depending on who it hit, short stories would be fashioned. These stories were usually centred on the colour of the student's underwear!

A more printable incident in secondary school happened with Chhaya Naayak who was our classmate throughout primary and secondary school. She would get noticed due to her plain looks, richly oiled pony-tail, braces and a more than prominent mole near her left nostril. It must have been 1979 when post-recess, 15 of us, all boys, were trotting back to the class room to attend Mrs Chopra's English lesson. Just as we were about to enter the class Sanju said, 'Whoever enters the class first shall marry Chhaya Naayak.'

All of us came to a screeching halt. Nobody wanted to 'marry' Chhaya Naayak. Mrs Chopra was puzzled at the assembly of her students outside the class when she and 25 others were sitting inside. She came out and said, 'What's wrong with you boys, get inside!'

None dared to. The corridors of TAPS would have never seen a stranger sight. The dignified Mrs Chopra was getting exasperated. No, none of us wanted to get 'married' to Chhaya Naayak. She felt she could persuade the always quiet Devavratt to enter but even he didn't want misfortune befalling him and so stood his ground. Another stentorian order resulted in nothing more than some of us exchanging glances. Sanju stood as if he was participating in a solemn solidarity march. His expressionless face magnificently disguised the puckish schemes in his mind. Mrs Chopra, perplexed and stupefied, looked around to find some method or some man to break this inexplicable congregation of serious looking students outside her class. She tried to grab Goldie by his arm which led him to wrestle it out of her grip and scoot off like an arrow towards the boy's toilet. All of us ran into the sanctuary where women don't enter. Mrs Chopra came and stood outside the boy's toilet and shouted at all of us. We came out but none had the courage to go past the classroom door. Almost half an hour would have elapsed before Mrs Chopra threatened Manekjit Dalal whose mother was a teacher in our school, and known for her firmness. 'I shall report this matter to the principal,' she firmly said to all of us, 'and as far as you are concerned, Manekjit, I will make it a point to bring it to the notice of your mother.'

Poor Manekjit, was now caught between his mother and a 'wife' he didn't want to marry. But he finally relented and behind him strode 14 more to the utter bewilderment of our other classmates. It took precisely 10 more minutes for a paper to be flying around our class on which was scribbled: *Mr and Mrs Dalal request the pleasure of your company on the auspicious occasion of the marriage of their son Manekjit with Chhaya!*

Notwithstanding the blissful oblivion I was living in before my schoolmate explained the 'sensational' act which leads to childbirth, I too was getting fascinated by the female form. I recall I was often on the lookout for a sight of cleavage and middle-aged Indian women who we used to address as Aunties were the only live source for this 'sexual' satisfaction. The other two sources for viewing some cleavages were Hindi movies—where the vamps would oblige with a little show of thighs and a brief show of some cleavage—and film or lifestyle magazines where on a lucky day I would chance upon a picture or two of some bold women. I think I always brought up the rear within the circle of my friends vis-à-vis understanding of this human act which from time immemorial has made the world go round and round, and up and down!

During our years IX and X, it was decided that after the assembly the entire school would be put through physical exercises. The announcement to this effect was prefaced and marketed with the platitude that healthy minds reside in healthy bodies. It was an unpopular decision and one that led Billa to express his displeasure in a way only he could have. He decided to pee 'on' the entire school as it performed routine exercises under the hot sun! The drill was that after the morning assembly students would be allowed to run up to their classrooms to leave their school bags. We had to reassemble in the grounds within 10 minutes and start the exercises under the instructions of our PE teachers. On one such day Billa, the short and stout mathematician with a squeaky voice, went into the boy's bathroom that overlooked these grounds, climbed atop the urinal, removed a glass fishplate and stuck his by-now-famous penis out of the building and towards the grounds! Of course, the PE teacher and all of us were a good 50 metres from the building. Goldie and some others had been informed the precise time when this act of defiance was to occur. As we moved our arms—forward, then sideways, then upwards—one of the class-mate shouted, 'Look, look straight up at second floor'.

Those of us standing close enough to hear him looked up to see the hideous sight of a piece of human anatomy, belonging to Manohar Pal Billa, leaking drops of defiant urine!

Meanwhile, Billa's foe-turned-friend Goldie had developed a voracious appetite for food. With everybody's tiffin lying in their bags, unattended for an hour while we did exercises, Goldie would polish off a few every time he decided to bunk exercises. We started returning back to the classrooms dreading the fact that hunger lay in store if Goldie had consumed our tiffin. The pillage was usually discovered at recess time when we opened our tiffin boxes. Billa was never the suspect since his food habits were both disciplined and different and he was not interested in other people's morsels. Amongst Goldie's few 'victims' was Ramkumar. When Ramu opened his lunch-box at recess time one day, he discovered that all four *dosa*s and entire coconut *chutney* from his tiffin was gone! In his entire school life, Ramkumar displayed non-saintly and normal, mortal behaviour only thrice! First the kick in the bottom; second, the failed collusion with Abhishek and now with his entire tiffin gone, an upset Ramu, knowing his short and slender frame could not take on the wiry and wild 'beast-cum-barbarian', picked up his empty tiffin box and smashed it at the classroom wall with frustrated livid ferocity. Goldie's torso vibrated with fiendish laughter while Billa's expression suggested he couldn't understand what the fuss was all about. All others in class were stunned at the sight of the 'devil seizing the saint'!

***

The loneliness that accompanies a human being at birth and in death haunts us throughout the time we are here. It is a stark brutal truth escape from which is a perennial motivation for man. Hindu scriptures describe the universe as *mahashunya* or the big zero. How can infinitesimal earthly people then have any significance bigger than zero? Yet all our lives we are trying ever so hard to shun that loneliness, and fill up that zero with distractions that are sometimes lofty, sometimes mundane.

As we spent time together sharing a desk, I started noticing that Devavratt never made an effort to be with rest of the boys. He seemed comfortable in his loneliness, or he was too shy to come out of his shell. Other than recess time cricket matches where there was a twinkle in his eyes, he was quite content to be by himself. He would cycle in to school unnoticed and cycle out unobserved. It didn't seem to bother him if he was not included in the boys' chat and prank group. He also felt hesitant while speaking to girls, something that many of us boys in India of the early-1980s frequently experienced. I could sense the effort he was putting in his academics, yet he had a strange effortlessness in his limited social ways. Each one of us, indeed, is a product of our upbringing and experiences.

From the emaciated barefoot peasant of Champaran tilling a parched piece of land to feed his children an evening meal to the rich barrister of Notting Hill Gate walking down Bayswater Road and flagging a black London cab with the index finger of his raised left hand; from the emotional bespectacled clerk in Calcutta ambling past the rickety tram lines towards a vegetable shop to buy three fresh potatoes, two tomatoes and a dozen ladyfingers that his unhappy wife might cook that night to the unemotional six feet seven inch tall company executive of Utrecht in Netherlands lamenting the falling share prices over a glass of milk on his lunch table; from the confident 28-year-old MBA driving her Honda City in Gurgaon knowing exactly what she wants out of life and rounding off the day with a glass of Merlot to the ever-relaxed store attendant in the mall in Barra da Tijuca saying '*Obrigado*' to customers and having a *caipirinha* with her friends before calling it a day—each one of us is a product of our upbringing and conditioning and experiences.

Big Boys Of Secondary School

My paternal grandmother lived 45 years of widowed life. While she had not studied many classes she was learned and narrated lovely stories from Indian history and scriptures to my brother and me. She would always cook her own meal and sit cross-legged on the kitchen floor and eat her food. She was stoic, morally upright and kind-hearted. It was only in my adult years, long after she was gone, that I wondered with deep solemn admiration how she must have brought up my father all by herself as a young widow. Happiness and pain are not evenly distributed in this world. Nothing is. She was an Arya Samaj believer and started every single morning with the *havan* and chanting of *Gayatri mantra*. I too learnt the *Gayatri mantra* from her, but only recently understood its entire meaning. I have chanted it on my occasional visits to temples, before all kinds of exams and interviews, and during turbulence in flights. After she succumbed to cancer in 1979, while the daily early morning *havans* at my parental home stopped, my father would still have a little *havan* organised at home once a year. He would invite the Shastriji from nearby Arya Samaj to conduct it.

Shastriji was a very lean man of medium height and always wore white *kurta* and *dhoti*. He had grey hair, a very prominent forehead, and the gentlest of smiles. He would bow and say namaste to everyone who would be at home for the *havan*. I used to find his way of sitting on the floor, in front of the *havan-kund*, remarkable. His spine would be majestically straight and he appeared like a sage meditating on the wisdom handed down through the centuries. His face radiated with decency, honesty and with the knowledge of his subject. It radiated with self-respect, with respect for people around him and with moral rectitude. I would see the same radiance on my father's face, and indeed on the countenance of a few of my friends' fathers. I would see that on the faces on some public figures of the 1960s and 1970s—Dr Karan Singh, Homi Bhabha, Atal Behari Vajpayee, Verghese Kurien. I tend not to find that same radiance on middle aged and elderly Indian men known to me today. It is not a generational lament. We are much richer now than we were in those few decades after Independence, however, the higher standards of living and commercial dazzle—a case for which must also be made—appear to have come at the cost of affability and humility.

In later years of life, my father and I often discussed this social and cultural change. While he would first think aloud and ruefully wonder, 'When we have descended from spiritual intellectuals like Buddha and Vivekananda and fearless warriors like Shivaji and Prithviraj, when our ancestors were not marauders but foragers of truth and scientific discovery, where a promise was honoured even at the cost of one's life, where then did this greed creep in?' He would then reflect and himself add, 'But it is a finite few, only a finite few and their mendaciousness will never totally besmirch the land of the Vedas.' His point of view was: 'Why did we let the avarice, even of those "finite few" traumatize national consciousness; when there is such loftiness in the collective spirit and fibre of the country why did this duplicity come to pass?'

Social morality and individual virtues never stay static. I have no doubt that the decency, honesty and honour with which Shastriji's face radiated will inspire Bharat again. It may, however, take some time for that sun to fully rise and for its glow to become eclectic, the light though is already on the horizon.

During the *havan*, Shastriji would recite *mantra*s in Sanskrit and at the end of the *havan* my father would offer him a small sum of money—a sum that respected Shastriji's time and knowledge, but never caused burden on my father's modest pocket. Shastriji would accept whatever was offered with folded hands and a tender bow of the head. He would then sit with us for a while and partake in the *havan prasad* that was prepared and answer any questions that my brother or I or any of the relatives and friends present might have. On one such occasion he explained to me the meaning of the Upanishad *shloka* '*Purna-madah purna-midham purnat purna-mudachyate*'. In reference to an individual and the ever-expanding universe, the Upanishad says, 'You are complete and I am complete, from completeness comes the complete, and if completeness is taken away from completeness, you are still left with the complete'. From the infinite universal energy emerge human souls and plants and animals, the universal energy remains infinite and we, the microcosm of that energy, immerse in it only to perhaps appear yet again! The 108 Upanishads are part of the 4 Vedas. After the *havan*, my father would drop Shastriji back to the Arya Samaj in his second-hand car.

***

After being Dev's desk partner for about three months, I recall asking him, 'Why are you so sober?' I remember Dev looked at me puzzled. 'I mean, you don't mix freely with everyone; you don't speak too much you and you don't laugh too much.'

Dev replied with an ever so gentle smile 'Now that you are my desk-partner, I will learn these qualities.'

As he opened up with me, I realised he had a subtle sense of humour. Once in the boy's room I said to him, 'Is there really a need to wash hands with soap after urinating?' to which he laughingly said, 'I know, it's a particularly clean area.'

It was during the vacations after we had finished year IX that Dev came to my house for the first time. I had invited him just before the school closed for summer vacations and he had readily agreed. Dev cycled down all the way from Bapa Nagar to my place a week after the vacations had started. My father's cousin's children Gautam and Geeta were also over. Gautam was my age and Geeta two years younger. They studied in a different school. After introductions and lunch was over and we sat chatting in the living room, Dev asked me, 'How old is your carpet, Sandeep?'

I was surprised and asked him 'Why?'

'I saw a large marble lying on the shelf of your bedroom,' said Dev.

That marble was five times the size of normal marbles. 'You don't want us to play marbles at this time, do you!' said Geeta incredulously.

Dev shook his head. 'If the carpet is old and you don't mind, would you like to play cricket on it?'

For the next two and a half hours there was fervent activity going on in the house. Dev pulled out a sports magazine from his bag. He then asked for bottle caps, scissors, wedding or greeting cards, a seven inch by two-inch piece of wooden plank, some wool, tape and he picked up a discarded piece of thermocol.

I worked with him in preparing whatever this game was going to be, while the others joked and laughed at what was going on. Dev cut out the faces of Indian and English cricketers who had played in the Jubilee Test of 1980 and some who were active Test cricketers at that time and whose pictures had appeared in the *Sportweek Cricket Quarterly* he was carrying. These pictures were then pasted on a little piece of the greeting card or wedding invitation card, cut out with the firm background, and then taped on the bottle cap and the picture turned upwards as it was stiff paper. Thus, we had 22 two-inch players—Ian Botham, Kapil Dev, Sunil Gavaskar, Geoffrey Boycott and others were all ready!

The carpet was to become the pitch on which the extraordinary 'Indoor Carpet Cricket' or ICC was played that afternoon. The little piece of thermocol was the 'stumps', the wooden plank with padding of wool on it and tape on the edges was the 'bat', the big white marble was the 'ball'! Eleven two-inch-high players were the fielders. And Devavratt then went on to explain the game to us.

One of us, the batsman, was to sit on his or her knees with the bat, next to the stumps. From a distance of about 5 metres, which was close to our dining table, the bowler would sit on his knees and bowl to the batsman. The bowling couldn't be overarm; the 'ball' had to be thrown to the batsman. If the 'ball' hit the stumps one of the 11 players who was being represented by one of us would be out and a new player from either the Indian or English team would come in to bat. The 11 fielders from the fielding team would be spread out on the carpet and if the ball rolled on from the bat, hit one of those fielders resulting in its fall and then rolled further out of the carpet onto the floor, the batsman was out caught. If it rolled out without hitting any fielder and went and hit the walls of the living room the shot would result in runs. Thus, if we were to play defensively the chances that it would dislodge a player were minimal and even if a player got dislodged the chances of the marble rolling out of the carpet were limited. Just as in real cricket the chances of getting out were higher if you were playing aggressively; similarly, to make runs, you had to take calculated risks and play shots judiciously! Devavratt had introduced us to an addiction!

I initiated Ramu into ICC as well as some boys in the neighbourhood. Whenever we met at Gautam and Geeta's house for a sleep over, or any of our neighbourhood boys or Ramu would be over, we would invariably play ICC. Gautam and Geeta became very fond of Dev. Once we all met at their house in Greater Kailash and they invited Dev too. Till today most of them fondly remember Dev and the ICC we played together! Immense delight is available in the many insignificant objects thrown around and overlooked in our own homes! Indeed, immense happiness is to be found in simple and trusting relationships.

I was still struggling with Mathematics, and Devavratt, now my steady desk partner, was foxed by those chemistry equations! My former desk partner and Maths test lifeline Ramkumar was serving poetic justice and changing his desk partners every three months; and Abhishek and Billa made the oddest desk-couple of all time. I was beginning to find flashes of impish humour in Dev too, though it surfaced occasionally. During chemistry lessons we would sometimes be playing dots and crosses and sometimes book cricket. Once around Holi time, our chemistry lesson was made colourful by a wicked Sanju prank.

I had seen Sanju enter the class room with water balloons all over his person. There were water balloons in his rolled-up sleeves, inside his shirt and even in his socks. As our chemistry teacher Miss Trehan turned around to write an equation on the blackboard with a piece of white chalk a water balloon smashed splash on the board! She turned around and demanded in shock and bewilderment, 'Who did that, who threw the balloon!' There was a hush in the class. She again shrieked, 'I will not teach you till you tell me who threw this balloon!'

Sanju's reputation for mischief had travelled a little, and though as always, he sat with a poker face, Miss Trehan now addressed him, 'Sanjeev, who threw that balloon?'

Sanju looked at her in as matter of fact way as he could and said, 'Miss, I don't know, probably came from outside.'

Now our classroom was on the first floor and for that naughty Holi balloon to have come from outside not only would it have had to travel thirty feet upwards but also make a bend of at least forty-five degrees! 'How can it come from outside!' Miss Trehan fumed, 'Tell me now or I will report the entire class to Dr Oberoi!'

Friendship is a cocktail that comes in many colours and tastes. And it was one of Sanju's gang of pranksters who stood up and placing his hand on his chest, admitted, 'Miss, I did it.'

He was made to go down on his knees in front of the class as punishment which he smilingly did. Even today when we remember this incident Sanju says with exactly the same poker face, 'I don't really have too much of a guilty feeling.'

Sanju had also told the innocent Billa that every man has been granted only a finite quantity of sperm, this information was received by the short and burly Billa as a colossal injustice of nature, and for the period when he lived in this belief his self-gratification got curtailed and life was no longer worth living. I suspect the day truth must have dawned would have become a red-letter day in the life and times of Billa! Soon he was in his element again. He told us how he had taken his semen load on a piece of paper and then tried to light fire to it, something which I bet is untried even till today by the best of chemical engineers.

Another standard antic of Sanju's was that as we would be walking in the corridors of the school, he would suddenly put his right hand between our legs and lift us a good 3 feet from the ground in a *mann-mauji* crushing act! The only ones who had been spared this experience of a lifetime were Ramu and Dev; for some reason, Sanju's right hand had not shown interest in reaching between their legs. While Sanju seemed ahead of all of us in terms of 'worldly wisdom', he still retained boyish humour. He once asked me with twinkling eyes why words like 'partnership' and 'membership' had the suffix which meant the posterior of a human being. Every time 'partner*ship*' or 'member*ship*' or 'apprentice*ship*' came up during a class, he would look at me and stroke the side of his bottom!

We were now big boys in secondary school soon to write the class X Board exam! Most of us shot up in height and hair appeared in seen and unseen parts of the body. And suddenly a strange magical unexplained sensation would journey through the mind every time a good-looking girl with new body parts walked past!

The most important festival, especially in north India is Diwali. On this day some 7000 years ago, Lord Ram had returned back to Ayodhya with his wife Sita and brother Lakshman following 14 years in exile and after slaying Ravan, the demon king of Lanka. The day Ram, Sita and Lakshman returned to Ayodhya was marked by celebration with people lighting up their houses with lamps and distributing sweets.

To this day on Diwali people light up their houses, distribute sweets and burst crackers.

The story of Ram is contained in the age-old epic *Ramayana* which was first written by Valmiki, and centuries later the story of Ram was recited again by Kamban and Tulsidas. In fact, there are almost a hundred different versions of the *Ramayana* written and recited by scholars in different parts of India at different times. An educated, super analytical, ideologically-torn society possessed of several technical tools which can supposedly validate or disprove historical facts has in recent times questioned the heritage not just of India but of several ancient civilizations. For the leftist intellectuals, historical events are described in terms of power and class struggle, men of science seek proof for everything though physics cannot explain the cosmos before the big bang happened, men of religion use fear of the unknown and fascination of the unexplained to juxtapose their eminence, the modern philosopher or guru tends to dismiss the old beliefs with newly packaged clever concepts appealing to the rational, and history stands captive in the hands of the victor. Man is always eager to lend his ear to new theories and hypothesis.

As a child, I did not see all these angles to a beautiful festival. I would wonder how they must have lived 7000 years ago; how did ordinary men get supernatural powers through boons and how so many miracles described in our epics happened. Diwali for me meant holidays, festivity and decoration in town, sweets at home and crackers of all sorts on the Diwali day. During my mid teen years, it also meant many visitors and some more cleavage to look at! And by now I had even started noticing the bigger derrière of women.

But what gave me even greater joy was the festival of Dussehra which precedes Diwali by 20 days. Dussehra is the day when Ravan was actually killed and to this day, Ravan's effigy is burnt all over India, thus signifying that if you are evil and cast a baneful eye on the property or wife of another, the end will be annihilation. My cousins and a few neighbourhood friends, my brother and I looked forward to Dussehra because we would, year after year, make an effigy of Ravan and then blow it up in the little park outside our house on Dussehra.

Fifteen days before Dussehra we would start going around the blocks in our locality collecting contributions from neighbours for the making of the 'Ravan'. For the Ravan of 1980, we appointed the gentle Geeta as our treasurer carrying the contribution box into which the donations would go. During the Dussehra break, Dev too joined us in the making of the Ravan on the terrace of my house.

A mixed group certainly had greater credibility than an all-boys group did. Sixty percent of the contributions went towards buying the bamboos and colours, paper and crackers for Ravan. The remaining forty percent was lavishly spent on buying snacks and ice creams from the hawkers and was consumed by us with a sense of naughty satisfaction derived from the fact that hard earned money of the neighbours was going towards satisfying our appetite for junk food! A little bit of immorality was fun.

And when Dussehra would arrive, there would be incessant revelry throughout the day with someone commenting on Ravan's moustache and others poking fun at his paunch. By evening, the free standing 20-feet-high Ravan would be planted in the park outside our home and just before sunset the demon would go up in flames. Crackers big and small would blast off from his body and neighbours would come out from their houses with suppressed smiles to see their contributions in bamboo and cardboard burn in front of them.

The most delightful part was the creativity and thrill associated with our effort. In actually seeing a creature contrived by us, in working on giving him shape and ensuring that he stood up and that his arm holding the sword remained skywards and didn't go limp. The coming together of cousins and friends meant that there was no interlude in laughter.

My Desk Partner

Dev and I had been desk partners for a year when our academic year for class X started in the July of 1980. He was as sober and introverted as ever, though not as excruciatingly restrained as he had earlier come across. There was usually a gentle smile on his face but his laughter never reached his eyes. He was curious about academics but showed little curiosity in the people around him. There was something bottled up inside him which never came out. He seemed happy keeping to himself, but was neither unfriendly nor unpopular in the class. He avoided confrontation, his face was still and his eyes were sunken and contrasted between sadness and an intensity with which he was searching for something. He was always happy to share with me whatever he knew about history and current affairs and sports and science and literature, but didn't quite seem open to go beneath that layer and talk about his life. He seemed simple at heart yet somewhat complicated in his thoughts. He spoke so well when he did in both languages, yet when he would come home, he would listen more to my parents and my cousins than talk himself, which he did only in short sentences. He never discussed girls in the way other boys would but did not look away whenever I brought up the topic, and with the most subtle of humour he gently changed the subject. He never bad-mouthed anyone but appeared not to like everyone either, his lips seemed to purse just a little whenever he encountered someone he didn't fancy.

Often, I would see his face turned away, looking out of the window and away from the class in an intriguing mingle of thoughtful aloofness. It appeared to me that he could not lie nor was he comfortable saying no. He had mentioned to me the poetry and rendition of Gopaldas 'Neeraj' which he had seen on Doordarshan twice and found mesmerising. He had loved reading Sunil Gavaskar's autobiography *Sunny Days*, liked the Five Find-Outers mysteries by Enid Blyton, and intended to read Mahatma Gandhi's *My Experiments with Truth* after Boards. He used to enjoy the Phantom and Mandrake comics, and Amar Chitra Katha comics on stories from Indian history. He would write 'Om' in Hindi in very small font at the top right corner of the examination answer sheets. But when I asked him if he believed in God, his reply was, 'I am not sure', and when I quizzed him the reason why he then wrote a letter of prayer, he looked at me very intently and expressionlessly but did not answer my question.

For the compulsory vocational subject at that time referred to as Socially Useful Productive Work or SUPW, he had taken sculpture. He would never ask me for anything, and never refuse if I asked him to lend me a book or comic though he seemed a trifle uncomfortable in temporarily parting with *Sunny Days*. He, like a few others, had become quite tall and a newly-sprouting moustache completed the clean-cut face of Devavratt Pratap Rajvansh. In those early years, the only things I was certain about Dev were his passion for cricket, his growing fondness for Hindi poetry, and an arcane feeling inside me that I could trust him completely.

***

From prehistoric times till today majority of humankind has held some belief or the other which has helped them relate to each other and to society, to nature, to the immense universe and which has attempted to provide an answer to the eternal mystery of death, and life after death. In our times, this belief system has been called religion. Despite their divisive nature at global level, religions old and new have survived thousands of years, reflecting man's deep need for God. Dev and I and about 80 per cent of India of our time were born Hindu. My father would tell me of Hinduism as one of the oldest religions whose origins went back over 6000 years to the time when the Vedas were written. The four Vedas written in Sanskrit contain a body of knowledge which the wise sages of that time revealed upon meditation in the form of hymns and prayers and rituals. '*Rig Veda* is the oldest known book in the world and its opening *shloka*—"*agni meele purohitam*"—in reverence of the fire that dispels darkness and gives warmth is the very first verse of the most ancient text known to mankind', said my father. From the Vedic tradition emerged Hinduism, also referred to as *Sanatana Dharma* or the eternal law. Contained in the Vedas are the 108 Upanishads where the essential principles of Hinduism reside.

I grew up understanding Hinduism as pluralistic and liberal which taught that there are various paths to truth, different ways to seek omnipotent God, where *shastrath* or debate was encouraged and there was freedom to question, where time is believed to move in four great cycles or *yugas*, each of millions of years, where there is harmony and order in the universe with which human beings can align by performing simple *pujas* and where human life itself has four goals i.e. *dharma* or rightful duties, *artha* or working for livelihood and prosperity, *kama* or human desires and *moksha* that is salvation and liberation from the cycle of birth and death. Death is nothing but end of the physical body for the soul is everlasting and part of the Supreme Being. *Moksha* can be attained through the right *karma* or actions in one's lifetime and also through practice of *Yoga*. Accordingly ideal human life is divided into four phases or *ashrams* of twenty-five years each beginning with *brahmacharya* or student life, followed by *grihastha* or life of a householder, then *vanaprastha* or age of retirement and withdrawal, and finally *sannyasa* or renunciation.

Our sacred texts are either *Shruti* which is 'heard directly from God' and is the heart-centre of Hinduism, or *Smriti* which is remembered and can be attributed to an author. Our main scriptures are the Vedas, Upanishads and *Bhagavad Gita* which are all *Shruti* and the *Ramayana*, *Mahabharata* and Puranas which are the *Smriti*s. *Smriti*s are the narratives and stories through which *Shruti* comes alive! These scriptures contain the righteous way of life, the moral fabric of society, codes of conduct and philosophy, theology, *yoga* and *puja*. Intrinsic to them are the concepts of *atma* or spirit and *brahman* or the essence of creation. Little did Dev or I know then that the 'Om' he was writing on examination answer sheets is the most sacred *mantra* of Hinduism, it is the eternal sound within which all sounds reside, which represents universal energy or God itself. In recent times I heard of NASA's satellites capturing vibrations of the solar system and those vibrations seem to produce a sound similar to 'Om'!

***

The various choices for compulsory SUPW vocation classes were sculpture, photography, music, painting and carpentry. I had taken photography while Dev had chosen sculpture. We would often jokingly refer to SUPW lessons as 'Some Useful Periods Wasted'. Be that as it may, the SUPW classes were enjoyable and helped us to at least make an introduction with a craft.

Dev appeared to enjoy sculpture certainly more than he enjoyed chemistry lessons! I vividly recall the image of Dev working on his sculpture: intently looking at his emerging piece of art, using a chisel and hammer to give it shape and proportion, concentrating hard to attain perfection and beauty in his creation, a little smattering of plaster of paris on his drape, and so immersed in his craft that his 40-minutes SUPW period would get over in the blink of an eye and Mr Thapa, the sculpture teacher, would have to tell him that he could complete what was left in the next class. A man immersed in a moment of time is the most fulfilled and happy human being. Hinduism mentions *moksha* and salvation, the one way I know how that might be attained is for human beings to immerse themselves in pursuits where they lose track of time and whose creative completion is its ultimate reward!

A five-stanza poetry rhyming and touching the most tender of human emotions, a painter bringing her canvas alive with colour and sensation, a teacher delivering a lecture where the listeners are held spellbound with the depth of knowledge yet simplicity of its conveyance, a batsman crafting a chanceless innings of character with sublime stroke play, an entrepreneur meeting the identified need of the target segment with a smartly-priced product marketed with the intention of not just of profit but of organisational development and community service, a doctor using his deep understanding of human anatomy and medicine to alleviate the patient's pain, a lawyer arguing, a designer fabricating, a priest reciting, a cobbler mending, and a writer letting his pen flow using the words of his chosen language to express his innermost thoughts and building a fervent relationship with his unseen readers—every activity can lend itself to an art form so long as its roots are in passion and sincerity. That activity ceases to be an effort. Time, the supreme dimension, has to smilingly sit back to allow a human being so immersed to create and complete his universe.

The Ashwath Public School was celebrating its silver jubilee in 1980 and amongst the many events planned was an exhibition of students' achievements. In a little corner of the front grounds on a five-feet-by-three-feet tripod board were mounted four of Dev's sculptures. On the top right corner of the board was inscribed: *Devavratt Pratap Rajvansh—Xth-E.* A few parents and some students and teachers stopped at the sculpture corner too and complimented Dev. He smiled and thanked them, and frequently looked back at his sculptures admiring his own work and re-living those SUPW periods when he had created them. SUPW ended at secondary school level, and those were the last sculptures that Dev ever made.

At this point in time, the start of a new decade, my parents and Dev's guardians were giving us exactly the same advice! The year X Board exam was all important, not only would a good performance help us choose our preferred subjects for senior school but these grades would show up on our certificates and in CV forever! This decade of the 1980s was going to set the foundation for the direction our careers and lives would take.

But while Dev was trying his best at academics, and dabbling in sculpture and getting interested in Hindi poetry, his deepest passion lay elsewhere. His eyes twinkled and his stride became purposeful only on the cricket field. He was a different person in the field and on that patch of twenty-two yards that he would later in life describe as a territory where 'riveting game of outdoor chess' was played. Throughout secondary school years, Dev had motivated the boys in our section E to show up on winter month's Saturdays at the school cricket ground for matches. The two pitches on TAPS cricket ground were only used by the school cricket team to practice on, for inter-class cricket matches of years X and below to take place, and indeed, for the year X Sub-Juniors

Cricket Tournament that helped in selection of the senior school cricket team. Recess time cricket matches could be played anywhere but not on 'the square' where the two pitches were laid. But Dev and Goldie had taken permission from the school vice-principal and school cricket coach for us to play on one of those pitches on Saturdays during winter months. Usually, 10 to 12 of us would show up in assorted clothes for those Saturday cricket matches. It was delightful to see each other in non-school uniform clothes! We would all pool money to buy a new cricket ball, and while some were independent enough to reach the school on their own, others would have one of their parents drop them.

Dev was the traditional opening batsman and Goldie the traditional opening fast bowler. They would always be captains of opposite teams and in those two years both of them came for every single match. My faint recollection from those enchanting morning games includes Dev taking some astonishing diving catches, and bowling his off-cutters at such nagging length that made it difficult for anyone to score off them, Goldie's and Raghu's bowling having that menacing zip about it, Gopi's incredible throws from the boundary line into the keeper's gloves, Ramu's mild grunt as he got into his delivery stride, Sanju's cute bowling action, Gurpreet's little dance every time his team got a wicket and Dhiraj's superb stroke play.

The one match I remember till today is when Dev's team was chasing 99 runs to win. We were playing seven a side with both sides fielding! I was in Goldie's team that day, and Dev's team was suddenly 6 down with not even 10 runs on the board and their last player who came in to join Dev was Satinder who had a polio affected arm. We were certain to win. But Dev kept hitting fours and picking up singles off the fifth or sixth ball of every over. I could hear him say to Satinder, 'This ball is like a dog, if you get scared it will scare you; just keep your eyes on it, put your bat-pad together and play forward.'

Eventually, Dev cut a short ball past me at point to win that match. He was 90 not out and Satinder 9 not out! What had also happened just when Dev and Satinder got together was that we saw two of our female classmates walk past. They used to live just across the road from the school and might have come for a walk. We had always seen them in navy blue skirt and white shirt, but that day Nita and Ira were looking most attractive and smart in jeans and t-shirt. Gurpreet concluded that Dev had got inspired by Nita! Why Nita and not Ira is a question Gurpreet never answered! During the school-week, he scribbled Nita's name on the back pages of Dev's notebooks, which Dev would labouriously try and scratch out. A little love-tale had been supposedly started!

Despite all the cricket that section E boys used to play, when the Year X Sub-Juniors Cricket Tournament started, it was section U who were the favourites. The Year X inter-class cricket matches, or the Sub-Juniors Cricket Tournament as it was called, always took place in early November. Each team would get four matches and play all the sections once in a 25 over-a-side game. There used to be two matches a day and the top two teams would then play the 30 over a side final.

Dev, of course, was our captain, and Goldie was the vice-captain. It must be said for Goldie's sportsmanship that he never resented Dev being the captain and came across as a true team-man. A week before the matches started, Dev would keep discussing the strategy with me even during lessons. I told him we were not playing Test matches and while the games were competitive, in the end it was all for fun. His reply was, 'It would be fun to win as well.'

The sub-juniors cricket tournament was actually watched by several teachers and a large number of class IX and X students. Some of the TAPS cricket team players—who were all from the senior school—would also see the matches in order to select the players for the school cricket team. Picture and names of the winners would go up in the reception of the school building and stay there for two years. A few days before the tournament the chatter in corridors was all about the cricket matches that lay ahead. Dev had told me that when we step out, I should loudly talk about how good our spinners were. Once back in the class and on our desk when I asked him, 'But you are the only spinner; Goldie, Raghu, Vinod, Indranil are all pacers;' he looked at me with an expression I had never seen before. His eyes were twinkling and he had a mischievous smile on his face. Ah! He wanted the other sections to believe that our strength was spin while it was actually our fast bowling! I generally used to feel somewhat protective about Dev given his quiet nature, but for once, I felt he knew exactly what he was doing. He seemed in-charge and for the cricket week, I felt safe knowing Dev was strategising.

Delhi Winter And The Golden Sun

Delhi winters are always glorious and romantic. The golden winter sun is gentle and charming, and it makes a promise of friendship that I have not known any Delhiite to ever resist. The gardens of Delhi, as indeed our school, would always be full of lilies and roses during winters. The air has a scent of crispness, and particularly if the body is youthful its spirit soars for the life-giving sun in the skies during Delhi winters!

The first match of the sub-juniors' cricket tournament was always between sections A and E. When Dev went out to toss for the first match, that golden sun was shining brightly. Just as his tall frame was about to step out from our changing area, Raghu asked him what we would do if we won the toss. Without any hesitation he turned around and said, 'Of course we'll bat. We'll always bat first if we win the toss.'

I think that was the time he realised that he should communicate with his teammates more. From thereon, he would always make it a point to sit together in the morning before any match and discuss the game plan. He seemed utterly confident of what he was doing. I had found him rather hesitant several times in class but here he seemed to know just what he was up to.

'By the time 25 overs are finished, everyone will be tired. Batting second with the added pressure of chasing runs is always difficult. Unless it is very chilly or the pitch is too grassy, we should bat first. And here it's not grassy,' Dev explained his logic for batting first, pointing towards the two wickets we were supposed to play the matches on.

Devavratt lost the toss and section A batted first. In no time, Goldie and Raghu, our opening bowlers, had them in deep trouble and at the end of seven overs section A were 32 for 6. The wicket seemed quite fast even though it wasn't grassy. Both Raghu's wickets were catches held by Dev, one in the covers and the other at mid-off. The mid-off catch was unbelievable. It was a hard flat hit shot which was travelling very fast but was a couple of feet from the ground. From the slips where I was standing it seemed about 10 feet from where Dev was standing, the next thing I saw was Dev a couple of feet from the ground and parallel to it, in the air, lunging to his right with his right arm fully stretched. He tumbled once as he fell to the ground with the ball in his right hand and joy on his face. We all ran to Dev and he retorted with a smile, 'I usually don't drop those.'

Goldie and Raghu made way for Vinod and Indranil. Dev told Vinod to bowl well pitched up deliveries on the toes of the section A captain. From mid-off, he said he had noticed him shuffle a bit too much to his off stump and not roll his wrists while flicking the ball. 'His head falls over a bit to the right,' as Dev put it. If he played a shot, chances were that he would overexpose the flick and Dev put a fine leg, a deep square leg, a mid-wicket, a backward short leg and a mid-on for that overexposed flick. If he missed, he would get bowled behind his legs. He also told Vinod to bowl his fourth ball really slow. But when Vinod tried it, it was too slow and almost bounced twice before it reached the batsman. The batsman ferociously drove it through the covers but Gurpreet dived to his left and disallowed any run. I could hear Dev clapping and shouting, 'That's it, they won't even get to 60 if we field that way.'

I was seeing a brand-new Dev! The next ball was clipped by the batsman off his pads. It soared high in the air and came down straight into the lap of our deep square leg fielder. We had trapped their captain! This was perfect bowling, perfect catching and near perfect tactical thinking. While I was not a fraction as cricket crazy as Dev was, I could play reasonably well, but it was then that I really began to feel how tact and strategy was required at every point in cricket. Indeed, cricket is one sport which is played more in the mind than on the field and Devavratt had a tactic up his sleeve at almost all times throughout the tournament.

Devavratt brought himself on and kept the mid-on up, thus inviting a shot. He bowled fast-ish off spinners and was deadly with his line and length. His first over cost him one run, his last ball was slow looping and flighted and as the batsman went down the wicket, I knew that could be a catch. But Raghu couldn't hold on to a high skier which seemed to be in the air forever. He told me once that when you bowl a high-flighted ball what happens is that the balance of the batsman's head is disturbed for his head goes up as he follows the ball in its flight and once 'you lose your head, it invariably results in a lofted stroke'—in cricket and in life!

Section A was 80 for 8 in the 21st over. Dev's first ball of his next over was bowled from wide off the crease. It pitched seam up on the middle stump at a nagging length. From the first slip I saw the batsman just hanging his bat out, instead of cutting in the ball cut away and *click*—the off bail was rudely dislodged. The bail went spinning high over my head and the score was 80 for 9. Dev bowled a fast well-pitched ball to their last batsman which was smartly driven back. But Dev leapt to his right to field the ball and even without looking back, threw the ball reverse-handed at the non-striker's stumps. The non-striker who had taken a start was left stranded. As we walked back having dismissed section A for 80, Goldie also appreciated Dev's run-out. He usually didn't praise Dev but for a change he did. We all cheered Goldie as we walked back to our changing area.

Devavratt decided not to open the batting that day. 'I'm happy with my batting,' he said. 'Why don't some of you get practice in the middle?'

As we munched some sandwiches, we spoke about the morning. Dev felt that the wicket was a very good one to bat on and that Goldie and Raghu had bowled skilfully. 'Just your normal game', he kept saying. 'Play your shots.'

When Gopi and Gurpreet went out to bat nobody could guess that the game would be over as soon as it ultimately got over. At 15 for no loss in four overs all of us felt the game was going completely our way. But it wouldn't be cricket if nothing strange happened in a game. From 15 for no loss, we slumped to 30 for 4. All the wickets fell while the batsmen were playing their shots. Some of them were injudicious shots. Dev had padded up along with me when Dhiraj got out to make it 29 for 3. And when Gopi departed Dev with a little pensive look on his face stood up and asked me to wait. 'Finish this off, Dev,' said Gurpreet as Dev picked up his bat.

He took a single off the first ball he faced. We were 31 for 4 when the eighth over began, we were 81 for 4 at the end of the 10th over! Overs 8, 9 and 10 were treated with such authoritative contempt that everyone seeing the match that day stood up on their feet to see Devavratt in that murderous mood. He seemed to despatch anything even remotely in his vicinity to the fence. His arrogant 42 came off 12 scoring shots, he hit 4 fours in the eighth over from Kumar, another 4 in the ninth over from Vikram and two more followed in the 10th over of the innings that Bhatia bowled. Section A seemed utterly helpless as Dev flashed his bat like a mace. He just pulverised those three bowlers. The boundaries he hit off Kumar were all cover drives and were brutal in their execution. As he trotted back from the ground the section A guys applauded his batting. He gently nodded his head to them once. In the changing area Sanju who was not playing in the tournament said, 'That was sensational.'

Dev smiled a little.

Later in our life, Dev and I discussed cricket so many times. The sport remained his fascination throughout. 'Whoever invented cricket was the ultimate genius; it's like chess being played outdoors.'

While every sport is thrilling for those who enjoy it, perhaps no other game is impacted by so many factors from weather to nature of the pitch and the toss to how old the ball is. The combinations and situations which can arise in cricket are endless, and the ever-evolving laws of the game are always trying to keep a fine balance between the bat and the ball. 'The cricket laws are handed down to us by the gods,' said a cricket enthusiast to Dev much later in life and he narrated that to me with boyish delight. Dev always found Test match cricket the, 'Most riveting form of the game, like a three-hour classic movie drama'.

On another occasion, Dev read out from the book *Corner of a Foreign Field* how 'cricket has been both a mirror and catalyst for social change in India'. He paraphrased an illustration from the same book on Palwankar Baloo, a so-called 'lower caste' player who at the beginning of 20th century used to play in the Quadrangular cricket tournament in Bombay and who faced so much discrimination that during tea interval, he had to sip his refreshment outside, and not in the pavilion with other players, and then wash his own cup. Despite being the best player, he was never made the captain. Dev went on to tell me with the book still in his hand, that years before the movement against 'untouchability' started in India, Palwankar Baloo's brother Vithal became the captain of his team in the Quadrangular, his team members even carried him on their shoulders in jubilation! As he kept the book away, Dev shook his head and said, 'This caste discrimination must have been so terrible; any form of discrimination is so dreadful.'

Goldie, Raghu, Gopi and Dhiraj were our stars for most of the tournament. We were beaten by six wickets by Section U in our second game but we won our other matches quite comfortably. At the end of the round robin league Section

U had won all their games and we had won three. Thus, the finalists for the 1980 Sub-Juniors Cricket Tournament were Section U and Section E. We suffered a crippling blow when Goldie pulled his calf muscle running in from long off to take a catch in our last league match. We got the school doctor to examine him but it was hopeless; there was no way he could play the final.

On the morning of the final, we were all sitting in the changing area when Dev said, 'I wish Goldie was well' and he continued after a pause, 'but it may not be a huge loss that he is unable to play. Both wickets are worn out; we are playing today on wicket 1 that is worn out even more since so many games having been played. It will be on the slower side and at Goldie's pace, the ball would have come on to the bat nicely. Slower bowlers will be more difficult to score off now. Gopi you start as the keeper but mid-way through if the ball is keeping low and not coming onto the bat, let Gurpreet keep and you bowl as well.'

Gopi said, 'Fine, Dev, but Goldie was our best bowler and honestly, U section is very strong.'

'Cricket is a strange game,' replied Dev. 'On this slow wicket, you and Sandeep will be perfect substitutes for Goldie.' I had not done much in the matches and wasn't sure if I will play the final. Dev continued looking at me, 'I think your spin and front foot play will be really useful today.'

He then said to Raghu, Vinod and Indranil, 'Let's keep it just a bit short today, on a slow pitch that is keeping low batting won't be easy. Let's surprise U section today!'

It was a lovely crisp morning. We had been in the field since 8:30 am, warming up, doing some catch practice and feeling the ball on the bat. It was fairly cold and the hard cricket ball really stung on the hands. The final match of the 1980 TAPS Sub-Juniors Cricket Tournament was scheduled to start at 10 am.

By 9:15 am the ground was really packed. This was always a special event in the year's calendar for the school. Dr Oberoi, our school principal, arrived at 9:25 to meet the teams. He too was fond of the game and always supported sports activity in the school. As we and the Section U team lined up to meet the principal, I had not imagined that 40 years later I would be re-living that day again by writing about it.

At 9:40 am, Devavratt and Deepak, captain of Section U, went out to toss. Section U were favourites but Dev seemed very relaxed. As they walked back from the wicket Dev and Deepak shook hands, Dev looked at us in the changing area and with his left hand signalled that we were batting.

Gopi picked up his pads, he and Devavratt were to open. As Dev got back to the changing area he said, 'It's definitely going to be a slow wicket, and I think the ball will stay low. Let's try and get on the front foot as far as possible. Occasionally the ball will misbehave due to the cracks. 150 will be fighting.'

Among some excellent players the Banerjee brothers were section U stars. They were both fast bowlers and although they were not brothers, they were known as the 'Banerjee brothers'. During our recess-time friendly games with tennis ball we had played with them a few times, and even with the tennis ball they were not easy to play. Dev and Goldie and Dhiraj with their good techniques had played them well, but neither was Goldie playing that day nor were the Banerjee brothers going to have a tennis ball in their hands!

School Cricket Final

The Tall-Banerjee bowled the first ball of the final match at 10 am and it took Gopi's off stump with it. There was a hush in the ground. Gurpreet had barely put on one of his pads when Gopi returned back to the change area. At the end of first over we were 0 for 1.

The first ball of the second over from the Short-Banerjee wrapped Dev on his half stretched left leg, from where we were sitting, he seemed plumb in front. But the umpire ruled him not out. On the next ball Dev opened the account for us with a glance down to square leg. The last ball of the second over again kept low and wrapped Gurpreet on his half stretched left leg. The vociferous appeal for leg before was this time upheld, we were 1 for 2.

The wicket was keeping low and at 15 for 2 as Dhiraj went for a drive he played early to give cover a simple catch. 15 for 3 looked like a desperate situation. But 15 for 4 was worse as the next ball of that over from the Tall-Banerjee to Raghu again kept low and he was late in coming down on the back-foot. Dev square drove a low full toss to the cover point boundary and then half glided half cut a wide half volley for 3 to the third man. Vinod tried to hit out of trouble and his two lusty blows took us to 30 for 4 in the seventh over. When he tried another big hit, he only managed to connect with the root of the bat and lobbed an easy return catch to Tall-Banerjee. Indranil was the next batsman in and was exceptionally unlucky to get a shooter from Short-Banerjee that wrapped him plumb in front of the wicket.

When I stepped out to bat, I realised that the 200 odd students and teachers who had come to see the match seemed very disappointed. As I crossed a grim looking Dev at the non-striker's end, I smiled at him; he looked at me and said, 'Front foot please.'

I played the two balls remaining in the over on the front foot. As the field changed, Dev came up to me and said, 'Let's try and play the overs at least, please play on the front foot. Don't worry about the score or the six wickets which have fallen. Just the front foot full stretch.'

This was over number eight. Deepak for some reason removed Tall-Banerjee from the attack, perhaps to save his two overs for any eventuality later on. I saw Dev was standing a few inches outside the popping crease and just as the ball was delivered, his front foot would go lunging forward. His brows were knitted but his forehead seemed like steel. The Devavratt of the first match had bludgeoned a near half century in merely three overs. But here he was playing copybook defensive shots. Ball after ball, over after over, his bat would block every ball hurled at him. It remained as straight as an arrow, and not even the air blowing in The Ashwath Public School could penetrate his bat and pad that morning. He had asked me to be prepared from the fourth ball of the over for a single. We started scoring in singles and sometimes an odd two.

I had never realised how engrossing the game of cricket could be even if runs were not flowing or wickets were not falling. I felt really important batting that day. Dev and I were fighting with our backs to the wall. But we were fighting. We had neither given up nor were we foolishly trying to hit out. We had to play those overs out. Runs would perhaps start coming. We had to keep our heads down. Matches like these teach lessons for life. At the end of 18 overs, we were 58 for 6. But I was feeling confident at least in staying on with Dev.

We started accelerating from thereon. Dev was on the front foot and beginning to drive the ball now. For the first 18 overs he had only pushed or nudged the ball. 'Concentrate now, Sandeep, their shoulders are dropping. They will tend to overpitch as they try harder. Let's aim for five per over for a few overs.'

We had only 12 more overs to make a match of it. In the next five overs, we got exactly 25 runs. I was seeing the ball really well and found that although I was committing myself on to the front foot, on one occasion when the ball was really short, I was able to get back on the back foot and pull it to the mid-wicket fence. Dev meanwhile was at his elegant best, driving fluently, with a bat as straight as his character.

'You are batting well now,' Dev said to me, 'so I won't farm the strike anymore, but let's not do anything silly. After one of us leaves, we may not get too many.'

Dev off-drove the first ball of the 24th over and started running hard. 'Three Sandeep, three', he shouted. The fielder had the ball in his hands at the long off fence. It was their fast bowler with a strong arm. I was hesitant but Dev was shouting, 'Run, run', and so off we went.

The throw narrowly missed the non-strikers end and resulted in four overthrows. We got seven off that ball and Dev had a half century. I saw everyone at the ground stand up and give a huge applause to Dev. As we crossed each other on the wicket I was clapping the bat with my left hand. He merely looked at me with the slightest of smiles and winked at me!

That wink said so much. It was the first time I had seen Dev wink. Who knows it may have been the first time in his 15 years that he had done so. He raised his bat for a split second; his celebration was as understated as him. But that wink has stayed with me ever since, it seemed to say that we are winning because we are trying, and while we are with each other, this game may still be ours.

We got 16 off the 24th over as I flicked two half volleys on my legs for boundaries. 99 for 6 off 24. At the end of the 26th over we were 119 for 6, Dev batting on 68, I was on 31 and there had not been a single no-ball or wide-ball by section U that morning.

Tall-Banerjee returned to bowl the 27th over, and this was to be the battle royal of the tournament. Tall-Banerjee was the fastest and most successful bowler of the tournament. Devavratt was never more determined on the cricket ground. Section U were still the favourites, although Dev and I had put up some sort of resistance. Banerjee's first ball was overpitched on the off stump, Dev went forward and played defensively, the ball went to the point boundary! The next ball was fast and pitched at a good length on the off stump. Dev went forward and gently drove it, ever so gently that the bottom of his bat merely got above his knees. The ball raced to the cover boundary! Deepak ran in from mid-on to have a word with Banerjee. Banerjee came tearing in and bowled a short off-length ball which was deceptively slow, Dev seemed beaten for a split second on his front foot but quickly adjusted himself, stood up and on drove the ball between Tall-Banerjee and Deepak. Another four!

The fourth ball was pitched on Dev's pads and he went forward and sent it scurrying to the mid-wicket fence, his bat was as high as his shoulder when he finished executing the flick. Deepak was shouting at his tall bowler! Banerjee decided to come round the wicket. Yet again, he pitched on Dev's legs; Dev left his signature on TAPS Cricket Tournament with that shot. He came forward, picked up the ball, flicked it and sent it soaring way over the square leg boundary through the bushes hitting the junior school building wall. His bat went a full circle this time and was pointing over third man when he had finished, both his hands were over his head. His right leg was off the ground and if that bat was taken away from his hands, he would seem like Lord Shiva doing a war dance! Banerjee slumped to the ground. There was loud cheer from everyone at the ground watching the match, and an even louder one from our team. Dev had moved from 68 to 90 in five balls! We were 141 for 6, Dev and I had put on 111 for the 7th wicket. As he straight drove the last ball I was backing up, Banerjee's left hand would have just touched the ball which deflected off his fingers on to the stumps. I was a few inches out of my crease and my innings ended there, run out for 31.

I have never heard such a loud applause for me as I did that early afternoon. It left me with a lesson for life. In any new situation try and see what is happening, play with a straight bat until you are established, never underestimate anyone but never be overawed by anyone either, patience usually bears fruit which is sweet. And the man who had implored me to play that way was behind me, I just looked back at Devavratt; he was standing at the wicket applauding my effort.

I had barely got my batting gear off when I heard another loud roar. As I looked up, I saw the ball sailing over us and landing near Dev's sculpture area! He tried another big hit and this time it was finally the turn of Section U to be jubilant. Gurpreet standing beside me muttered, 'Caught behind.'

If my applause was a loud one, this was deafening. Dev was walking back after a sensational knock of 96. It had been 28 overs of pure classical batting. He had a very relaxed and satisfied look on his face as he got back to a thundering applause. Our innings folded at 149 in the 29th over.

During lunchtime, our school cricket coach came to our huddle area. He looked at Dev and said, 'In my 12 years with this school, I have never seen a better innings during this Tournament.'

Dev gently smiled and pointed towards me.

'Well played', said our coach shaking my hand. 'I am proud of both of you; cricket is all about character you know! Best of luck. It is an open game now.'

Dev looked at him and nodded. He was really tired; I was really tired too. That morning brought Devavratt and me together in more ways than one.

We all sat down together to plan out the afternoon. 'This is a slow, low wicket. We shouldn't sacrifice length for pace, third-man and long leg should be square and not fine, a widish slip will be enough. Raghu, Vinod, Indranil—just keep it up slightly short of a length in line with the off and middle stump. We'll open with a spinner on one end. It doesn't matter whether we win or lose but let us give our everything in the next two hours.' Devavratt Rajvansh, who we started calling Skipper Dev after that match, drew out his last strategy for the Tournament.

Section U was 40 for no loss by the middle of ninth over, and Tony the opener was batting solidly, as was his partner. Dev persisted with Raghu and Gopi for the first 10 overs. On the last ball of the ninth over, Dev put a deep square leg along with a long leg. In addition, there was a mid-wicket, a backward short-leg and a mid-on. Devavratt shouted from covers to Raghu, 'Get it on top of his right shoulder.'

Raghu charged in and instead of bowling a bouncer around the striker's right shoulder bowled a toe-crushing yorker. We saw to our delight the leg stump cartwheeling. A good old trick! The field was set for a bouncer but instead a yorker is bowled. Gopi gave away six runs in his fifth over and the scorecard at the end of 10 overs read 46 for 1.

The first change in bowling was made only after Raghu had bowled his sixth and last over, with Vinod replacing him. Dev asked me to bowl a few overs as well of my military medium and got Gopi back as wicket-keeper. We were beginning to worry and at the half way mark Section U looked comfortable at 71 for 1. My last ball of my second over was a full toss that Ramandeep pulled through mid-wicket, instead I found the ball looping high over his head and almost half the field ran to the skier. Gopi shouted, 'Mine, mine,' and we all waited for a long long time to see the ball eventually descend into his safe gloves. I was thrilled to get a wicket but was surprised when Dev came to me at the end of that over and said, 'Thanks, Sandeep; that will be all.'

Indranil replaced me and with his first ball that kept really low had the new batsman plumb in front. This was over number 17 and Section U were 82 for 3. Dev was trying to ensure that everybody was on their toes and not allowing the good shape of Section U innings to demoralise anyone. Vinod's fifth ball in the 18th over was pushed between mid-off and covers by Deepak, and as I tried to run behind the wicket-keeper to cover the throw, I could see Dev sweep on the ball and in the same action, with a flick of his wrists, break the striker's stumps. Yes! We had got Tony run out! We were jubilant. This was the wicket we wanted and at 94 for 4 the game was open again.

Dev eagerly took the ball after Vinod had finished the 18th over. This was to be his day. He marked his short run up and ran in gently and immediately pitched the ball just outside the off-stump at perfect length. Deepak played forward and the ball came in and hit the bail over his leg and middle stump. 94 for 5 and the captain gone! His third ball again pitched on the off-stump and cut in sharply; Short-Banerjee played forward and was hit on the pads. We instinctively went up in appeal and were a little surprised when the umpire raised his finger. Dev, Gopi and I all thought that the ball would have missed the leg stump but then this was a leg before wicket decision. Short-Banerjee wasn't happy at all. For more than a moment Dev thought if we should withdraw the appeal but then both Gopi and Indranil were adamant. Gopi said assertively, 'Forget it! It's an LBW and he didn't touch it. The umpire knows best.'

Dev said nothing but quietly went back to his bowling mark. The fifth ball of his over was a beauty, he bowled it from close to the stumps with the seam up but an off-break action. It pitched on the middle stump and the batsman expected it to move in a little. Instead, it moved away and hit the top of the off-stump. It was music for us as we reduced Section U to 94 for 7.

Our tails were up and we knew that we were going to be champions that day. Vinod bowled his next over at express speed but kept the ball short. He got an LBW decision with a ball that scooted and so when Dev took the ball for his second over, they were 99 for 8. Again, the same sharp in cutter and yet another clean bowled occurred! As their last batsman, Tall-Banerjee pushed the next ball to short mid-off, there were loud 'Yes-No-Yes-No' and the batsmen started running. Gurpreet grabbed the ball in his hand and ran to the striker's end. As he took off the bails, Banerjee, who had been sent back, was stranded in the middle of the wicket. I saw Dev pull out two stumps and run towards the striker's end where all of us were hugging each other. All 11 of us and two of our classmates who were not playing were shouting with joy and deliriously hugging each other.

'I got this for you', said Dev, giving me one stump. We hugged each other again. Triumph is so essential for team spirit. Section U team came to congratulate us and Deepak got all his team to applaud for us together. There was amazing noise coming from where rest of our class was sitting. Goldie, who could not play but had come in to see the final, seemed crazy with joy. We all picked Dev up, ran out in the field and hurled him in the air three times amidst loud cheer. Then Goldie shouted, 'Sandeep'; and they all grabbed me and threw me up thrice. We then did that to Raghu, Gopi, Goldie, Dhiraj and Vinod as well. It was unadulterated happiness flowing ever so effortlessly.

There was no surprise as our cricket coach announced the player of the match. Dev went up a second time to receive the winner's cup and said, 'If you don't mind Sir, I would like the entire section E team to receive this lovely trophy.' As we all stepped up and received the cup, Dev whispered in my ear, 'Wouldn't have been possible without you.'

We all congregated as the photographer arranged us for a memorable picture that hung in the reception of TAPS for two years. Each one of us was also given a print and Dev and I framed our copies. In my old house in Delhi, family photographs have now pushed that picture out though it lies tucked away carefully in one of my cupboards and I intend to someday display it in my Gurgaon apartment. Every time I look at it, it makes me feverishly nostalgic. But the past is frozen in time. No institution is ever the same once we leave it and try and return to it to re-live a few moments from the past. But it lives in our minds; it creates warmth and occasionally soft agony at the time which has slipped away.

Though Sanju never played cricket seriously, he was there that day cheering us throughout. After the match and presentations and all the congratulations from the teachers were over, we went to Sanju's house in Green Park to celebrate. 15 to 17 of us in his living room—sitting on the sofa, on the settee, on the floor, on the dining table chairs—re-lived how Gopi got out or Banerjee bowled, how Indranil had dived or how Dhiraj had hit a shot, how Short-Banerjee got a dubious decision or how Deepak had lost his cool! We laughed and laughed. After every few minutes that evening at Sanju's someone mentioned Dev's name and mine! Twice I happened to see Dev looking a little lost, but soon he joined the laughter and banter. It had been a memorable day and it was a memorable evening too. As we bid goodbye to go back to our respective homes and I said to Dev, 'Well played, skipper Dev!'

He smiled back with pursed lips and then said to me, 'We should have called Short-Banerjee back, he was not out.'

Notwithstanding that sober reflection and compunction of guilt, those few days had an impact on Dev's demeanour. From then on, he wasn't as aloof as he had been previously. He never cycled back home unnoticed and would say bye to a few class mates. There were many more in the class wanting to engage him in a conversation and as always, he would speak in short sentences but converse with everyone. I managed to find a marker pen and scribbled on that stump Dev had given me—*TAPS 1980 Cricket Winners*. It took me some persuasion but I eventually got him to sign it as well—*Devavratt Pratap Rajvansh*, he wrote in full! He refused however to put in brackets the word 'Captain' which I wanted him to!

A week later the senior school cricket team selection took place and there were some 20 odd hopefuls. The senior school cricket captain and Cricket Coach were going to do the selection. Dev was in the field just taking some high catches when the school captain called him and said, 'You're in! No need for you to spend the day here today. Just join us after school hours for practice every Monday, Wednesday and Friday.' Dev was absolutely delighted.

The Ashwath Public School's cricket team was known all over Delhi as one of the best. Three of our school mates went on to play international level cricket as well. Though he never said so, but Dev's biggest dream was to play Test cricket for India. In December that year, Dev played two matches also for the school cricket team. He made 20 in one of the matches and bowled well in the other without picking up a wicket.

Just before the school shut for Christmas and New Year's break, he seemed the Dev of old, more withdrawn and aloof than usual. He had had a chat with his uncle about pursuing cricket seriously who had told him, 'Son we are a country of 600 million people, and only 11 make it.'

Dev didn't argue with his uncle but felt very sad. Middle-class India was very risk averse then; it has moved forward a fair bit since. It was not in the cultural upbringing of our time to argue with our elders: the respect for elders is a fine social value but when it begins to inhibit free thought it hinders individuality and arguably progress. We knew very little of life at that time and were guided by our parents. Dev didn't go for the cricket practice after school hours from then on nor did he play any further matches for TAPS.

Dev's Conundrum

Man's endless quest is for happiness. We chase it with all our might all our lives. Every person develops his or her own formula for happiness. Qualifying for the best possible educational institution, finding the dream job and earning lots of money, consuming nourishing food to stay healthy, wearing comfortable but trendy clothes to look appealing, finding and enjoying the company of like-minded friends and for most Delhiites making friends with socially relevant people, travelling to exotic places, reading intellectually stimulating authors, finding escape either in a pub or a place of worship, seeking fame through an industry adored by the masses, or becoming a source of happiness for others through social service. All our actions and pursuits—physiological, social, emotional, intellectual, religious and finally self-actualising seek happiness and bliss. It is in nature that most things we chase and desperately try to cling onto tend to elude us. The formula for happiness begins to show errors at various stages of life and requires correction. A new formula is then developed, then another, then yet another.

The search for happiness brings a large number of people into contact with religion. The origin of religion was to help human beings self-reflect and be conscious of ourselves—instead, religious practices have tended to focus on the preacher or the icons or the holy books and in many ways, got reduced to rituals, beliefs, dogmas and dos and don'ts. That which was meant to free through enlightenment has become the grand incarceration. That which should have united human beings has become hugely divisive. With every 'mine' and 'thine' comes a sense of superiority at least for some. Like the pecking order in hens, human beings are always looking to look down on fellow human beings. Marketers and politicians exploit this intriguing fallibility fully.

Every institution and action, every choice for those who have one, is based on what might enhance status more. Man seeks to distinguish himself from others and looks for superiority in the hope of finding happiness! Intelligence ends where the idea of superiority begins, and yet the thought of having status over others is such a delicious concoction that generation after generation has drowned itself in it. It is scrumptious to study in privately run public schools and look down on boys studying in government schools, to find admission in prestigious Delhi University colleges and look down on those in less exalted colleges, to work in a multinational company or American bank and think of employees in Indian companies and banks as less capable, to live in Golf Links or Vasant Vihar and consider those in Punjabi Bagh or Karol Bagh as less sophisticated, to work in New York or London and pontificate about those working in India—be it race or colour or caste or education or residence or club or passport or religion, every source of superiority conceals a hidden inferiority and complex.

With every complex there comes the death of intelligence, with death of intelligence there is smothering of inquisitiveness and acceptance of the holy book, the holy man and the holy rituals. A vicious cycle of again looking only outside for answers. Meanwhile the alpine chough flying at 25000 feet effortlessly and harmlessly is neither capitalist nor communist nor did he sit wondering about mixed economy! The cuckoo and the koel sing lovingly despite never knowing the verse of church or *shloka* of temple or *ayat* of mosque. And the sparrows chirp happily despite attending neither government schools nor Kendriya Vidyalaya or English speaking privately run public schools!

Man's continuous search for happiness is understandable but often in vain. If only he could live without 'mine' and 'thine', without clinging onto his 'sources' of happiness so aggressively, treating each day as the last day of his life, and identifying himself perfectly and totally with Nature, it would be happiness that would be finding man! That single *shloka* of The *Gita* seems to provide more than a hint on the essence of happiness—*Karmannye vadhikaraste maphaleshu kadachana*—doing the right act without worrying about the reward! However, man seeks rewards for his actions and also answers to his eternal questions which are ultimately ascribed to God.

Science solved many puzzles that religion had no answers to; the two have not necessarily and always been in conflict though. In fact, the origins of *Sanatana Dharma* or Hinduism were in science, the *Sanatana* principles are an exploration into nature and how human beings relate to it. Indeed, ancient Hindu texts refer to zero and infinity and the decimal system. The *Dashavatara* or ten incarnations of Vishnu is a reference to evolution of human beings. The Rig Ved alludes to The Big Bang and Ayurveda, the ancient form of medicine passed down to us from that era. Valmiki's *Ramayana* refers to the *Pushpak Viman* suggesting the knowledge of flying. The sacred Hindu number 108—the number of beads in the *mala* and the number of Upanishads—is the ratio of sun's distance from earth to sun's diameter! In the first *shloka* of *Mahabharata* which dates back to around 3000 BCE the blind king Dhritarashtra asks Sanjaya, his charioteer, to narrate live commentary on the battle of Kurukshetra. Thus, at the very least, the concept of a live telecast was conceptualised then! Kalidasa's *Meghadūta*, written in about the 4th century CE, is suggestive of wireless communication, with the *Yaksha* sending message to his wife through the cloud!

The divergence between Science and Religion happened when Science failed to answer the eternal questions, and also when religion became a source of political power. Science discovered natural laws which must have perplexed our ancestors. Technology has made our lives comfortable and, in many respects, safer. But despite finding answers to several timeless mysteries of the universe and making inventions most of which improved human life, neither Aryabhata nor Newton or Galileo or Einstein are worshipped as holy men. Nor are Shakespeare and Neeraj or Premchand and Wordsworth given the same place even though they provided nourishment to the soul. Poetry and literature are intangible and poets and authors can neither harm nor benefit happiness seeking man, and scientists can explain the ways of the cosmos only after the Big Bang with which 'time' began.

Nonetheless, science & technology were planting the seeds to make India into a push-button society at the start of the 1980s. All my friends and neighbours owned a transistor or Murphy radio by then, most had a black and white Televista or Dyanora TV and a Kelvinator fridge as well. A lot of them had a Bajaj mixer and a few households had at least a second-hand

Fiat or Ambassador car. I felt a little special because we had a telephone too, and several of our neighbours had passed on our number as PP or '*Padosi* Phone' to their kith and kin! I had got a blue coloured 'Speedwell' bicycle on my previous birthday and owned two watches—a HMT watch and one with a mickey mouse dial. My father promised me a Click 3 camera after the all-important year X Board exams! The freshness and fragrance of unbranded water coolers made summer afternoons merrily enjoyable for those who considered themselves a cut above the middle class. Calculators were not yet in vogue though ownership of slide-rules made a student distinguished. Of course, all of us carried compass and protractor in our Camlin geometry boxes.

There was no dearth of big news in India even as the board exams of class X loomed large on us. The Janata government which had come to power in 1977 lost the mid-term general election and Indira Gandhi-led Congress returned to power in early 1980. Her son Sanjay Gandhi died in a plane crash later that year. Amitabh Bachchan with his 'angry young man' image was at the height of his popularity and we would all discuss his movies as though we were analysing state of the economy! Boys started breathing heavily when they saw Zeenat Aman on film screen. Her song in movie *Qurbani*—*'Aap jaisa koi meri zindagi mei aaye'*, sung by Nazia Hassan—had all of us drooling with desire. Having gone medal-less at her national sport hockey for 16 years, India went onto win the Hockey gold in 1980 Olympics. Prakash Padukone put India on the international badminton map by winning the All England Championship. Sunil Gavaskar had recently led India to Test series wins against Australia and Pakistan and had become India's first sports brand icon with the famous advertisement—'While Sunil Gavaskar was perfecting his square drive, Palmolive was perfecting his shave.'

Doordarshan, however, was the only TV channel and we dreaded the demise of any political big-wig as it would mean three days national mourning and no telecast of sports or Tele-match, movies or *chitrahaar*, or English comedy serials like *Here's Lucy* or *Father, Dear Father* or *Yes Minister!* The blinding of over two dozen criminals in jail in Bhagalpur in Bihar was a hotly discussed subject in newspapers and in my parents' social circle. Also discussed by my parents and their friends was choice of subjects to be taken by their children as they moved from year X to senior school!

The year X Board exam was the biggest event about to happen in our young lives. We were to write exams in English and Hindi; mathematics, including geometry; sciences including physics and chemistry and biology; and social studies including history and civics and geography. In addition, there would be science practicals and a letter grade awarded for SUPW and physical education. The Board exams syllabus covered all that we had studied in year IX and X and the five groups of subjects carried an aggregate of 150 marks each. I was reasonably confident though mathematics exams did give me butterflies in the stomach. In the run-up to exams, I would be on the phone with my cousin Gautam, and Sanju and Dev and Ramu exchanging notes on difficult questions. There was exam fever in the air! Finally, that day arrived in the March of 1981.

I used to see Devavratt make notes since we became desk partners. He had a notebook for all subjects—separate from the classwork notebook—where he would write answers or practice questions and diagrams or some interesting facts that he would pick up from his uncle or a reference book. It was a habit I too picked up and during exams, I was realising the benefit of it. Smart, hard work never fails and all my exams went well. Dev did well too, and Ramu and Abhishek were always expected to do well.

After the last exam we all came back to TAPS for a class photograph, there were so few pictures taken in those days that I still have vivid memory how the tall Dev stood in the extreme right corner in the back row and I was next to him.

My father's publisher had his office in Kashmiri Gate and my brother and I would look forward to driving with my father to the publisher's office as they would always offer us Campa-Cola! Usually, we would pick up Gautam and Geeta from Greater Kailash to accompany us. My father's publisher's 40-year-old son Bansidhar used to lisp while talking and pronounce the 's' in any word as '*th*'. 'Nara*th*ima Rao is a very good bat*th*man' he said for a debutant Test cricketer. When Bansidhar asked me what subjects I intended to take in senior school I simply told him, 'Not science'.

To this, Bansi rather incredulously remarked, 'You are not taking commer*th*?'

Throughout our drives back Gautam, my brother and I would mimic Bansidhar and lisp away to delirious laughter.

All of us moving into year XI were soon to be confronted with the first choice of our lives: choosing a set of subjects. Gautam was clear that he would take sciences with mechanical drawing in senior school. Ramu too wanted to do engineering and was taking science with mechanical drawing. I was clear that I was not taking science as mathematics and physics was too frightening for me! And Dev had told me that he would take humanities!

'Why humanities?' I had exclaimed when he told me his intention. After all humanities was usually taken by the girls and only those few boys who were kissing the bottom of the class. Dev's uncle, who had brought him up, was in a government job. He used to work for the Indian Audit and Account Service and had inspired Dev to aim for the civil services, the Indian Administrative Service in particular. His opinion was that liberal arts subjects like history and political science make entry into the IAS easier. And so, Dev seemed rather clear that he would take humanities. His aversion to chemistry made the choice easier. I thought I should go for commerce without mathematics but a few of my father's colleagues—who were all university teachers—categorically told me that 'there is no career without mathematics'.

Our results were declared by end May. We had to go to the school to see the results. I saw Dev as soon as I entered TAPS.

'Congratulations, Sandeep!' he said looking relaxed.

'How much?' I asked him nervously.

'You got 70%.'

I was happy to hear 70% in those days was a very good score. 'You?'

'For our section Abhishek has 572, Ramkumar 549, Shweta and Ira are in the same range too.'

And you?' I repeated.

'I got 540, that's 72%.'

I congratulated Dev. He had to leave as his uncle was waiting outside. 'Come over for ICC next week,' I told him before he left.

He nodded.

The next few days were really lovely. I was the centre of attention in my home. A number of relatives called and came over to congratulate. In our neighbourhood there were all kinds of families. One of the families was dry-fruit merchants and their children studied in government schools. Their son Bittoo had also appeared for class X board exam. Every year that aunty would trudge to our home and ask me in her dismal soft voice with a depressed expression, 'Have you passed?'

'Passed!' I would mumble to myself, 'What does she mean 'passed'! Of course I would pass!'

Later I understood where she was coming from. Her son was academically poor. And theirs was a family where education was not accorded the same importance. A few days later, I saw her labouriously walking towards our home. She had that same depressed expression all her life! She opened the gate and I said namaste to her.

'Have you passed?' she muttered in her dismal voice.

'Yes,' said I.

'Fine. Our Bittoo failed,' she lamented and went away.

When the schools re-opened, we were all split up into sections based on subject categories i.e. two sections of sciences, one with mechanical drawing and the other with biology; two of commerce, one with mathematics and the other without mathematics; and finally, one section of humanities. The school principal was surprised that Dev was opting for humanities. While most of the administrative discussions at that time were to discourage students who had not done well from taking sciences and commerce with mathematics, Dev's was a unique case where he was being encouraged to take either sciences or commerce with mathematics. However, he seemed clear and walked into the humanities section where there were 40 girls and four boys seated in one corner of the class room. I was sad that Dev was not with me since I had taken commerce with mathematics, as had Sanju and Abhishek and Shweta. Commerce without mathematics was the less distinguished section as it was meant for students whose performance had been average in the class X Board exam.

Manohar Pal Billa, as always, had just about secured pass marks in all subjects; however, he got 99% in mathematics. After some discussion amongst the teachers, he was allowed to join science with mechanical drawing. Ramkumar too went to science with MD. Nita joined the science with biology section, while Ira and 39 other girls were in humanities with Dev and three other boys. Goldie had requested for science but the school regretted since he had not achieved the grades required for taking science subjects at senior school level.

In the India of 1981, which was just about breaking away from her socialist present and conservative past, boys and girls didn't interact freely, and Dev with his reticent nature was that much more hesitant in talking to girls. And the three other boys in his section could talk about films and smoking and fashion and girls, but would stare so blankly at the mere mention of calculus or fundamental rights or rain shadow area or demand curve or Newton's laws of motion that Dev was caught in a web of his own making! He was the centre of attraction in that section even though the most attractive girls of TAPS happened to be in humanities. To make matters even more hilarious, in that torrid month of July, in the back corner of the class where Dev was sitting with Gurinder, who walked with a funny limp, the ceiling fan was not working! Every five minutes, Gurinder would climb on the desk and give the ceiling fan an all-mighty push, after precisely thirty seconds the fan would come to a helpless stop leaving a perspiring Dev wondering if the pursuit of Civil Services was after all worth it!

After five days of mental and physical and emotional torment, Dev could handle it no more and he went up to the senior humanities teacher—who had been very proud that a good student like Dev had joined the section—and requested for a section change! She referred him to the principal who told Dev that he could pretty much choose whichever section he wanted. Given that Dev disliked chemistry, his only choice was commerce. And with the section commerce without mathematics having become the abode of the academically mediocre and untamed, he opted to join commerce with mathematics! Dev was back in my section and in my classroom!

A few days later my younger brother joked with Dev and me, 'So ultimately both of you took Ban*th*idhar's advice!'

Senior School

'*Beta paneer kha*,' fathers could be heard urging their sons at dinners during north Indian marriages to have the cottage cheese dish instead of the commonplace potato or cauliflower. Paneer was a delicacy! Food at marriage parties was the most talked about feature by the guests who cared more about *shahi paneer* than the bride and groom! Food was the single most important factor around which socialising happened in India at that time. Food still remains the major building block of socialising in India and indeed around the world—golf, literary festivals, Resident Welfare Association meetings, exotic holidays with like-minded friends, shopping malls and prayer meetings notwithstanding. Of course, in today's India there has been an explosion in the cuisine types. The typically voluble happily married north Indian couple along with their two turbo-charged kids no longer set out on weekend evenings nowadays only to devour *shahi paneer* and butter chicken with *naan* at a Mughlai food restaurant, but have Italian, Chinese, Mexican, Continental, South-Indian and other cuisines to choose from. Not just food, but retailing in general is coming of age in the India of today. Since man arrived on this planet, food and survival has been the most basic desire. Complexity starts once basic desires are fulfilled, and legal, religious and social norms have to be established to manage man's unlimited and complex desires.

Almost all of us studying in year XI in The Ashwath Public School did not have to worry about food or our next meals, that was provided for by our parents. Most of us were looking to succeed in the XIIth Board Exam and secure admission in good colleges so that we could be gainfully employed. There were a few who were seeking a career in sports and some who had family businesses; nonetheless, everyone wanted at the very least a university graduation degree. And everyone wanted to look nice to get attention from the opposite gender—a 'hello' or smile from the pretty girl, an occasional phone call from the girl with sexy legs, some form of titillation, and some remote or even vicarious sexual experience. The greatest of philosophers and poets, from Buddha to Krishnamurthi and from Keats to Neeraj, all have thought and written on human desires. Small desires of the little human being help him live on this tiny blue planet with its enormous cargo of society, religion, knowledge, ideology, laws, norms, conventions, and the heaviest of them—ego.

Abhishek was now with us in the commerce with maths section, his parents wanted him to become a chartered accountant. Nita, Dev's supposed 'heart-throb', was in science with biology section and doing brilliantly well! She was never the topper during secondary school but blossomed so much during senior school that her teachers were certain she would qualify for AIIMS, the finest medical college in India. Goldie was just not his effervescent self in those early days of senior school since he had been denied Science subjects. As I had already paired up with Sanju to share the desk, Dev who had arrived a week later into our section had to find a new desk partner. Soon, Abhishek told us that his father was getting transferred to Hyderabad and that he would be leaving school. When Abhishek bid us goodbye, Dev said to me, 'I wonder if we will ever meet Abhishek again.'

Every meeting on this planet is ultimately for separation. In a few days' time, however, it all seemed usual again; nobody is indispensable in this world.

The boys of year XI were interested in building their bodies. Everybody could be heard talking about weights and how many push-ups they could do. Some boys tended to wear half sleeve shirts and then do a couple of folds even in the cut sleeve to show their muscle! Goldie claimed that he could do 500 push-ups non-stop, and that thrice a week he would jog from South Extension to Qutub and back, a distance of 16 kilometres! We would take it with more than a pinch of salt.

Everyone including Dev was experimenting with styled stubble and some were wearing their hair in fancy ways. The girls, some of whom had braces in secondary school, had since got them removed and were flashing perfect smiles. Their skirts seemed just a couple of inches shorter than before and their faces glowed in the 16th year of their life. A couple of girls who had joined TAPS from convent schools seemed even more interesting; they engaged in conversation more readily and looked smarter. The new body parts of our female classmates were even more prominent now! Meanwhile, we were discovering, in addition to our own adolescent hormones, new subjects—economics, commerce, accounting, mathematics of a higher level and viewpoint-based English literature lessons.

Murari Lal Bhola, our geography teacher in year VI, was now teaching us economics. And his elder brother Bihari Lal Bhola who sported a goatee beard was taking commerce. Our accounting teacher was Shamsher Singh, and it was because of both his name and an upturned handlebar moustache that we used to call him *Sher* or lion. His arrival in the class would be preceded by one of the student muttering, '*Sher aaya, Sher aaya*.'

A few weeks into the new school-year, I received a call from Goldie. He sounded unusually solemn and asked me to come over to a fast-food restaurant in South Extension; Goldie mentioned that he had called Dev, Sanju, Ramu and Billa as well. When we met, Goldie told us that he was leaving TAPS and moving to The Defence and Honour School, which had offered him science. He said that both his choice of subjects and the school would help him pursue his dream of joining the Air Force and becoming a pilot. Goldie had been with us since early childhood, his mischievous pranks and boundless boyish energy and occasional self-deprecation made him a unique person. And behind his rough and self-proclaimed 'beast-cum-barbarian' exterior lay a soft person! 'You all are my brothers and I will stay in touch you,' said Goldie.

Dev started enjoying the new subjects: year XI economics focused on Indian economy and statistics; commerce was about learning forms of business organisations and business functions; accounting started with the very basic principles of 'debit what comes in, credit what goes out' and covered journal entries and financial statements and cash flow; mathematics included algebra, coordinate geometry and probability. Dev's habit of making extensive notes worked very well for him. He used to read a little beyond the syllabus in order to give his answers more richness. Soon he became Murari Lal Bhola's favourite student—the same Murari Lal Bhola who had erroneously slapped him in class VI and then 'taken his slaps back'! In fact, Mr Bhola started telling all the three sections where he used to teach economics, 'If you have any doubt, first ask Devavratt Rajvansh; if he cannot clarify then come to me.'

We were therefore not surprised when class XI results were announced and the teacher distributing report cards mentioned the name of the student who had stood first—it was Devavratt Pratap Rajvansh!

It was during the same summer vacations after year XI that I went to Dev's house in Bapa Nagar for the first time and met his aunt and uncle. His uncle was a gentle person who listened intently and spoke softly. He suggested to me to keep a private mathematics tutor to prepare for the life defining year XII Board exams next year. A high score in mathematics will propel the aggregate upwards. When I spoke to Dev a few days later, he mentioned that for the first time ever, he now had a private home-visiting mathematics tutor: Mr Mohan Raj Midha.

Mohan Raj Midha was a bespectacled, somewhat balding man in his 30s with a pigeon face, who would travel on a two-wheeler scooter. The very first thing he told Dev was, 'Maths is my best friend!'

The first thing he wrote in Dev's notebook was: 'Do you want 90+Δ?' In other words, he asked Dev in writing whether or not he wanted more than 90% marks in the mathematics board exam.

Obviously, Dev had nodded. However, Mr Midha made Dev write a 'Yes' against his question, scribbled on the first page of his notebook! In the months to come, anytime he found Dev playing cricket in the park near his home just before his tuition, Midha would open the first page of the notebook and point out to Dev that he himself had written that he wanted 'ninety plus delta'! Clearly, 'cricket was not going to get him those marks'—was the message he wished to deliver not so subtly.

The Asian Games of 1982 were organised in New Delhi and the Nehru Stadium was constructed at that time to host the games. Colour TV had just been introduced in India, though as for the old B&W TVs, the antenna fixed on the terrace had to be properly adjusted to get a sharp reception. Often, I would be sent to the terrace by my parents to adjust the antenna, I would shout from the terrace 'Is it okay now?' or '*Theek hei*?' and a voice from downstairs would come, 'Adjust a little more' or '*Thoda aur, thoda aur*'.

In the Delhi of that time, Nirula's, the fast-food restaurant in Connaught Place, was gaining recognition and suddenly, we had a choice in ice-creams which hitherto had been restricted to Kwality and Gaylord! In our homes we were still bathing using a bucket and mug and while shampoos had been introduced, the concept of 'conditioner' was unheard of. We were never asked what we would have for breakfast or lunch or dinner—we ate whatever was cooked, though most of us did not relish green vegetables like *ghiya* or *tindda*. Flying kites, especially in the run up to Independence Day, was a favourite recreation, and simple games like *gulli-danda* and *pitthoo* and hide and seek were very popular. Many an afternoon was still spent playing chess, ludo and Snakes & Ladders. In due course, I realised that not just chess but even Snakes & Ladders originated in India several centuries ago—it was called *Moksha Patam* then, where 'ladders' were found on squares that represented virtues like faith or kindness or knowledge and 'snakes' bit on squares that represented vices like arrogance or anger or greed. The 100th square represented *moksha* or salvation!

The day the President of India declared the Asian Games open, in his rather halting tone, Midha was supposed to reach Dev's home at 6 pm. Midha was exceptionally punctual but that day reached half an hour late. He mentioned that he had got late due to 'the match'. Dev looked at him incredulously and Midha, who used to live in Kotla near Nehru Stadium, said with his straight pigeon face, 'There was match today at Nehru stadium; I got late because of the traffic there.'

Dev mentioned to his tutor that there was no 'match' and that, 'Today was opening ceremony of Asian Games.'

Midha wryly remarked, 'Never mind. Our spelling of "match" is in any case different; in our spelling of "match", there is no C.' *Touché!* His idiosyncrasies notwithstanding, Midha was clearly an excellent maths tutor, as became evident with Dev now beginning to excel even at mathematics.

***

A large number of Indians around this time were flying to Thailand—most would bring back a Video Cassette Recorder from there and the men, when they had the opportunity, indulge in a bit of paid sex offered in different enticing guises! Throughout the 1980s, Colour TVs along with VCRs and video shops hiring out original or screen prints of film videos were the most popular in-house entertainment in cities and semi-urban areas. Sanju was one of the first friends to have a VCR in his house; he would also manage to get X-rated films and his prank gang would assemble in his house, at judicious times, to feast their eyes on mind-blowing, eye-popping, jaw-dropping sex gymnastics on TV screen! Billa had told me that after he saw his first blue film at Sanju's place he could neither sleep nor control the blood supply to famous parts of his body for days unto end. In due course I also made my 'educational films' debut at Sanju's house and like others, I too remained astounded for days at nature's amazing creations and what they could do with different parts of their incredibly sexy bodies.

While Sanju had refocused on academics, this being the all-important year XII, he remained the merry prankster leading his pack of fun-loving classmates and neighbourhood boys. He would make deep humming noises with a straight poker face while the teacher was teaching—soon the boy sitting behind him would do the same and the one behind and so on! Usually this would happen during Mrs Chopra or Murari Lal Bhola's lessons. Mrs Chopra would say with the stern expression, 'Stop these juvenile noises'; while Mr Bhola would purse his lips, ignore the impishness and say, 'Take down one, one-and-a-half questions'—we still don't know what the half question meant!

It has been a sad irony of urban India that sometimes smart young people don't wish to speak in fluent Hindi even if they are able to do so! It is almost as though well-spoken Hindi diminishes their status. Thus, on one occasion a female classmate, who had joined TAPS in year XI, requested the canteen vendor, 'Jawahar, *pachhas ka chola dena*.' She wanted a plate of chick peas for fifty paise, now 'chola' is singular and 'choley' is plural. What she meant was: '*Pachhas ke choley dena*'. Her request, translated in English, meant: 'Jawahar, give me a chick-pea for fifty'! Sanju overheard this and before our classmate could get back to the class, he made a paper 'chola' the size of a tennis ball, put a sticker on it that read 'Pachhas ka chola' and kept it on her desk! Bemused on seeing a 'pachhas ka chola' on her desk she promptly tossed it back towards Sanju who grabbed it and started nibbling on it!

The Ashwath Public School in the early-1980s must have had some of the prettiest girls of Delhi on its rolls. School time crushes carry with them a scent that stays in later years of life bringing both a tender smile and a gentle remorse of what may have been had we shown a little more pluck in those young years gone by and never to return. The one or two students who boldly formed boyfriend-girlfriend relationships became folklores. Every year at the TAPS annual farewell party, a Mr TAPS and Miss TAPS would be announced—the handsome boy and the beautiful girl. In the two years that I attended the farewell party, it was never the girl generally thought to be most pretty who won the Miss TAPS recognition. Perhaps because they were openly seen hanging out with their school time crush and I suppose a senior member of the school staff might have preferred the second or third runner-up, presumably because she had displayed better 'character'. Character, morality, reputation are nothing but words to describe a fabric that people try and wear which may have little correlation with the simplicity of the heart and straight-forwardness of the human being.

The few weeks after our farewell party the all-important year XII Board examinations started in the March of 1983. The examination was immensely satisfying for me; I felt I couldn't have done better. Dev seemed happy with the papers too. My cousin Gautam had appeared in the Board exam as well, however like Ramu, his aim was to pass the IIT entrance examination and become an engineer. It was six weeks before the results were declared. Dev and I went together to the school to get our result. It was a lovely moment in my life and the 79% I secured was the highest I had ever scored in any school examination. I felt that Delhi University's Kautilya College for Commerce, one of the best Commerce colleges in India, was within my reach. I also thought how proud my parent would be. 'Well done, Sandeep', Dev tapped on my shoulder as I came out of my momentary reverie.

'Oh Dev!' I said and instantly tried to see the result sheet pasted on the wall in front. His face was radiant; when I saw his marks, he seemed to have topped the school in almost every subject. On a piece of paper in his hand was scribbled 415-75=340, and beneath that, 85%. The universities in India would consider English and best of three subjects, which for Dev was 85%.

'Wow Dev!' I exclaimed and both of us hugged each other instinctively. Dev topped the school in commerce stream, Shweta was second and I was third. We had driven to the school in my father's car and he was waiting outside anxiously. Dev and I stepped out of the school as students for the last time.

'79 percent', I said to my father who was standing beside our ambassador car. First I, and then Dev, touched his feet. '85; school topper,' I said to my father, with my hand on Dev's shoulder.

'Wonderful, wonderful', he said, 'well done both of you!'

Mohan Raj Midha was waiting at Dev's house. '98%, Sir', said Dev, mentioning his mathematics marks to his tutor and then touched his feet.

'Overall?' My Midha enquired.

'85 percent.'

'Very good,' said Mr Midha with a genuinely happy expression on his face.

'Welcome, Midha sahab,' said Dev's uncle.

Mr Midha folded his hands and said modestly, 'Sir, I hope no complaints with me?

Dev's uncle smiled, 'We have never had any complaints against you'; and then with a pause, 'Please come in and have some sweets.'

'I usually avoid sweets but today I will definitely have a small piece', said Mr Midha; and then turning to Dev, 'Please get your very first note book.'

Dev's aunt got some *barfi* for Mr Midha and Dev pulled out his first maths tuition note book on the first page of which was scribbled 'Do you want 90+Δ'. Mr Midha smilingly had a piece of *barfi* and casually took the note book from Dev's hand, and while speaking with his uncle, wrote something on the first page. As Mr Midha took leave from Dev's place, Dev saw the first page of his notebook. Next to the 'Do you want 90+Δ', Mr Midha had written 'Achieved. Congrats!'

The combination of freedom, success and youth is a heady cocktail. There were innumerable congratulatory phone calls at my house too. My mother was delighted at my result and I could hear my brother occasionally say '79 percent' to his friends enquiring about my result. My father said to one of his colleagues who lived in the neighbourhood and had come home to congratulate us, 'Let's hope so', in response to the latter's observation, 'He will definitely get Kautilya now.'

The world was just about opening in front of me and I thought my first step into it had been good enough. I felt such a sense of elation and relief. Our school years were over and so was 'the long childhood'. I had been successful in the all-important year XII examination; the freedom and youthful excitement of college life lay ahead. The combination of freedom, success and youth is a very heady cocktail!

Part II

College Days

My mother had lived in Calcutta in the early 1940s. She would describe what she saw during the 1943 Bengal famine—totally emaciated men, no more than skeletons, were fighting with dogs amidst garbage for morsels of rotten food. Bharat–where the light of universal consciousness reflected off the Himalayas onto the minds of sages and translated into the Vedas, where the greatest of men put honour above kingdoms and stoically walked in her forests for 14 gruelling years, where the wisest of souls played the flute and whose celestial words inspired the finest scripture of spiritual knowledge and whose GDP well into the 18th century was 25% of the world's income; in that same Bharat I still saw much deprivation in my growing up years, though thanks to agriculture science with the White and Green Revolutions, the country had overcome to a large extent that abject misery of the 1943 famine.

In the 1980s almost half the country was poor and most of the remaining half was middle-class. Amongst the poor some were so impoverished that occasionally there were news reports from tribal areas in Orissa of a destitute couple selling their newborn for a bowl of rice! 'We are 'middle-income', not middle-class', Dev told me once. 'Middle-class suggests low self-esteem and mediocre ability but we as a people are as good or as bad as any other in the world.'

Even the so-called 'middle-income' people living in big cities had to put up with water shortages and frequent power cuts in the 1980s. On the 25th of June 1983—when we were still enjoying that wonderful time between school and college—as we sat glued to our TV watching the Prudential World Cup Cricket final between India and West Indies being played at Lord's, there was a power cut! The entire locality would moan loudly when there was a power outage and come out of their houses; there would again be a loud humming cheer in the neighbourhood when the power would get restored. Somewhere in that deprivation of the 1980s, there was happiness. Today, there are hardly any power cuts—generators and inverters are available to ensure constant supply of electricity—yet in today's power-sufficient, mobile-phone-connected, WhatsApp-driven Bharat, there seems to be somewhere a deprivation of *that* simple happiness. Beyond that material which is needed for survival and basic dignity, all else appears to bring only ephemeral pleasure.

Thankfully, on that fateful 25th June, the power was restored after half an hour and we saw history being made as India defeated the all-powerful West Indies in the nail-biting final! The 1983 Cricket World Cup win lit up such a brilliant torch that it changed Indian cricket forever, and in more ways than one, it was set to change India.

***

Delhi University and in particular, DU's north campus, was an integral part of the captivating life of a largely 'middle-income' and some high-income Delhiites at that time. North campus still remains as charming, even though students have much wider choice of universities and vocational institutes today and with the rise in prosperity, several choose to travel overseas for higher education. Education is the locomotive that Indians have used to improve their lot, and still do, notwithstanding internet start-ups and the cricket IPL.

Founded in 1922, DU has more than 85 colleges and faculties affiliated to it spread all over Delhi. Some of the finest DU colleges are in the northern part of Delhi—the north campus that stretches over 10 square kilometres. The Augustus College, Kautilya College of Commerce, Ved Vyas College and Lady Thakurdas College for Women in north campus being some of the best regarded institutions in the country for under-graduate education.

Given my year XII marks, I was confident of getting into Kautilya College of Commerce; however, my father's colleagues who were visiting our home, sometimes to congratulate me, suggested I consider pursuing Economics (Honours) instead of B.Com (Honours). 'If economics is so much,' said one of my father's colleagues who was incidentally a professor of commerce, extending his hands wide apart, 'then commerce is this much', he spread his thumb and index finger three inches apart.

Ultimately, I decided to apply only for two courses: Economics (Hons) in Augustus College and B.Com (Hons) in Kautilya College of Commerce.

Meanwhile, despite his capability, Ramkumar had not managed to clear the IIT entrance exam or qualify for Brahmagupta College of Engineering in Delhi. The other surprise was that Nita did not pass the entrance exam to All India Institute of Medical Sciences nor did she get into the medical colleges affiliated to DU. Instead, she had decided to pursue Economics. Sanju narrowly missed the grades required for Kautilya and had thus applied to Rajguru College in Delhi's south campus, which was regarded as the next best college for commerce. My cousin Gautam, who had also studied science with mechanical drawing and wanted to become a computer engineer, also did not quality for IIT, and thus, both Gautam and Ramu decided to move to South India where there were several engineering colleges.

Dev was keen to study Economics and he applied for an Economics (Hons) course to Augustus, Ved Vyas and Kautilya colleges. His uncle, in a moment of insecurity, did suggest that Dev apply to some South Delhi colleges as well. He feared that at the north campus, students get into drugs and if Dev was in a South Delhi college, he would be closer home and the chances, if at all any, of someone as upright as Dev of getting into drugs, would be minimal. There are moments in every young person's life when she or he breaks the proverbial umbilical cord and begins to get less dependent on his parents. Dev decided that he was going only to north campus and he accordingly applied only to the three top DU colleges for Economics.

My application for an Economics (Hons) course at Augustus College was rejected; however, I comfortably made it to B.Com (Hons) in Kautilya College of Commerce. Dev got admission in all the three colleges he applied to, it was an easy choice for him, Augustus was the elite college of DU and had produced top civil servants, industry executives, noted journalists and eminent people in several other fields over the past several decades.

We were set for the next chapter of our lives.

***

Delhi Transport Corporation or DTC as it is better known as would ply University Special buses from different parts of the city to and from the north campus. The U-Spl was as much of an institution as any top college in DU was! Only University students could board these buses.

I skipped the first day of college fearing ragging from senior students. On day two, with dreams in my heart and apprehension in my mind, I walked 10 minutes from my home in Nehru Enclave to the spot where the Kalkaji U-Spl started from. Stepping into a new world is always a thrilling experience: to see so many boys and girls, the latter in particular, in casual non-school-uniform clothes, was new for me. Amongst so many pretty girls in the U-Spl, I wondered if I might be able to make acquaintance of a few!

I still have some memories of that first day at Kautilya College—the walkways from the two entrance gates towards the main U-shaped building, classrooms on ground and first floors, the neat front lawn inside with a mounted bust of Chanakya, side lawns too, the canteen behind the main building, the swimming pool and cricket ground and the boys hostel at the far end of the college; those initial introductions with new classmates, all topper-types from various schools across India, some of whom would go onto become lifelong friends; and the diverse backgrounds of students in Kautilya, something to which public school educated Delhiites had to adjust to. I looked around to see how many pretty girls I could spot; there were a few, just very few!

Later that day, I decided to walk to Augustus College in the hope of meeting Dev. This was the July of 1983 when even landlines were a bit of a luxury and even our wildest imagination would not yield the thought of a sleek mobile phone which is more important than our limbs are today! Augustus College was a 10-minute walk from Kautilya and adjacent to Ved Vyas college. Being at north campus gave me a sense of vitality. There was energy and colour and youth and hope. After strolling around in Augustus for a few minutes, I saw Dev. He was with, presumably, a classmate of his.

'Hi Sandeep,' he greeted me warmly, 'How is Kautilya College? Any ragging?'

Dev mentioned that on his first day, he was asked to queue up in front of some seniors one of whom said, 'Devavratt Pratap Rajvansh—couldn't you have a longer name!' The senior continued, 'Ah, Economics! So, tell us Mister Long-name, precisely what is the impact of the rise in population of cockroaches in Siberia on the Indian economy?' Dev had also been asked to go down on his knee and propose to a first-year female student!

I curiously asked Dev how he answered the question, he simply smiled.

'And how did the girl you proposed to respond?'

'She rejected me', he said with a laugh.

Just then, I saw Nita who was now Dev's classmate. 'Hello Sandeep,' she said.

'Hi Nita, what a pleasant surprise! Are you in Dev's class?' I enquired.

'Dev is in my class!' she said with a gentle wink. She was looking so smart in her jeans. She always had a very pleasant demeanour and intelligent looks.

***

The lectures in college would usually be held, but not always. I learnt how lectures are different from tutorials which were held less frequently. As the weather got cooler, occasionally, we would sit out in the lawn and chat with the teacher there. I and the few friends I had made were all quite conscientious about attending the lectures in the first year. Soon, different college festivals started. These were the two to three days in every college's annual calendar when students would organise social–cultural–literary events which all DU college students could attend. The Kautilya College and Lady Thakurdas College festivals were very popular. This was an occasion to make friends and I was still looking to make the acquaintance of some girls.

While I studied accounting, business management, business law, statistics and basic Indian economy, Dev was studying micro-economics, macro-economics, mathematics, Indian economy and developmental economics. Later that year, Dev introduced me to some of his friends from Augustus—Ajay Jaiswal, Vikrant Rajput, Gulshandeep Singh Kohli, Anshuman Pant and Dhananjay Dayal. They were addressing each other as Jaiswal, Tank, Gullu, Anshu and DD respectively. Gullu seemed like a happy-go-lucky Sikh, always game for a laugh; others looked studious though Tank was strongly built. Jaiswal, Anshu and DD all wore glasses.

In the company of his college friends, I found Dev becoming more outgoing. His sunken eyes seem to have life now, he was developing a sense of humour which could be described as somewhere between subtle and sparkling, and he no longer avoided the topic of girls.

'There comes Dev's "clean-heart"', I heard Anshu once say, referring to a female collegemate who, presumably, Dev might have referred to as a 'clean-hearted girl'! Gullu would often talk about '*Bhabhiji*'s class' in reference to a young female teacher who Dev had called 'graceful' and thus, Dev's name got associated with her and she became 'Bhabhiji' or 'sister-in-law' for his other mates! In the mid-1930s, we would find 'chick-charts' pasted on the walls in a lot of colleges. I doubt if they allow such overt gender objectification nowadays; and as social norms change, most youngsters today would probably find it distasteful. I recall Dev and I reading the 'chick-chart' pasted in his college and Dev use the words 'stunningly beautiful' for one of the girls named on the chart!

Life's many phases phase out and phase in gradually. Slowly, the school friends were getting relegated to memories of the past. Dev and I were very much in regular touch, and Sanju and I would still meet and even study together, I would often get a letter in the post from Ramkumar; and Shweta was in Kautilya College while Nita in Augustus. But the others seemed to have all gone different ways. I heard little about the legendary Goldie as well, till one day Dev told me he had run into him and thereafter been invited for lunch at his Munirka house. Goldie had not qualified for the National Defence Academy the previous year and was preparing for a second attempt. This was sometime around mid-1984, after we had finished first year of college. Goldie's father ran a successful white goods dealership on ring road between South Extension and Defence Colony, and they had lived in a rented house in South Extension for many years. Goldie had a younger brother Nona who was in secondary school, also at TAPS, and had then moved to the different school along with his elder brother; he was nearly six-feet tall though still in his early teens!

'Very interesting,' is how Dev put it when I asked him a few days later, about his lunch at Goldie's new home.

'How is Goldie?' I checked with Dev.

'As uncomplicated as ever,' he said.

'And the younger brother?'

'Very sweet. Adores his elder brother', said Dev.

When I asked Dev to narrate in detail what happened he described the afternoon to me; it so reflected those simple times when we used to laugh ever so easily!

Just as Dev had rung the bell, Nona came running out and gave Dev a ribs-crushing bear hug. 'Bhaiya!' Nona welcomed Dev. 'Bhaiya, you taught me maths', Nona reminded Dev of their previous meeting over a year back; however, Nona's statement just ended there. Dev had looked at him quizzically. 'Goldie bhaiya is here', Nona showed Dev into the living room.

The living room was barren. Goldie's family was in the process of moving from their rented home to their new Munirka house and the furniture was presumably still on its way. '*Aa bhai*', Goldie also welcomed Dev in his deep scruffy voice.

Dev had been pleasantly surprised at the lunch invitation; perhaps it was because of the mutual respect both Goldie and Dev had for each other's cricket skills. There was just a two-in-one lying on the floor with no furniture at all. Dev, Goldie and Nona all sat down on the floor. Michael Jackson's famous song

'Beat It' was playing on the two-in-one. Goldie was moving his head from side to side along with the rhythm. Nona sat quietly, gazing intently at 'Dev bhaiya' and smiling uninterruptedly.

'Rewind', Goldie instructed Nona after 'Beat It' had finished playing. Again and again, 'Beat it, beat it, beat it, beat it, just beat it' played. Dev realised that Goldie had not quite caught the lyrics of the foot tapping song, for as Jackson sang 'Beat It', Goldie sang alongside, '*Fidey, fidey, fidey, fidey, ja-fidey*'.

'I can do non-stop exercises on this song', claimed Goldie. The topic changed to body-building. 'A man should have body', said Goldie, implying a man must do exercises and build a strong body, 'there is little in academics.' Of course, after half an hour, while Michael Jackson continued to 'Beat It', when Dev commented that Goldie had developed a lithe physique in the last year, Goldie countered his guest, 'There is nothing in body brother. By god's grace if a man can educate himself, nothing is better than that.'

Dev wisely decided not to point out that just a little while back Goldie had stated the opposite! As Nona excused himself for a few minutes Goldie got up and pointing to a flat across the street said, 'Devavratt, I have a crush on my neighbour. She lives in that house.'

'Does she feel the same way about you?' enquired Dev after thinking for a moment.

'I don't know bhai; I have never discussed this with her.'

'Why not?' wondered Goldie's guest.

'She is married with a grown-up daughter!'

Dev did not even have the side arms of a sofa to hang onto, he sat on the floor listening, wondering. As Nona returned, he was instructed to rewind the tape and for the 20th time since he had arrived, Dev heard: 'Beat it, just beat it'.

At about 2 pm, Goldie casually asked Dev if he would like to have lunch. Dev said, 'Okay.'

'*Nonae*, lay the plates and take out the curd, I will get the rotis,' said Goldie.

As Goldie stepped out to get rotis from the local *tandoor* and Nona went into the kitchen to get the plates, Dev sat alone on the floor in that barren room, it was just him and a two-in-one that continued to play 'Beat It'. Nona emerged from the kitchen with three steel plates and a bowl of curd. The curd seemed very watery! The three plates were placed on the floor, while the bowl of watery curd was kept in between the three plates. Nona didn't get any serving spoon or small bowls to contain the watery curd that fateful afternoon! The doorbell rang and Goldie entered holding a paper bag made from old newspaper containing 10 *tandoori* rotis. Lunch was about to get underway.

'Start,' said Goldie giving one roti each to Dev and Nona and keeping one in his plate. Then picking up the bowl of watery curd he poured a little in his plate! Nona and Dev did the same. The curd spread all over the plate and Dev picked up the roti in his hand to avoid it getting soggy.

'I had to put in much effort to break a chewable piece of roti, it was like hard rubber,' Dev mentioned to me while narrating the adventures of lunch party.

'And "Beat It"?' I flippantly asked Dev.

'It was constantly playing.'

While Dev struggled to first break the roti and then chew and then swallow it, Goldie and Nona seemed to be enjoying the meal. Dev checked if they had salt and black pepper to add to the curd.

'Everything is available,' said Goldie and Nona fetched the masala box. Despite adding salt and pepper, Dev was having one bite of roti dipped in curd and then drinking a few sips of water to wash it down! While he struggled to finish one roti, Goldie had devoured six and Nona two.

'This one is yours; it's yours, bhai,' Goldie told Dev.

'No, no, I can't have any more,' said Dev.

'Sure?' asked Goldie again.

'Absolutely sure.'

Goldie picked up the last roti from the paper bag, his seventh and looking at Dev, remarked, 'It seems you didn't enjoy the lunch!'

I couldn't help laughing loudly! Dev's afternoon, however, wasn't yet over.

It was impolite for Dev to leave immediately after the 'meal'. Also, Goldie commanded him to relax and that he would show him something 'nice' a bit later. At about 4 pm, Goldie asked Dev to come into another room where too there was no furniture except an almirah. Nona also came into that room holding a large towel. Goldie opened the almirah and showed Dev the poster of Sean Connery he had pasted inside the almirah.

Was this the nice thing he was going to show? Dev wondered.

Goldie then took off his t-shirt, stood just in his track pants and asked Dev, 'Whose body is better—Sean Connery's or mine?'

Dev was bewildered.

Before he could say anything, Goldie continued, 'Sean Connery, right?'

Dev nodded.

'Okay, now see…' said Goldie.

Goldie started doing push-ups; after he completed hundred, he stopped for a moment without resting his body and stayed on his fours. So, he was in the shape of an arch-bow with the palms of his hands and the toes of his feet on the floor but rest of the body lifted up. Awesome! Nona wiped the sweat off Goldie's torso with the large towel and after less than a minute of break, Goldie started push-ups again.

Another hundred! Again, he didn't ease his body but stayed on his fours. Again, Nona cleaned the sweat off his brother's torso. Dev watched disbelievingly. Goldie repeated this after 300 and then again after 400. Eventually he did 500 push-ups non-stop! Then he rose and tightening his body so that the muscles would get taut he asked Dev, 'Now tell me whose body is better, his or mine?'

'Whoa!' I exclaimed, 'so it's true Goldie can do 500 push-ups nonstop!'

'Seen it with my own eyes,' said Dev.

None of Dev's friends believed that one of our schoolmates could do 500 push-ups nonstop. I suggested half seriously that Dev should check with Goldie if he would be willing to give a demonstration. Goldie had no compunction whatsoever. Just before the university was to reopen and we were to begin the second year of our graduation, Jaiswal who used to live in Defence Colony invited Dev and their other friends to his place. Jaiswal's father, in an India when organised private sector jobs were not aplenty, was a senior executive in a multinational company. Dev and his other friends, except Gullu who couldn't make it that day, admired the new Maruti 800cc car that Jaiswal's father had gifted him. Maruti would go onto change the automobile landscape in India. They all also enjoyed Jaiswal's air-conditioned home!

Dev had reluctantly asked Goldie if he would come to Defence Colony's D-block park for showing his unique prowess. Goldie had happily agreed. As all of Dev's friends assembled in the park that evening, they noticed that someone was hopping around the park on his haunches! The periphery of D-block park would be nearly half a kilometre. Goldie was on his haunches and hopping, perhaps warming-up, around the periphery of the park. Jaiswal, DD, Tank and Anshu couldn't believe what they were seeing. Dev could! None of them could hop even 5 metres on their haunches! Dev introduced Goldie to his friends who were already wide-eyed as they shook his hand. Goldie started with his push-ups. And without any fuss or a towel to clean his torso, he did 500 push-ups nonstop!

'Wow!' said all of Dev's friends. 'That's amazing!' said Jaiswal to Goldie.

'Would you like me to do 500 more?' asked Goldie nonchalantly!

As Goldie made his way back to Munirka with an insouciant face, Jaiswal suggested the others drive with him to Connaught Place Nirula's for a pizza! They all enjoyed cheese, capsicum and onion pizza and laughed over just about everything, the evening in particular! Nirula's cheese capsicum onion pizza and vegetable burger with wafers and hash brown followed by Manhattan Mania and Nutty Buddy were to become the staple diet of Dev and his friends during outings through the university years.

'Daily thrilling cabarets', muttered Tank as they drove past some of those shifty restaurants in Connaught Place where this was prominently mentioned on tripod boards placed at the gate! This was enough for all of them to start laughing.

'Not just thrilling, also killing cabarets,' added Anshu lowering his eyelids to give a lustful expression.

'And extremely fulfilling cabarets,' chuckled DD.

The entire car burst out into a laugh riot. All our lives we are seeking happiness, but college days is that time in life of those who are fortunate to have access to higher education, when fun and happiness seeks us!

It was around this time that I received a call from Manohar Pal Billa. He had taken admission in Kurukshetra University and said, '*Sh*andy, I want to meet *unkil* for some advice.'

Billa had not got the mathematics course he wanted a year earlier and was trying his best to pursue the subject he so loved. My father wrote a letter of introduction to a professor in Kurukshetra University he knew. As I walked Billa back to the bus stop his somewhat innocent and uncultivated mischievous side soon surfaced when he asked me, '*Sh*andy, have you had sex so far?'

Seeing my shake of the head he proceeded to confide in me in a rather matter of fact way, '*Sh*andy, I *lowve* sex,' and then added, 'but only *womens* who do immense physical activity and have big hips can accept me.'

That was the last time I met Billa; in fact, nobody who I know saw him again, we did hear about him many years later and I shall mention about that at the appropriate place in this narration.

No Longer Teenagers

Organisations, societies, religions and nations that stop challenging and questioning themselves become stagnant, fail and eventually perish. Just as an individual who stops learning and reaches conclusions, and then clutches to those conclusions aggressively, starts losing vitality and friends. The flowing river silently shares with us the secret of living. Ever moving, ever assimilating from its environment, creating valleys and deltas, the silent river is beautiful and alive. It is alive even in its ultimate and inevitable fall into the vast mysterious sea. Man's thinking faculties allow him the fountain of curiosity, indeed the tempest of inquisitiveness. Bit by bit we chip on the puzzles of nature, on the mystery of creation. It is no surprise that as boys and girls become young men and women, they start questioning social norms as have been introduced to them. Is a living being just matter or also a spirit? If there is spirit, then is the spirit immortal and whatever happens to it upon death? Does it immerse itself in the vast flow of universal energy or does it find a resting heaven or hell? Is time linear from minus infinity to plus infinity or cyclical as Hinduism suggests? Newton amazed the world with his brilliant discovery and explanation of mechanical physics. Till Niels Bohr and Albert Einstein came along and quantum physics and theory of relativity re-explained the truth. Their tempest of enquiry gave the silent river of living beings the vigour of knowledge and truth, potentially wisdom.

As we moved into the second year of graduation, my interaction with Dev somewhat reduced. He had become more social and enjoying college life with his friends. He invited me to his Bapa Nagar home for lunch once in mid-1984. Like most 'middle-income' homes at that time, they had water coolers to keep the intense heat out. His uncle chatted about the Operation Bluestar that had happened a few weeks back. Dev's aunt asked me if we were watching *Hum Log*, the first of its kind Indian TV serial the telecast of which had just started, and which wonderfully captured the aspirations of a 'middle-income' India.

Later in the afternoon, we went into Dev's little room which, like everything else about Dev, was neat and orderly. A study table with four piles of books and notebooks with neatly-labelled stickers that read: Microeconomics, Macroeconomics, Mathematics and Indian Economy. A bed adjacent to a cupboard, two small comfortable chairs and a side table with a cricket bat in the corner. And a book shelf; inside it a small picture of his parents and some school time light reading: Sherlock Holmes, Alistair Maclean, The Hardy Boys, Five Find-Outers, Phantom, Tintin and Amar Chitra Katha comics. And then two books on philosophy by J. Krishnamurti, C Rajagopalachari's *Ramayana* and *Mahabharata*, several books on cricket with everything that Gavaskar had authored, a book of Neeraj's Hindi poetry and a book on Theory of Relativity and modern physics. He would still not speak much, preferring instead to listen and reply in short sentences.

As I flicked through Commentaries on Living by Krishnamurti, I asked him what the book was all about.

He said, 'Philosophy of life.'

I asked him, 'And what is Krishnamurti's philosophy of life?' He said smilingly, 'Trying to understand that, Sandeep. He guides towards self-reflection, no direct answers; it is liberating, though.'

I reminded him that in school during exams he would write 'Om' on the top right corner of the examination sheet. 'Do you still do that?' I asked him.

'I have been wondering since that day,' he said smilingly.

'Wondering what? Whether or not God exists? And have you reached any conclusion?'

Dev pointed his hand towards his head, 'With this mind and its limitations, chances are I never will.'

Just before I left for my home, Dev's aunt requested us to get some milk from the nearby DMS milk booth. As Dev inserted some tokens and milk started pouring out into the steel container he asked me, 'How is Sanju doing?'

Sanju was studying in Rajguru College doing the same course which I was pursuing in Kautilya College. He and I had kept in touch and were both searching for a good accounting tutor. Quite a few DU professors would offer private tuitions in their personal time. Hariom Lal Trivedi was an accounting lecturer in Rajguru College who, we learnt, offered private tuitions for B.Com (Hons) students. He would charge Rs. 300 per hour, but if two students studied together, he would charge them a combined Rs. 500 per hour. Sanju and I decided to approach him through my father; we thought that since my father too was a DU professor, Hariom Lal Trivedi might give us some concession! Trivedi addressed my father most respectfully but said, 'Guruji, my fees is fixed but I will give the children a long one hour, your son is my son.'

'And your money is my money,' Sanju quipped when he heard what Trivedi had said.

We started going to Hariom Lal's small house in Chittaranjan Park twice a week. He was a good accounting teacher and in between would narrate some interesting stories from Gorakhpur where he originally came from. He was short-statured, balding, clean shaven and had a bulbous sort of face.

He would reveal his *paan*-stained teeth when laughing with his little paunch wobbling. I used to carry my slide-rule scale for drawing straight lines in my notebook register for making a P&L account and Balance Sheet. Trivedi loved my slide-rule for some reason and would pull it away from my hand saying, 'Do give this to me!'

He would keep tapping the slide-rule scale on his left palm with his right hand and return it after our tuition hour was over! Occasionally, when we would come across a difficult accounting problem and lay it in front of Trivedi, he would refer to his own old master textbook. Once, while discussing a problem we couldn't solve, our tutor looked up and found the same problem in his book as well, he had circled it and next to it written the word 'Difficult'. '*Deefee-cult*,' he cackled, 'I too had found it *deefee-cult*,' his paunch wobbled and his paan-stained teeth gaped at us.

He had a son and Trivedi introduced him as a boy who could whistle very melodiously—the pride displayed in his son's *surili seeti* we imagined would have been more appropriate if the lad could play the piano very well or sing well! *Surili* took the compliment smugly. One day as Sanju and I stepped out of Trivedi's house, laughing as usual, we saw two pigs locked copulating. This added further fuel to our bursting lungs. We instinctively picked up some stones and starting pelting on the passionate pigs. Just then a middle-aged passer-by on bicycle stopped and said with a suppressed smile, '*Kar lein deo babuji, kar lein deo*', meaning 'let them do it, O Sir, let them do it'!

After nearly 40 years of this incident, Sanju and I are still laughing. That passerby whose looks suggested he might never have been to school, I thought on reflection, was more kind-hearted than us. Literacy and wisdom have not been synonymous in any language of the world!

A few years after we had stopped taking those tuitions and were reminiscing several funny incidents in my father's presence, he said, 'Wonder what all Trivedi and his family might have had to endure in their journey from Gorakhpur to Delhi.' On more than one occasion my father narrated incidents of large-heartedness of people from small towns; and so often in my life spent in big cities I have seen pettiness in the manner of the wealthy. The man of modest means is ever willing to share the limited food on his plate, while the affluent think twice whether or not refrigerated water should be offered to their guest, even during torrid summers, based on the guest's social status! That man of modest means is truly richer of the two!

The university had re-opened and as second year students we were immensely enjoying our carefree lives. Both Dev and I had an established circle of friends in our respective colleges now. We knew the fun spots and eating places in and around the north campus, and the Nirula's and Wimpy's outlets in

Connaught Place. The U-Spl rides were as delightful as ever. I felt more confident and would strike a conversation or two with girls in the U-Spl who were not even in my college.

The Delhi autumn plays the starting music of a love song, the lyrics of which are put to harmony during the romantic Delhi winters. As we entered late October in 1984 the annual festival of the Lady Thakurdas College was ongoing, and the air had the beginnings of a love song. On the 31st of October I was walking from Lady Thakurdas college towards Patel Chest, where all the U-Spl buses would be parked, around 2 pm with three friends chatting about a concert we had just seen at the festival; at the same time Dev was coming out of Augustus College with Gullu. Just then several passers-by were discussing that India's Prime Minister Mrs. Indira Gandhi has been shot at! Some said she had been shot dead, others said she has been critically wounded. My friends and I were stunned to hear this.

'Bluestar,' said Gullu pensively.

'What?' enquired Dev.

'Bluestar,' said Gullu again, implying that the assassination attempt might be linked to Operation Bluestar that took place in June that year.

As I reached home, my father had the radio on.

'Did you hear the news?' I asked him.

'Yes,' he said.

The news was that Mrs Indira Gandhi had been shot at by her own bodyguards who happened to be Sikhs. It was only late in the evening that news of the Prime Minister's death was confirmed on TV. A discernible fear seemed to be gripping the air that evening. I woke up next day to find that the city had become a most ghastly place.

What I saw on the morning of 1st of November 1984 still sends shivers down my spine. There was smoke of fire in every direction of my home and loud screams heard in the distance. Those were not days of instant communication, there was no 24-hour TV either. Suddenly a worried looking neighbour would be rushing to his house and tell us that shops of Sikhs are being burnt in Kalkaji; an elderly lady from the adjacent house would tell my mother, 'In Greater Kailash, even houses of Sikhs have been attacked.' A school-going boy living a few houses away would tell me, 'Bhaiya, people are being killed, burnt alive.' Suddenly there was commotion and a man signalled to all of us, 'Get into your houses, a mob is coming'. We were petrified.

News started coming on radio of riots in the city. The Sikhs were being targeted. Even by evening time, I could see smoke of fires, this time from Chittaranjan Park side. It was the same on 2nd November as well as into 3rd November. At night time a rumour would spread—*the water of Delhi has been poisoned.* On the night of 2nd November, the rumour was—*there will be a counter-attack, go up on your terraces and lock the house.*

Then next morning we realised the riots had spread beyond Delhi to north India, in some parts not just the Sikhs but even Punjabis were being looted and killed. It was gruesome. What must partition time have been like? I shuddered to think. All the great men in whose names religions of the world are established, they all preached love and kindness. Yet in the name of religion every river of the world has seen its waters turn red. How much pain must humanity endure to realise that every living creature is born from the womb of the same universal energy?

By the 3rd of November, the Indian Army had been called in to control the situation. We were able to breathe with a sense of security. It was reported that 3000 Sikhs had been killed in Delhi alone, and several thousand more in other parts of India. To this day I cannot get the mayhem and agony of those days out of my mind. How must people who saw their near and dear ones killed in that chilling havoc have lived through all this time?

Mrs Indira Gandhi's son Rajiv Gandhi had been appointed Prime Minister after her death. Soon the general elections were announced and the young PM won a landslide victory. Around the same time 74-year-old Ronald Reagan was re-elected as the US President. Two of the most remarkable democracies of the world had just elected their youngest ever and oldest ever leaders. India is often referred to as the largest democracy of the world and USA the oldest democracy. Our history books taught us that democracy had its roots in the Greek city-states of Athens and Sparta; and yet there is mention of *Sabha* or assembly and *Samiti* or committee in the Rig Veda which dates back to around 4000 BCE. And the Indus Valley civilisations is known to have had independent republics as far back as 6th century BCE!

As India slowly came out of the shock of assassination and the deathly riots that followed, our colleges resumed and Dev and I started getting on with our university life.

If we got an interesting professor to teach us Business Organisation at Kautilya College, Dev had an amusing teacher for Econometrics at Augustus. We nicknamed our teacher '*Barfi* Sir' which is a popular sweet in north India, made of dense milk known as *khoya* in Hindi. '*Khoya*' also means lost, and indeed, *Barfi* Sir was both a sweet person and had a lost look about him. We would often say, '*Barfi hamesha khoya khoya rehta hei*'—'Barfi always looks lost'.

Barfi Sir was in the habit of repeating the second part of every sentence with hilarious effect. When upset with our class for not concentrating, he would say, 'When a batsman purposefully takes a ball on his pads, sir, purposefully takes a ball on his pads, it means he is not interested in batting, sir, in batting, sir; same is the situation with your class, sir, with your class.'

Meanwhile, Dev's teacher for Econometrics was popularly called 'Zero Marks'. He would often explain the difference between mathematics and econometrics thus, 'Mathematically right, econometrically wrong—zero marks!'

My friends and I would come out laughing from Barfi Sir's lecture, just as Dev and his friends would chuckle incessantly after their econometrics session. In the interest of full and balanced disclosure, both Barfi Sir and Zero Marks were excellent at their subjects.

The day I wrote my final exam of the second year, in April 1985, my father received a call from his cousin brother, Gautam and Geeta's father. He informed my father that they were immigrating to Canada. He had got a job with a Canadian oil company and would be based in Calgary. Geeta had finished writing her class XII Board exam and Gautam was completing his second-year engineering in a Madras college. They were to move in June. I was slowly getting used to this emotion of friends and relatives who I was close to getting transferred. It was dawning on me that every single meeting eventually results in parting.

I mentioned to Dev that Gautam and Geeta would be leaving India. He was quiet.

'Have you been in touch with them?' I asked him.

'Have spoken to Geeta a couple of times, she too wanted to study Economics in college, but it's been a while since I heard from Gautam.'

My parents invited Gautam and Geeta and their parents' home for dinner an evening before they were taking the flight to Calgary.

'May I also come Sandeep?' Dev asked me, 'Would like to say goodbye to them.'

We had a nice dinner that evening in June with reminiscences of old stories coupled with laughter but the underlying ambiance was one of sadness. As everyone was bidding goodbye, my mother and aunt with tears in their eyes, I asked Gautam and Geeta to stay on a little longer. It was their last night in India! I had learnt to drive by then and offered to drop them at their Greater Kailash home. After another hour of good cheer, I hugged Gautam and Geeta goodbye and Dev shook hands with both. As we drove off, Dev looked back from the front seat of the car to wave goodbye to them again.

Dev was spending the night at my place. We spoke a little as we lay down reminiscing, amongst other things, the Ravan we would make and the indoor carpet cricket we all used to play together. I don't know when I got sleep but when I momentarily opened my eyes, I found Dev still awake reclining on the pillow.

'Sleep, Dev, it's going to be morning soon.'

'Yeah,' he said with that gentle smile of his.

Career Choices

Death is a certainty, at least till today, but even more certain than death is uncertainty. And if uncertainty possesses potential force, then change is its kinetic manifestation. Man begins to die as soon as he is born and time changes relentlessly, ever so relentlessly. In its sweep every aspect of human life is as transient as a railway station seen by a passenger in a fast-moving train.

In the early 1950s, my father used to live in Chhipiwara in Old Delhi; there were 30 people in one house and since a number of family members were engineers, their home was called 'Engineer's House'. By the mid-1980s, we were a nuclear family of four living in South Delhi and meeting with most of the extended family was infrequent.

Even as reasonably well-to-do households like Dev's and mine still had ration cards to access fair price shops for buying food grains and sugar, and primary and manufacturing sectors were still contributing bulk of India's national income, the

Maruti 800cc car was signalling the start of an automobile revolution and we were no longer surprised to find female drivers at the wheel of Maruti. The launch of colour television a few years ago and *Hum Log* had drawn family audiences to the TV and marketers started using it as a medium for advertising: the jingles and advertisements of Nirma: 'washing powder Nirma'; the 'laa-lalalalala' of Liril waterfall girl; the Onida TV Devil's 'neighbour's envy, owner's pride;' 'Buland Bharat ki buland tasveer, Hamara Bajaj scooter;' and Thumps Up featuring Sunil Gavaskar, Sandeep Patil and Ravi Shasti are still fresh in my mind. The government had given impetus to the computerisation programme in the country with the establishment of Department of Telecommunication. And with the Prudential world cup win in 1983 and then the victory in early 1985 in the World Championship of Cricket in Australia, there was vigour in the air in India.

Hindi cinema has always reflected the changing society: the social dramas and struggle against poverty themes of the 1950s and early '60s had made way for musical romances shot in Kashmir in floral sweaters and lost and found formula in late 1960s and '70s; then came the 'angry young man' of the 1970s and early '80s fighting against social prejudices and childhood trauma. Now Hindi cinema was turning to political corruption and the vamp of the 1970s who would oblige with some sizzling cabarets and cleavage show was being replaced, and the lead heroine herself would wear short dresses and do titillating hip swinging dances in the first half of the film and appear in saree in the second half of the movie providing family strength! The lingering literary lyrics of Sahir and Neeraj had been supplanted by 'couldn't care less' words to fit boisterous tunes that lent themselves to dance steps that old timers would describe as 'PT steps'! Jeetendra and Sridevi were the archetype and hit lead actors during mid-1980s, with Kadar Khan and Shakti Kapoor and 'Mogambo' Ambrish Puri adding cheeky comedy and striking villainy for the masses. It sold!

Large multinationals like Burmah Shell and Coca-Cola had exited from India around 1977. While organised private sector was not massive in mid-1980s there were still several transnational corporations like Hindustan Lever, Richardson Hindustan, ICI, Citibank and Grindlays, and Indian industrial houses like Tata and Birla and fast-growing Reliance.

Dev in his Economics (Hons) course and, to a lesser extent, I in B.Com (Hons) was coming across articles on much needed economic liberalisation in India and were writing essays on it. Dev found the term 'Hindu rate of growth' to describe India's ongoing 3% annual GDP growth as inappropriate, in one of his class-tests he struck a diagonal line in the space provided beneath the question 'state key reasons for India's Hindu rate of growth'. The Indian economy professor asked him when he had answered every other question so well why had he not answered—in fact, struck off—this particular question.

'Sir, I do not find this phrase to describe India's slow growth appropriate.'

The Professor rested his eyes on Dev for longer than usual; to his credit, he then softly said to Dev, 'Okay, I understand.'

The discussion on decontrol and increasing competitiveness, internationalisation of business and economic liberalisation was gaining traction more so with India having sought $6billion IMF loan recently.

It was with this backdrop that Dev and I found ourselves in the final year of college with the big decision of 'what next' to be made. Having had some academic success and made a good circle of friends gave us confidence and a sense of pride especially when junior students would seek advice. The enchanting Delhi winter, the lilies in the gardens and the glorious golden sun gave us romantic hope. The world was young and full of anticipation, and erectile dysfunction was a term to be laughed at and not an ailment to be at all concerned about.

As Dev contemplated what to do next, IAS was not the only option he considered. In fact, most of his batch wanted to do MBA. Masters in Business Administration had emerged as a glamorous alternative to IAS. The idea of a 'high flying multinational executive' was delectable. It was a professional degree and if a candidate could get into one of the top management schools his or her 'future was secured'! It was not very easy to get in; but once someone did, the effort-to-reward ratio for MBAs was improving at a dramatic speed. An MA in Economics sounded too academic to Dev and he felt he wasn't suited for Chartered Accountancy.

Dev and his friends would sit in those lounging chairs of their cafeteria in Augustus college and discuss these options over scrambled eggs and toast; I would do the same with my friends in the canteen of Kautilya college eating veggie hotdogs with orange-coloured sauce. In my final year while I was studying Auditing, Company Accounts, Indian Economy and Income Tax, Dev was studying, amongst other advanced Economics subjects, Monetary and Fiscal policy. While our Auditing teacher was telling us that an auditor must be a 'watchdog, and not a bloodhound', Dev's famous Economic Policy teacher Dr Brijmohan was teaching them how central banks use interest rates as an instrument to control money supply and inflation in an economy.

Dr Brijmohan was an institution. He was slim and of medium height and acknowledged as an authority in his subject. He was always smartly turned out, had keen grey eyes and walked purposefully. 'Young men and women sitting in heavy jumpers with drooping shoulders and closed windows, open these damn windows will you!' he would roar on arrival in the class.

'How is Mr Devavratt Pratap Rajvansh today?' Dr Brijmohan would invariably say. He had taken a liking for Dev. 'Not going to answer "Hindu rate of growth" is it?' The word had spread that Dev had purposely left such a question in the class assignment. 'So, Mr Rajvansh, if you were the Governor of a country's Central Bank, and the economy was reeling under double digit inflation and registering 3% GDP growth pray what will you do with interest rates?' he would ask puckishly.

'Sir, I would need more information before I can answer this.'

'Fire away young man,' would be the retort. Dr Brijmohan's story-like lectures were usually packed out. Those who have mastered their subjects are able to simplify them and narrate them with anecdotes in story form.

The most talked about film when we were in final year was *Ram Teri Ganga Maili*; it had a great script, superb music and amazing photography. For 20-year-old boys what was most alluring was that the heroine's breasts were clearly visible in more than one scene! During our final year, Dev and three of his friends once walked to my college when our annual cultural festival was going on. After attending a speed debate, we went to the canteen. I asked them if they had seen *Ram Teri Ganga Maili*.

'We were planning to go last Friday Sandy, but because of this fellow we couldn't,' said Jaiswal, pointing at Dev.

I knew Dev only too well. I could sense he didn't quite like being referred to as 'this fellow'. A few days later I asked Dev, 'Your friend Jaiswal, he can be a bit brash, isn't it?'

Dev only said, 'He is a friend, Sandeep.'

Dev started preparing for the MBA entrance examination like many of his friends. In my college too there was a craze for MBA. Most aspirants wanted to get admission either in one of the four IIM's or Delhi College of Management Studies or The Management School of Delhi or Jamnadas Patil Institute of Management in Bombay or Zoilus Human Resources Institute in Jamshedpur—IIMs, DCMS, TMS, Patil and ZHRI as they were commonly known as. The MBA entrance comprised of a 120–150-minute multiple choice written examination, and for the fortunate few who got shortlisted the second stage involved a group discussion and interview. The multiple-choice exam tested quantitative ability, logical reasoning and verbal and comprehension skills. About 150–180 questions had to be answered in the time allotted and given negative marking this was a high-pressure test.

We bought special thick MBA entrance books and also picked up practice tutorials from private coaching institutes in India to prepare for the first stage of the exam. Nothing in life could have been better at that stage than getting a first division in our university bachelor's course and securing entrance to a premier business school.

***

In the indefinite journey of life, we all experience some moments that stay with us throughout our transitory time in this hotel lodge called the world. While happiness and sorrow, like night and day, present themselves as two sides of the same coin, those for whom there have been more moments that have brought happiness view existence on this planet as light of the morning, those who have encountered more struggle and pain see life as an evening with setting sun where the tired toiling bread-winner must return to his impoverished home in the hope of finding some rest. For Dev and his friends, who decided to make a car trip to Shimla in the October of 1985, their four-day vacation was so fun-filled that it kept bringing a smile to their faces long after they had all left college.

Anshu's father owned one of the largest car dealerships in Delhi. After some persuasion, he decided to lend his son a second-hand Fiat car for the long weekend in October. Jaiswal managed to book his father's company's holiday home in Shimla. And so, the six of them—Dev, Jaiswal, Anshu, DD, Gullu and Tank—decided to drive up to the hills even though

Dev's uncle was reluctant to see his nephew go away for the first time on his own.

Waking up at the crack of dawn and starting a long drive with friends was a novel adventure for all of them. There was no road atlas or GPS in those days and they relied on signposts and fellow travellers to guide them. After about an hour and a half of leaving Delhi, they stopped for breakfast at Murthal which was famous for road side *dhaba*s serving *parantha*s in particular. Along with the *parantha*s they asked for large glasses of *lassi*.

Gullu dipped his straw in Dev's mango-*lassi* as well while drawing Dev's attention to the large sweets corner in the restaurant. How come I am not getting any *lassi* in my mouth? wondered Dev when he next tried sipping his drink. Gullu had punctured his straw with the strike of his middle finger while Dev had been distracted and was now thoroughly enjoying all of Dev's *lassi* while Dev kept sucking at the straw and getting nothing in it! Dev laughed on realising and poked an elbow into Gullu who was cackling with the carefree spirit of Punjab.

They sang popular Hindi songs as the bespectacled Anshu drove on the Delhi-Chandigarh highway with lovely green paddy and sugarcane fields all around and the golden sun slowly rising up. Often the words would be changed to alter the meaning of the song and render it with naughty innuendos. As Tank moved to English songs and started humming Laura Branigan's 'In the night no control', Gullu interjected with, 'In the day all control,' and then laughed happily with his modification!

After about a five-hour drive, they started the 88-kilometre ascent to Shimla. Half-way up as they stopped amidst the hills for a comfort break, DD looked out into the valley. He had a crush on a girl in Augustus college whose birthday happened to be that very day, with his legs spread apart and arms lifted up he shouted, 'Happy birthday Sanjula!' The valley echoed with his voice.

'I don't love you, *Deendayal*,' squealed Jaiswal from behind in a girl's voice!

From the time they arrived at the holiday home later that afternoon till they left three days later, it was nonstop thrill and mirth. Somewhere on the Mall Road in Shimla they bought a set of playing cards with nude pictures. At night as they would spread out on the double bed to play a game of cards where every hand played created hilarity as the picture would get compared with famous people! And he who played the card was focus of the banter. Being rich in idle time is never added in national income estimates. Aimlessly wandering on the Mall amidst salubrious hills with mischievous trustworthy friends, enjoying *tandoori* rotis with *daal* and chicken curry at local *dhabas*, shooting balloons mounted on a white thick sheet with an air-gun in a tourists' stall, riding on a *tonga*, sitting on a bench overlooking the distant mountains occasionally discussing a serious topic and having that soberness broken by Gullu's amusing quips, making morning tea with condensed milk, taking pictures in quaint poses with scenic backgrounds and breathing that crisp unsullied air of the fresh mornings were priceless then and are priceless now!

DD was very keen to play video games in the local video games parlour. Every day after lunch he would get into a shop with colourful lights and start playing *Space Invaders*. On the third day, Jaiswal told him, 'If you go into that video games place again, I will break your balls.'

Dev smilingly said, 'That won't affect him; he will play with his hands.'

Tank laughed with his head buried in Dev's back.

At about midnight the day before they were supposed to leave, Gullu said loudly, 'I want to eat sweets, I can't sleep without some *meetha*.' He woke up everyone. 'Come Dev let's get some sweets.' He pulled Dev out of the bed and in the October night chill of Shimla they wandered on the Mall Road looking for sweets.

There was one sweets shop with shutters down but they could see lights on from the crosspiece window above the shutter. Gullu was not wearing his turban nor had he fixed his beard at that late hour. He climbed on top of Dev's shoulder and peeped inside the window and called out, 'Open, open! We want some sweets.'

The shopkeeper must have been scared; Dev didn't expect him to open the shutter but he did! In one large mud earthenware pot Gullu and Dev carried back 48 *rasgullas*! Six final year Economics (Hons) students of DU polished off all 48 that night with significant contribution coming from Gullu! All that remained in the pot was sweet syrup.

'Whoever can have that shall forever be called Badshah-Salamat,' said Dev.

They took a picture of Gullu drinking the sweet syrup remaining in the container! A memorable picture for years and years to come!

Back in Delhi, Dev started working hard for the MBA entrance exam. The first MBA entrance didn't go well for him. Some of the other written multiple-choice exams were better. I realised I needed more practice too, not just in the numerical section but also with comprehension. The results would get posted home—I didn't receive a single interview call! Dev qualified for an interview with TMS and ZIRI.

I remember speaking to him on phone after his TMS interview, their group discussion was on 'Drawbacks of Computerisation following which was an interview. 'What did you say in the GD, Dev?' I asked him.

'My point of view was there are hardly any drawbacks I see with computerisation.'

'And in the interview?' I enquired.

Dev said, 'I was asked about Planning Commission, deficit financing, backward sloping supply curve of labour,' he continued, 'whether or not I would actively seek to go abroad for work and finally the difference between googly and wrong 'un.'

I laughed!

'I am sure they regretted asking you that last question!'

By early April the result was declared. Dev was waitlisted at ZIRI but had qualified for TMS; turned out that Tank and Nita Rajagopalan had also qualified for TMS.

'Nita again!' I laughed, talking to Dev over the phone, 'She can't live without you!'

My friends at Kautilya talked about the big vacuum there will be in life once college is over. Sunil Gavaskar too had announced his retirement and Reliance World Cup in India was going to be his swansong. No college, no Gavaskar; it was going to be huge vacuum! Dev's last exam and my last exam fell on the same day around end of April in 1986. I told Dev that in case he wasn't going out with his friends I could pick him up from the gate of Augustus, as I was driving to Kautilya, and we could drive back together and have a pizza at Nirula's.

I waited in my car outside the Augustus college gate that early afternoon and saw the lean and tall figure of Dev coming out. He stopped about twenty metres from the gate to greet a professor. It was Dr Brijmohan! From my car I saw Dr Brijmohan place his hand on Dev's shoulder. They stood like that for a few minutes with the Professor saying something to a gently smiling Dev. He then shook hands with him as Dr Brijmohan gave him a pat on his back.

Before Dev exited from the gate towards me, he stopped and turned around to look at his college for one last time as a student. He had not had the easiest of childhood; his college had cradled him and made him somewhat more outgoing and definitely more confident. He looked at the silent walls of his college which had affectionately embraced him, those gentle lawns which always welcomed him cheerfully, that cricket ground where his energies had expressed in the game he was so passionate about, that merry cafeteria where his friends and he would endlessly banter, those wooden desks in the classroom which in spite of being lifeless had cherished his young life, that sombre quiet library that had cuddled him with knowledge of his subject, those hallowed corridors which had given him the assurance to dream. With that one last look at his temple of happiness, he turned around, came out of the gate and walked towards me.

Master Of Business Administration

Indians have held education as sacrosanct from times immemorial. Education has been the locomotive for knowledge, excellence and livelihood in Bharat. Goddess Saraswati, in fact, represents learning. In all my association with Dev, he never categorically talked about political ideology nor initiate discussion on religious beliefs. But I could infer that he was spiritual without being religious. However, he devoted some of his time in later years to understanding different religions. 'Just as mathematics is the language of modern science, Hindu gods and goddesses are symbolic of virtues that help human beings relate better to society and nature.' I remember asking him if there is convergence between modern science and Hinduism, to which he had said, 'There is very clear convergence between modern science and Hinduism and Neeraj's spiritual poetry. The reason why traditionally Hinduism was called *Sanatana dharma* is because its origin was in the scientific discovery of nature and its ways including man; since laws of science are unchanging, hence the name Sanatana or everlasting for the traditional principles some of which are contained in the 5000-year-old scriptures.'

Universities of ancient India like Nalanda, Takshashila, Shardapeeth and Vikramshila amongst many others were centres of higher learning where scholars travelled from faraway lands like China, Japan, Greece and Persia to seek education—much like the top American and British universities today. Indeed, some of the big temples of India also doubled-up as Universities, where not only were advanced subjects like Vedas, surgery, astronomy, mathematics and statecraft taught but these temples-cum-universities also encouraged open debates like the top Universities today. Adi Sankara, the great Vedanta philosopher and debater, studied at Shardapeeth and took the art of debating to highest levels including *purva paksha*, that is, debating from the opponent's point of view! Bhaskaracharya the great mathematician of the 12th century, who developed calculus much before Newton and contributed significantly to Pythagoras theorem, taught astronomy and mathematics at Ujjain University.

These temples of high learning in India were destroyed by conquering emperors between the 13th to 17th century CE and with them went India's immense literary treasure of Sanskrit and colossal knowledge of science. Later, English was introduced in the 19th century and went onto becoming the 'status' language with local Indian languages getting pushed to secondary importance. Of course, knowledge of English has enabled India emerge as one of the outsourced IT services-centre of the world, and made Indian technology and management graduates valuable human resource assets in transnational corporations. However, not being able to speak one's mother tongue fluently—for those who can't or feign not to—is inexcusable. Despite all the upheaval that happened in the sub-continent in the past millennium, pursuit of knowledge and learning remained sacred and Saraswati *puja* is performed till today. Dev and I and our many friends seeking master's level education and post-graduate professional courses were carrying on in this centuries-old revered Indian tradition of higher learning!

My parents, brother and I went to Dev's house for evening tea a few days after our graduation results were declared. Dev had secured a high first division, and I had a first division as well. Dev treasured his admission to TMS, he was relaxed and cheerful and we discussed options for me. My parents and Dev's aunt and uncle got chatting about the new TV serial *Buniyaad*, a story of post-partition India. They all related to the character of Haveli Ram and Lajoji. We laughed when they started talking about 'mileage' of each other's cars—we would observe the inanity of this question and chuckle. Dev's smile would still not reach his eyes—something was missing.

I had the option of sitting at home and preparing for MBA entrance again or joining a professional course like Chartered Accountancy. I decided on the latter. Chartered Accountancy was as good a course as MBA. However, I thought I should try for MBA entrance for a top business school one more time. Thus, even though I had offers from a couple of big CA firms I decided to approach a mid-size firm. I reached the Connaught Place office of Surendranath Vedprakash & Co. When I told Mr Surendranath the purpose of my visit he laid his eyes on me and said, 'You have finished your graduation and are now knocking from door to door?'

My nod was met with the second question, 'What does your father do?'

I told him he was a professor in the University.

Mr Surendranath smiled, 'You are the son of a teacher. Children of teachers must get the best of education.' I thus got an article-ship with SNVP.

The Management School was located just off the National Highway 8, near Rajokri village, about 20-minutes-drive from DU's south campus in Dhaula Kuan. While TMS was not affiliated to DU, it would synchronize its calendar with DU and operate a bus shuttle service twice in the morning and twice in the afternoon to connect students and staff to DU's South Campus. Thus, in the middle of July, The Management

School opened along with DU, and Dev reached TMS for his first day of Master of Business Administration course.

Nestled amongst Gulmohar, Ashoka and Neem trees the TMS was like a faculty building, much smaller than our college building, made of red bricks with ground plus two floors. There was a small lawn in the front along with space for car parking and a small lawn on the back side of the building behind which was Dean's bungalow, teachers' cottages, the canteen called Ridge and a hostel for 30 odd students. It was located not too far from Delhi-Gurgaon border.

Dev was slightly nervous. When he moved from school to Augustus, he met school toppers from all over India. Now, he was again encountering the sharpest brains from all over the country at TMS! The first-year batch of 55 students had almost half the students with an Economics-Commerce and liberal arts background and the other half were engineers from top engineering institutes of India. There were 16 students from Kautilya and Augustus colleges and notably nine engineers from Brahmagupta College of Engineering. There were only eight girls in their batch including Nita Rajagopalan!

TMS excelled in Marketing, Business Strategy and Organisation Behaviour. They were well regarded in Finance, HR and IT Systems as well. In the first year all subjects were compulsory while students could specialise in the second year. Apart from Tank and Nita, Dev recognised Pranav, who was a year senior to him in primary school in Jaipur. 'Good to see you here Deva,' said the burly and bearded Pranav in his deep voice.

Their classes got underway straightaway; the teaching methodology was absolutely new for Dev. They had case studies, team projects, group discussions, role plays, surprise quizzes and of course, home assignments and end of semester exams.

Students of both first and final years would be heard using expressions like 'funda', 'maxed it', 'cracked it' and 'oh fucks'. The corridor chat would be about seniors who had got placed in top MNC's or American banks. Some of the Professors too had great pedigree and were considered legends in their respective fields.

The Marketing professor Dr Rajeshwar Desai was a middle aged slightly built man with a quaint gait. He had sharp eyes and ready wit and would always ask a student his or her name during class discussions, 'Without a brand name there is no customer recall,' he said. He introduced the batch to the 4Ps of marketing: Product, Price, Place and Promotion.

'Sir, what about People as the fifth P?' asked a student in a gentle effeminate voice.

'Name?' asked Dr Desai.

'Sir, I am Rakesh Mutreja,' said he in a very measured, almost drawling effeminate way, adjusting his hair with his right hand.

'That way you can add several Ps—packaging, processes,' said another throaty voice in the class in a rapid fast tone.

'*Naam, naam*,' checked Dr Desai again.

'Jeet, Jeet Tandon,' said he clearing his throat. 'The 4 Ps that Sir mentioned are the core Ps, you can keep adding to them,' said Jeet again clearing his voice. Jeet always spoke with his right hand half up from the elbow and the right index finger fully raised while the ring finger and small finger half raised.

'How is People not a core P; it is people who are developing the other Ps?' countered Rakesh Mutreja in a slight tone, again daintily adjusting his hair.

Dr Desai softly laughed. He asked one of the girls for her view.

'Sir, I am happy with 4 Ps,' she said and the entire class laughed.

'Name please?'

'Simrin Avasthi.'

As the lecture ended Dr Desai gave the class a lesson that none of them ever forgot. 'A manager is often wrong but never in doubt!'

Meanwhile, I wasn't quite savouring my auditing work. While the seniors in the firm were helpful and professional, the nature of the work, especially for a junior article trainee was a bit tedious. I was usually just tallying numbers and applying tick marks in different ways to the ledger accounts. Of course, as auditors we were looked after really well by the clients. My sense of weariness made me one day call Sanju. He had not yet decided what to do with his life and I asked him to consider joining SNVP.

Dev began finding his feet at TMS and getting comfortable with the new livewire classmates. Jeet Tandon would travel from Rajendra Nagar on his 100cc bike and immediately start seeking bets on various matters going on in the world! 'Give me the odds, what are your odds,' he would say in a throaty fast tone with his right index finger raised. He wore dark photochromatic glasses and sported a moustache.

Rakesh Mutreja would come also on a 100cc bike from Patel Nagar and adjust his hair ever so gently and greet everyone most courteously. He was clean shaven and his eyes seemed lacking sleep and hid the punchy streak in his personality. Nobody knew of the storm that was to hit them!

Pranav Chaturvedi would sometimes delightfully banter but when it came to academics none was as serious as he was. There were two more class-fellows who Dev got to know a bit. Aakash Samarth was the most clean-cut guy, he was from Mussoorie and his serene temperament epitomised the hills. Sudhir Kapoor was a Delhiite, in fact, he was my batch from Kautilya and had completed B.Com (Hons) though I didn't get to meet him at college. Sudhir was quite sober but could also use some typical Delhi phrases with enthralling effect, he dressed smartly but in an understated manner and instead of extending his hand with thumb facing skywards he would open his hand with the palm facing skywards while offering a handshake. He had the typical decent boy next door looks. Students who were not Delhi based were given preference for hostel accommodation and thus Dev, Sudhir, Pranav and many others with family homes in Delhi used to commute daily to TMS.

Dev did his initial projects with Tank and Nita, his friends from Augustus college. They worked on the 'marketing mix' of Yamaha RX100 bike. Sudhir was working with Rakesh and Simrin Avasthi on analysing why the drink Happiness had not done well. The day various projects were to be presented in the class, Jeet Tandon ran into Simrin and quipped, 'You know why Happiness didn't do well?'

'Why?' she looked at him intriguingly.

'Because it has only 2 Ps,' said Jeet and walked away briskly with hushed laughter. Obviously, this was a pun between 4Ps of marketing and the spelling of Happiness, but Simrin didn't get the joke! Since that day Jeet started calling her 'Happiness' and in no time the entire class would refer to Simrin as 'Happiness'!

Tank organised the first party for the MBA class on the terrace of his home in Nizamuddin. The limelight was stolen by Rakesh Mutreja. After a couple of beers, he broke out into a dance, and stopped only after two hours and eight beers during which time he also went and hugged Dev, Tank, Sudhir and Aakash and told them exactly what he thought of them, thus enhancing their self-awareness! His electrifying Travolta like dance earned him the nickname Volt which was later expanded to Voltage after his spirited discussion on 'depreciation as a non-cash expense' with the Financial Accounting teacher.

Jeet had developed the reputation of being a super 'salesman'. His spoke fast often bamboozling his classmates.

'Tandon can sell Taj Mahal to anyone,' remarked a student. He was particularly brilliant in Quantitative Operations Management lectures. As an engineer from Brahma, his mathematics was exceptional. He got nicknamed 'Jigsaw' by Sudhir whose glossy magazines including a *Playboy* and *Debonair* he borrowed in the first semester and, despite twice committing the place and time, never showed up to return them! Jeet was an enigma which couldn't be unravelled. Towards the end of first semester Dev found everyone addressing Jeet as 'Jigsaw'.

In the meantime, I was delighted that not only did Sanju land an article-ship with Surendranath Vedprakash & Co but we both got assigned to the audit of a five-star hotel on Africa Avenue, The Blue Emerald. Sanju's presence gave me a sense of strength and of course, unlimited fun. I would take the Mudrika and reach Blue Emerald invariably by 10:30 am with guilty feeling of being late. Sanju would reach at 11 am with no feeling of guilt! He always lived life on the edge. Once in the auditor's room, Sanju and I would order cold coffee.

'Auditors need refreshment,' Sanju would say mischievously. After 'ticking' a few ledger accounts, we would proceed for lunch in the staff canteen of the hotel at about 12:30 pm. Back in after a hearty meal, Sanju would arrange the well cushioned chairs next to each other in order to stretch himself! I would be inspired to do the same.

'Auditors are resting,' he would say softly as I would burst out laughing. Post the gentle siesta, we would get back to checking some account totals while chatting about girls and films. At 3 pm we would order tea with pineapple pastries and by 4 pm we would call it a day! All meals and snacks at the Blue Emerald were of course complimentary for the auditors.

Not every audit that I got assigned to was as tranquil or as much fun! The time had also come for me to make my second attempt at MBA entrance. After a few weeks I was happy to hear that I had been shortlisted for the next round by TMS. Dev called me and said he would come over to my place on the weekend to share some tips for the interview. He came three consecutive weekends, had lunch with us, and not only did he talk me through how to approach group discussion and interview but did mock interviews with me as well. I had an ordinary interview and was thrilled when Dev called me in the

March of 1987 to inform me that I had qualified for the MBA degree programme at TMS!

I didn't quite know how to break the news to Sanju, on my imploring he had joined the CA course and now I was going to leave him. He took it very sportingly as did Mr Surendranath.

Dev would now become my senior at university! I was looking forward to July when I would board the U-Spl again, albeit to south campus this time and take the connecting shuttle to a premier business school of India. The world seemed such a terrific place again. I was also looking forward to personally meeting Voltage, Jigsaw, Pracha as Pranav Chaturvedi was popularly called, Happiness and the other names who I had heard from Dev while he was preparing me for the TMS interview.

Dev was having his share of excitement at TMS. He was quite enjoying the Organisation Behaviour sessions with the role plays and discussions on Leadership and Motivation using 2x2 matrices developed by management researchers! On one occasion Dev, Voltage and Pracha were asked to step forward by the OB professor in a tower building role play. Wooden blocks were laid out on the table with Dev sitting blindfolded and Voltage and Pracha giving him directions on how to place one block over another.

Dev didn't know whose instructions to follow, 'Can you please speak one by one?'

Voltage and Pracha decided that they would instruct Dev one by one on reaching out for the blocks and the care he needed to take lest the tower falls down. As the tower began to tilt the pressure rose on Voltage and Pracha! The team with highest tower was to win. Voltage decided to take matters in his hand, '*Prachey*, let me tell him now.'

The amusement in the class was more than audible to Dev. As Dev gingerly placed another block the tower tilted precariously. He felt a slap on his shoulder with Voltage telling him, 'This is going to fall if you are not careful!'

'I can't even see. How can I be more careful?'

The class was loudly laughing now.

'*Arrey* Dev, believe me this is going to fall,' said an exasperated Voltage in his drawling manner.

And then someone harshly pulled off his blindfold.

'I told you it will fall,' Voltage exclaimed, Dev saw the fallen wooden blocks on the table and the entire class in splits.

Somewhere around the beginning of the second semester Sudhir and Dev had started chatting a fair bit, they were somewhat similar in temperament and family background. Sudhir was sober and studious but had a streak of 'breaking-loose' occasionally and saying the wackiest of things. He used to love the dramatic aspects of life! When the weather would be cloudy and cool, he would say, '*Aaj tho kat-kat ke mar rahe hein log*', translated fuzzily in English 'it's the weather to die for'. Sometimes he would look at Dev and lower his eyelids as if to fill them up with lust and then bite his lower lip like a seductress in films! Dev found Sudhir the most unfussy and straightforward of people. Sudhir's whacky touches brought out further light-heartedness in Dev's still largely abstemious personality. '*Bhery* much possible'—an expression used by their Business Economics professor when Dev hesitatingly checked if it was at all possible for him to have got low marks in final exam having scored cent per cent in internal assessment, went go onto becoming part of Sudhir and Dev's conversation for many decades to come.

Summer of '87

The world today respects power—a stark reality of our times! The idealism that existed largely between the two great wars was shaken on 1st September 1939 and 'realism' dawned. Reason and philosophy as instruments for world peace were replaced by economic and military might as sources of power and 'balance of power' became the cornerstone of international relations. National interest became the single most important guiding principle for foreign policy of nations and remains so till today. While nationalism at the broader philosophical level might be divisive, at the worldly plane every nation must strive for power and instilling national pride amongst its citizens.

For an individual, 'power' and pride comes from exclusivity, as young university students our pride was emanating from the prestigious colleges, we were succeeding in getting admission into. When my parents' friends found out that I had qualified for The Management School the contrast of their eyes changed and the congratulatory messages carried warm admiration.

Since that day, I have always advised anyone who has cared to seek my opinion, that aspiring for the 'best brand' in any aspect of life should be a no-brainer! Of course, no amount of power or pride, is a sufficient condition for happiness.

While I was basking in what was till then my most significant success, Dev had succeeded in finding summer placement with another top brand. The placement season in TMS would get underway soon after the New Year holidays around early January. At the end of the first year, students would seek summer placements just as graduating final year students would be looking for final placement. Dev got a summer training offer from a large foreign bank, The Meridian Promissory, at their Madras branch. Two of his batchmates, Aakash Samarth and Jigsaw, got placed with another top foreign bank, The Capital Green, also to be based down south in Madras.

The Meridian Promissory was located on Mount Road, the main commercial road of Madras, and Dev's uncle was able to find a student's hostel accommodation not too far from there. The Spurtank Students Hall was just over 2 kilometres from Mount Road towards a pleasant area called Nungambakkam. The Hall was meant for students from around the world and with nearly 160 twin rooms spread over four floors. It was open to both boys and girls and attracted, amongst others, overseas students travelling in and around south India, summer trainees, college sports teams and student researchers looking for temporary stay at nominal prices. Samarth's bank The Capital Green was also on Mount Road, hardly 100 metres from Meridian Promissory, and Dev and Samarth decided to share a twin room in Spurtank Students Hall. The room charge per person was Rs. 10 per day! And so, towards the end of April 1987, three students from TMS flew to Madras for two months summer training. With Jigsaw with them and youthful sparkle in their eyes, anything could happen in the coastal city!

Dev and Samarth checked in to Spurtank Students Hall on the afternoon of a Sunday, a day before their summer training was to start. Jigsaw checked-in later in the evening. A pathway from the gate of the hostel led to the reception area where there was a man in a loose white shirt and white *dhoti* with *vibhuti* smeared on his forehead and a young bespectacled girl in a plain *salwar-kameez* with jasmine flowers in her hair and two gold bangles around her wrist. The man dolled his head from side to side when Dev told him they had a booking. 'Vaasanthi will help you,' he said. Vaasanthi was very courteous and often said 'seri' and 'aama' and checked in Dev and Samarth.

Dev and Samarth's twin room was as basic as a subsidised student's hostel in those days could be, the bathroom-toilets were common and located at the end of the corridor on each floor. This was Dev's first time in a hostel! Dev looked out of the window of his room on the fourth floor and the scent of Madras filled him captivatingly. In front of the hostel was a big sports ground with large banyan and neem trees, behind the hostel was a somewhat soiled canal with wild green plants floating in its smudgy waters. Breakfast and snacks were available in the canteen below, which was next to a neat little lawn within the compound of the hostel. The road outside looked cheerful and there was a little bakery called Harring's just beyond the students hall.

'*Chal*, let's go to the beach,' said Samarth to Dev in the evening. They took an auto to Marina beach quietly absorbing the sights of a new city with wide discovering eyes. It was with some difficulty that they communicated to the auto driver that they wanted to go via Mount Road and see their Banks en route. The auto drove past Pantheon Road crossing Taj Connemara Hotel to their right onto the Mount Road or Anna Salai as it was called. Mount Road was broad and clean with very few high-rise buildings; it stretched from Madras Central Railway station which was now well behind them, all the way to Guindy which was much ahead. To their right and across the road they first saw The Capital Green and soon thereafter The Meridian Promissory. Dev smiled to Samarth. Their auto turned left onto Dr Radhakrishnan Salai driving straight towards Marina beach. The sea breeze carrying with it fragrance of the local trees—palms, coconut, tamarind—was enchanting. A short argument followed with the auto driver over his fare, which the MBA students lost.

This was the first time Dev was seeing a beach. He was spellbound by the vastness and serenity of the glittering sea in front of him. The sun had still not set and its last rays were reflecting off the grand blue allure of nature which at once mesmerised Dev. Samarth too was quietly gazing at the magnificent waters. Words were not needed. As far as he could see and as deep as he could sense Dev felt an almost celestial energy which the sea was pulsating with. Energy which could subsume human energy effortlessly, yet it had such a calming influence on human souls. As the smell of phytoplankton reached Dev's lungs, he saw waves rising and ebbing then rising again then ebbing again. Like a human life, rising for a few seconds and then disappearing, then rising and receding again. How very small the physicality of human beings is. A single temperamental wave could sweep all of them, rich and poor, at the beach that evening in one go. Yet that one solitary boat in the distance, like that one bird flying home in the infinite night sky, appeared so strong in her solitariness in the boundless sea.

Did he love the mountains more or the sea, Dev thought to himself. Wave after wave would come lapping to his feet taking a bit of sandy ground from under them as it left. Like a toddler standing up on his feet without support for the first time, astonished at the magical ways of nature, so stood Dev feeling the waves come and go and every time, take some ground from beneath his feet. The sun was going down at the horizon with a promise to return again, it seemed reachable just as the moon does on a still night, the sky around it saffron with renunciation. The evening sea waves were whispering the secret of living—not to be found in words or books, not to be found in ideology or organised religion, not to be found in today's mobile phones or technology driven theme parks and not even to be found in our minds. The secret treasure lies in the heart. In the carefree laughter of those children who were playing bare-bodied on the beach, in that cup of tea had with friends under the village banyan, in effortlessness, in freedom and in love.

Dev and Samarth came out of their trance to look around at the beach. Several people were strolling but none in beachwear. On the beach sidewalk middle-aged and elderly couples were walking, in many cases the lady just a step behind her man. Most ladies were dressed in saris, the middle-aged a little heavily built and the ones with grey hair of frail frame. All wore gold in some form; all had jasmine flowers in their hair. The men were in plain shirts with either a trouser or in some cases a *dhoti*, walking in rubber *chappals*.

'Take flowers, Sir,' said a lady in her thirties to Dev, she was carrying a basket full of jasmine flowers that rested on her hip. She had dark burnt skin, frilly hair with flowers in them and wore a *bindi*, a gold bangle too, and her saree was tucked differently to the other ladies walking on the sidewalk. 'Take, Sir,' she repeated.

Dev looked at her and smiled. He found it hard to shake his head.

'Very nice flowers Sir; take Sir,' she said again.

Dev gave her a five rupee note and she handed some pristine jasmine flowers to him. Before walking away, she too gave Dev a shy smile.

Dev and Samarth sipped south-Indian filter coffee at the beach and checked with the coffee stall vendor if he knew of a nice place to eat.

'*Aama*, Sir, Saravana Bhawan, *straaaeeght* you go,' said the vendor, dolling his head and dragging the first syllable of the word 'straight'.

Madras seemed more orderly than Delhi; on surface it appeared more emotionally collected, perhaps because of the sea, arguably because north India had been so tumultuous since times immemorial. People were polite, though there was again a little argument with the auto-driver when Samarth and Dev got back to Spurtank Students Hall late evening.

'We must decide on the fare before we step in, Aakash,' said Dev to Samarth. He didn't like confrontation. Their friend, Jigsaw, who never blinked in a street fight, met them in the lawn of the Hall. He was shouting at another auto-driver who was just leaving from the gate. The driver was shouting back in Tamil at Jigsaw. Jigsaw was unflustered and smiling. He relished confrontation!

'Coming from a *mujra*?' said he naughtily, looking at the flowers in Dev's hand.

Dev smilingly shook his hand.

Before sleeping that night, Dev pulled out an inland letter from his suitcase and wrote a quick letter to his uncle and aunt informing them of his safe arrival in Madras, the telephone number of the reception and the postal address of the students' hostel.

The next morning, dressed in a dark navy blue trouser, a white shirt, a tie which matched the trouser and black shoes Dev got ready for his first day of office, albeit as a summer trainee. After *idli-vada* and coffee in the canteen below, Dev and his two batch mates got into an auto for Mount Road. The Meridian Promissory was a high-profile international bank and its Madras branch reflected that quality in every way. The décor of the bank was stylish and sophisticated, there was soft piped music playing, the air-conditioning seemed rather effective and Dev sensed professionalism when he saw the smart young employees working at their desks or walking around in the office area. He asked for Mr N. Parameswaran who was the Vice President Operations and was directed to a middle-aged man with salt and pepper hair.

'Good morning, Sir, I am Devavratt Rajvansh from The Management School in Delhi. I am supposed to do my summer training here and was asked to report to you,' Dev introduced himself.

'Good morning. Call me Param,' the gentleman replied with a polite smile.

Param took Dev around and introduced him to the officers in the branch. Two jovial managers in the Foreign Exchange trading room on the first floor shook hands with Dev and then chatted a bit with Param, twice using the word *chumma* which in conversational Hindi means 'kiss'. Later Dev learnt that in spoken Tamil, *chumma* meant 'generally' or 'without any apparent reason'. That afternoon Dev was introduced to the branch head, a dynamic looking young man in his mid-thirties who Dev learnt later was an MBA from one of the IIM's.

That evening Dev walked to The Capital Green branch to see if his friends were still there. They indeed were and seemed very quickly settled in. Jigsaw introduced Dev to two girls who too were summer trainees at Capital Green and were staying not very far from Spurtank Students Hall. They were MBA students from IIMs.

They all settled into their work routine. Dev was supposed to contact 30 institutional clients of Meridian Promissory during his summer training and introduce the bank's cheque discounting scheme to them. At the same time, he was supposed to spend a few days each with the various teams within the bank—retail banking, corporate and investment banking, foreign exchange trading, credit cards and even the teller—to understand all aspects of banking. Frequently, Dev would walk to Capital Green branch after his day was over, and usually he and Samarth, occasionally Jigsaw as well, would take an auto back to their hostel. He would often get a Swiss roll from the Harring's bakery on his way in to their hostel room. They started discovering restaurants in the Nungambakkam and Egmore area. Jigsaw would narrate astounding tales over dinner on how he was approaching his summer job.

'If you introduce yourselves as summer trainees, clients will not take you seriously,' he told Samarth and Dev in his distinctive speedy tone. Jigsaw understood the ropes much better. He seemed to master the situation in no time. He would then chat about the female summer trainees staying not too far from their hostel, 'Saritha said she found Dev very sweet. "So sweet! So sweet!" she said.' Jigsaw let out a short throaty laughter.

After about a fortnight, two groups of girls' sports teams checked into the hostel and the TMS trio could see pretty girls all over in the hostel. Around the same time a summer trainee from Lokakrithi Institute of Management in Calicut also checked into Spurtank Students Hall. He was told that Jigsaw was alone in a twin room and after meeting each other, Muthuraman became Jigsaw's room partner. Muthuraman looked exactly like a shorter version of Lionel Richie, the famous singer. He was very slender and of medium height, with a deep voice, large eyes, his lips would usually be parted revealing his teeth, he had thinning hair which bared a large forehead. Muthuraman was a simple person and his sharing a room with Jigsaw seemed like a real-life manifestation of dialecticism. Friendships are struck relatively easily during student days. Muthuraman started joining the TMS trio during their evening walks and late-night bantering sessions.

In every part of the world there are some informal words that are used casually in statements usually with friends or acquaintances of similar age profile. 'No problem *yaar*' in Delhi; '*aw-right* mate' in England; '*Kidhaan*' in Punjab; '*aur beedu*' in Bombay. The TMS summer trainees too would keep hearing the suffix '*da*' in Madras, not the soft sound of 'da' as in brother in Bengali but the bold sound of 'da' as in the word 'dash'! '*Enna da*' in Tamil loosely meant 'what's up'. Muthuraman in his own accent would often say 'sure *da*' rather '*shooar da*' or 'going to *aw-feez da*', and thus Samarth started greeting him in the evenings with 'Muthu da'. Soon Muthu was addressing his new friends as Samarth da, Jigsaw da and Dev da. Dev would address Muthu as Muthuraman at which Muthu would haltingly laugh. 'Call me Muthu, da,' he would say. Muthu was doing a market research project as part of his summer training with a large South India-based FMCG company.

The girl's badminton team had caught the eye of the three TMS trainees and the one LIM trainee. Some of them were really good looking and in their short skirts looked even more striking. There was never a better time for some mischief, some light flirting, some yarn for young lives to knit, some unearthing of their earthly desires. But Dev and Samarth were not exactly the most gregarious of characters, Jigsaw was evidently not into harmless pursuits of life and Muthu was a simple small-town boy. Yet Jigsaw and Muthu chatted at night as to how they could get an introduction with the girls, while Samarth and Dev smilingly looked on.

'Dev da, give us some idea da,' said Muthu.

'Samarth is the intelligent one,' said Dev gently laughing.

'I saw Dev saying hi to the tall girl this evening,' said Samarth with a wink and they all laughed.

'Prepare a questionnaire Muthu and get them to respond to it,' suggested Dev impishly.

'Great idea, great idea,' said Jigsaw clearing his throat, 'you are in any case doing a market research project, you can tell them you are looking for customer preferences for chocolates.'

'Ha-ha,' laughed Muthu, 'you guys are cruel smart da,' he continued, pronouncing 'cruel' as *crool*! 'So, I should get their names and what else?' asked Muthu of his three north Indian friends.

'Get their names, which place they are from and tell them all of us are executives in multinational bank,' said Jigsaw, raising his right index finger with the ring finger and small finger only partially lifted, 'don't say we are summer trainees.'

Muthu laughed heartily.

He prepared a questionnaire to be 'administered' to the good looking athletic 'baddy girls' and for several evenings the summer trainees, to more or lesser degree, got vicarious pleasure listening to their Calicut friend debrief them on his encounters with the pretty young girls. 'The girls are mainly from south though there are two from Gujarat as well. They are all university level badminton players trying for state selection. This is a coaching-cum-selection camp, it's for a fortnight but could get extended.'

Muthu had been a tremendous sleuth! 'Dev da the tall one you like; her name is Aparna and she is from Mangalore. One of the Gujju is Aaheli and the other Gujju who will suit Samarth da is Shubhanshi.'

The TMS students were laughing in admiration at Muthu's 'market research.'

'Muthu, who is the girl who carries a navy-blue kitbag?' asked Jigsaw.

'She is a *kurnoo* da, I think the one you are referring to her name is Namitha.'

'*Kurnoo* meaning?' asked Jigsaw.

'From Kurnool,' laughed Muthuraman.

You told them we are all executives?' said Jigsaw.

'I did da, I think a few of them like Samarth and Dev,' said Muthu as the laughter of the summer trainees got louder, 'they were enquiring about them during my questionnaire sessions.'

'Tell them I am senior to Samarth and Dev,' said Jigsaw leading to hysterical laughter in that hostel room on the fourth floor of Spurtank Students Hall!

This was Madras and India of the 1980s. Muthu's efforts ultimately only resulted in the bright TMS students exchanging some pleasantries with the lovely young girls. The LIM student from Calicut and Samarth and Dev did not have the chutzpah to go any forward. Their fourth friend, who was a few years elder to them, had the nerve and was less self-conscious but chose only to derive gentle kicks from this memorable but infertile encounter.

Meanwhile, at work, Dev was conscientiously meeting the clients and discussing Meridian Promissory's cheque discounting scheme. He even started getting some business for the bank. The managers and staff in the bank who were local to Madras seemed a bit distinct from the other 'MBA types' from different parts of India. It seemed to Dev that for the locals, 'god, work and sea' defined their life. One day, while returning from work, Dev couldn't find an auto and hence decided to hop into a public bus. He was amazed to see that the seats on the left side of the bus, earmarked for ladies, were all unoccupied even though several men were standing in the aisle. In Delhi, even on ladies' seats, men can be seen sitting while women might be standing. Ladies were certainly respected in Madras. Often, he would hear boys and men addressing ladies they didn't quite know as 'Ma'. People in Madras appeared more emotionally composed to Dev than the Delhiites, till he saw mob frenzy outside a cinema hall where a popular Tamil actor's film had just been released.

As the summer trainees entered their second month in Madras and had become familiar with their surroundings, Jigsaw took the initiative of organising a weekend trip to Mahabalipuram. About 60 kilometres from Mount Road, Mahabalipuram was a popular get-away with several beach resorts and seaside hotels, cave temples and even a crocodile farm. Apart from the three of them, there was Muthu and the other four summer trainees from Capital Green which included three young ladies and a young man. Saritha who was studying at IIM and doing her training with Jigsaw and Samarth got two more female friends of hers. The group of ten—five girls and five boys—got into a mini bus on a Saturday morning for a weekend trip to Mahabs, as it was popularly called. They had booked a beach resort near Shore Temple in Mahabalipuram with two large duplex rooms, one each for the boys and girls. The hour and a half drive to Mahabalipuram was along the sea, and with the enchanting waters to their left and a bus full of smart, intelligent, single men and women with ready wit, the journey seemed much too short!

Staying on the beach was another first for Dev. After checking-in to the beach resort he just kept looking at the sapphire sea from the balcony of their duplex room. Jigsaw was in a hurry to eat something and have a beer and implored the group to come down to the restaurant, only to find that the restaurant was full with a waiting time of about 45 minutes. Delhiites don't easily take no for an answer and Jigsaw used all his persuasion skills to jump the waiting queue and in 15 minutes all of them were seated by a large window in the restaurant overlooking the beach and sea. Dev and Muthu and three of the girls didn't drink beer and ordered a soft beverage to go with their snacks, while the other five said 'cheers' and exclaimed that friends, beach and cold beer created paradise on earth! They spent the remaining morning and afternoon discovering Mahabalipuram. In the Tiger cave temple Saritha asked Dev, 'Who is your favourite character from Indian mythology?'

Dev said to her courteously, 'For me all this is history and not mythology. The historical personality I admire the most is Krishna.'

The girls were feeling a bit tired and the entire group returned to the resort late afternoon and agreed to re-assemble at 6 pm. After a round of tea and banter they stepped out on the beach walking towards the sea. They scattered a little on the beach and Saritha asked Dev if he would like to see the rocky part of the coastline and the two started moving in a different direction to where their friends were going. They must have walked about half an hour before turning back to their resort and by the time the two got back their friends were already in the restaurant having beer and juices. Dev told Saritha that he would have a quick shower and then come to the restaurant. As Saritha joined the others in the restaurant they all started making mischievous sounds.

'Hmmm we were expecting the couple to come together,' said one of the girls and everyone laughed including Saritha.

'Where is our friend?' asked Samarth.

'He has gone for a shower,' she said.

'All alone!' remarked one of her friends.

Saritha laughed and gave her a gentle whack on the shoulder.

'Did you like our pal?' smirked Jigsaw.

Saritha thought for a moment, 'He is very nice, but there is something aloof about him.'

'You mean you didn't like our Dev?' Jigsaw was not giving up.

'He is sort of detached, his mind seems elsewhere; but deep down, he must be a romanticist,' said Saritha.

'Romanticist! How do you know?' pried Jigsaw.

'My sixth sense,' winked Saritha.

'Did he compliment you on your smile?' checked Jigsaw naughtily.

Far from it, Jigsaw He was only interested in knowing about my summer project and the activities in IIM. The closest personal thing he said to me was to ask whether I liked the sea!'

All of them softly laughed. Soon they were loudly roaring as a well-groomed Dev walked towards their table. They did more sightseeing the next day and started back for Madras at 4 pm, stopping at the famous Elliot's beach in Besant Nagar near Adyar on return.

Five weeks into their summer project, Dev and Samarth had started writing their reports. Muthu too was beginning to think how to compile his market research results into a report. Jigsaw wasn't bothering with one. 'Show them some business, what will they do with reports,' he said to his two younger batchmates and room partner.

Dev's boss Param seemed very happy with the way Dev had approached the project. 'You have worked like an officer Dev, not like a trainee,' he told Dev. Dev felt really uplifted with the recognition.

***

One evening, with just about 10 days to go for the TMS students to return back to Delhi, when Muthu had not yet got back from his office, Jigsaw told Dev, 'I am now getting bored here.'

Dev suggested, 'Let's go for a film.'

'That we can,' said Jigsaw, 'but in your kingdom there should be something more exciting to do.'

After a minute's pause, Jigsaw got a brainwave and asked Samarth and Dev to be his accomplices in playing a practical joke on Muthu. 'Bhaisahab, tell Muthu today that I am a homo,' said Jigsaw with a wicked chuckle. 'Then after two days, check with him if all is going well. Then after two more days I will scare him a bit!' Jigsaw shared the outline of his stunt.

The two tall clean-cut room partners exchanged a glance and agreed to enjoy a bit at Muthu's expense. Later that evening, as they were walking back from a restaurant after dinner, Dev was strolling with Muthu a few metres behind the other two.

'Muthu, is all going well with Jeet? I mean Jigsaw?'

Muthu looked a bit curious, 'Yes da, why do you ask?'

Dev kept looking in front, 'No, no, just like that.'

'That's an unexpected remark, Dev da,' said Muthu sounding intrigued.

'There is a little rumour, and I am not sure at all, just that our institute boys sometimes say, that Jigsaw has some homosexual tendencies,' said Dev, discovering an acting ability in him.

'What!' exclaimed Muthu, half laughing, half reflecting.

'As I said, I am not sure, but just thought I would let you know,' said Devavratt.

Muthu was now thinking more and laughing less, 'He has been fine da, not tried any hanky-panky with me.'

Dev changed the topic as they walked back on a lovely full moon night feeling the pleasant sea breeze on their faces.

The next evening Jigsaw got a film magazine and instead of peering at the pictures of female actresses in sizzling dresses, he kept gazing at shirtless photos of male actors ensuring that Muthu noticed it! As they set out for a walk the day after, Muthu said to Dev, 'I think you were right da, I need to be careful of Jigsaw.'

On their last weekend in Madras they decided to dine in the famous Rain Tree restaurant eating food served on banana leaves, looking back on what had been such an enriching two months in every possible way. During their half an hour walk back to the hostel occasionally Jigsaw would place his hand on Muthu's shoulder, the latter would instantly step away and position himself such that either Samarth or Dev was between him and the 'gay'. They reached the Spurtank Students Hall and Muthu decided to come into Samarth and Dev's room for a chat. Muthu looked a bit concerned. 'Since you told me about Jigsaw, I have removed my bed from its original place close to his bed and shifted it as far as I could.'

'Ah, you mean Jigsaw's rumoured tendencies,' said Samarth hanging his shirt in the cupboard.

'I don't think it's a rumour da, he was kissing the photo of a male actor in that film magazine and even now while walking he constantly wanted to walk close to me,' said Muthu sounding worried.

'And today is weekend, he might just be in the mood,' said Samarth with a straight face.

'He has never made a move on you, has he, Muthu?' asked Dev.

'Since the day you told me, not only have I moved my bed away but I also cover all parts of my body with a sheet while sleeping so that I am not exposing any skin to him,' said a visibly-shaken Muthu.

'Aakash is right about this being a weekend, be careful tonight and tomorrow, Muthu,' cautioned Dev.

Muthu was almost trembling now. 'Dev da, let me sleep in your room tonight.'

'Oh, don't worry so much, Muthu. Jeet, I mean, Jigsaw won't approach if you are not consenting,' said Dev, scaring their simple friend a little more.

'Hey please da, I don't want to sleep there tonight.'

'You have taken all precautions, Muthu, don't be so scared,' said Samarth stretching himself on his bed.

'I will come with you to your room Muthu,' offered Dev.

I can't help laughing to myself every time I think of the image of Jigsaw, as Dev described to me, when they reached Muthu's room. As Dev opened the door with Muthu a safe step behind him, he found Jigsaw half reclining on his raised pillow wearing just his shorts, no vest or t-shirt on his bare-body. He had his dark glasses on though even at that late hour, his left leg folded up with its sole resting on the bed and the right leg crossed and placed on top of the left leg. For that complete and dramatic effect, he had a key ring on his index finger which he was twirling.

'Hey you! Stay away from me,' shouted Muthu without any provocation from Jigsaw who was only looking at his room partner through his dark glasses.

'Hi Muthu, come, come here,' said Jigsaw patting the mattress right next to his hip.

'I know all about you, you bloody Jigsaw; stay away from me,' yelled a frightened Muthu.

'I won't hurt you, Muthu, come here, come,' said Jigsaw softly. In a swift action Jigsaw got off his bed and reached out for Muthu.

'*Aayy*, no, no,' shouted a perspiring Muthu and turning away towards the door he started running in the corridor. Jigsaw instantly ran after him with a devilish smile. Dev was stunned. He didn't expect that Muthu would get so frightened with this prank. He too ran after both of them fearing that Muthu might, in that frenzy, jump off the window from the 4th floor of the hostel! A 5'7" thin Muthu followed by a 5'9" wiry Jigsaw followed by a 6-foot slim Dev were all running on the 4th floor corridor of Spurtank Students Hostel that Saturday evening in the June of 1987!

After a chase of some thirty meters, Jigsaw caught up with Muthu who threw himself on the floor and folded his body like a baby in sleep. 'Get away, get away please!' shouted a traumatised Muthu with tears in his eyes.

Dev too caught up with them. 'Muthu we were just playing a prank. It's just a joke,' said Dev bending down on his knees to comfort Muthu. Jigsaw too comforted Muthu placing his hand on his shoulder which the latter brushed away. After a few minutes Muthu collected himself.

'It was just meant to be a practical joke, Muthu, we are really sorry,' said Dev. He waved to Jigsaw to say the same.

'Just a prank Muthu da,' said Jigsaw. Dev took Muthu to his room; Samarth opened the door and saw the three of them in. They all comforted Muthu and chatted for half an hour explaining to him how they had conceived the practical joke.

On the last day of summer training, Dev handed over his report to the VP Operations Mr Parameswaran. 'I hope you will join us permanently next year Dev,' said Param, shaking Dev's hand. He also gave Dev a letter from the bank certifying the successful completion of his summer training. With a feeling of utmost fulfilment, Dev bid goodbye to all his colleagues one by one. His flight back was next morning, though Samarth and Jigsaw were only flying two days later. He decided to go to the famous Nalli store to buy a saree for his aunt, after which he went to Victoria Technical Institute on Mount Road to pick up souvenirs for his uncle and cousin.

That evening Muthu and the three TMS students went to a new restaurant on Harrington Road. It was their last evening together in Madras since Dev was flying the next morning. Dev didn't quite know when he would meet Muthu again; they chatted and laughed about their adventures over the past few weeks. As they were walking back, Dev gently placed his hand on Muthu's shoulder, the Lokakrithi Institute of Management student said to him, 'Dev da, I didn't expect you to play that prank on me; you guys treated me like a toy.'

Dev felt dreadful. 'I am sorry, Muthu; we thought it would be a harmless joke. Do forgive me.'

Muthu smiled at him, his eyes reflecting a touch of hurt and also sadness that Dev was leaving the next morning. 'Stay in touch da, do write to me,' he said to Dev giving him a hug.

The next morning Dev said bye to Jigsaw and Samarth, of course, they were to meet shortly back in TMS in a couple of weeks' time. 'This has been memorable Aakash,' he said to Samarth who had come with him to the gate of the hostel to see him off.

Samarth who used to speak very little said, 'It's been wonderful two months with you, Dev. Have a safe flight.'

As Dev sat in the Indian Airlines flight, he wished his time in Madras had lasted longer. He was going to miss the zestful Students Hall, their *idli-vada* breakfast and filter coffee every morning, the food on banana leaves, the presence of friends all the time, the swanky bank office, the sea and the beach and that enthralling fragrance of Madras, the evident simplicity of the people and the way he felt the coastal town had embraced him. He felt enriched with the experience, he felt confident as a management student.

He couldn't help comparing Delhi with Madras, this was the first city he had actually felt and comparison was inevitable. But Delhi was his home. He was looking forward to meeting his aunt and uncle and cousin, his room which was his little place on Earth, the lovely monsoons about to arrive in Delhi and the *jalebi*s and *samosa*s, Lodi Gardens and Khan Market and those tandoori rotis in the little *dhaba*s. He was looking forward to speaking with Sudhir and me and sharing the happenings of last two months. He wished he could carry a little bit of Madras with him, he wished Delhi too would be less aggressive and safer for women, and that human interactions in his home town could be simpler and more courteous. Yet he didn't want Delhi to trade its greenery and parks and wide roads, its lively amalgamation of cultures, its whacky humour, its never-say-give up attitude and energy, and its great-heartedness bestowed in rainbow colours!

Trying to understand India with all her diversity is a demanding and ceaseless occupation. He who sets out to comprehend the world can stay busy for more than a lifetime. But he who sets out to understand life must become enormously, if not eternally, poignant.

"Master of Business Administration"

Dev was chatting with someone at the porch of the building when I stepped into The Management School for my first day as an MBA student. Standing slim and tall as I had always seen him, he was not that excruciatingly sedate school boy anymore. He looked composed, confident and accessible; his eyes were no longer sunken but had a purpose about them, his thick black hair as always perfectly groomed. His long chiselled clean-shaven face with that prominent nose turned towards me as he saw me walking towards him. He gave me a warm smile. 'Hi, fresher,' he said. He kept smiling gently as we shook hands; his look revealed how genuinely happy he was for me, though as always there was a part of him that palpably lay concealed.

'Meet your classmate Sandeep,' Dev softly gestured towards the person next to him who he was chatting with.

I held the extended hand. 'Eklavya Malhotra,' he said.

'I am Sandeep Khanna.'

'Khanna!' exclaimed Eklavya. 'We are same family,' he said with a beaming smile that, unlike Dev, at once radiated to his eyes. Eklavya was just a couple of inches shorter than Dev with a demonstrative and handsome face. He had cropped hair, was clean-shaven and laughed easily. His ears seemed to be sticking out and his eyes were gleaming though a bit narrow and on their outsides, he would instantly show skin lines while laughing. He was casually though smartly dressed and his voice—unlike Dev's somewhat coarse voice—was pleasantly striking.

Just then a classmate of Dev's walked up the three steps onto the porch and lay open his hand which Dev clasped. 'Bhaisahab,' said he, giving Dev a half-hug.

Dev introduced Eklavya and me to him, 'Sudhir, this is Eklavya, joining first year today. I have known him for about 15 minutes.' Sudhir and Eklavya shook hands. 'And this is Sandeep who I have known for longer than fifteen minutes.'

'Sandeep Khanna,' said Sudhir, indicating that he had heard about me from Dev.

'And you are Sudhir Kapoor; Dev has often mentioned,' I reciprocated the familiarity even though we had met for the first time.

'Kapoor!' exclaimed Eklavya again. 'This is one large family! Khanna, Kapoor and I am Malhotra,' he said, pointing towards himself perkily.

'That's a unique name,' remarked Sudhir.

'Which one—Eklavya or Malhotra,' asked Eklavya with glint.

Sudhir laughed.

'You can call me Luv.'

I felt a gentle hand on my shoulder and this time it was a female voice who said, 'Hi fresher.' It was Nita Rajagopalan.

'Lovely to see you Nita,' I greeted her.

'Eklavya Malhotra,' said Luv at once introducing himself to Nita, even as Dev and Sudhir side-stepped to meet their other classmates arriving to TMS for the first day of the new academic year. '*Khannae,* what time is the orientation?' asked Luv, addressing me in a way I had hitherto not been.

The orientation was in the large classroom on the first floor, all of the first year and most of the final year students and faculty members were there. The Dean welcomed us all, he then spoke briefly about the teaching methodology, the high standards of TMS and what the industry had come to expect from the institute's graduates. He took a few questions and then just before the faculty members and he left us with our seniors he said, 'Make friends with your seniors and next year, your juniors as well, and take care of each other.' Then looking at our seniors who were sitting on the back benches of the classroom, he said with a pleasant smile, 'Only light-hearted GTKY; no ragging.'

I learnt later that day that GTKY meant 'Get To Know You'.

The Dean then looked at Nita and said to her, '*Samosas* and tea on their way?' and looking at us he said, 'Only for today, only today!'

Each of the first-year students were supposed to come to the front of the class and introduce themselves; the seniors would then pose a couple of mischievous chewy questions. There were about 50 students in my batch, since I was sitting in the second row from front with Eklavya, our turn came quickly. I was surprised to learn that Luv had done two years of engineering at Prayagraj Technology Institute after which he 'got bored' and didn't complete the degree, and then shifted to Ved Vyas College in DU for a Psychology (Hons) course.

'The Eklavya of ancient India gave away his thumb, what do you intend to give away?' asked a girl from the final year. It was Happiness who posed the question!

'Since there are some good-looking girls in TMS, I might give my heart away,' said Luv. There was massive clapping and whistling in the class when Luv said this. He came back and sat down with a grin and smile lines around his eyes.

When I came forward, Nita asked me, 'What are you most looking forward to here?'

I wanted to give an amusing reply but nothing came to my mind straightaway. Hesitatingly I started, 'Well, there are many extraordinary characters in your class. I don't mean to offend anyone…' And suddenly I heard two seniors saying 'Don't be defensive;' I continued, 'What I am looking forward to most is meeting Voltage and Jigsaw.'

Once again there was loud cheer from our seniors and thumping of desks. I could see Dev sitting 15 rows back smiling evocatively. Then one of the seniors said, 'I am one of the two names you mentioned—guess who I am! If you get it right, I will treat you to a beer, but if you get it wrong you will have to sing a duet song from a Hindi film in both the male and female voices.'

The entire first year and final year started laughing loudly! I had heard a little bit of the description of both Jigsaw and Voltage from my not too voluble friend, the senior asking the question had a mellow way of speaking and so I guessed, 'You must be Voltage.'

Once again there was a roar in the class from the seniors sitting on the back benches! I had guessed correctly. Amidst a lot of clapping, I came back and took the seat next to Luv. I looked back and over my right shoulder, Dev was smiling radiantly at me. Sudhir sitting next to him gave me a thumbs-up while Voltage was wagging his right finger at me in what appeared a good-natured manner!

As the introductions proceeded, I looked out of the large window to my left. The monsoon clouds had gathered and the cool breeze was blowing the tall gulmohar and neem trees in majestic abandon. The zephyr carried with it fragrance from a distant land, the chirping of cuckoo and koel announced nature's carnival as the grey curls in the sky opened up into a light rain and the grass-attired lawns, the innocent plants in the hedges and the fountain trees in the forest, all embraced the shower as a child embraces her nurturing parent. As the drizzle turned somewhat heavy it sang a song whose lyrics hit the heart instantly. There were still some red flowers on the gulmohar trees, the rains turned them scarlet, it was a colour that neither man nor technology could reproduce; the chaste green leaves had turned emerald, it was a colour whose freshness could be matched only by the sinless first beam of a new born baby. Just then the canteen boy arrived with *samosas* and tea to welcome us on our first day. A new institution that excelled in its field, two years of learning and discovery ahead, exceptional batchmates, some of whom would become friends, very little to worry about and the sensation of nature's miracle: if a person could experience even a dozen such moments in his or her time, the memories of such instances would be enough to see through a life even if it became deprived of every other endurance that human beings need to survive in this mortal death-ridden world where we have been sent for an unknown period by an unknown power.

While I got into the routine of lectures, case studies, projects and surprise quizzes, the real thrill lay with Dev's final year batch. In the final year there were several electives that students could choose from and decide their specialisation. The popular electives were Strategic Management, Consumer Behaviour, Marketing Communications, Corporate Finance and Investment Management. There were still a few compulsory subjects like Game Theory and Business Statistics, International Economics, and Government Business and Society. In the fourth and last semester of the course, students had to write an original dissertation under the guidance of one of the professors of TMS; the dissertation would be followed by viva. The final placements, those ultimate dream jobs, would happen, as ever, in early January a good four months before the final year students graduated.

There were incidents and mini-scandals galore with the final year batch, news would spread fast in TMS. Dr Partho Lahiri was the Government Business and Society professor, he was very frail and short and, while quite learned, he was not an effective communicator and gave the impression of being somewhat meek. Dr Lahiri used to almost wrap his thin leg around the podium in class and his threadlike fingers would hang from his hand leading Voltage to describe them as *jadi-bootiyan* or herbs! He had the ability to make the most interesting of topics somnolent. Once, after quarter of an hour of a drowsy monologue on governments' role in business in developing countries, he looked at the class and said, 'Have some views.'

What he meant was 'share your views'; instead, he repeated 'have; have some views.' For some reason he used to address Rakesh Mutreja—the famous Voltage—as Ramesh Kukreja! 'Yes, Mr Ramesh Kukreja, have some views,' he said looking at Voltage.

'Rakesh, Sir,' corrected Voltage in his soft manner, self-consciously adjusting his hair.

'Have some views.'

'Sir, I have none,' said Voltage.

'Have some,' implored Dr Lahiri.

At this Voltage remarked, 'Sir, actually I come to your class only for attendance. I will really appreciate if you don't disturb me just as I am not disturbing you.' The entire class looked down at their desks even as laugher was stirring within them.

The teacher was taken aback; his Adam's apple shuffled up and down as he collected his wits and tried to find his voice. Looking dejected he quietly said, 'This is India today!'

***

Sometimes relative strangers recognize personality traits of people we are close to more readily. Luv would have met

Dev in TMS only a few times when he said to me over a cup of chai one morning, 'Devavratt is very helpful, twice I have asked him for some guidance and both times he has patiently and clearly explained to me.' Luv continued, 'I believe he did his summer training with Meridian Promissory,' Luv looked at me enquiringly.

I nodded.

'That's fantastic, he has leadership qualities,' said Eklavya.

'How did you make that out Luv?' I enquired.

'Just the way he carries himself and speaks.' Luv's father was in the defence services and due to his frequent transfers Luv had studied in seven schools, in all parts of India, and two colleges before getting to TMS. He was a free-spirited person with malice towards none and a whacky sense of humour. Since he had already travelled so much and met people from all over India, he could judge a person really fast. He also relished in creating the cultural stereotypes! 'East India is predominantly emotion, north India is about power, west India is very business-like and the south is systems and processes.'

If Dev was restrained, measured and careful, Luv was free-wheeling, gregarious and extroverted. '*Khannae,* I have grown up with some biases, one of them is that when I see a man with a comb in his hip pocket, I can't help feeling he is a bit tacky,' he said during that same early morning conversation and then broke out into a giggle.

'Thank god I don't carry one Luv,' said I joining him in the chatter.

'But this cream shirt that you wear with a black collar,' he said looking at my shirt, 'makes you look like a waiter.'

I laughed at his charming directness. 'I will warn Dev never to carry a comb in his back pocket,' I said jokingly.

'Dev is elegant, I can bet my pyjamas he has never carried a comb,' said Luv stroking his bottom.

Quite a few of my classmates had admiration for Dev; and Sudhir, Samarth and Nita were very well regarded too. However, the legends in TMS were being scripted by Voltage and Jigsaw as well as Pracha. Dev had mentioned to me that Pranav Chaturvedi was the most hard-working student in their class. Due to my surname, Pracha started calling me 'Praji,' which means 'brother' in Punjabi. His manner of speaking was rather provincial. 'You have to consider the *impli-caashunn* of the *liberali-saashunn*' was a line Dev's friend Sudhir would use while trying to mimic Pracha, stressing on the second syllable of the words 'implication' and 'liberalisation'! It was well known that Pracha was keen to join the government civil service post MBA. In fact, Sudhir also wanted to take the civil services examination. A few teachers at TMS were not too enthused about the idea of MBA graduates, who were being prepared for industry, joining civil services. On the other hand, there were teachers who were of the view that management education and industry understanding would come in handy in government jobs.

Dev's Strategic Management professor was a young and smart man who spoke impeccable English. He was one of those who didn't quite approve of MBA students considering civil service options. Pracha's unpunctuated way of articulating meant that he now had two red flags as far as the Strategic Management professor was concerned. One of the projects for students who had taken the Strategic Management elective was to do a book review of any general book on business strategy. Pracha reviewed a book called *Marketing—The New Warfare*. While giving the synopsis of the book in class Pracha spoke in his booming voice thus, 'Sir, basically what the book says is that marketing is just like war, as in war you can attack from left flank or right flank and throw the enemy into confusion. Similarly, marketing is about attacking the competitors with different schemes and ideas and springing surprises.'

The Professor looked through Pracha and then turning his face to the others with a wry smile that betrayed dismay at the just-expressed summary, said in his clipped accent, 'How would you rate the social conversation value of that synopsis on a scale of 1 to 10?'

Dev and Sudhir and Nita exchanged glances at the sharp comment, Voltage couldn't suppress his smile, though it appeared that Pracha was unconcerned and sat down having, in his opinion, given a reasonable synopsis of the book! On another occasion as the burly frame of Pracha carried a tripod stand for a project presentation, and his heavy torso shuddered under his thick beard, the Strategic Management professor commented, 'Are we going to have a cabaret in the class!'

Meanwhile, Voltage and Jigsaw had crossed swords at the start of the final year, perhaps due to Voltage's super candid nature or Jigsaw's mystifying ways or both. In the Game Theory and Business Statistics lecture, as Jigsaw sat in front of Voltage in class and obscured his view of the blackboard, Voltage requested him, 'Jigsaw can you move your coconut a bit.'

Jigsaw looked back sternly. 'Addressing your Pa?'

Not to be outdone, Voltage shot back while tenderly adjusting his hair, 'Jigsaw, I will have you kidnapped from Rajendra Nagar.'

The Business Statistics teacher—who used to pronounce Simrin as *Shimrin* and Jeet as *Zeet*—had to intervene, 'Rakesh and *Zeet*, please don't *zoke*.'

The following week, during a Business Statistics class test, Jigsaw who was a genius at mathematics, decided to cut the chase and copy the answer from the book! When the professor saw Jigsaw, sitting beside the window, copying the answer from the book he at once confiscated his answer sheet and the thick yellow book. Jigsaw protested, 'Sir if you find anything common between my answer and the book, I will resign from TMS,' said he.

For the first time a student was threatening a 'resignation' from an educational institution! 'You cannot have the book on your desk while writing a test,' said the Professor.

'Sir, it's not my book. I will resign from TMS if you can prove that I was copying,' continued Jigsaw clearing his throat and with his right index finger raised.

'Whose book is it?' demanded the Professor.

'Sir, it is Simrin's book,' said Jigsaw arguing spiritedly with the teacher.

'How did *Shimrin*'s book reach your desk?'

'Sir, the window is open, the breeze is blowing, the book has come to my desk,' remarked Jigsaw bewildering the professor.

'Oh ho, so the window is open and the breeze is blowing, so *Shimrin*'s thick book flies 20 feet and comes to your desk and then that same page opens from where I have given the question! How come all this never happened in our times?' said the Professor brusquely.

'Sir, at your time the breeze must not be blowing!' pronounced Jigsaw almost yanking his answer sheet from the Professor's hand.

***

Dev had decided to major in Marketing. When I asked him that with his economics background wouldn't Finance have been better, he mentioned there were many more marketing jobs in the employment market and that he was taking some credits in finance as well. The two Finance subjects he had taken as electives were Corporate Finance and Investment Management.

The Investment Management teacher was a young lady who had recently been appointed following completion of her PhD. Quite of few of Dev's batch, including Voltage, had done their summer training with foreign banks and therefore had exposure to some sophisticated parts of modern banking like international finance, foreign exchange trading, merchant banking, mergers and acquisition etc. During one of the lectures on 'structuring an acquisition' the young teacher discussed the book value of a target firm's equity share, market value of a target firm's equity and then the acquisition price of the target firm. She got a little confused with what the difference between these concepts represented and how they were to be treated in financial accounting.

'Ma'am, if the difference between market value and book value is goodwill, then what is the difference between acquisition price and book value?' asked Voltage adjusting his hair. It was an intelligent question.

'I think that's acquisition premium,' conjectured the teacher.

'Then what does the difference between acquisition price and market value represent?' posed Voltage again in his halting gentle tone.

The young teacher got flustered. 'I think there is a problem with your class. You either don't understand simple concepts or are too smart for these sessions. Somehow with your class I have had problems from day one,' she lamented.

'Ma'am, can you please explain again what the difference between book value, market value and acquisition price represent?' Voltage was not giving up. He was sitting next to Dev that day who could sense the teacher's discomfort, he tried signalling to Voltage not to belabour the point, but it was too late.

The teacher was really upset, 'Just with your class I seem to have problems,' she snapped.

'From day one', whispered Voltage to Dev with a tone of derision.

'I feel like physically lifting you up and throwing you out of the window,' the teacher was at the end of her tether.

'Oh, what a pleasure, Ma'am!' murmured Voltage again, thinking that he was inaudible to the teacher.

None of the students could understand why but the teacher walked out of the class room looking visibly tormented. Simrin Avasthi, or Happiness, as she was better known as, followed the teacher presumably to comfort her. Back in her office the teacher mentioned to Happiness that 'the chap sitting next to Devavratt' was constantly murmuring which led to her getting agitated. Happiness apparently mentioned Voltage's name to the teacher. The message instantly reached the head of the Finance department Dr Tarneja who instructed Voltage to apologise to the Investment Management teacher. Throwing his legs as he always did, Voltage ambled into the teacher's office, where he also found Simrin. Instead of apologizing and realizing that Simrin had gone behind his back, he said to her, 'Happiness, you back-biter, I will wreck your happiness, I will make everything about your life sad.'

Voltage instantly found himself in the company of two very perturbed young ladies in that room. Later Dr Tarneja summoned Voltage to his office room for a closed-door meeting, it was widely believed that the former was actually impressed with Voltage and his compelling logic on Investment Management and life in general, not only did Voltage emerge unscathed from that meeting but along with Pracha, he was now Dr Tarneja's favourite student!

We were in the December of 1987 and the semester exams were upon us. Luv and I were to write the first semester exams and Dev his third semester. But before that, the final year students had to choose their guide for dissertation. The dissertation carried high credits. Most of the students were choosing a Marketing or Finance professor as their guide. In their third and ongoing semester Dev's batch had been taught International Economics by Dr Dastur who was a very suave and well-spoken teacher in his mid-thirties with back-swept hair and a disarming smile. Dr Dastur was an alumnus of a top British university, he appeared very calm and good-natured, and his articles on economics used to appear in financial newspapers in India.

Dev's mind was made. He telephoned Sudhir one evening and said to him, 'Sudhir, do hear me out, don't react instantly. I have a suggestion regarding our dissertation guide.' Dev persuaded Sudhir that they do their final semester dissertation under Dr Dastur.

Dr Dastur had a British way of speaking; using soft words, understating his remarks and posing his statements in the form of questions. 'Well, why don't you consider factors which might determine foreign direct investment in India in the coming decade,' he said to Dev. And then looking at Sudhir, he suggested, 'Processed Foods exports in a macro-economic perspective, does that sound interesting for a dissertation?'

Dev and Sudhir came out of Dr Dastur's office on the second floor of TMS. Dev seemed assured about the dissertation though Suchir was still unconvinced about an economics-based project. However, he went along with his friend. Of course, soon after the winter vacations the placement season was to start. It was the biggest event in the calendar of TMS and what all the MBA students had worked for nearly two years. If they got one of the best companies—a top multinational or a foreign bank or a couple of the most respected Indian business groups—then their life would be put on a successful and comfortable trajectory.

Placements started two days after TMS re-opened in early January. The best of companies used to visit The Management School and the popularity of the company determined the day of the placement season, which usually spread over a fortnight, they would be invited on. An evening before the day one of the placements, Jigsaw was given a pre-placement offer by The Capital Green on the basis of his performance during summer training! It was quite an achievement to receive a pre-placement offer.

'Congratulations, Jeet,' said Dev to Jigsaw.

'Thanks brother,' Jigsaw gave him a hug.

Dev too expected a similar offer from Meridian Promissory, they were scheduled for day two of the placements; however, he had not received any such offer by late evening on the day before the placements were to start. Dev applied to all the companies visiting on the first three days which included foreign banks, FMCG multinationals and a respected Indian industrial group. Sudhir urged him to also apply to Torsh Chemicals, scheduled to come on day three, it was a blue-chip chemicals manufacturing and marketing company and one of the largest multinationals operating in India. Dev thought he was better suited to consumer marketing, however even Samarth and Voltage told him that it was a 'career company'.

Dev was shortlisted by nine of the top ten companies visiting on the first three days. By the end of day one, Nita and Samarth were amongst the 10 candidates placed in addition to Jigsaw. Dev cleared all group discussions however got rejected in all interviews. He was most hopeful about Meridian Promissory on day two. Once again he sailed through the GD. He discussed his summer project with the interviewers and on being asked his 'strengths and weakness' spent time mentioning his strengths and then 'packaged' a few other personality traits like 'feeling weary with routine tasks' as his weakness! At the end of the selection process, he was very disappointed to learn that Meridian Promissory had drawn a blank after interviewing the shortlisted candidates. Nature has its ways of denying to men what they desperately crave for. Five students got placed on day two; Dev did not clear any interview that day either. Nor did some of his friends like Sudhir, Tank, Voltage and Pracha get a firm offer from any of the three companies that visited on day two.

Sudhir and Tank told me that Dev was very effective in GDs. Once again, I couldn't help thinking of that reticent fretfully sober school boy: but by now I had seen how he could lift his game at crunch time. Successful human lives evolve through a series of similar trials and challenges. By day three, Dev was being referred to as 'GD King' as he again shone in the group discussions. His first interview that day was with Ellinson Hindustan Ltd. a high profile American multinational marketing FMCG products. It proceeded along expected lines and was more of a profile match. Before conclusion of that interview one of the four interviewers asked Dev, 'So what are your interests?'

Dev said, 'Sir I play a little bit of cricket and have some interest in Hindi poetry. In school I also used to do a little bit of sculpture.'

'A little bit of everything?' remarked another interviewer.

'Yes Sir, just my hobbies,' said Dev.

'So, you are jack of all trades?' he said.

Dev smiled very slightly, 'You can say that, Sir.'

'And master of?' quizzed the first interviewer peering through his glasses.

Dev paused of a moment and then said, 'Master of Business Administration.'

Two of the four interviewers laughed aloud, one of the other two also nodded in acknowledgement at the repartee.

When the result was declared, Ellinson Hindustan Ltd. was also not making a final job offer to anyone from TMS that year.

Dev had two more interviews lined up that afternoon; one was with a consumer durables company and the other with Torsh Chemicals. Sudhir and Voltage were also shortlisted for Torsh along with four others. The Torsh interview was not just a profile match but the panel asked Dev questions about salesmanship, marketing and business strategy. The distinguished looking Sikh gentleman in the panel asked Dev, 'If you as a Sales Manager have been missing your targets for three months, and with a little bit of workaround you could achieve it in the fourth month, what will you do?'

Dev instantly checked, 'Sir, what exactly do you mean by workaround?'

'Mr Devavratt Rajvansh, what is more important to you, means or the end?'

Without batting an eyelid Dev said, 'Means.'

At 8 pm that night, the placement secretary of TMS announced the results. Dev, Voltage and another batchmate of theirs had been selected by Torsh Chemicals. Further, Dev and Voltage were also being offered jobs by the consumer durables company. Voltage came and hugged Dev, Torsh was Voltage's dream job! Sudhir looked disappointed; he had not yet got any offer. But he was very happy for Dev. Dev asked him which of the two offers he should accept.

'Torsh! No question about it,' said Sudhir. 'It's a blue chip European MNC; the chemical engineers would give their right hand for a job with Torsh.'

Dev wished his parents were alive. He had almost no memory of his parents and had often wondered what they would have been like.

Sudhir got into Dev's Fiat car; Dev was to first drop him at a convenient bus stop. Sudhir was understandably quiet during the drive though spoke to Dev about his interviews. When Dev told him about the interview with Ellinson Hindustan Ltd earlier that day, especially the bit where they asked him what he was master of and he had said 'Master of Business Administration', Sudhir heartily laughed. 'You should have got EHL' he said.

Dev dropped Sudhir on outer ring road as the latter again congratulated him; he then went to a sweets shop in Sundar Nagar before turning around for his Bapa Nagar home. He kept attending to congratulatory phone calls that evening and the day after. He had decided to accept the Torsh offer and with placements still ongoing at TMS and no regular lectures, he treated himself to relaxing at home. A couple of days later, he dropped by at TMS to meet Dr Dastur regarding his dissertation and soon left for home.

A further three days from then, he got a call from Nita Rajagopalan. 'Hi Dev, haven't seen you at the campus for a few days,' she said.

'Yes Nita, I have accepted the Torsh offer and since hardly any classes are going on I am just taking it easy at home,' he said.

'Can you come to TMS tomorrow?' she enquired.

'What happened?' he was curious.

'I need to speak to you,' she said.

Dev was surprised. Nita had never spoken like that with him earlier. 'Can we speak on phone?' he checked.

'I'd rather meet you and talk.'

That night Dev kept wondering what might Nita might to speak about.

He took the U-Spl next morning, then the connecting shuttle and saw Nita at the porch.

'Cup of chai?' she said.

'Certainly,' he gestured with his left hand for her to lead the way to the quaint tea stall right outside the campus.

'Why haven't you been coming to the institute?' she said looking straight into his eyes.

'I told you yesterday, there are hardly any classes during the placement time.'

Nita went on to give a lesson to Dev that he remembered for the rest of his life. 'You realise that Sudhir and Tank are still not placed,' she said.

'Yes.'

'So, Mister, do you have no responsibility towards your friends?' she said admonishingly. Dev was taken aback by her tone. 'Shouldn't you be with them, supporting them at this hard time? Either that or don't call yourself their friend,' she sipped her tea, 'Tank I can still understand; he is quite social. But Sudhir is close mainly to you. And you are nowhere to be seen,' she reprimanded Dev.

An odd teacher or occasionally his uncle or aunt might have rebuked him, but Nita's telling off was a new and numbing experience. 'Nita, it is my weakness, I just don't know what to say in difficult times like these.'

She softened her tone. 'You don't need to say anything Dev; just be with your friend who is facing a tough time. The test of true friendship is only during difficult times. Just be with your friend in person.'

Even the most earnest of human beings have their frailties. Dev absorbed every word of hers. He looked at her with embarrassed eyes, 'Thank you, Nita.'

She gave him a big warm smile.

The wiring of human beings is such, those who have had a somewhat disturbed childhood, lost a parent or didn't get enough affection and care in early years, struggle with their own emotions throughout their lives. A part of them dies. They find it hard to express especially their softer emotions and constantly feel insecure. Self-reflection helps only to an extent; such a person can come out of this childhood distress only if he or she finds true love at some stage in life.

Dev immediately went looking for Sudhir and Tank. After about half an hour he found Sudhir in the library. He put his hand on his shoulder.

'Where are you, Bhaisahab!' said Sudhir giving Dev a perplexed look.

'Sorry Sudhir, how are you?'

'How do you think I would be,' Sudhir said with a smile that betrayed a tinge of hurt.

'No breakthrough so far?' asked Dev.

'Waitlisted one with Gerbera Bank, Tank is two on waitlist, but I am not too keen,' informed Sudhir. After half a minute's silence, he continued, 'Your absence has been most surprising for me, Dev.'

Dev tried to explain, 'I just didn't know what to say in this situation Sudhir; it's my flaw.' It was to Sudhir's maturity that he empathised with where Dev was coming from. 'In fact, some of the least expected monsters have been egging me on.' Dev looked at him in quiet mortification.

After a further minute's silence, he said to Dev with his usual smile, '*Chaliye*, let's go to The Ridge and have a sandwich.'

The Second Birth

Sudhir decided to pull out of placements.

'That's a big decision Sudhir,' remarked Dev.

'I will focus only on the civil services exam this year; with a full-time job I won't be able to give my best for preparation of the IAS exam.'

On several occasions, Dev had mentioned to me that Sudhir was the most diligent and sincere person he knew, and alongside Pracha, also the most hard-working. Just before end of the placement fortnight, Gerbera Bank made a firm job offer to Sudhir, but by then he had decided not to take up employment that year. Tank who was next on the waitlist got the job! As human beings go through the intriguing journey of existence it is never quite possible to see destiny's bigger picture, which becomes evident only when various quirks of fate are joined together at milestone moments of life.

The fourth semester was by far the most relaxed and delightful time for Dev and Sudhir. It was mainly the dissertation they had to work on and Dr Dastur was the most wonderful of guides. The Delhi winter, the golden sun, lilies in the garden, a few months of near idleness, youthful energy and companionship of friends was the perfect icing on five years of higher education. Yet both Dev and Sudhir also wanted to do well at dissertation since it carried high credits. Despite his brilliant academic record, Sudhir was a bit uncomfortable with higher mathematics applied to economics and when Dr Dastur handed over an econometrics-based paper to Sudhir to review and include its findings in his dissertation, he felt a little stumped.

'Think intuitively,' suggested Dr Dastur to Sudhir.

An evening later when Dev called Sudhir, the latter was on the terrace of his house in Priyadarshini Vihar. 'What is the economist up to?' Dev joked.

'Gazing at the sky and trying to think intuitively,' said Sudhir sardonically.

Dev's project turned out relatively straightforward, Dr Dastur told him to include a chapter on current FDI policy as well, for which Dev referred to a book written by Dr Majumdar, a former Dean of TMS who had since retired. Sudhir and Dev would often meet Dr Dastur outside the campus; their generous guide would treat them for lunch or a snack at Asian Games village in Hauz Khas and also provide a steer on how to put the dissertation together. The other students were not having as delightful a time with their dissertations. Dr Tarneja, Pracha's guide, told him off on his draft, 'Mr Pracha, what gibberish have you written.' The hard-working and burly student was left red-faced.

In that final semester, I would frequently see Dev and Sudhir with some of their batchmates sitting in the front lawns of TMS soaking in the morning sun and sipping a cup of tea. That reticent school boy who would cycle in and out unnoticed had become fairly sociable! Meanwhile, I had come to know Luv quite well in the few months that we had been together, and both of us would sometimes join Dev and Sudhir over a cup of chai in the lawns or on an odd occasion for bun-omelette in The Ridge.

Luv was the youngest of three children and clearly an afterthought since his eldest sister was fourteen years his senior. She was married and Luv knew nearly all her friends. One of his sister's friends, Purnima, had caught Luv's eye. He had found himself ogling at her cleavage and ample hips several times.

'What do you address her as, Aunty or *Didi*?' I asked Luv when he would tell me about his fantasies.

'Neither! I jokingly told her that I would call her girlfriend, she calls me boyfriend. We have a healthy relationship,' he replied.

'Healthy relationship!' I couldn't help laughing.

'Yes, she is quite healthy. I mean, she is fairly heavy.'

I couldn't stop my laughter. 'And she is married?'

'Yes, with two daughters.'

I told Luv that this is called 'puppy love'.

'*Yaar*, it has happened twice now that when we met at my sister's home, and she gives me a hug my hand has touched her hips.'

'You are a scoundrel, Luv,' I told him, laughing non-stop.

'I know,' he said with a straight face.

'Then?' I enquired further about his bizarre fantasy.

'She didn't object to it; she kept chatting with me jovially,' Luv completed his queer tale of imaginative romp and bodily flirtation.

Given his penchant for cultural stereotyping, generalizing and theorizing, a few months later he came and told me, '*Khannae*, I have a theory.'

'I am all ears,' said I.

'I think women who are heavily built and laugh a lot; they are keenly interested in sex.'

'So says Dr Eklavya Malhotra; put it in a two-by-two matrix,' I said.

It must have been late February in 1988 for it was still very pleasant outside, I was chatting with Sudhir sitting in the lawns. He was telling me about the final year electives and tips for summer training. Just then Nita joined us, 'Where is Mr Torsh?' she enquired.

'I think he is at the photocopiers,' said Sudhir.

We chatted a bit about their dissertations and then Nita mentioned she was to start with Capital Green in Bombay in May. 'What's with Dev these days?' she asked looking at both Sudhir and me.

'He is doing fine, why?' said Sudhir, wondering where Nita was coming from.

'Looks preoccupied,' she said.

'What's new, Nita?' I remarked.

'Is there a girl scene?' she queried without smiling.

It took Sudhir and me a moment to understand Nita's question. 'You mean there is a girl in Dev's life!' exclaimed Sudhir.

Now Nita smiled, 'I mean there *is* a girl in Dev's life,' she said affirmatively.

'Did he say anything to you?' I asked Nita.

'Does he ever say anything to anyone?' she too knew Dev quite well.

I narrated the incident to Sudhir, in Nita's presence, how one of our school mates had scribbled Nita's name on Dev's notebooks after she had walked past while all of us were playing cricket in school many years ago, and Dev went on to score 90 runs and win the match single-handedly! 'Most of our classmates in school thought that Dev had a crush on you, Nita!' I said to her not non-seriously.

'Oh, how I wish, Sandy!' she said with a longing expression, looking at me engagingly with her chin resting on her right palm.

Sudhir and I didn't know how to respond to her plain statement and frank body language.

'So, you are just surmising?' said Sudhir.

'A girl has a sixth sense, remember!' said Nita.

'How come neither of us has ever noticed?' I wondered aloud.

'Do you boys ever notice anything other than girls' boobs and posteriors?' said Nita, not exactly tauntingly.

Sudhir and I looked at each other; we were in the company of a very intelligent, confident and perceptive young lady.

I don't know if Sudhir mentioned anything to Dev about this conversation, but a few days later Dev and I were sitting together in the shuttle bus returning back home in the afternoon. 'Did Sudhir speak to you about a chat we had with Nita?' I asked him.

'What happened?' said Dev.

'She reckons you have a girlfriend!'

'How did Nancy Drew discern that?' said Dev, not surprised.

'So is Nancy Drew right or wrong?' I continued.

Dev turned his head towards me and said, 'We have our dissertation viva this Friday.'

Sudhir and Dev had completed their dissertation write-ups and except for that econometrics paper Sudhir had enjoyed learning about the processed foods industry. The econometrics paper referred to statistical tests like the F-test and T-test whose implication to his project had been a challenge for him, nonetheless only page 47 of his project report made reference to these econometric variables and statistical tests. Dev too deepened his understanding of foreign direct investment and factors determining its flow into India. The FDI policy chapter that Dr Dastur asked him to include was very dry and Dev had referred to the ex-Dean Dr Majumdar's book for the same.

On that memorable Friday in the March of 1988 our senior batch were all dressed for their viva. Dev couldn't believe that the retired Dean Dr Majumdar was chairing the panel assessing their dissertation! He was certain that he would be questioned on FDI policy for which he had referred to Dr Majumdar's book, and which was not his strength. The ex-Dean was a pleasant elderly man and made Dev very comfortable in the viva. He didn't ask a single question on FDI policy, instead focused on how India could increase her FDI inflows. Dev answered self-assuredly mentioning domestic research and development as a factor as well which made the panel admiringly nod. Dr Majumdar then checked with Dev why he had chosen to work on FDI, to which Dev said that since he was keen to join a MNC he thought knowledge of

FDI will help him later in his job as well. After 15 minutes he found Dr Majumdar looking at his fellow panellists and saying, 'I think we'll grant it to him.'

Sudhir was in next and Dr Majumdar commended him for the project report. Dr Om Kapoor, another economics professor at TMS, was also in the panel and was browsing through Sudhir's dissertation report. As fate would have it, he stopped on page 47! Dr Kapoor asked Sudhir, 'What do these F-test and T-test values signify?'

Sudhir's only prayer that morning was that he should be questioned on anything in his 100-page report except the statistical tests! 'Sir, what the F-test means is…'

Before he could complete the sentence, Dr Kapoor interrupted, 'I don't need to know what F-test means, I am asking you what these numerical values of F-test and T-test imply in the context of processed foods exports.'

Sudhir wanted to rewind time and not agree with Dev's suggestion of doing an economics project! 'Sir, these statistical tests help understanding the variance.'

Once again Dr Kapoor stopped him. 'Sudhir Kapoor I am not asking you what these statistical tests mean, I am simply asking you that what do these negative and decimal values of F-test and T-test imply for India's processed foods exports.'

Sudhir looked at Dr Om Kapoor with pleading eyes that seemed to say: *I am Kapoor, you are also Kapoor, why must you put me in this insufferable position!* Finally, Sudhir mustered some courage and said, 'Sir I have done many other things in the project also, why don't you question me on those.'

Dev feared for his friend; once again he didn't quite know what to say to Sudhir, but this time he called him and said, 'All will be well.'

Dev ended up with 77% in the dissertation and even though his friend didn't have a good viva, he received 64% which was higher than a lot of their batch who had worked on marketing and finance projects! Sudhir pulled Dev's leg, 'I am sure when Dr Majumdar saw the section on FDI policy in your report he would have thought to himself—our views are quite similar!'

Dev had immensely enjoyed the two-year MBA course, as had most of his batch. He was ready for graduating and starting his job with Torsh Chemicals as a Management Trainee. A person takes a second birth when he or she steps out in the world to earn a living and make a name for him or herself. All that remained was a farewell party which the first-year students used to throw for the graduating seniors.

We organised a farewell party in a five-star hotel in Chanakyapuri. The entire first year and second year students and most of the faculty were there. Jigsaw and Voltage, aloof with each other in the best of times and at each other's throat when normalcy prevailed, were in their element thanks to a few drinks.

'Jigsaw you are my best friend,' said the three-beers-down Voltage.

'No, Voltage, you are my best friend,' replied the two-beers-and-a-vodka-down Jigsaw.

'No, Jigsaw, you are my best friend,' said Voltage.

It seemed Jigsaw had been admiring one of the girls in my class, he held Dev by his hand and said to him, 'Get me an intro with Anurima.'

Dev said, 'I don't know her, Jeet.'

'I have seen you say hi to her,' replied Jigsaw.

Dev laughed.

The second vodka in Jigsaw gave him enough strength to directly approach Anurima, 'Hi, I am Jeet,' he said introducing himself to her.

'Hello,' she said.

'I have been admiring you for two years,' said Jigsaw in his throaty voice.

'But I have been here only for a year,' she remarked with twinkling eyes.

Never at a loss for a repartee and boosted with sufficient spirit Jigsaw said, 'Well, it seems like two years!'

As the party reached its crescendo, a high Voltage requested Dev, 'Dev we will be colleagues also now, do get me some food in a plate.'

Dev smiled and obliged. Voltage, Luv, myself, Dev, Sudhir, Nita, Happiness, Jigsaw, Samarth, Pracha, Tank, and a few others all stood together with our dinner plates at one side of the hall. Voltage's hand holding the plate tilted and tilted as he freely laughed at every inane comment by anyone. The butter chicken gravy started dripping down his arm and onto the carpet.

'Voltage, straighten your plate please,' said Sudhir.

'Why?' asked Voltage, coming very close to Sudhir and looking at him with glazed eyes.

'The gravy is dripping.'

'So what? Let it drip,' said Voltage with an elated expression.

'All the professors are around Rakesh,' remarked Dev.

Voltage falteringly strode towards Dev. 'Who is around?' he said in his peculiar soft tone.

'Dr Dastur is here, Dr Tarneja is just behind you.'

Voltage picked up one of the chicken legs and ecstatically threw it in the air. '*Oye* Tarneja,' he screamed.

Most of us, in sober state or happy, chuckled with shock.

Seeing our reaction, Voltage continued. He picked up a piece of tomato from his plate and flung it high up. '*Oye tamatar!*' he yelled this time. Then it was the second piece of chicken leg on his plate that went flying across the party hall, '*Oye haddi!*'

Unfortunately, whatever starts in this world has to end. The Dean said a few inspiring last words and we shook as many hands as got extended, and it was time to go home. It was time for us to become the senior batch and for our seniors to take a 'second birth'.

As the 1980s were coming to their inevitable end, we had seen so much change in the country. The demand for economic liberalisation was contesting a socialist India. The term 'license-permit raj' was ubiquitous with a negative connotation. Maruti 800 cc car first, followed by Omni and Gypsy and Maruti 1000 cc had offered a choice to Fiat and Ambassador. Nirma was a household name that had challenged Surf detergent powder, just as Nirula's ice-creams posed competition to Kwality and Gaylord. Doordarshan was now showing more than just the one channel and the TV serials *Ramayana* and later, *Mahabharata* had created mass viewership. The television in the process became not just an important marketing medium but also a foundation for strengthening the unity of a diverse nation. From Bhimsen Joshi and Lata Mangeshkar to Amitabh Bachchan and Prakash Padukone all lent their illustriousness to the never-to-be-forgotten video song on national integration: '*Miley sur mera tumhara*'.

Most households with at least one well employed member had a telephone. The STD/ISD booths had just about started sprouting up. Reliance had led in the creation of a new asset class and the stock market offered an option to the risk free good old bank fixed deposit. Gavaskar had retired after a brilliant career with the Reliance World Cup being his swansong, the mantle was soon to pass on to Sachin Tendulkar. Corporate careers and MBA qualification were becoming increasingly popular especially in urban India. New young actors like Aamir Khan and Salman Khan and Madhuri Dixit and Juhi Chawla were making their debuts with romantic films. A new Janata Dal government was soon to be elected. Internationally we were on the eve of the collapse of Berlin Wall and dismantling of USSR, the political and economic reforms of USSR were best recognised in the words 'Glasnost' and 'Perestroika'. India too was thirsting for unshackling of the economy and cessation of 'license permit raj'. The worsening trade deficits and balance of payments position exacerbated by the Gulf War and increasing oil prices in 1990 leading to the point where India had to pledge nearly 50 tonnes of her gold with Bank of England, ultimately resulted in the historic economic reforms of 1991 when 'license permit raj' was dispensed with and industry and interest rates substantially decontrolled.

Thus, as Dev began finding his feet as an employee with a multinational company, on the much larger canvas of the world India was beginning to experience a new birth.

The social change in the late-1980s however was not as discernible. Marriage was a much needed and worthwhile institution. Loneliness was still just a word in the dictionary and people were unreservedly visiting each other's home unannounced. The frequent weekend get-togethers, usually held at the home of the eldest member of the clan, would find the closely related extended family with siblings, cousins and all the children in one large living room. Brands were not terribly important, only togetherness was. We were still going to the neighbourhood tailor shops for stitching of clothes though ready-mades had hit the market. In those days people usually didn't leave elderly parents at home and adventure out for the weekend. Today, of course, friends are the new family and people prefer to go out and discover new restaurants, talk about health foods and exotic drinks, new apps, RWA matters, streaming services like Amazon Prime and Netflix, high politics, foreign holidays and top international universities.

***

Torsh Chemicals had been incorporated as Torrent & Shakers Chemicals International in Europe after World War I. Since then, it had grown to become one of the best chemicals companies of the world including eight large petrochemicals complexes, four in Europe and one each in USA, Brazil, South Africa and Malaysia. Torsh Chemicals as it was referred to now, was largely into manufacture and marketing of downstream chemical products like Plastics, Agri-products namely Fertilizers and Seeds, Coatings and Polymers, Textiles and Dyes. In India they did not have a petrochemical complex but were manufacturing and marketing all the downstream chemical products. The plastics plant was in Bhavnagar in Gujarat, coatings and polymers were manufactured in Durgapur in Bengal, textiles and dyes in Nagpur in Maharashtra, urea fertilizer production and seeds treatment plant were in district Barabanki near Lucknow in Uttar Pradesh, and DAP and MOP fertilizers were made in district Alwar near Jaipur in Rajasthan. Torsh was one of the most sought-after employers in India and attracted the best of talent from engineering and technical colleges, management schools, agriculture universities and rank holding chartered accountants. Their Indian headquarters was in Madhavan Building on Barakhamba Road in Connaught Place in Delhi where they occupied three floors.

Dev received a letter from Torsh Chemicals confirming his appointment as a Management Trainee to be placed in the Agri-products business; he was to report in mid-May to the Marketing Manager of the business. His starting salary, handsome for late-1980s for a fresh management graduate, was Rs. 5000 per month including House Rent Allowance.

What is there in human life without celebration! And merrymaking doesn't require riches, it only requires heart.

In happiness or in pain, in achievement or in fiasco, in recognition or in disregard, in reciprocation or in heartbreak, at high-noon or with setting sun, in youth or dotage, in that exclusive club or by roadside, on an Atlantic cruise or by Gomti, in a Santorini resort or under the village banyan, with a champagne or a glass of lemon water, wherever a few friends assemble happiness joins them uninvited.

'Such a good job calls for a celebration Dev,' I said to him a few days before he was to start with Torsh, 'and something a little more thrilling than pizzas in Connaught Place.'

Dev called me the next day and suggested we meet at Hotel Taj for club sandwiches and cold coffee. 'I will call Sudhir too,' he said.

'May I ask Luv as well?' I enquired.

'Certainly.'

Dev and I were the first to reach Taj hotel and we took a table for four in the coffee shop. As we waited for our other two friends, Dev told me he had been placed in the Agri-products business, something he was a bit concerned about. 'I had consumer marketing or a foreign bank in mind,' he said as we were handed the menus, 'never imagined agriculture marketing.'

I told him he could always move within the organisation or a few years later, as job-hopping MBAs were known to do, move to a different company. He nodded.

'So, Dev, is there a special girl?' I asked him again.

He looked at me with an expression I cannot describe. 'Is it Nita?' I was trying to comprehend that expression.

Dev laughed, 'No no, Sandeep.'

I waited for him to continue; he kept looking at the menu. 'Come on old boy, you need to tell me at least.'

He kept smiling.

'Is it that girl last year who took you on a beach walk in Mahabalipuram? Who is the happening one?' I thought I had pushed enough.

Dev looked at me for a moment and then lowered his eyes, he then said quietly, 'She neither happens nor lets anyone else happen.'

Just then we saw Sudhir walking in through the entrance of the coffee shop. He opened his palm facing it skywards, as he always did, to shake hands. Dev enquired how his IAS preparation was going; Sudhir modestly underplayed the intense hard work he was putting in. We ordered some club-sandwiches as Luv was never known for punctuality. But when he joined us an hour later our group was suddenly enlivened.

'Have you been hugging your sister's friend?' I remarked to get him started.

Luv was by now comfortable with Dev and Sudhir and shared his cuddling experience with perambulating hand. '*Yaar*, I feel because of her I am becoming an ass-man.'

We all burst out laughing.

'What kept you so long?' Sudhir checked.

'One of my school friends, Raja, from the time we were in Secunderabad, was over. He left late.' Luv then narrated how he and Raja, now working in an IT company in Manchester, did a train ride to Secunderabad a year before. They got booked in a coupe with just two berths, a lower and an upper one. Late evening Raja got into his sleeping bag in the buff. He felt uncomfortable on the upper berth and asked Luv to swap. Since he was not wearing anything, Luv gave him a towel to wrap around and step down.

Dev, Sudhir and I were waiting to gush out in laughter.

'He wrapped that towel and put his legs on the lower berth while he was holding the straps of the upper berth for support,' continued Luv, 'his legs and hands were spread apart so he looked like a large X. Just then his towel came off!'

The three of us were already erupting with a cackle.

'So, I was standing waiting for Raja to step down, and he was standing with his feet on the lower berth and hands holding the upper berth straps and just as his towel fell off the ticket checker knocked and I opened the door.'

Sudhir's mouthful of cold coffee almost came out as he laughed.

'The ticket checker was shocked to see a naked man standing in the coupe. "What's going on?" said he in disbelief.

Raja replied turning his head towards him, while still standing naked, "I am a computer consultant from Manchester." The ticket checker looked at him from top to bottom and remarked in Hindi, "*Kya personality hei!*"

***

On the 16th of May 1988, Dev reached the Madhavan building in Connaught Place. No sooner had he reached the reception of Torsh Chemicals office that a jovial short statured man in his mid-30s with drooping moustache also entered behind him. 'Devavratt?' he said.

Dev nodded.

'Hi, I am Bhagatveer Bhatia,' he extended his hand. 'Welcome to Torsh! Come in please.'

Dev entered a large well-lit posh office where he saw a large number of desks and chairs placed in the middle in an arrangement that extended from one end to the other of a 100 feet corridor, and all around on the periphery of the office there were cabins most of which were still unoccupied as it was 8:45 am. By 9 am, most of the staff had come in, some were sitting on the desks outside while a few were entering their respective cabins.

'We do a 9 am to 5 pm here,' said Bhagatveer Bhatia to Dev.

'Yes, Sir,' said Dev.

'By the way, call me Bhagat, and I suppose most people would be calling you Dev', he laughed amicably. 'Congratulations on joining the right company Dev. I am the marketing manager for Agri-products which includes mainly urea, that's the cash cow, but we also do Di-ammonium Phosphate and Muriate of Potash and have recently started with Seeds.'

Bhagat was going to be Dev's mentor during his one-year management trainee time. He had drawn up a comprehensive induction plan for Dev.

'Top of the morning, Mr Bhatia', said a deep voice outside Bhagat's cabin.

'Morning, Sir,' said Bhagat standing up, 'this is Devavratt Rajvansh, joining us today as a management trainee.'

Bhagat introduced Dev to Inderpal Singh Sodhi, the General Manager of the Agri-products business. Mr Sodhi was immaculately dressed in a tweed jacket, he seemed in his early fifties, held a briefcase in his hand and his manner of speaking suggested he was a man of both style and substance. 'Let's meet later in the day young man,' he said to Dev.

Bhagatveer Bhatia then explained to Dev that the Torsh urea brand Apna Gram was one of the most popular in north India; the company had also recently started treating seeds. The DAP and MOP plant in Alwar was very small. Bhagat reported to Mr Sodhi. The National Sales Manager Debashish Biswas also operated from the same office. 'We have two categories of staff—the management staff like us and cadre staff. The cadre staff is unionised.'

'So, the staff sitting outside…?' checked Dev.

'They are cadre staff; I will tell you more about the dynamics over lunch today,' said Bhagat.

Agri-products business had four branch sales offices in north India—Delhi, Lucknow, Allahabad and Patna. Each branch office had one or two small area offices attached to it. Thus, Delhi Branch Office had two attached area offices in Chandigarh and Meerut, Lucknow branch had a medium size area office in Kanpur, Allahabad had the area office in Varanasi reporting to it, and Patna branch had an area office in Calcutta. Jaipur office was designated an area office with independent charge. The four Branch Managers and Jaipur Area Sales Manager reported to Biswas and the other ASM's of course reported into the BMs.

'We can sell only in north India; urea is an essential commodity controlled by the government,' said Bhagat. 'From the outside you might feel urea marketing is unglamorous but believe me your learning curve will be steep and one that will stand you in good stead throughout your working career.'

Dev was to have introductory meetings with various managers including a few Board members in his first week in Delhi. Thereafter he was to spend a week in Chandigarh followed by a few days in the Jaipur area office. This was to be followed by a formal induction programme for all management trainees across India, thereafter a few days in the plant in Barabanki and then he was to work in the Lucknow Branch Office for four months.

'By around end-October, we will take a call on where we should finally move you.'

Bhagat took Dev for lunch to the Meridian Hotel on his first day. Dev remembered Jigsaw telling him in TMS that Torsh had a 'royal lifestyle'. Bhagat explained to Dev that the cadre staff both in offices and at the plants was unionised. They did routine tasks and scope for their promotion was limited. 'They report to us, we deal with them respectfully and in a friendly manner but have to maintain some distance—basic people management. Be assertive but a little careful, you will learn in no time.'

The cadre staff seemed to be in their forties and fifties. 'In the plant it can get dicier, it's a continuous process plant, can't be switched off and on easily, so if workers strike there it gets serious.' The field salesmen called Agri-products Marketing Associates or AMA were not unionised but they too were close to the cadre staff as in their professional growth opportunities were limited, most of them had twenty years' experience in selling fertilizer and seeds. 'Some of the sales managers also have an agriculture background and have come up the ranks, you will find their approach a bit different from the young MBA types,' said Bhagat. But the BM in Lucknow Rohit Sahni is a young MBA; he is highly regarded in the company and a good human being, that's why I am sending you there for field training.'

Part III

Young Manager's Dreams Of Love

I could manage to read in my lifetime a very small fraction of the literature of the two languages that I learnt. Two words that recur both in Hindi and English literature are 'death' and 'love'. Love is the only element in universe that never diminishes, the more it is 'spent' the more it 'accumulates'. Knowledge too grows with sharing, but if love is the owner of the heart, knowledge is a tenant in the mind.

How does anyone capture love in lexicon? It is in the notes of music, in the lyrics of a tender song, it is the word that completes an incomplete poem. It is the sun during English autumn, cloud during Indian summer, melody of the evening breeze; it is the star that shows direction. It is the *tulsi* and camphor on a *puja* salver, the snow on distant hills, the rain shower in famine; it is the faith and the thousand lamps that float on the Ganges, and the hedges of the back gardens of homes which bow into the Thames. It is the magnetic energy of a temple and the prayer that is said and unsaid, it is the smile of the innocent child and her doting dart into her father's arms, the sinless eyes and the earnest lips. It is far beyond religion; it is beyond spirituality too. It is the shyness of the lowered eyelashes, the helplessness of all senses, it is the deserted sleep and that which can both wreck empires and build kingdoms. It is the deliverance where winner is not necessarily the victor and loser is not necessarily the vanquished. He who hasn't loved hasn't lived. It is what was simmering within Dev, for whom—he had not shared with anyone.

Late afternoon on his first day at Torsh, Dev had a brief meeting with Mr Sodhi the GM, who gave him the bigger picture and said in his deep seasoned voice, 'I spend large part of my time chasing supplies like naphtha and coal and attending meetings in the Ministry for our sales allocations and various subsidies.' He then looked keenly at Dev and said 'I dislike the word "subsidy". Bhagat will tell you why. I would like to spend more time in the market with our sales people and the trade, but that's why we have you. You come with a Master's in Business Administration. Try and learn quickly how fertilizer is marketed, how to deal with the distributors, when to push product and when to ease off, why working capital is so important and the economics of distribution of the white prills. And any problem—shout—my style of management is open,' he spread his hands apart as he finished his last statement. He then puffed on his cigar and checked with Dev, 'Any questions?'

'None at this stage Sir.'

'Thank you,' said the GM.

Before Dev started his induction tours to Chandigarh and Jaipur area offices, he met Debashish Biswas the National Sales Manager. Mr Biswas was a slender looking man in his late forties, plainly dressed and with a full head of black hair. He had clearly cut his teeth in fertilizer sales and had a terrific understanding of rural marketing in general.

'Ah *Debabratt*!' said Mr Biswas in a Bengali accent as Dev knocked on the open door of his cabin. Pronouncing 'so' as '*sho*', he explained to Dev, 'Sales team earns the money for the business, *sho* we have to handle them rather carefully, particularly dealing with AMA's—they all have over 20 years' experience and you will be like their senior. Your acceptability depends on your competence and how you treat them.' In reference to the head office he said, 'I am rather very happy that you will be in the field, this place is meant for old people like us,' he smiled without parting his lips, 'here you will become a paper tiger, real learning is in the field. Remember that urea is the money spinner. If you meet your urea fertilizer sales targets, all crimes are forgiven.' He smiled meaningfully at Dev and wished him good luck.

A white ambassador car picked up Dev from his Bapa Nagar flat and dropped him at New Delhi railway station, another white ambassador received him in Chandigarh and ferried him to an upscale four-star hotel. The Area Sales Manager of the Chandigarh area office was a happy-go-lucky man, he seemed to have come up the ranks and wasn't the 'glamour boy MBA'.

'We have no problem in meeting our sales targets even in these dry *kharif* months,' he said to Dev, 'the issue is we don't get product on time. I have got two people in the team here just to chase Distribution in Barabanki.'

In the large hall outside the ASM's cabin were six cadre staff, managing billing, accounting, cash and distribution. One of them seemed to be like the local union leader, he didn't smile much and during introductions asked Dev, 'So with whose approach did you get into Torsh Chemicals?'

Dev was surprised with the questions and said, 'It was through campus placement.'

'So, nobody's approach?' it was turn of the local staff leader to look surprised.

Dev shook his head just a little.

'Very good, *yaar*,' said he, pronouncing 'very' as *vaary*.

The ASM suggested to Dev that they do a day's field visit to give Dev a 'flavour of the market'. So, the day after two of them drove to the small town of Mandi Gobindgarh. A few kilometres before the town was a village that the Area Sales Manager mentioned had been 'adopted' by Torsh under their village adoption programme. Torsh Chemicals used to fund a school there, help maintain the roads and frequently provide the villagers with best agriculture practices. As they walked in the village the ASM wished a middle-aged man sitting on a *charpai* in the front mud-soled yard of his home. The man enquired where the passers-by were coming from and was obviously pleased to know they were from Torsh. He invited the ASM and Dev for lunch! Dev was surprised when the ASM accepted the invitation. A minute ago, they didn't even know the man in whose home they were about to have lunch! A second *charpai* was laid out for the two Torsh Chemicals managers and the ladies of the house cooked *paranthas* for them, they plucked fresh lemons from a tree under whose shade the three men were seated and prepared lemon-water. The villager introduced his family to the ASM and Dev, told his guests about their agricultural practices and the harvest of the previous season. After a cup of tea, the ASM and Dev took the villager's leave thanking him and the ladies in the home for lunch and their generosity. Dev never forgot that afternoon. Having lunch in someone's home who was a complete stranger! How large-hearted the villager with modest means was. The afternoon epitomised Punjab—its free-flowing mighty rivers, expansive bountiful fields and gregarious large-hearted people.

In his hotel room in the evenings, Dev's thoughts would knit dreams of love. In those younger years the purity and intensity of love is so self-consuming that Dev would find himself applying conscious effort to keep his focus on work during daytime. Whenever he would be by himself his mind, helpless at the altar of his heart, would wander into the eyes of someone whose identity was buried in the deep recesses of his spirit.

At the induction programme that Dev attended at a five-star hotel in Delhi, prior to his departure for Lucknow, all the management trainees from across India were invited. The senior most managers of Torsh Chemicals were making presentations about their business or function. The HR Director of Torsh asked the trainees during plenary, 'So what is your expectation from the organisation?'

A majority of the MBA's gave extravagant replies. One of the Management Trainees from Plastics said, 'A fast track career.' When the Director HR probed further, he replied with a clipped accent, 'If I feel I cannot become a GM by the age of forty I will quit this company.' He pronounced the word 'quit' as '*koo-wit*' and his tone was arrogant and pretentious!

Throughout his life Dev avoided 'machine-made' people; he enjoyed the company of people with normal vulnerabilities and imperfection and those who were original in some respect. When the HR Director glanced at him, Dev said, 'I am looking for practical experience in sales and marketing.'

Voltage, who had also joined Torsh from TMS, said in his soft tone, 'Fairness,' in response to the HR Director's question.

In the middle of June, on a Friday, Dev went to say bye to his mentor Bhagatveer Bhatia. Dev was leaving for Lucknow by the overnight train the next day. Torsh Chemicals did not have accommodation for sales and marketing management trainees in Lucknow. Dev's aunt had spoken to her cousin, who Dev would address as Sushma Masi, and the latter had insisted that Dev stay with her in their home in Indira Nagar. 'Didi, Dev must stay with us, we have a room on the terrace which is vacant, if he so wants, he can look for a place on rent later on, but let him start with us.' Family ties in India in the late-1980s were still strong!

Dev found his way from Lucknow's Charbagh railway station to Sushma Masi's house in Indira Nagar. She used to live with her husband, a teenage son and her mother-in-law. They were very welcoming and after checking everyone's well being showed Dev around their small but warm home and offered the sparsely furnished room on the terrace to him, it went without saying that Dev would have meals with the family. Post lunch, Masi's son Kunal took Dev to Aliganj where the Torsh Branch Office was located, so that he knew exactly where to reach the next day. They went by a cycle rickshaw that charged Rs. 15 since they were a twosome. Kunal would address Dev as 'bhaiya' and every time Dev told him something that surprised the teenager he would exclaim '*arrey ghazab*'. The following morning Dev again took a cycle rickshaw for Aliganj, paying

Rs. 10 for the ride, and arrived in twenty minutes at the large villa that housed the Lucknow Branch Office.

Rohit Sahni, the Branch Manager, was in his late twenties. He had an affable and intelligent face, prominent moustache, wore glasses, was about 5'8" tall and had just that additional inch on his waist. He made Dev feel very comfortable and after both of them had exchanged customary information on their backgrounds, he introduced Dev to the 12 cadre staff whose desks were outside in the large hall. Dev found most of the staff chewing *paan masala* and several of them pronouncing 'Delhi' 'as '*Dehli*' while getting to know Dev. Rohit showed Dev his cabin which had a small window that opened into the former's larger cabin. He had mixed feelings as he settled into his little office cabin. Dev had struggled with chemistry in school and here he was in a chemicals company. He hoped to do FMCG marketing or work with a multinational bank, instead he was set to do agriculture marketing. From that air-conditioned swanky office of Meridian Promissory in Madras with piped music and smart young colleagues, he now found himself in a typical large house in Lucknow rented as an office and, with Rohit's exception, the other staff members were all middle-aged men wearing loose fitting trousers and playing cards at lunch time. From the hall outside his cabin, he could hear staff mentioning his name—'one Mr Rajvansh from *Dehli*'—and then talking to each other loudly with the prefix '*ama yaar*'.

'Come over Dev I will introduce you to two of our tigers,' said Rohit through that little window between their respective cabins.

Dev found two middle-aged men sitting across Rohit in his cabin. 'Mr Arup Sanyal is the boss of Lucknow and Barabanki districts, and this is Meghraj Singh our man in Hardoi district. Mr Devavratt Rajvansh has recently joined Torsh as a management trainee, he will be in your care for a few months.'

Both Sanyal and Meghraj Singh got up and shook Dev's hand with the former addressing Dev as 'Sir'. They were the Agri-products Marketing Associates or AMA posted in Lucknow and Hardoi respectively. They reported to Rohit.

'Raghunandan ji is also here, Sahni sahab,' said Sanyal. Raghunandan was AMA for Sitapur. Rohit greeted him as the substantially-built Raghunandan ji entered his cabin. Raghunandan ji seemed to be in his early fifties, he was short, had a large round face with big innocent eyes, a crew cut of largely grey hair and he was wearing a safari suit. The fourth and fifth buttons from the top were open as his bulging paunch forced itself on the fabric. 'Sir, sir!' he said and almost doubled up as he shook Rohit's hand. 'Happy to meet you,' he said to Dev and very respectfully shook his hand.

'May wasn't bad, Raghunandan ji, given the weather,' said Rohit to him.

'*Ji ji*, all your guidance and blessings.'

'We all take guidance from you Raghunandan ji,' laughed Rohit.

'*Ji ji*,' said Raghunandan not understanding Rohit's slender compliment.

Sanyal and Meghraj were addressing Rohit, 'June sales will be a challenge Sahni sahab, not a drop of rain and Khushaal is coming in plastic packing with two months credit.'

Khushaal was a urea brand and the main competitor to Torsh's Apna Gram. Rohit was giving them a patient hearing, while Raghunandan was talking to himself, sometimes smiling and occasionally frowning with his own thoughts. He burped loudly as Meghraj commented 'There roars the lion.'

'They will do all the selling, Dev,' said Rohit after the AMAs had left, 'but we need to give them respect, listen to their views and be nicely assertive when needed. We almost never meet the distributors without the AMA.'

Dev was going to the Barabanki plant next day for his induction visit; he was to be there for three days. 'Stay on there on Friday, Dev, Sanyal and I have to visit the Barabanki distributor and we will pick you up from the company guest house on Faizabad Road, and you can start understanding the distributor and sales dynamics.'

Dev got onto a cycle rickshaw and feeling the summer evening breeze on his face rode back to Indira Nagar. He saw some nice villas in Aliganj and Mahanagar and also some vacant plots with wild grass. There were almost no high-rise buildings. He crossed Gole Market where there were a few restaurants, grocery shops and a dental clinic. A rickshaw coming from the slip road said to Dev's cycle rickshaw rider, '*Badhiye, arrey pehle aap badhiye,*' meaning 'move on, you move on first please'.

Tiny makeshift shops, a few stray puddles of water, semi-constructed houses, tempos exhausting diesel fumes, a little pull called 'pulliya' by the rickshaw rider, a crowded main road and horns and bells were the sights and sounds as Dev reached his Masi's home. After half an hour of pleasant chat with his large-hearted hosts he went up to his little room. He walked on the terrace soaking in the sights of Indira Nagar by the setting sun, and slipping into thoughts of a girl whose mere one picture was in Dev's bag, several in his heart, and who was 'neither happening nor letting anyone else happen', whatever Dev meant by that statement to me a few weeks back.

While Dev tried to appreciate the chemistry in the massive urea manufacturing plant the next day, the pungent smell of ammonia bothered him no end. He couldn't get rid of the smell even after a long bath in the plush company guest house located near the Torsh township just off Faizabad Road. Dinner on all three nights and breakfast in the mornings was served by waiters wearing white gloves and the most exquisite crockery and silver cutlery was laid out. On Friday morning, he checked out of the guest house and waited for Rohit and Sanyal who arrived precisely at the given time. As he opened the front door of the car to sit, Sanyal stepped out from the rear door and requested Dev to sit behind with Rohit. 'Please, please,' said Sanyal and urged Dev to take the rear seat. The roads were dusty and potholed and the little market they crossed en route to meet Banwari Lal Gupta, their distributor, looked disfavoured. The fields outside looked barren since paddy had not yet been sown. Any idyllic image that Dev had of rural India was blown on that first trip.

Rohit explained to Dev that Torsh distributors in north India were, 'The second most important persons in the district after the Collector'. They were financially very sound and on the back of Torsh name they would get agencies of other large companies.

'*Chacha* is on the *gaddi*,' said a boy to Sanyal as their car slowed down near a narrow street.

'Let's get off here Sahni sahab,' said Sanyal and the three of them entered the narrow street on foot.

Just then a man in his late forties wearing a *dhoti* and *kurta* came briskly towards them and exclaimed 'Ah ha, welcome, welcome.'

'How are you, Banwari?' said Rohit to him.

Sanyal introduced Dev to Banwari, 'This is Rajvansh ji, he is also *bara* sahab.' The managers of Torsh Chemicals were known as '*bara* sahab' or 'big boss' amongst the distributors.

Banwari and Sanyal led Rohit and Dev to the *gaddi* or the office room with mattress where the distributors sat cross legged and managed their business from. Banwari ordered tea and some snacks for his visitors, and he and Rohit first chatted about local politics. Banwari was in the habit of finishing every sentence with the word '*samjhe*' meaning 'understood', and '*samjhe*' would always be said softly, almost under his breath, and a few seconds after finishing the rest of the sentence. 'Khushaal is giving two months credit, Sahab, *samjhe*, and their supplies are in plastic packaging, *samjhe*, while we are mainly jute packing, our company will lose out this way, *samjhe*.'

Rohit gently pushed Banwari, 'Banwari has never missed his target and this month can't be an exception.'

Banwari wanted the price dropped and at least 45 days credit, Sanyal intervened and laughingly told the distributor, 'Thirty days will work Banwari ji. In July the offtake will pick up as sowing starts and today there are two *bara* sahabs here so you cannot refuse. I am telling you a factual thing.' Just as Banwari used '*samjhe*' at the end of every statement, Sanyal used to often say, 'I am telling you a factual thing'.

Meanwhile the tea and snacks arrived; neither was to Dev's taste but Rohit indicated to him quietly not to refuse.

With the sales negotiation done, Banwari asked Rohit how their distributor in Sitapur, Mannilal Agarwal was doing. He went onto add, 'He is a very *pakka baniya, samjhe*;' meaning he is an astute trader. Being a '*pakka baniya*' was a compliment.

Mannilal Agarwal, a distant relative of Banwari Lal Gupta, also had a cement dealership and according to the latter he rotated his money such that he availed credit from the principal companies and collected his dues from his buyers, the retailers, very early; thus, his investment was zero and his return infinity!

Before they left Banwari offered *paan* and *elaichi* as mouth fresheners. In no time they were racing down the highway. Krishnakant, the driver, stopped after 15 kilometres to relieve himself. As he went behind a tree Dev noticed that he pulled out his sacred thread from inside the shirt and rolled it around his ear.

'He mows at least two stray dogs each trip,' said Rohit with a blithe look, in reference to Krishnakant's rash driving. Dev smiled at Rohit.

They were to first drop Sanyal home, then Dev and finally Rohit. Just before Sanyal got off Rohit asked him what volume he was planning to do in June. 'Market is very tight Sahni sahab, I am telling you a factual thing, will be just a little over May.'

'Just a little over. I suppose it means you will double the May volumes,' said the Branch Manager.

Sanyal turned back and looked at us smilingly; he had a pleasant face, revealing his *paan*-stained teeth he said, 'Can't double, Sahab, distributors' April stock is not yet liquidated. I am telling you a factual thing, but I will be plus on May not minus, that I can assure you.'

'Hope you enjoyed that visit Dev?' checked Rohit just before Dev got off.

'Learnt more on this one trip than I did in all the lectures on Sales Management at the institute,' said Dev.

Rohit laughed. 'What are you doing this weekend?' asked Rohit.

'Looking for a room to rent in the Aliganj-Mahanagar area.'

'Good luck! Let's go *ganjing* once you are settled in.' '*Ganjing*' was a colloquial term that meant leisurely strolling around in Hazratganj which was Lucknow's main market.

Dev went to half a dozen houses on the weekend, near his office, looking for a room to rent. Everywhere he was asked where he was from and whether or not he was married. On learning that he was from Delhi and a bachelor all the landlords refused to let a room to him. Dev realised that landlords preferred a married south Indian, since the general impression was that south Indians were more decent! On the following weekend it was the same occurrence. That's when Sushma Masi told him, '*Beta,* why don't you just stay here for your four months training, all of us are so happy to have you.' Dadi ji too was elated when Dev, who was unable to find a suitable room to rent, decided to stay on with his relatives.

Rohit took Dev along for a few more joint trips and then in consultation with the National Sales Manager Debashish Biswas, the former gave Dev independent sales charge for the districts of Lucknow, Barabanki, Sitapur and Hardoi, indeed under his overall supervision. Dev's acceptability with the office staff and the AMA's had become high with his uprightness, courteous manner and patient listening, focus on organisational objectives and occasionally good business ideas. He had picked up various selling techniques as well. Dev had also realised the importance of that right mix of conviction, assertiveness and humour in leadership. Biswas was correct, the field experience had no substitute.

A few weeks later Dev did his sales trip to Hardoi and Sitapur where he was to meet, along with Meghraj Singh and Raghunandan ji, the distributors in Sandila, Hardoi, Sitapur and Mahmudabad. Krishnakant hit one dog that ran across their car as he raced from Lucknow to Sandila where Meghraj met Dev.

'Ah ha, welcome, welcome!' said the Sandila distributor on seeing Meghraj and Dev. A discussion on family's wellbeing and politics followed. When Dev asked him about state of business he said, 'Business later, first what will you have chai or *thandda*?'—'*thandda*' meaning cold drink. Before either Dev or the AMA could respond, the distributor thumped his desk and decided for them '*thandda*!' He then waved his index and middle finger to an errand boy, '*Do thandde*,' meaning get two cold drinks.

No matter how hard Meghraj or Dev tried the distributor refused to give an order, he said the rains were not coming and with no offtake of urea in the market his money was all stuck in the May and June stock he had bought. After half an hour, the Torsh employees left Sandila and Dev asked Meghraj, 'I was a bit thirsty but the cold drinks never arrived.'

Meghraj explained to Dev, 'Rajvansh ji, you didn't notice when he signalled for the *thandda* he shook his two fingers? It meant don't get them. That's because he didn't want to buy any material from us since he can't on sell to retailers, and we weren't really welcome today!'

This interplay of hospitality and commerce was a revelation for Dev.

'See how he behaves during rabi season, they run after us for material during winter months and will lay out the red carpet for you then.'

When Dev reached Hardoi town and could find a landline, he called Rohit to suggest that if equations reverse in rabi then they should link what the trade bought in *kharif* with what they needed in rabi. Rohit told him that he was working on such a scheme and they could refine it when he was back. The Hardoi distributor was also reluctant to buy any more product but Dev told him, 'I have come to your *gaddi* for the first time, will you let me go empty-handed?'

Meghraj an ace salesman himself was delighted with Dev's sales push and kept saying to him, 'Guru, too good, too good, Guru.' The word 'guru' was used as a distant synonym for the word 'boss'.

'Sir, sir!' greeted Raghunandan ji when Dev met him next morning.

Dev complimented him for June performance and remembering what Rohit had told Sanyal, he said, 'Double it in July Raghunandan ji!'

Raghunandan could not defy authority, his face turned red as he said, '*Ji ji*,' but when Dev was checking out at the reception, he saw the AMA muttering angrily, though softly, to himself.

Dev and Raghunandan first met Mannilal Agarwal, the Sitapur distributor. Raghunandan had cautioned Dev that Mannilal Agarwal will offer full breakfast which they must decline. Dev was curious to understand this new correlation between hospitality and commerce. Raghunandan explained, 'Sir the breakfast will prove to be very costly, Mannilal will not give us any order if we accept his breakfast, we will only have a cup of tea.'

Dev did as suggested. After the usual sales talk during which Mannilal Agarwal didn't give an order at that instant, though he promised to 'do his best' during July, he told them how in the previous month there had been a burglary in his house just before 5 am. 'The thief was nabbed,' he mentioned. 'He also stole our alarm clock. We had set alarm for 5 am on it; *chowkidar* in a nearby house heard it.'

Mahmudabad was Dev's last stop during that sales trip. The Lucknow Branch Office had planned a *kisaan mela* or farmers fair in Mahmudabad, and Rohit was also joining in from Lucknow. Indernath Maurya, the Sales Promotion and Advertising Manager, who was one of those few AMA's who had got promoted to management staff, had organised it. Maurya ji was in his early 50s and in Rohit's words was 'neither fish nor fowl'; he had been an AMA till recently so neither did he quite fit in with the young 'MBA type' managers nor was he a cadre staff anymore. Maurya ji was a jovial person who would sometimes call Dev *bachcha* or 'child'.

'How are you, *Bachcha*? Completed your target?' said Maurya ji as he and Rohit got off from their car. The *kisaan mela* was organised in an open field in a village near Mahmudabad, a raised concrete platform was the makeshift stage from where Maurya ji, Raghunandan ji and the local distributor were to give speeches and explain the benefits of Apna Gram urea and Torsh DAP and MOP.

A magician had been called from Sandila and there were two elephants which had been walking the little *mofussil* town since the previous day with large coloured sheets on them showing Apna Gram logo and announcing the *kisaan mela*. A photographer had been organised by the distributor, and Apna Gram wall paintings in large numbers had been completed in the run-up to the *kisaan mela*. There was much excitement in the village and about 200 farmers including some women and children were enjoying the magic show while the Torsh employees were getting on the stage. Just then a few villagers pointed to one of the elephants—it had got an erection! The farmers started laughing while the few women in the crowd covered their faces with their *dupatta*s. Dev thought just how uncomplicated the animals were when compared with human species that killed each other over property, supposed love and difference of ideology.

The Mahmudabad distributor spoke first and introduced the Torsh company employees. Then Raghunandan got up from his chair with some help from the distributor. No sooner had he started speaking that all the villagers started running helter-skelter. Dev heard Rohit say loudly, 'Swarm of bees!' They had been attacked by a massive swarm of bees!

'Run, Devavratt!' shouted Maurya ji. All the villagers including the women were running really fast, Rohit and Maurya ji and Dev all got off the stage and started running towards a stream of water flowing past the village. Raghunandan ji was too heavy to run; the distributor put a piece of plastic on his head and helped the large AMA somehow get away from the bees. Maurya ji and Dev got into a little mud hut where the former lit a straw fire to keep the bees away. Dev saw a villager covered in bees jump into the stream. He had never imagined as an MBA student in TMS, solving case studies and thinking strategically like a CEO, that the real world meant having sugar powered tea with distributors who haggled over ever rupee, organising magic shows in small villages and dodging attack by a swarm of bees.

Dev learnt later that his urging Raghunandan to double his sales in July had led the latter to pull out a pistol at his distributor who couldn't comply with the 'order' and for the National Sales Manager to show tactical annoyance to Rohit for not 'appropriately training Dev'.

The weeks in Lucknow rolled by. Sales trips, dusty little towns, scattered patches of beautiful green countryside, returning late at night and feeling a bit lonely on the terrace of his Masi's home, hearing an odd snide comment from a middle-aged cadre staff in office, *ganjing* with Rohit and an occasional film in Hazratganj, a couple of visits to the Barabanki plant, a few conversations with Sushma Masi who also enjoyed Neeraj's poetry, and thoughts and dreams of a girl whose name Dev would write alongside his on pieces of paper and wonder if she had any idea, any idea whatsoever that somebody's entire being was seized in her love.

Almost every third week, Dev would take the overnight train to Delhi, he would miss his home in Bapa Nagar and the sights and sounds of the metropolis. Despite the beginnings of the STD/ISD booths they were still not used as much by us in the late-1980s and Dev would call me and Sudhir only when he would be back in Delhi for the weekend once a month. Sudhir was preparing for his IAS Mains exams and I was enjoying my last year at university. Once Sudhir, Luv, Dev and I met in Greater Kailash I, M block market for dinner, we all felt that Dev's body had filled in a bit. He was still slim but was looking nicely muscular. His eyes seemed purposeful, his manner was gently confident and anything but withdrawn, his humour was more evident and he was respectfully assertive whenever his opinion was at variance with others. I didn't approach the subject of the 'girl in his life' either when he would call or when we met in GK I.

By the October of that year, the Agri-products vertical of Torsh Chemicals had still not decided where to move Dev next. Bhagat and Rohit had indicated to him to carry on for a few more months in Lucknow.

Meanwhile, Dev started noticing a change in the attitude of Sushma Masi's husband towards him. He was always a man of few words but would sit together with rest of the family and check on Dev's wellbeing in the evenings and share an odd anecdote or incident with him. However, in recent days Dev found him to be totally aloof and whenever Dev would return from office, he would excuse himself and go in the bedroom without exchanging any pleasantries. Dev learnt a big lesson of life—he had overstayed his welcome!

That very weekend, despite house owners in Lucknow being reluctant to rent rooms to unmarried north Indians, Dev decided he had to vacate Sushma Masi's home. The best he could find was an unfurnished room in a modest neighbourhood a couple of kilometres from Aliganj office. Not given to over-the-top expressions, Dev said to me on more than one occasion many years later, 'Nothing, nothing at all should be more important for any human being than self-respect.' In this world, poverty and emotional distress and sometimes greed, causes people to barter their self-respect, yet, and again as Dev told me once, 'If we can find a small roof with our honest money and live and die there with self-respect, even alone if fate so decrees, it would be a life reasonably well concluded.'

Dev had stayed with his gracious hosts for four months, Sushma Masi and Dadi ji had cooked for him caringly, Masi's husband was not being impudent in silently giving him the message that it was time. A decade later an English friend of his used the expression in some context 'guests are like fish, they get stale after four days', that's when Dev could put a tangible definition on his lesson and no matter how close a friend or relative he adhered to the four-day limit like a non-negotiable moral commandment.

There was no kitchen with the absolutely bare room that Dev had to rent, and he discovered to his horror that the bathroom had broken plaster at the corner on the roof exposing it to the skies, which meant that cold winter mornings were unbearable. A million mosquitoes would welcome him whenever he opened the ancient style twin wooden doors. A folding cot, a mosquito repellent coil, a bucket and an immersion rod to heat water were the immediate things he bought. The uncertainty about length of his stay in Lucknow, having to depend on oily restaurant food and total lack of any comfort in his rented room made his next few months in the city very distressing. The ordeal reached such an extent that when he was to board a train on New Year's Eve for Delhi, he read 20:40 hours departure time printed on the ticket as 10:40 pm! He was totally thrown when the ticket checker—who he had to call since someone else had occupied 'his seat'—told him he was in the wrong train. Fortunately, even the 22:40 hours train was for Delhi and Dev had to spread his sleeping bag next to the entry doors of the coach on the floor and endure near freezing temperature all night.

Dev had availed a part of his earned leave and was going to be in Delhi for a week and a half. Our placements in TMS had started and Luv and I both got placed early on. Luv got an offer from Ellinson Hindustan Ltd. and I too succeeded in getting into a good multinational company. Dev would call me every day during placement time and was delighted with our news. 'Let's meet tomorrow, Sandeep,' he said after congratulating me.

'Anytime, Dev; anytime and anywhere you say,' I told him, most relieved and glad with my placement.

We met in a fast-food restaurant in South Extension, it was a cold January morning. 'Happy New Year, Dev!' I greeted cheerfully.

'Congratulations, Sandeep.'

I checked how his first year of job and apprenticeship in Lucknow was progressing and Dev enquired on outcome of the placements at TMS. After we had been chatting for about 15 minutes, Dev said, 'You have asked me a question a couple of times in the last year.'

It took me a moment to understand what he was alluding to. 'Anyone I know Dev?' I realised that Dev was perhaps meaning to tell me about the special person in his life.

'Yes,' he said almost forcing himself to speak. I had seen Dev's journey from a reserved and withdrawn school boy to a personable and self-assured young professional, but the man sitting in front of me seemed to be struggling to tell one of his closest friends the name of a girl who I reckon meant a few worlds to him. I sat quietly waiting for Dev to collect himself. For a change that stoic exterior could not hide the vulnerability and strain within, it seemed like a sincere man's impasse with his own emotions. 'Yes,' he said again.

'I will be here till you feel comfortable to speak Dev.'

There was a confounded expression on that truthful face. After another long minute he finally said, 'Geeta.'

'Who?' I looked at Dev in disbelief; I think I saw his hand tremble a bit. He was quiet, looking at me as though he had confessed to an offence. 'Which Geeta?' I asked him almost grappling with my own senses.

He said nothing.

My mind was whirring as I exclaimed 'My father's cousin's daughter!'

Dev sat looking at me motionless though his face was slowly gathering its colour.

'Dev, Dev, I can't believe...! Are you telling me you are in love with my distant cousin?' I reconfirmed.

Dev spoke nothing at all, his silence said everything. Old images flashed through my mind. That day in the summer of 1985 when Gautam and Geeta were leaving for Calgary, of course it was so out of character for Dev to invite himself to my place to bid them goodbye. And then when I woke up when it was almost morning, I had found Dev, next to me, awake!

'Goodness! Since when?' I asked him.

'Since when?' he looked at me trying to understand my question.

'Since when have you been feeling this way?' I said, a little more collected.

'Since I can remember,' said Dev. I was still trying to fathom.

'Are you in touch with her?' I asked.

'No.'

'Does she have any idea?' I enquired further.

'No,' said Dev, and then after a pause, 'unless telepathy works.'

'Are you in touch with Gautam?'

'No,' said Dev again.

'So, for years, you have had Geeta in mind and you haven't mentioned this to anyone?'

'No'.

'Why didn't you tell me earlier?'

'I didn't know how you will react.'

'And why would I react in any way other than with happiness—because she is my cousin?'

Dev again said nothing.

'Oh Dev, she is a distant second cousin; and even if she was my sister, would I be anything but delighted that one of the finest people I know likes her! Which era are you from!'

For years, five, perhaps six, Dev had grappled with the most beautiful emotion known to man without sharing with anyone. 'And what do you want to do now?' I asked him as my mind settled down a little.

'I don't know.'

'You want to marry her? What if she is not interested; what if she has someone else in mind? What do you mean you don't know?'

'Sandeep, I suppose in our families, marriage is the most respectable thing to do. But it all depends on her.'

'And how will you break this to her?' I asked Dev.

'I have spoken to my aunt this morning; she is going to talk to Aunty, your mother, today.'

I couldn't help frowning. 'I wish you had spoken to her directly Dev'.

'I wish so too,' he replied.

'Why can't you call her?'

'And say what? It will be too abrupt; it will sound specious.'

I shook my head. 'Official channels through parents will complicate it; how my parents will react, how her parents will react, whether or not it will get conveyed to Geeta properly. This is a one-way love story Dev. Nothing, nothing would make me happier, but one-way love stories usually don't have a happy end.'

We were in India of the late-1980s. Letters via 'Air Mail' was still the most common way of international communication. Long distance calling was rare and costly. Dev had never made an international call in his life, nor had I. Even my parents had never called, nor received a ring, from Geeta's parents even though her father was my father's first cousin. I would receive an odd letter, once a year perhaps, from Gautam. I wanted to do my best for Dev, I trusted him more than my life; he deserved happiness.

We paid the bill and came out of the restaurant soaking in the warm sun just about appearing on that cold morning.

'Till when are you in Delhi?' I asked Dev.

'Five more days.'

'You've put us in a bit of a situation.'

'I am sorry for that, Sandeep,' he said.

I shook my head, 'That's not what I meant at all. I looked at Devavratt Pratap Rajvansh; I remember telling him, 'I will never come across a man like you.' We hugged each other for longer than usual. 'I will call you tonight, Dev.'

A Beautiful Marriage

In the mathematics of life, love trumps all divisors. It is the most sublime and headiest of feelings. What I saw on Dev's face that January morning, if the nectar of love and elixir of immortality were placed before him to choose from, all he would have wanted was a sip of the former. If only the sun, that radiates over India first before taking its luminosity to Canada, could have conveyed Dev's intensity to Geeta. I would have roamed around in the indulgent South Extension market but was in a hurry to get home. I did not want a situation where Dev's aunt calls my mother, and without speaking to me my parents call Geeta's father. I thought I would try and contact Gautam or Geeta directly and slowly broach the topic.

My worst apprehensions came true, as I stepped out of the auto and saw my parents' lit-up face. They immediately told me what I had just learnt but then they also mentioned that my father had called up Geeta's father.

'Why, why did you do that without asking me?' I felt so stymied.

My mother said that they were very fond of Dev and as soon as his aunt called her, she discussed with my father and in their keenness to help Dev and matchmake, they booked an international call to Calgary.

I held my head in dismay. 'I hope you didn't tell them that Dev is keen on Geeta?'

'Of course, we had to mention that,' said my father.

'And what did Uncle say?' I enquired on the reaction of Geeta's father.

'He sounded happy; they will get back to us.'

That night I called Dev and conveyed word to word what had happened. He was quiet. If nothing else, he could have written to Geeta. But now with three sets of parents in the picture, the situation was beyond us. He returned to Lucknow in a few days' time and once placements were over, I started focusing on my final semester dissertation at TMS and enjoying the last few months of student life with Luv.

The biggest lesson I learnt from my association with Luv, is not to take oneself too seriously. There is enough burden in life; a certain way to ease the journey is to recognize and make light of one's own frailties. Luv was in no way less sincere in his interpersonal relationships, but beyond a point didn't bother how others thought of him. While watching a zesty blockbuster Manmohan Desai film in a theatre I found him clapping in delight when the righteous character in the movie stops the villain's plane from taking off with a rope lasso or when the lion genuflects with folded hands in front of the hero's mother! He later told me how his sister's friend Purnima, 15 years his senior and for whom he nursed erotic fantasies, was getting transferred. 'I went to say bye to her and this time, non-accidentally felt her back side,' he said to me with naughtiness writ large on his pleasant face, 'she kept laughing and told me to stay in touch with her.'

What intrigued me no end about Luv was that he was also deeply religious. Having got a good placement, my father told me to visit our temple in Chhipiwara in old Delhi. When I mentioned this to Luv, he was very eager to come along. 'I love the energy in temples *Khannae*,' he told me.

Not only did he sing the *aarti* in the temple, but spent a lot of time with the priest understanding background of the temple which is so revered by all Khannas. I was still unsure how Dev felt about religion, his occasional visits to temples notwithstanding; I was quite sure though that he was searching for bigger answers. It was therefore paradoxical that a seemingly non-religious Dev, perhaps spiritual though, was the most straight-forward, non-intrusive and upright person; and Luv who was truly religious, while being very forthright, was also was given to tomfoolery, mischievous stereotyping of communities and carted more than a sprinkle of flirtation and lustful thoughts in his fertile mind. That they were both genuine made me value their friendship ever so much.

A couple of weeks later, I received a letter addressed to 'Devavratt Rajvansh c/o Sandeep Khanna' at my Delhi address. It was from Geeta's brother Gautam. I re-directed it to Dev in Lucknow. It was just a general letter checking on Dev's wellbeing and what he was planning to do in the near future. It gave some hope to Dev, though I suspect like most of us, he wanted to share love with Geeta and not necessarily, and immediately, matrimony.

During his next month's visit to Delhi, Dev shared two pieces of good news. Torsh Chemicals had decided to transfer him to Delhi as Assistant Marketing Manager reporting to Bhagatveer Bhatia and Sudhir Kapoor had cleared the written exam for IAS and been invited to appear for interview. Dev was to move to Delhi by end March 1989, operating from Madhavan building in Connaught Place. Sudhir's interview was also scheduled towards end of March.

Dev settled in quickly in the new job back in Delhi. He would take a chartered bus from Bapa Nagar to Barakhamba Road. Bhagat was a terrific manager balanced between 'concern for task' and 'concern for people'. He welcomed Dev and explained his responsibilities which included providing marketing support to the Agri-products business, primarily

Apna Gram, as well as assisting Bhagat with various matters related to interface with the government ministry. The National Sales Manager, Debashish Biswas, who also operated from Madhavan Building, advised Dev to 'represent the field in the head office.' By now Dev had sensed some strain between sales head Biswas and marketing head Bhagat.

Meanwhile, Sudhir had a good interview for civil service but with just hundred odd open seats, qualifying for IAS also needed the blessings of destiny. He was profoundly religious and keen to visit the Vaishno Devi temple, a little beyond Jammu, soon after his interview. Dev and Sudhir had become very close friends since their MBA days and so both of them got on a train on a Friday to visit Vaishno Devi. Dev later mentioned to me that it was one of the most 'divinely memorable' trip. From Jammu the two of them did a two-hour car drive to Katra, the temple is 13 kilometres uphill from Katra in the Trikuta mountains and most people trek up on foot, the deity is inside a cave. Dev said that it is 'the one place in India where everyone wishes each other' and walking up the hill amidst the clouds, stopping for refreshments along the way, pilgrims wishing each other and finally the *darshan* of the deity placed within a cave was 'one of the most fulfilling experiences for me.'

Luv was to start with Ellinson Hindustan Ltd. in Calcutta by end May. I too was joining my company around the same time, so for about two months the four of us were in Delhi and once Dev would finish his work for the day, we were only too eager to meet up and enjoy the charming restaurants of Connaught Place. 'I want a Connaught Place job *yaar*,' Luv would often say.

Once Sudhir and I landed up in Dev's office around lunch time. We were also surprised to see the clear demarcation between cadre staff sitting outside and management staff in plush cabins. After a cup of coffee in Dev's cabin, Sudhir wanted to use the toilet. Dev led him through the corridor, where all the cadre staff was seated, to show the facilities. Dev was a couple of strides ahead of Sudhir when the civil service aspirant entangled his right foot in the young manager's shin, a college time trick that usually over balanced the person ahead. As Dev lost his step, though didn't fall down, he looked back at Sudhir in astonishment, 'What are you doing!' and then gazing at the cadre staff, some of whom were watching the two young men, he continued in a displeased tone, 'they call me "Sir", what will they say!'

Sudhir retorted playfully, 'They will say: today Sir's Sir has come!' Sudhir and I laughed our way back to our homes that afternoon.

In the middle of May, the day Dev got his letter of confirmation from Torsh Chemicals having completed his one year of management traineeship, he received a call from

Sudhir who, after congratulating him, said, 'The civil services result is being declared tomorrow.' Sudhir was to be at the American Centre Library on Kasturba Gandhi Marg the next day and Dev told him he would meet him there at 3 pm. Sudhir came out of the American Library at 3:10 pm. Dev was waiting outside.

'Hi, I am Sudhir Kapoor IAS, mind giving me a hug!'

'Whoa!' exclaimed Dev. 'IAS proper—in top hundred?' Dev reconfirmed hugging his friend.

Sudhir smiled and nodded.

That weekend, the two of them did another trip to Vaishno Devi. By end of May that year, Luv and I left Delhi to start our jobs and by June end Sudhir too departed to start his civil services foundation programme.

The weeks started rolling into months, there was no news from Calgary. Whenever I visited Delhi I would call Dev, we also met a couple of times. He never asked anything further, though both times that year when we met, his eyes had an expectant look about them. There was much to discover in his head office job though—both constructive and downbeat—having an eye for detail, preparing thoroughly for meetings, keeping the boss in the loop and trying to do 30% of his job, importance of a learning attitude and listening skills in leadership. Dev was nominated for an in-house training programme on Situational Leadership in Bombay. The lessons

Dev learnt on that course, how a leader should alter his or her leadership style according to the competence and commitment of subordinates, he internalized and always tried to practice.

But despite Torsh being a top-class company, there were organisational games on show as well. The self-promotion certain managers would do albeit in a subtle manner, the line roles versus support functions tussle, the tactical show of disagreement, the good cop bad cop theatre, the sham of overtly motivating subordinates, the informal prejudice-based groups and the political games where the 'yes men' and sycophants despite low competence would pinch promotions. Dev and Bhagat also discussed the limitation but inevitability of normal distribution-based appraisal methodology and the usefulness of potential appraisal. Dev developed and ran a successful marketing campaign captioned 'Apna Gram Story Competition' that year and in December was nominated to represent Torsh in a competition for young managers to be organised early next year by Management Forum of India on 'Competitiveness and Internationalisation—Economic Imperative or Imaginary.'

By year end, Dev had almost given up hope on Geeta. The usual New Year greetings letter from Geeta's mother addressed to my mother had a passing reference to the fact that they had not yet 'discussed anything with Geeta'. I conveyed the same to Dev. Two days later, he asked me for 'one last favour'. He had written a letter to Geeta—presumably his last effort to reach out to her and reveal his heart—he wondered if he should put his name on the outside of the envelope under 'sender's name and address' or would it be more appropriate if I put my name and address. I thought it was better if I put my name; I posted that letter in early January of 1990.

Failure and rejection are the greatest teachers in life. Man's education is incomplete without them and dawn would not be valued till the dark shadowy night precedes it. He or she who has not known the disappointment of failure and the pain of rejection would never understand life as deeply as one who has come face to face with these austere teachers. Nature and society both have their ways to cope with setback but one of the finest instruments to prepare for life's vicissitudes is sport. The lessons on the cricket field or golf course or any other sport—of skill, teamwork, companionship and leadership, and above all being gracious in victory and sporting in defeat—are lessons of life.

Dev never got a reply to his letter, in fact he didn't even know whether or not it got delivered to Geeta. A few weeks into the new year though, the doorbell of his Bapa Nagar flat rang which his uncle answered. It was his colleague Mrs Anand and her niece Meher. Meher was in the final year of Economics (Hons) undergraduate course at Lady Thakurdas College and evaluating options like MBA, MA or going overseas. Mrs

Anand had once discussed career alternatives for her niece with Dev's uncle in office and the latter suggested that they come home and speak to Dev who had also studied Economics and not too long back appraised various career choices himself. Meher was a gorgeous young lady, tall, very well spoken and poised. Dev was struck by her beauty, as he conversed with her about the trade-offs between different career options. Meher laughed easily unlike the young man she was speaking with, who despite being self-assured and much relaxed in his mid-twenties, was sparing with his laughter unless in the company of his selected friends.

Sudhir's success in the IAS exam and his subsequent conversations with his friend had reignited a decade old aspiration in Dev. Over the years, as the appeal of the private sector spread and he secured admission to a top MBA school that aspiration within Dev had got subdued, though it wasn't dead. In the coming weeks Dev's mind was occupied with the Management Forum of India project his company had nominated him for, whether or not he too should try for the Civil Services and, not strangely, the image of Meher! The sadness of not even getting a response from Geeta was still lurking but the inexorable time seemed to be slowly breaking out into something resembling dawn.

Dev was the north zone winner of the young managers competition organised by Management Forum of India, his project followed by a presentation to and discussion with a jury also earned him the third position all India. He received the award from a former Union Minister for his work that made a compelling case for opening up Indian economy through decontrol and trade reforms, creating greater business competition in the interest of quality and price for customers and promoting export led industrialization rather than import substitution. The General Manager of Agri-products business Inderpal Singh Sodhi was delighted with Dev's achievement and said, 'You have made all of us proud.'

Meher telephoned after a few weeks and spoke to Dev about a Master's programme form she was filling and books she should refer to for MBA preparation. She sounded lovely on the phone. Dev offered to find his MBA entrance preparation book and lend to her. Mrs Dhawan accompanied her the second time she came home. Something dreamlike seemed to be happening and Dev was feeling drawn to Meher.

Dev contemplated whether or not to take the civil services examination. He had been living with the regret of not pursuing cricket despite being selected for TAPS cricket team, he didn't want to carry yet another regret in life. Somewhere deep within Dev also wanted to extend his time in Delhi, he sensed Torsh might move him into the field soon; he wanted to get to know Meher more. Dev's mind was made. He decided to take his boss Bhagatveer Bhatia into confidence and requested him for a week's leave before the Preliminary examination and said, 'Should I clear that, then a couple of months later, I will seek four week's leave for the Mains Exam.'

Bhagat was surprised and wondered if young MBAs, well employed, were still attracted to the civil service. He appreciated Dev's forthrightness and told him, 'You can do anything in your personal time Dev, and you are entitled to 28 days leave annually, but I will need to mention this to Mr Sodhi.'

A week later Mr Sodhi called Dev in his cabin and tried to describe the bright career that lay ahead for him in Torsh. Dev didn't change his mind. 'Sir I am keen to give civil services one serious attempt, in case you can consider my request I shall be very grateful.'

'You could have done this on the sly, Rajvansh, feigned sickness or whatever, it is honourable of you to be straightforward,' said the GM; he then continued, 'Your leave is your entitlement, but I suppose what you are requesting for is that your leave request should not be turned down and till about yearend you should not be transferred out of Delhi. Correct?'

Dev gently nodded, 'That's right, Sir.'

'You might forego promotion opportunity,' said Mr Sodhi.

'I understand that, Sir,' replied Dev.

'Okay, Rajvansh, go ahead; but I don't want any laxity on your job.'

By now, Dev was speaking to Meher at least once a week on the phone. He mentioned to her that he was going to attempt the Civil Services that year and then gathered enough guts to ask her out for a coffee. She called back the next day and declined. Dev wondered when was the last time he got something that he dearly wanted.

In addition to Sudhir, Dev was speaking to a few other people who had appeared for the civil services exam and they seemed to suggest that subjects like Public Administration, Geography and Sociology had in recent times been high scoring. Without fully appreciating that preparing two new subjects will be too big a bite to chew, Dev made a wrong decision. After clearing the preliminary examination, he checked with Meher who had finished her graduation about what Master's programme she was finally planning to pursue. During that conversation, Meher mentioned that she was going to Connaught Place for shopping with her parents and sister on the weekend. Dev, reluctantly but again, asked her if she would like to stop by at Khan Market for a coffee. Though she had rejected Dev's invitation once before, Meher accepted this second one. Dev got to meet Meher's father, a recently retired naval officer, and sister Meghna as well, as they dropped her at a café in Khan Market.

A man or a woman can fall in love at any time but what happens in those young twenties captivates the senses so intensely that even if it does not lead to a consummation, there are several who go onto live their entire life just by themselves with nothing but the memory of a few moments of this all-mesmerizing phenomenon. Dev too had spent years with one photograph and a tender thought. But he was realizing that Geeta was perhaps an image, whereas Meher was real. The more he tried to focus on his civil service study the less he was able to. His choice of subjects had all but sealed his fate in any case. This was the season for romance; everything else could wait or was dispensable. There had never been a lovelier monsoon and never had the following autumn 'blossomed' as much. Dev had experienced the happiest instances on a cricket field and so in the October of that year he took Meher to Augustus College and while walking in the cricket ground proposed to her.

Meher set aside her Master's plans and there was no way Dev was going to qualify in the demanding civil service examination. Nonetheless, he wrote the exam half ruing half smiling at not taking subjects like economics or management, and soon thereafter re-joined office. In early 1991, after the results had been declared and Dev had expectedly not qualified, a big organisation reshuffle was announced in Torsh Chemicals. Bhagatveer Bhatia was moving as General Manager

Textiles and Dyes based in Bombay, and the Branch Manager of Lucknow Rohit Sahni was replacing him as Marketing Manager of Agri-products business in Delhi. The Area Sales Manager of Varanasi branch Kamal Goswami was taking over as Branch Manager for Lucknow.

Dev found himself in the GM's cabin once again this time with Debashish Biswas seated beside him. 'So, Mr Rajvansh, can we discuss your next move?' said Mr Sodhi in his deep voice. 'How do you fancy ASM Varanasi?'

Dev felt a little cornered. He had already proposed marriage to Meher and she had accepted but the parents had not yet sat down—as usually happened at that time—and decided on a marriage date. In fact, Dev and Meher had not even exchanged rings till then! Dev was upfront yet again and mentioned to the GM, in the presence of the National Sales Manager, that he had fiancée now and would prefer to be transferred after marriage.

The GM chuckled, 'Were you studying last year or busy romancing?' He continued, 'Well, congratulations for that,' he extended his hand out to Dev who shook it, 'When do we hear the wedding bells?'

Dev felt a little uneasy, 'Sir, it should be in the first half of this year, though the exact date is not decided yet.'

Mr Sodhi was a large-hearted man, he smiled at Dev and said, 'Its two-zero, Mr Devavratt!' implying that Dev had sought two favours in recent times. 'You have heard of the saying that there is no free lunch?' said Mr Sodhi with a pleasant look on his face, 'I need to get a gentleman's commitment out of you.'

Dev looked at Mr Sodhi, 'Certainly, Sir.'

The GM said, 'Kanpur might come up later this year. For the next 18 months, I don't want you considering any job in any business other than Agri-products. So, if Bhatia wants to pull you into Textiles, not before 18 months! Agreed?'

Dev smiled at the GM, 'Agreed, Sir.'

Meher's parents and Dev's aunt and uncle all met and it was decided to have the wedding ceremony in end April 1991. Dev and Meher made a magnificent couple. Sudhir and I met them around the new years' time and we all dined together. Meher was a tall, beautiful and happy-go-lucky girl, always smiling and an intelligent conversationalist. She seemed to have that perfect combination of traditional values with a modern outlook. My friend, who wasn't dour any longer, was lucky to have her as his life partner.

As the wedding preparations started the fair-minded heretic in Dev began to question some of the rituals. Left to him, he would have just wanted to live with Meher as friends, but he realised none of the parents, not even Meher for that matter, would ever approve of that.

Marriage is as old as ancient civilizations, conducted in different ways in separate cultures and for multiple purposes with distinctive and sweet ceremonies. Around the world, since times immemorial, it is also an alliance between families and a reason for merriment. The Hindu marriage is a bond for 'eternity'; it is so positioned perhaps to congeal the relationship. Two individuals come together to jointly pursue *dharma*, *arth*, *kama* and perhaps even *moksha*, the core purposes of life.

'Do we really need to spend so much money on different ceremonies?' Dev asked his uncle. 'Can't we have just one joint function?'

'*Beta*, you get married only once; we are not going to overstretch but some dignified celebrations should be there. All these years we have attended a marriage ceremony and then a reception at weddings of friends and their children; it just doesn't look nice to have one common function. And our ceremonies and rituals all have a spiritual and scientific basis, what is it that is bothering you?'

Beneath the stoic exterior, there was a tempest within Dev which would question the established ways. He may not have been overtly religious but he had understood *Sanatana Dharma* as life's principles based on sense of enquiry, no wonder he told me years ago that there was convergence between modern science, Hinduism and Neeraj's poetry. Like the principles of science certain truths shall always be *sanatana* or everlasting, but man's curiosity and questioning must never stop. While it was difficult to ascribe any definition to Dev, a sense of equality and fairness drove his thinking and actions. He wanted Meher and himself to be equal in all ways, to be friends forever. He was swayed neither by established intractable patriarchy nor by explicit feminism.

Time moves, society changes, world modernizes, gadgets become more important than relationships, instant gratification and not *vilambit anand* or 'belated joy' is sought and so all rituals and rites come up for questioning—as they must—no belief should stay static, for the ever-moving river remains fresh only because of its locomotion. Yet, it's so easy to disbelieve everything and dismiss tradition as archaic or superstition; it takes effort and humility and an open mind to understand their basis. Dev applied himself again to appreciate that Hindu rites were not created for commerce but their two legs were philosophy and science.

Years later, returning from Neeraj's poetry concert he mentioned that he had never understood the symbolism in *Mahabharata* of Draupadi and her five husbands till that day. Dev paraphrased Neeraj's spiritual elucidation. Draupadi also known as Yagyaseni, one who emerges from *yagya*, represents consciousness for it is consciousness that emerges from *yagya*. The five Pandavas represent the elements of nature that is earth, water, fire, air and space. Life gets created only when the elements of nature are bound together with consciousness. Thus, the five Pandavas were all married to Draupadi. It takes effort and an open mind to understand Draupadi, it is easy and frivolous to dismiss her as a 'woman with five husbands'.

The *mangalsutra* or the auspicious necklace with golden and black beads that the groom ties around the bride's neck is for keeping the relationship ever blessed, the black beads to ward off evil designs of a third person. The seven *pheras* around the holy fire are the seven vows for always being with each other in happiness and sorrow and for sharing nourishment and health, prosperity and progeny and above all love and friendship. And then finally *kanyadaan* in Hindu marriages where the bride's father places his daughter's hand in the hand of the groom.

Dev asked himself if the daughter or *kanya* is an object that can be given in *daan* or charity. 'Why is the groom not 'given' in *daan*?'

'*Beta*, *kanyadaan* means that the bride's father is giving to the groom she who he loves more than his life, it is the ultimate charity and one that is supposed to not just enhance the prestige of the bride's father but also purge them of any sin. Are you bothered about the word *kanyadaan* or the custom?'

Dev replied with a smile, 'Perhaps you too could place my hand on Meher's after *kanyadaan*!'

His uncle smiled as well, 'I will place both your hands on Meher's!'

The engagement, marriage ceremony and reception were all evenings to remember without any ostentation. The engagement happened in the lawns of a large bungalow on Ashoka Road and the marriage in the lawns of a bungalow on Humayun Road. Dev's uncle threw a reception in Pragati Maidan.

Sudhir and I attended all three events. Luv reached Delhi late evening on the engagement day and insisted we all meet up. We picked up Dev first and then drove to Meher's house in Defence Colony.

'No, no,' said Luv, 'Devavratt cannot get such a beautiful girl,' he said to Meher. We then went to the coffee shop at The Taj Hotel where Luv said, 'We are Punjabis, we must sing and dance on marriage eve,' and requested the hotel staff to find a small band.

'Dev is not a Punjabi,' I reminded him.

'In the company of a Khanna, Kapoor, Malhotra and…' he looked at Meher who told him her surname was Dhawan; '… he is an honorary Punjabi,' said Luv laughingly.

Ramkumar and Sanju from our school also attended the wedding and reception. Sanju was already married by then. Most of Dev's Augustus College friends were there for the marriage and reception except Jaiswal who couldn't make the final event. All his Torsh colleagues came for the reception though at the wedding only the GM was present. Most of Dev's friends at TMS were there on the two main events, I had not met Samarth, Voltage, Jigsaw, Pracha and Happiness since mid-1988. Nita Rajagopalan was in Bombay, she couldn't make it.

The couple was spending their wedding night at The Blue Emerald hotel; Luv and I and Dev's cousin and Sushma Masi's son Kunal who had come from Lucknow went to drop them. Luv decided not to leave easily, 'Such a sanitized wedding you have had, Dev; at least get us a beer now.'

Dev pushed the giggling Eklavya out.

'Our friend is now officially good for nothing,' laughed Luv.

Dev touched my parents' feet when they went to greet the newlyweds at the reception. My mother hugged both of them. As my parents came and sat down my mother shook her head a bit and referring to Geeta's parents said to my father, 'I really wonder why they didn't respond to us;' and then looking at Dev and Meher some distance away, smiled at my father, 'so wonderful both Dev and Meher look.'

'Lovely couple, a beautiful marriage,' said my father.

Meher was smiling and laughing all through the various events, while Dev was Dev! Two days later, Dev and Meher left for their honeymoon to Manali.

Man Of His Word

'Whatever is true of India, its opposite is also true,' said the famous economist, Joan Robinson. Of the numerous ways to try and understand the heterogeneity of India, the simplest is to experience her sights and sounds in different parts of the country, the foods, the dresses, the predominant vocations and trade, religious beliefs, monuments, art and music, dialects and exclamations.

As was his wont, Luv had his own somewhat insightful somewhat amusing but always innocuous descriptions of various regions of India. He had mentioned to me a few years back that 'North India is about demonstration of power, emotion predominates eastern part of India, the west is professional and business-like, while south India is driven by systems and processes'. Anybody thinking of India in these terms would not be wrong but would also be far from correct!

Northern part of India is not just an expression of power; it is also not just hockey, paddy and wheat fields, *chole-bhature* and *rajma-chawal*, Ganga and Yamuna, *bhangra* and *dholak*, the revered Ayodhya of Ram and Mathura of Krishna, Taj Mahal, Ferozeshah Kotla and '*oye hoye*', '*maar suttiya*', '*bhaiya and paaji*'. Nor is East just emotion; it is also not just football, argumentative economists, fish curry and rice and *rasogolla*, the tea plantations, Rabindra *sangeet*, Brahmaputra and Hooghly, the venerated Durga Pujo and *pandal*s, Eden Gardens and '*khoob bhalo*' and '*orre baba*'. The western region of India is professional and business-like but not just that; it is also not just cricket, Bollywood films, *vada-pao* and *thepla*, industries and financial institutions, the *dandiya*, Somnath temple, Goa beaches, Narmada, Wankhede stadium, '*aai-shapath*' and '*kemcho*'. And south India with its systems and processes is much more and not just chess, scientists and engineers, IT parks and auto-manufacturing, *idli* and *dosa* and filter coffee, the shrines Tirupati and Sabrimala and Meenakshi temple, Carnatic music and bharatanatyam, Cauvery, Chepauk, '*aiyyo*', '*aama*', '*pah*' and '*cheh*' which are exclaimed in admiration and revulsion respectively. The states and regions of India have a richness in variety which when described would invariably require the qualification that 'whatever is true of India, its opposite is also true'.

Luv was a people's person, a friend for all seasons, whose purpose of life seemed to be to find a reason to laugh. Our just married friend Dev was a friend forever in trust, no longer introverted but not an extrovert either, whose purpose of life I daresay appeared to be to explore if life had any purpose at all. At Dev's reception, Luv annoyed my school friend Ramkumar a bit when he tried to hug him! Ramu was a reserved person and Luv had met him for the first time just the previous day. His discussion with Ramu on 'why is there resistance to Hindi in some parts of south' and his observation on learning that the person he was conversing with was an engineer that 'all my south Indian friends are engineers as are their cousins' didn't quite endear him to Ramkumar.

Luv's other encounter at the reception was with Debashish Biswas, the National Sales Manager of Agri-products business of Torsh Chemicals and Dev's senior.

'Ah, you are *Debabratt's* university friend! Where are you working?' asked Biswas.

On learning that Luv was in Calcutta, Biswas asked him if the city had grown on him. Luv mentioned that he was loving the food and clubs of Calcutta, and the fact that nobody dare say anything inappropriate to a lady most of whom were addressed as *didi* or sister; but struggling with the traffic and some of his team members in Ellinson Hindustan Ltd, 'Sir, they usually reach office only by late morning, and whether it's my boss or subordinates they speak in Bengali with each other in my presence, even though they know I don't understand.'

Biswas had smiled a bit, '*Sho* I have worked in Delhi and UP most of my life and adjusted to the language and habits here.'

On more than one occasion in our long association, Dev had said to Luv, 'Look at human beings as they are, without any cultural stereotyping or baggage.'

Luv would say to me in Dev's presence, '*Khannae,* even in marketing we were taught to identify common characteristics of target segments, life becomes simpler and more enjoyable through archetypes.' In fairness to Luv, he always made a lot of jokes on himself and laughed at the way his family members spoke and behaved. 'Dev bhaisahab says that relationships and decision making gets distorted if we stereotype people, but I have also found that by having open discussions with people from around the country about their background and culture I build more enduring relationships.'

Before Dev got back from his honeymoon, Luv, Sudhir and I had all left Delhi for our respective work locations. Sudhir had got his first posting in district Korba in Madhya Pradesh. Dev resumed office and a few days later, on the 22nd of May, Meher woke up Dev quite early and holding the newspaper in her hand, quietly told him the shocking news that former Prime Minister Rajiv Gandhi had been assassinated the night before at Sriperumbudur in Tamil Nadu. The country was passing through a severe Balance of Payments crisis at this time, the foreign exchange reserves had dropped to merely three weeks of import cover even though the crude oil prices which had shot up the previous year following outbreak of Gulf War had somewhat eased. High fiscal deficit, runaway inflation and prospect of a debt default loomed large. There was a caretaker government at the centre and parliamentary elections were underway when the alarming news of the former PM's assassination was broken. A month later a new government was sworn in at the centre and in July a significant national event occurred that was to impact millions of Indians including Dev and Luv and me.

Triggered by the critical economic situation in the country, when nearly 50 tonnes of gold had to be pledged with Bank of England, the then Finance Minister ushered in economic liberalization by abolishing industrial licensing for all except 18 industries. This dismantling of license permit raj, as it was infamously called, was a major step towards free market. There was a slew of other measures like readjustment of exchange rate, reduction in import tariffs, deregulation of industry and automatic approval of foreign direct investment in many sectors. Since then, successive governments have more or less stayed the course of economic reforms, and these policy changes have contributed to India registering relatively high GDP growth. From a $270 billion economy in 1991 India is now a $4 trillion economy! Amongst several other changes that the country has seen in the last three decades, the growth of a corporate elite class is notable. These corporate elite, discerning in their dress and subtly aggressive in their manner, outwardly easy-going but always on the look-out for 'better opportunities', enabled the growth of several cascading economic activities like foreign travel, smart condominiums, golf clubs, fine dining and up-market retailing.

Of the 200 odd multinationals in India in 1991 the big names were Unilever, ICI, Maruti-Suzuki, Citibank, Nestle etc. In the two decades that followed this number grew to over 800 multinationals. Some large MNCs like Shell, Coca-Cola, Pepsi, Ford and Honda entered fairly soon after the 1991 economic liberalization while others like Lafarge, M&S, Aviva, GE Money et al entered India in due course. I remember since that day in July 1991 for a long time to come, whenever Dev and I met or spoke on the phone the new economic policies and emerging employment opportunities were the hot topics of discussion.

As had been indicated to him earlier, in August that year, Dev was appointed Area Sales Manager for Agri-products business for Kanpur area office. The ASM of Varanasi branch Kamal Goswami had taken over as BM for Lucknow earlier that year and Dev had to report to him. Kamal Goswami was in his late 30s, bespectacled and almost bald; he wasn't the 'MBA type' manager and had come up the ranks. Goswami was known to be a 'shrewd strategist and super salesman'. He was a young man but an old-style authoritarian manager expecting deference. With Dev being too much of his own man and upright a clash between them was imminent.

Unlike Lucknow, Dev did not have much problem in finding a lovely little flat on rent in Kanpur, on Parvati Bagla Road close to Swaroop Nagar. His office was on the main Mall Road about 30 minutes from his flat by cycle rickshaw. For a newly-wed couple setting up their first home, unpacking the kitchen items and clothes and organising the cupboards, buying that first colour television and a water cooler, selecting a set of long living room curtains, placing the lamps on bedside tables, and getting their first cable TV connection was a blissful new beginning for the next phase of life. Cable TV has just been launched in India and soon Indian private TV channels like Zee TV and foreign channels like Star TV were telecasting news and entertainment programmes via satellite to millions of homes in the country. Kanpur, on the banks of river Ganga, is an old town once famous for leather and textiles, whose glory as 'Manchester of East' seemed well behind it by the early-1990s. But where there is love every town is a town of joy, every season is a season of happiness.

As ASM, Dev was responsible for not just sales of agricultural products of Torsh in the districts of Kanpur, Fatehpur, Etawah, Mainpuri, Farrukhabad and Bundelkhand region, but also management of the office and staff. There were six Agri-Marketing Associates in his team posted in the field and as many office-based staff. Even though he was far younger to them, Dev did not have any problem in managing either the office or the sales team; the combination of budding leadership skills and sense of fairness with focus on organisation objectives and people helped him grow in the new role in no time. His challenge was in managing his boss. But then Dev remembered the words of the National Sales Manager Debashish Biswas: 'If you meet your urea sales targets, all crimes are forgiven;' not that doing an honest day's job is described as 'crime' in any dictionary.

Meher would pack some *pulao* for Dev as he would leave for office in the morning, usually by cycle rickshaw and sometimes by an auto. He still couldn't afford a car. He would cross the historic Green Park cricket stadium to his left and after hitting the Mall Road swerve left on it, leaving two famous hotels of Kanpur behind him, Meghdoot and the relatively newer Landmark. Dev would smile when in the evening Meher would say, 'Come, dinner is ready,' and as she would lift the lid of the serving bowl it would again reveal *pulao*!

Dev and Meher made friends with two couples in Kanpur and it was with them that they would drive sometimes to Moti Jheel or Naveen Market. On a rare occasion when the young couple stepped out on their own and were returning home from Landmark Hotel in a cycle rickshaw, the latter rode past Gwaltoli market and the shut Victoria Mill. Seeing the deprivation in that part of town Meher broke down! Since that day Dev decided to go out with Meher in a hired car or with friends only. He would shop for the vegetables and groceries on his way back home in the evening and sometimes pick up *dhaba* food from New Raina Market on Company Bagh *chauraha*. Occasionally, they would join their friends for an evening meal and banter. Dev had a collection of board games like Pictionary, Cluedo, Battleships and Game of Life which they would play with their friends or any relatives visiting them. Every evening Meher and Dev would review their monthly budget; they had to manage their home and expenses in Rs. 6000/- a month. Once a month, they would go to Delhi to meet their parents. They would usually take the Friday evening Shatabdi and return by the same train by Monday late morning. Their Kanpur friends had introduced them to 'Thaggu Ke Laddoo,' a famous sweet shop, and the young couple would invariably carry a few boxes of sweets from this celebrated shop.

Dev would speak to his boss only on a 'need to know' or 'need to check' basis. There was still no email or mobile telephony or even pagers. As the sales graph of the region managed by Dev began to rise, even though the business of Kanpur area office rolled up into Lucknow branch, Kamal

Goswami started getting almost resentful. He checked Dev on the fact that every time he went to Delhi leaving on a Friday and returning on Monday, he was missing a day's work. Dev accordingly started taking official leave whenever he was travelling to Delhi for the weekend. As Dev doubled the sales from previous years, the area's travelling and communication expenses also went up, though in much lower proportion; Goswami ticked off Dev for 'laxity in controlling expenses'. Every time Goswami called it was only to point out lapses, which seemed to the ASM more conjured than real. Dev didn't want to leave Meher alone at home at night, so he would start his sales tours very early in the morning and return by late evening. Goswami started calling Dev 'fly-in fly-out ASM'. This infructuous relationship with his boss dampened Dev's own enthusiasm with which he was creating a strong area team. He had made a commitment to the General Manager that he would serve for at least 18 months in the Agri-products business and thus had to endure the stress of, as he saw, an irksome and belligerent boss for some more time.

His sales trips were usually adventurous. Dev found his AMAs competent, interesting and simple people with distinctive individuality. Once on an early morning trip to Bundelkhand, he reached the house of Pramod Kumar Upadhyay, his AMA in Jhansi, who invited him inside for tea. Dev found a little bird cage with a few parakeet and canary birds in it placed on the coffee table in the living room! The AMA offered Dev an album while he was preparing tea, a typical act in middle-class homes in India at that time, when a guest was treated to the host's family photos. As Dev turned the album cover, he saw a newspaper clipping on the first page whose heading read 'Pramod Kumar appointed Home Minister.' The article started: 'Pramod Kumar of Jhansi was today appointed the Home Minister for the state…' The next page had another newspaper article with the heading 'Pramod Kumar hits brilliant century against touring West Indies'; still another article stated: 'Pramod Kumar wins Filmfare award for super-hit *Suraj Ki Chandni*'. As a bemused Dev flicked through the pages, a laughing Pramod Kumar entered the living room holding a tray with tea and some snacks, 'This is my hobby, Sir. I create my own articles by cutting words from newspapers and pasting them on a paper and then have it photocopied.' Dev couldn't help laughing.

On a sales trip to Mainpuri, Dev was told by Vinod Kumar Srivastava, the AMA there that he must leave back for Kanpur early. Dev would in any case try and get home latest by 9 pm but he was curious why the AMA was stating so specifically. 'Rajvansh ji the drive from Mainpuri to Kanpur includes an hour on a non-highway road between Mainpuri and Etawah, there have been incidents where dacoits tie a rope across the narrow road from one *babool* tree to the other. As you stop the car they will loot you. You must cross that road before sunset.'

Dev asked him if he had ever encountered any trouble on the road. The AMA puffed on his cigarette and said, '1974', he then exhaled the smoke and continued, 'I was nabbed by dacoits and made to sit on railway tracks, they then asked if my company will pay 2 lakhs ransom for me. I told them to kidnap the GM since I was just a junior salesman for whom the company would not pay even 200 rupees!'

Dev was all ears to the Mainpuri AMA's tale who apparently was enjoying the anxious look on his boss's face.

'How did you come out of the situation?' asked Dev.

'Rajvansh ji, if their captor doesn't pay ransom, they usually pluck out his eyes and hang him on a tree. In my case, it was my wit that saved me,' he puffed on the cigarette again and without looking at Dev, said, 'when one of the bandits suggested to the leader that they shoot me, I folded my hands and told them not to waste their bullets; given my weak body, a couple of slaps would finish me off! At this the leader of dacoits laughed and let me go.'

When Dev mentioned this semi-chilling story with a lucky end to the two senior AMAs based in Kanpur they heartily laughed and told Dev, 'Rajvansh ji he must have moved product out of the stock point without invoicing, and didn't want you to visit the Mainpuri godown.'

***

The Agri-products business of Torsh would annually organise a two-day Key Tasks Workshop for its senior commercial staff in an exotic location. All Sales Managers, Supply and Distribution Managers, Marketing and Finance Managers and General Manager would be present; the workshop helped break silos and build teamwork as all concerned managers were under one roof. There had been a rumour doing the rounds that Torsh Chemicals was likely to be taken over by another European company and most of the discussions on the sidelines of the workshop were around this rumour. Dev met Rohit Sahni in the evening by the poolside of the hotel they were staying in.

After chatting about the families Rohit asked Dev, 'How is Kamal G getting along?'

Dev mentioned, for the first time to any colleague, that he wasn't comfortable what with all the nitpicking.

'I sensed that Dev.'

'Any suggestions Rohit?'

'What do you want to do?' asked Rohit.

'Either seek transfer or look out,' said Dev, 'difficult to continue like this.'

Rohit was thoughtful, 'Ideally, you should go up the line, but then speaking to Biswas won't help too much.'

'Why not?' wondered Dev.

'For starters, Kamal Goswami and Biswas are aligned on all issues; and then you, even I for that matter, are seen as part of the Sodhi and Bhatia group!'

'Really?' Dev was surprised. 'Why should we be seen as part of any group! Here to just do a job and build a little career.'

Rohit looked intently at Dev, 'Wish it was that simple, organisational politics is an inevitability,' and after a little pause he said, 'Never mind, I might just put it in Mr Sodhi's ear over breakfast tomorrow morning.'

Back in Kanpur, things came to a head between Dev and his boss following the former's next trip to Lucknow for the monthly sales meeting. Dev would hire a car for his visits to Lucknow Branch Office and, as always, did the same. He asked Meher to come along since she had never been to Lucknow and was keen to buy some *chikankari* suits from there. Dev suggested he would drop her at Sushma Masi's house who could take her shopping; he would attend his meeting and then pick her up on his way back. A couple of days after the meeting Kamal Goswami called Dev and told him that he did not approve of 'company assets being used for personal purpose.'

For middle-class Indians, rather 'middle-income' to use Dev's term, brought up on a diet of honesty and loyalty, even the slightest question on their integrity hurts them sharper than King Arthur's Excalibur! Dev instantly called Mr Sodhi's secretary and requested for time, he then bought Shatabdi tickets for Meher and himself for an unscheduled Delhi trip.

'Sahni mentioned in Udaipur that your boss was being a pain,' said Mr Sodhi to Dev in his office, 'Why didn't you tell me earlier?'

'Sir, I would request to be moved to some other team if possible,' said Dev plainly.

Mr Sodhi reclined his chair and put both his hands behind his head. 'You have done very well, Devavratt, both in the marketing and sales job, you should be confident about your performance and not be sensitive about every crack-brained comment your boss makes.'

Dev looked at his GM in the eye and said, 'Sir, I will not be able to ignore a comment against my integrity.'

Mr Sodhi lit his cigar then looked at Dev and said 'You are a man of your word,' and then after a little pause continued, 'You are or you are not?'

A serious-looking Dev responded, 'I try my best to honour my commitments.'

Mr Sodhi laughed softly, 'Good. I am going to share something with you in utmost confidence; if you mention it to anyone outside this room I will deny saying it.' Dev wondered where the GM was taking the discussion. 'You have heard all the rumours of Torsh Chemicals being taken over. Well, they are not rumours. The big boys in Europe are in an advanced stage of finalizing a MOU with the European company Roqsanto. Very old and well-established organisation. You have heard of it?'

'I have Sir, they are a large chemicals company if I am not wrong,' said Dev.

'One of the biggest chemical companies in the world, started about 60 years back by a Greek businessman from Santorini, that's where the 'santo' in the name comes from, 'rock' of course meant oil in the olden days. They started as Rocksanto, used to refine crude oil initially, but later got out of that business and focused only on manufacturing and marketing of value-added chemicals. That's when their name changed to Roqsanto, with a 'q'. So Roqsanto Chemicals International Ltd. is sitting on a cash mountain and wants to diversify. You see where I am getting to?'

Dev wasn't quite certain, 'Not entirely, Sir.'

'Roqsanto is doing due diligence of Torsh's assets worldwide to arrive at a takeover price. We have formed a team in India of some of our executives who will help in the due diligence, data room and valuation. The team still needs a couple of people. Once the MOU is signed the due diligence will get kick-started, if the takeover goes ahead then people working in this team will stand a good chance of being absorbed directly in Roqsanto, which incidentally will become a very large global corporation then.'

'What will happen to our businesses in India?' enquired Dev.

'Can't say, Roqsanto is currently in several product categories like Adhesives and Resins, Paints, Industrial-Construction products like additives and sealants, Cleaning-Polishing you know car cleaning products and drain cleaners and solvents, also an Agrichemicals business mainly pesticides. What I hear is that Roqsanto wants to stay in value added chemical products. So, in India they may retain Plastics, I am not sure about fertilizers and textiles or even coatings polymers for that matter. These commodity type businesses might, if the takeover goes ahead, get spun off to other buyers.'

Dev enquired further, 'So, what does Roqsanto really gain by taking over our India operation?'

The GM said thoughtfully, 'Well, an easy entry into one of the biggest emerging markets of the world. Also, when it's a global takeover you acquire the full organisation and then chop and change slowly. Specifically in India, Roqsanto will get our large Plastics business; they will get access to our distribution network and customer lists and manufacturing facilities including land. Plus, they can pick out the cherries from our highly accomplished staff like yourself! If you want me to put your name forward, I can do so, they will start fairly soon after the MOU.'

Dev agreed to Mr Sodhi's idea, he thanked the General Manager for his support and returned back to Kanpur the next day.

Human beings blossom when they are genuinely appreciated, not that false praise that mediocre managers resort to, or the sham that a lot of motivational speakers indulge in, but authentic recognition is like unadulterated sandalwood whose fragrance lingers for a long time. Dev felt happy after his meeting with the General Manager. In two weeks' time he got a call from Mr Sodhi.

'Mr Rajvansh,' said Mr Sodhi in his gravelly voice, 'pack up your bags and move to Delhi.'

'Is it the same job you mentioned Sir?' enquired Dev.

'Yes, it is.'

'By when do I need to move?'

'Let me discuss the exact date with Biswas, you should get a letter soon through your line.'

One of the last things Dev did while still being in Kanpur was organise a trip to Khajuraho with friends in the latter's car. Dev and Meher and another couple halted at Jhansi for the night before continuing on their little weekend get-away to Khajuraho, famous for temples with erotic sculptures. While at Jhansi, most of the Bundelkhand distributors came to meet

Dev, news that he was leaving Kanpur had already spread. The two couples spent a full day with a tour guide seeing the temples of Khajuraho built during the Chandela dynasty's 400-year rule. 'Sir, if you look around there is lots of other symbolism on the temples in addition to erotic sculptures. It reflects the balance of life—*dharma*, *kama*, *arth* and *moksha*—there are sculptures depicting all purposes of life. These are 1000 years old; India was liberal and sex was a celebration then, over the ages we got conservative and also a little morally confused and view sexual activity as debased now.'

Dev agreed with the guide and said, 'I did not realise that the Chandela dynasty ruled for 400 years.'

'Sir, not just Chandelas; Gupta and Mauryan empire lasted for well over 400 years each, Ahom dynasty ruled over 600 years, the Pandyas 800 years, the Cholas for 1000 years.'

Their guide continued to share facts about Indian history and temples that none of the four tourists knew about. 'Sir the Vijayanagra empire spread all over Deccan plateau, its capital was Hampi where, thousands of years ago, Lord Ram met Hanuman. The Hampi rocks date back to prehistoric times.' The guide continued, 'Do you know about the Great Wall of India?'

Dev and Meher and their friends shook their heads.

'There is a 36 kilometres wall in Kumbhalgarh fort in Rajasthan; it is the second longest wall in the world after Great Wall of China and Rana Pratap was born in the fort.'

'How do you know all this? I mean, these are not Khajuraho facts,' enquired Dev.

'Sir, I am a history teacher, I do tour guide work only on weekends to earn some more money.' Their tour guide joined them for lunch and enthralled the tourists with more interesting facts. 'Madam, you must be knowing about GMT, the Greenwich Meridian that passes through London. Hundreds of years ago the zero meridian, which indicates time centre of the world, was believed to pass through Ujjain in Gujarat. It is not just old Indian astronomers who mention this but even ancient Greek maps show Ujjain as zero meridian. That's why the Mahakaleshwar Temple dedicated to 'endless divine time' is located at Ujjain.'

'That's amazing!' said Meher. Dev and Meher and their friends were fascinated with all these historical facts.

'The *Ram Setu* that connects Rameshwaram with the northern tip of Sri Lanka is the wonder of wonders, but we don't find it in the list of ancient wonders of the world. I can bet all my ancestors that its carbon-14 dating will show it to be 7000 years old, coinciding with the times of *Bhagwan* Ram.'

'Is it true that the design of our Parliament building is also based on a temple?' checked Meher.

'Absolutely, Madam,' asserted the guide, 'it is designed on the lines of the Mahadev's Chausath Yogini Temple in Madhya Pradesh which was built in the middle of 11th century.'

'Are there more temples in India with erotic sculptures?' asked Dev's friend.

'The Sun temple at Konark in Orissa, Sir', said the guide.

'Why is it called Sun Temple?'

'Sir, the temple is designed in the form of a chariot being pulled by horses, and the wheels of the chariot are actually sun-dials, we can establish the precise time by seeing their shadows! Ancient India temples are not just wonders of unbelievable architecture but they contain nature's mysteries hidden in them.'

Dev's friend added, 'In Himachal, where I come from, there is a Jwalaji temple…' and before he could complete, the guide noted, 'Yes Sir, there are nine natural flames that constantly burn there, nobody has been able to find out their source.' He smiled at Dev, 'Where do I stop, Sir, our old Vedic culture was so rich and evolved and the temples I mentioned are just small examples. I could go on and on.'

Meher then asked the guide, 'When you say 'our old culture'—how old do you think it actually is?'

The guide replied, 'Madam, India is the most ancient continuous civilization going back at the very least 10,000 years.'

Meher's friend wondered, 'Continuous?'

'By "continuous" I mean that old culture has continued to evolve, despite external conquests it was never entirely destroyed, the excavated *Shiva linga* which dates thousands of years back is the same that you worship today; the artefacts excavated from Indus Valley cities show women with parted hair just as you and Madam here have parting in the hair where you apply *sindoor*!'

'Apart from the temples architecture that you mentioned, how developed was our ancient civilization in other fields?' asked Meher's friend.

The guide's face was glowing with the self-esteem of his heritage, 'Which field would you like to hear about Madam? We all know that it was Aryabhata who first propounded that the Earth is round and goes around the sun; you have all studied about the town planning in Indus Valley civilization; our *Mahabharata* is more than twice the size of *Iliad* and *Odyssey* put together; the kathak is the oldest dance form in the world; the zero, the *pi*, the decimal system were all invented here, Madam; the theorem we know as Pythagoras was discovered by Baudhayana in 8th century BC; plastic surgery was first done by Sushruta who lived around the same time as Baudhayana, steel was first produced in India. Bharat has nurtured democracy for centuries; our heritage is not just rich, Madam; it is truly glorious!'

There are several interesting and inspiring people who we meet in our lives and feel at that instant that we shall meet them again, but never do. Dev took the contact details of the guide but neither he or Meher nor their friends ever met him again. On their drive back Dev's friend switched on some old

Hindi film songs. Whenever a song written by Neeraj would play—'*Rangeela re*', '*Ae bhai zara dekh ke chalo*', '*Karvaan guzar gaya*'—Dev would share the history of how that song came to be created.

'Dev, you could become a music and poetry guide,' said his friend at the wheel.

'The two subjects we were just not introduced well to in school are history and Hindi poetry,' remarked Dev.

'And it has been amply evident today,' said Dev's friend with a smile.

'How would it have helped if we were taught these subjects better?' asked Meher from the back seat.

'You have heard the saying that those who don't know their history risk repeating it,' said Dev. 'For building national pride and also unifying a diverse country proper instruction on history can be so useful, if only it was taught to us in story form.'

'And Hindi poetry?' asked Dev's friend.

'Poetry is the most sublime form of entertainment; it nourishes the soul. There is so much wisdom and melody—if we were just taught Bachchan and Neeraj well in the Hindi speaking regions—it is lessons of life, would even help enhance national character.'

As they neared Kanpur, they passed by some villages where, let alone electrification and proper roads, even the thatched roofs of the huts seemed to be at the mercy of a heavy rain. A few kilometres down the road a two-wheeler scooter had run into a car, the pillion rider had sustained an injury and she was sitting on the road-side with a bleeding arm. The scooterist and driver of the car were bitterly quarrelling. About 25-30 passers-by had stopped and were just gazing at the ongoing argument, with nobody even checking on the injured lady. Behind the crowd two men were urinating against the wall of a house and hardly two hundred meters beyond this melee was a crazy traffic jam as everyone was jumping the traffic light! For a moment Dev and his friend thought of stopping and offering help, then they realised there were two ladies with them and it would be risky to get off the car amidst the fracas. It took them 45 minutes to get past the crossroad with the traffic signal and no sooner had they got into a narrow street that a heap of garbage landed near the bonnet of their car, someone from a higher floor of the adjacent house had thrown it.

'I wonder what is true!' said Dev's friend's wife, 'All the fantastic culture that we saw and heard about in Khajuraho or what we are seeing around us now?'

'Both are true,' said her husband at the wheel, 'what do you say, Dev?'

Dev had a pensive look on his face, 'Time doesn't stay still.'

***

Shortly thereafter Dev moved to Delhi as part of a 'special project' team that reported directly to the Managing Director. He had spent a year and a half in Kanpur and the indicated time-frame for the new assignment was one year. Roqsanto Chemicals International Ltd. and Torsh Chemicals Ltd. wanted to close the deal by end of 1993.

In the March of 1993 Dev had to meet with the central Roqsanto team, from UK and Germany, working on the takeover of Torsh assets in India. The meeting was in Bombay and since he had quite a few days of earned leave left he took a week off prior to the meeting. Meher accompanied him and they enjoyed the first few days of their holiday week in Bombay; on the 12th of March they were scheduled to meet Dev's TMS friend Aakash Samarth and his fiancée in Bandra by early evening. Just post noon on the 12th, Dev and Meher decided to take a cab and see the town starting from Nariman Point. The driver of the cab pointed out the stock exchange and Air India building to the couple, they then drove on Marine Drive past Chowpatty, onto Pedder Road where the cab driver pointed out Lata Mangeshkar's home; the car went past Worli's Shiv Sagar estate, the Siddhi Vinayak temple and onto Dadar. Dev was keen to see Shivaji Park the cricketing hub of Bombay, where several great cricketers used to play during their early years; the cab driver drove around Shivaji Park and then crossed Mahim on way to Bandra. Dev and Meher waited for Samarth at the designated meeting point but he did not arrive. The millennial generation must wonder how we survived in those days without mobile phones or email.

After two hours of waiting when Dev and Meher were about to leave, they saw Samarth walking towards them. Dev greeted him with a smile as Samarth said, 'Apologies, nice to see you both safe.'

'Got late at work?' Dev asked politely.

'No, no; don't tell me you don't know what's been happening in the city!'

Dev and Meher gave him a blank look. Samarth told them, 'There have been 10 to 12 bomb blasts in the city!'

It was later that Dev realised that he and his wife had providentially and narrowly missed several of these blasts by not more than half an hour. More than 250 people were killed in these bomb blasts.

The 1990s was as tumultuous a decade for India as it was splendid. It was a time of both enormous opportunities and immense turmoil when my friends and I were establishing ourselves in our respective professions. Never before was reading the newspaper and seeing TV news as exciting and as distressing. Barely three years into the decade, India had already seen mayhem in Kashmir and assassination of a former PM, severe financial crisis and landmark economic reforms, satellite TV and arrival of teenage prodigy Sachin Tendulkar whose talent was getting indelibly stamped on the world. Kashmir, that most strikingly picturesque part of the world, whose beauty evoked romance in poets, honeymooners, tourists and film-makers, was ripped through violent militancy beginning in 1990 that tormented its soul and from Dal Lake to Gulmarg every alluring feature of the blessed land of Chinars wailed in agony.

Dev's new assignment did not have month-end targets and the work would come in spurts. But there was a lot of insight on business strategy in the project, and Dev got to know the representatives of Roqsanto quite well. Of the four member Roqsanto team that was spending considerable time in India, there was a British gentleman, a Belgian and two Indians. One of the Indian representatives of Roqsanto was Karan Singh Varma, a tall and handsome man in his early forties with a regal presence; there was instant rapport between Karan Singh Varma and Dev. The acquisition process overran the expected timeline and it was only in early 1994 that a joint communication went out to the press and employees of both companies. Roqsanto Chemicals International Ltd. was taking over Torsh Chemicals' businesses world-wide. A new company was being formed in Europe: Roqsanto Torsh Chemicals Ltd, and the acquired company assets were getting absorbed in this new company.

As Dev contemplated his next job and whether or not to stay with Torsh Chemicals several of whose businesses in India were likely to be sold off, and about a month after the takeover announcement, there was a call on Dev's office phone: 'Hi Dev, this is Karan.'

He was calling from UK. After exchanging pleasantries Karan told Dev that Roqsanto Chemicals International Ltd. was planning to enter India. 'Not Roqsanto Torsh Chemicals Dev that is a ring-fenced entity. I am talking of RCIL. If you are keen for a change, send your CV to me.'

Hindustan Roqsanto Ltd. was incorporated as a wholly owned subsidiary of Roqsanto Chemicals International Ltd.; Karan Singh Varma was to be its Managing Director. The British person in the takeover team Howard Sadler was to be the Head of Business Development and the Belgian team member Adam Wouters was Head of Sales & Marketing designate. An experienced HR manager was hired locally and all four of them were in the interview panel when Dev entered the chambers in the Taj hotel in Delhi.

Karan looked at the HR manager and said, 'Zubin, we all know Dev well, you may make his acquaintance and check on any details.' The HR manager asked a few general questions after which Karan went onto explain RCIL's India plan, 'RCIL plans to enter India through Hindustan Roqsanto Ltd. with two product categories, Adhesives and Resins and a suite of what we call Cleaning and Polishing products that is car cleaners, drain cleaners, solvents, polishes etc. Over time, the portfolio team in Europe will decide which assets from the acquired company will be retained; those will then transfer to HRL. Once we establish ourselves here the entire range of our international Paints and Industrial products and Agri-chemicals will be potentially available to be launched here. There are a couple of vacancies in Howard's team that is business development and quite a few in Adam's team who will head Sales and Marketing. If we decide to go ahead with you, which is a distinct possibility', Karan laughed a little as he said this, 'and you are happy to come on board, what would be your preference?'

Dev looked at them, 'I have experience both in Sales and Marketing roles.'

'Okay, so Adam's team then,' said Karan

On the following weekend there was a telephone call on Dev's home number. Meher told Dev, 'Zubin Tarachand from HRL.'

The HR Manager said to Dev, 'Hi Devavratt, we are preparing your appointment letter and will post it to your home address. Your cost to company will be around Rs. 18,000 a month. Do you wish to discuss details?'

'No Zubin, that's very generous and perfectly fine,' said Dev. Never in his working career did Dev negotiate on his salary or perquisites.

'Karan is with me and wants to speak to you as well,' said the HR Manager. Karan told Dev that they intended to appoint him Zonal Sales Manager for either South or West or North India, but had not yet finalized. 'We would like you to start in Delhi, work with Adam and understand the new products and their attributes, and do the product launch in Delhi and Bombay first. Then evaluate the Eastern India market—we are not sure if we need to have a full office and team there—after which we will post you either in Delhi or Bombay or Madras.'

The Hindustan Roqsanto Ltd. offer was better than the other employment offers Dev had at that time. Dev resigned from Torsh Chemicals giving three months' notice as per his employment contract; he was to start with Hindustan Roqsanto Ltd. on 3rd October 1994.

A Polarized Horoscope

Marriage is necessary for most people, as humans find it hard to live alone. They have a need to share their emotions and feelings, and taken care of. Matrimony is also one of the biggest changes in peoples' lives which not only impacts daily routine, living situation and way of speaking of partners but becoming a spouse also alters one's personality. There was subtle change in Dev too post his marriage to Meher—he became more relaxed and confident than I had ever known him to be. He would laugh easily, speak and socialize much more, and while mentally he might have negated most elements and ideologies of existence, viewing human life as an unrelenting cyclical process of germination and decay, as a householder now he would take interest in buying the right appliances for his home, finding new restaurants to dine out with his wife, select gifts for extended family members, holiday with Meher and dream together of the times that lay ahead. Meher's warm simplicity and cheerful spontaneity had a blossoming impact on my friend.

Most MNCs that entered the price-sensitive and complex Indian market in 1990s went through a collective learning curve. Hindustan Roqsanto Ltd. too had a roller-coaster start-up phase though Karan's striking personality and Roqsanto's growing international profile ensured that HRL was always getting good press. Dev joined Roqsanto in October 1994 to find a team of 30 people in the company. HRL had tied up with India Rasayanik Ltd, a mid-sized state government company to procure from them adhesives and resins it intended to market locally and post quality check, package and sell them under Roqsanto brand name. For distributing the adhesives and resins, and the cleaning and polishing products which were to be imported, the vast distribution network of erstwhile Torsh Chemicals was available. Most of the old Torsh dealers were to become Roqsanto's retailers as well, and a few large ones could be offered distributorship and thus they could on-sell in open market.

The Roqsanto branded adhesives and resins, and cleaning and polishing products, were first launched in Delhi and Bombay amidst much excitement and some confusion over pricing strategy and channel margins. It took a while for Roqsanto to agree on the job titles for its India operation. Wouters was surprised that job titles was such a big issue in India and the front-line sales staff who had been given business cards that read 'Team Members' came back with the predicament that they were finding it hard to get married! As indicated to Dev, in early 1995 he was assigned to evaluate the prospects for Roqsanto in Eastern India, though he continued to maintain his rented house in Delhi. He carried a business card that read 'Zonal Sales Manager' with Delhi office address and telephone number and that distinctive blue and grey Roqsanto logo.

In the following few months, Dev spent every alternate week in Calcutta. He decided during his second visit itself that Roqsanto should launch its products in Eastern India. The GM of erstwhile Torsh Chemicals in Calcutta, now called Roqsanto Torsh Chemicals Ltd. whose distribution network HRL was to use, became a friend of Dev's and was most helpful and excited about adding the Roqsanto branded products to their portfolio of coatings and polymers and dyes in Bengal, Bihar, Orissa and North-East.

Dev started getting familiar with the drive from Dum-Dum Airport to Hotel Taj Bengal where he stayed during his first few visits. Coming out of the airport and driving past Salt Lake to his left, turning next to Science City with Tangra and China Town to his right, reaching Park Circus' Five-point crossing, past Park Street and Russel Street onto the Maidan area, the lungs of Calcutta, seeing Eden Gardens from one window of his car and Victoria Memorial from the other, then the delightful Race Course and finally turning into the pleasant Taj Bengal hotel. Calcutta had been the capital of British India till 1911, and for better part of the 20th century the most 'happening city' of the country, where all the old MNCs had their headquarters. By mid-1990s though a number of big companies had moved out of Calcutta and the city seemed to be crying out for infrastructural investment and modernization. 'In Calcutta, you measure the distance in terms of time taken and not kilometres, Sir,' said the amiable lady at the Reception when Dev told her that it had taken him nearly two hours that day to get to the hotel.

Eklavya had been in Calcutta since 1989 with Ellinson Hindustan Ltd., though as Brand Manager he had a hectic travel schedule. Luv was away when Dev visited Calcutta for the first time but during his second trip Luv came over to the hotel to meet Dev. 'Pack up your bags and come to my house,' he told Dev. 'I am in Alipore Park Road, hardly 15 minutes away.'

Dev smiled, 'During one of my next trips, Eklavya; have a few meetings lined up in the hotel business centre this time.'

'Dev how can you even think of being in a hotel when I am here,' said Luv, 'I am by myself in a three-bedroom furnished flat, I have a visiting cook, just stay with me. Even if I am travelling you can stay at my flat.'

'Certainly Eklavya, during one of my next trips.'

'Stay with me every time you are here Dev, I come to your house as my right, so should you.'

Dev gently touched Luv's shoulder.

That evening Luv took Dev to Kusum Rolls on Park Street for dinner. 'There is a place just beneath Kwality's on Park Street, they make the best chicken and veg-rolls in Calcutta,' said Luv. The all-yellow-coloured Ambassador taxis were conspicuous as were the traffic police personnel in their distinctive white uniform. 'You know that the traffic direction reverses at 2 pm in the Chowringhee–Park Street–Camac Street area,' remarked Luv, and then as they were driving on Russel Street, he pointed out to Dev a little outlet where people were standing and having tea, 'the best chai in the world at this place.'

Dev loved the old-world charm of Calcutta, those narrow streets, that frequent drizzle, that fragrance coming from marriage between water and earth and grass, and the evident simplicity of the individual on the road. People in Calcutta did not seem to be in any kind of rat race whatsoever! As they were enjoying the rolls Dev saw a human rickshaw where a frail man was pulling the cart with two passengers sitting on a small seat. Dev himself had sat on a cycle rickshaw a few times in Old Delhi and indeed used them frequently in Kanpur, but here a man was running barefoot carrying two persons behind him for a few rupees. Dev was gripped by the irony: Bengal had been at the forefront of India's national movement yet the Victoria Memorial stood in the centre of the city in splendour, the state had had the longest serving Communist government and here was a human being pulling a rickshaw and the passengers didn't seem to have any compunction on their faces. At least the rickshaw puller was earning his livelihood, not begging for it! Everything can be justified or criticized in this world, there are takers for all ideas and ideologies and beliefs, except perhaps human pain.

On one of his subsequent trips to Calcutta, Dev took the Sunday afternoon flight and drove straight to Luv's apartment on Alipore Park Road. Luv was chatting with a young lady in the building lobby as Dev reached his place. He gave Dev a warm hug and introduced him to the lady, 'This is Devavratt, my very close friend from Delhi, and Dev, this is Asha, they live in the flat opposite mine.'

Asha gave Dev a warm smile and said to Luv, 'Do get your friend over to our place while he is here.'

'Nice neighbours you have, Eklavya', said Dev as he and Luv walked into the latter's flat.

'Yes, Asha in particular is very friendly, her husband is reserved,' said Luv.

'They are from Bengal?' enquired Dev.

'They have been living in Calcutta for ages, but they are Garodia—*Marwaris*. *Marwaris* are very successful business people in Calcutta. Her husband is busy with his business all the time. Asha is originally from Allahabad, she is our age and a smart girl, wonder how she got stuck with a pot-bellied man.'

Dev laughed. 'Someday we all will bald and be embarrassed about our waist size!'

'Gosh', said Luv, 'the guy seems almost 15 years elder to her.'

'Haven't you found any nice single woman here?' asked Dev as Luv showed him into one of the bedrooms.

'You freshen up and then I will tell you about the women in my life.'

Dev had recently started having beer. After he had unpacked his bag, Luv showed him rest of the apartment and poured a glass of beer both for his house guest and himself. 'So wonderful to have you over Dev,' said Luv touching his beer mug with Dev's.

'To your happiness, Eklavya.'

'How is Meher?' asked Luv.

'She is well, feels a little sad that I am having to travel every second week to Calcutta.'

'Get her along on your next trip, this little flat is always yours.' Dev warmly smiled at Luv.

'So, six years in Calcutta; home for you now!'

'It took me a while to settle down here Dev, but I have had a lovely time. Professional life has been good, won't say great, but the social life is terrific,' said Luv finishing almost half his glass of beer in two gulps.

'Can't wait to hear about that,' said Dev with just that little hint of mischief in his smile.

Luv laughed. 'I have to be careful what I say, don't want to be told off for—what's that term you use—cultural stereotyping.'

'Your home, your city,' said Dev with a big smile.

'My colleagues in EHL here are really easy going and get to office around 11 o'clock. But they are exceedingly well read and articulate. Do you know the biggest book fairs happen in Calcutta and parents gift Encyclopaedia Britannica to their daughters in marriage!'

'I recall you also told Biswas, my senior in Torsh, that your team members and boss speak in Bengali even in your presence,' said Dev sipping the beer.

'Oh yes, I experience that even during social get-togethers, but now I am able to understand Bengali.'

'I think people here have a lot of pride in their culture' said Dev, 'this is a land of great culture and creativity.'

'Dev, my colleagues tend to argue so much even over simple procedural matters, but you know, outside office if I ask them for any help, not one of them will refuse.'

'There is very strong community feeling also here, isn't it?' enquired Dev.

'Absolutely, great sense of community, people stand up for and look after each other, something that I find missing in north India.'

Luv poured himself another glass of beer while Dev was still nursing his first glass. 'Now that I am feeling slightly high let me tell you about my experience with the women here,' said Luv as Dev laughed. 'Once again, only about the ladies I have interacted with in office, our advertising firm and my little social circle, lest you check me for—what's that term you use—cultural archetype!'

Dev was smiling at his straightforward friend.

'Most of the ladies in office, our ad firm and women I know socially are smart and cultured, very feminine and well spoken, confident and uncomplicated.'

'Yes, women are quite liberated here and men are *bhadralok*, they give a lot of respect to the ladies,' added Dev.

Luv looked at Dev, 'Though my middle-aged landlord and his wife, staying in the apartment just above, quarrel every night after both have had their drink.'

'When men and women are equal in all respects then some clash is inevitable,' Dev thought aloud, 'in fact, hasn't the society here always been quite liberal!'

Luv was almost half-way through his second glass as well, '*Yaar*, I don't know about the past, but you are very right about the respect that women are given here. Any lady, who people don't know, in the street or market or tram, is addressed as *Didi*; when a girl child is born the male members of the family address her as "Ma". I think it comes from the fact that Mother Goddess, Durga and Kali, is so deeply worshipped.'

Just then the doorbell rang, it was Luv's cook. '*Kemon achen dada*?' she greeted Luv.

Luv introduced her to Dev; she folded her hands and greeted him. Dev got up and folded his hands as well, 'Namaste.'

After a brief chat, Luv told Dev, 'She will make *khao-suey* for you, it's a Burmese dish and she makes it so well I could die eating it.'

The lady looked at Dev, 'Dada, fish curry?'

'This Dada doesn't eat fish,' said Luv pointing towards Dev, 'just make *khao-suey* today and tomorrow you can make fish for me and some *daal-chawal* for Dada.'

The lady cook laughed a little. 'Dada, *mishti*?' she checked with Luv if she should prepare a pudding.

'*Mishti doi*, *rasogolla*, *chamcham* from that New Alipore shop—in fridge,' said Luv with a wink.

The lady cook laughed and said in English to Luv, 'Very good, Dada!'

Luv would generally make people around him happy.

Luv picked up his third beer, 'Dev you are too slow.'

'I have just one glass, Eklavya.'

'I am having so much because I am so thrilled to see you, but your limited consumption indicates how happy you are to see me,' remarked Luv pulling Dev's leg.

'Sit,' said Dev waving his left hand, 'and pray continue.'

'Did I mention the plunging necklines of the lady who is our Account Manager in the ad firm and Mrs Chatterjee whose husband I play golf with?'

Dev smiled ever so slightly and said, 'Women can express themselves freely here, they are equal in all respects, what you are describing is an outcome of a healthy liberated society.'

'How I wish north India too was like this!' continued Luv, 'Unfortunately, there is crime against women everywhere but the prevalence of eve-teasing in north India is shameful. You know we lived all over India as my father was in the services, my sisters were fearful only in Delhi. My younger sister is in Bombay now, at times she comes home past midnight in an auto, she feels absolutely safe, no problem.'

'Even in north, Eklavya; you remember on *ashtami*, my uncle washes the feet of little girls who are called home for *puja*.'

'Yes, my father does the same,' said Luv.

'We all north Indians go to Vaishno Devi, in fact, in *Sanatana Dharma* itself, one of the conceptions of the supreme power is *Ardhnareshwar* or 'half man half woman'. India must be one of the few democracies, if not the only one, where universal adult franchise was granted to all adult men and women immediately upon Independence with the enactment of the Constitution.'

Luv looked enquiringly at Dev, 'So you are saying that women have always had equal status, perhaps even preeminent in some respects, across India. Then why is there such a perceptible difference in Delhi and north India as compared to say Calcutta and Bombay?'

'We should ask a sociologist Eklavya,' said Dev, 'I don't know what the numbers are in terms of crime against women in different metros of India, but my perception is same as yours. Very clearly places like Calcutta and Madras, and to a large extent Bombay, have a strong homogenous culture. They are capital cities of culturally rich states, but Delhi is a melting-pot, large floating population too, literacy levels in surrounding areas of Delhi are not as high as Calcutta or Bombay or South India. But you are right, community here is steeped in reverence to Ma Durga.'

'There is no doubt that Bengal has very rich culture,' said Luv.

'You know you were earlier saying that your colleagues are easy going when it comes to work,' said Dev thoughtfully, 'I think people here are more into the finer things of life—art, literature, Rabindra *sangeet*…'

'Satyajit Ray, Suchitra Sen…' added Luv.

Dev continued, 'We have had the greatest of thinkers and playwrights—Swami Vivekanand, who said in the previous century that space and time are the creators of creation, and this was much before Theory of Relativity or Quantum Physics.'

'Fascinating, Dev!' said Luv.

'"Vande Mataram" was composed by Bankim Chandra Chatterjee in *Anandamath*.'

'I always associated art, music, literature and films with Bengal but it had not crossed my mind that this land has given great religious leaders too,' noted Luv.

'Religious leaders and social reformists Eklavya, not to forget the leaders who spearheaded the national movement,' said Dev as Luv nodded. 'Chaitanya Mahaprabhu started ISKCON,' Dev continued, reflecting on the history of the land which he and Luv had been discussing for nearly two hours.

'Ah, the ISKCON society, they have a centre here in Mayapur, would you like to visit Dev? Oh, but you are not religious right?'

Dev gave Luv a gentle look and said, 'Krishna is all inspiring Eklavya, the fountainhead of The *Gita*. Ishwar Chandra Vidyasagar the renowned educationist who championed widow remarriage in the 19th century; and then of course, Subhash Chandra Bose. This is an amazing cradle of nationalists, artists, reformers and great thinkers. On my last visit here, I was meeting the GM of our old Torsh Chemicals, we got chatting on similar lines and he reminded me of an old saying—What Bengal thinks today, India thinks tomorrow.'

'*Esho*, Dada,' said the cook, calling Luv and Dev for dinner.

'You know, Dev, in all these years I have never heard you speak as much as you spoke this evening, you should have beer more regularly.'

Dev laughed, as they both got up and started moving towards the dining table.

'Secondly, I understand why you caution against cultural stereotyping. I used to tell Sandeep that you are a kill-joy, but I suppose every city, every community, every country must be having lots to be proud of which we should try and appreciate.'

'Eklavya, I never meant that we should not objectively evaluate or have a good-hearted laugh at the diversity and unique differences of various regions. Humour is the oxygen of life and mature societies should be able to laugh at themselves; all I have implied is that we should not let cultural differences become prejudices because that impedes both professional decision making and personal relationships. Of course, humour should not offend anyone, that's why the best jokes are those that we make on ourselves.'

Luv nodded in agreement. 'Sit', he said pulling out the chair at the dining table, 'and let me tell you about Poulomi Sen.'

'Poulomi is in the HR team in EHL, same office,' said Luv, 'we have been going out for about six months now; it's become a romantic involvement, she is lovely.'

'Romantic involvement as in?' enquired Dev.

'It's not a fling or a passing affair. We are both serious.'

'Someone in office is generally avoidable, Eklavya.'

'I know, Dev, if things progress then one of us will have to leave EHL.'

'Are you saying you are contemplating marriage?' Luv nodded.

'What's holding you back?'

'*Yaar*, I met her mother a couple of months back, she is a very polished lady but scary looking. Big piercing eyes, long frilly hair, mouth gets twisted when she speaks and when she laughs her heavy shoulders go up and down. And I believe girls start looking like their mothers over time.'

Dev laughed loudly, 'And how do you think you will look a quarter century later!'

'That's for Poulomi to worry about,' said Luv deviously.

'If this is the reason, this is no reason.'

'This and the fact that we are both in the same company and one of us will have to leave EHL.'

'Jobs come and go, Eklavya. If you both like each other then what can be better than having a nice life partner and a happy family!'

'Yeah, you are right, and for either of us finding another job won't be difficult, she too is a qualified MBA.'

'Pour me just two sips of beer,' said Dev, and then lifting his glass he toasted, 'To Eklavya and Poulomi!'

Luv looked at Dev with affection and smiled warmly.

Luv asked Dev to come into his room for coffee; he got onto his bed and reclined on a few pillows against the head-rest, while Dev took the single sofa chair lying next to the bed. 'What's this?' said Dev looking amusingly towards Luv's writing table on which, amongst other things, was a plastic straw with lipstick mark on it!

Luv had a sheepish look on his face. 'Mrs Chatterjee's,' he said.

Dev had a bemused look.

'I told you—that one of the persons I play golf with; his wife, she wears low cut blouses!'

'And?' Dev was curious.

'She has the most prominent and shapely bum! I can't get it off my mind. A few days back I had called my golf friends home for dinner with their wives. Sharmistha Chatterjee, she insists I call her Sharmistha, was also over and she sipped coke with this straw!'

Dev was still dazed, 'So what do you do with this straw?'

Luv gave him a wicked look, 'Cheap thrills, Dev.'

Dev put his hand to his forehead and laughed. 'How old is she?'

'Mid-forties,' said Luv.

'You have a thing for older women.'

'I do,' accepted Luv. 'But it's not my fault, this older woman fantasy and the fact that I have become an ass-man is all due to Purnima, my sister's friend.'

'Of course,' remarked Dev, 'you are as innocent as a rose.' The two friends laughed. 'Does Mrs Chatterjee know how fortunate she is to have a young handsome admirer?' said Dev wryly.

'I think she does, Dev, I do that typical flirting with her—"you know, I can't believe you have a 20-year-old son" —she laughs every time I say something like this.'

Before this strand of chat finished Dev asked Luv, 'By the way how old is Poulomi?'

'She is exactly one month older to me.'

Dev smiled ever so gently.

'Incidentally, I was thinking Dev, of all the great thinkers, artists and leaders you spoke about, you didn't mention a single cricketer.'

'There have been some good cricketers also from here, and who knows the next cricket star might come from Bengal.'

Dev was right. A year later, Sourav Ganguly made his Test debut for India and not only did he get a century in his first match, but in a few years' time went onto becoming one of the finest Indian cricket captain of all time.

As the two friends sipped coffee, Dev saw the *Gayatri mantra* embossed on a beautiful wooden plate hanging on the wall in a corner of the room and beneath it on a small table were kept framed pictures of gods and goddesses. Luv had always been very religious. 'My mother chants the *Gayatri* 108 times a day,' said Luv as he saw Dev intently looking at the *Gayatri*.

Dev smiled back at Luv, 'It is the most powerful *mantra* and prayer.'

Luv's expression turned a little solemn, 'What exactly is a *mantra* Dev?'

'*Mantra*s are transcendental expressions discerned at very high levels of self-reflection or meditation, usually by the *rishi*s and sages,' said Dev, 'the *Gayatri mantra* was given by *Rishi* Vishwamitra.'

Luv was listening to Dev absorbedly, 'Tell me more Dev, what does it exactly mean and why is it chanted 108 times?'

Dev shared whatever he knew about the *Gayatri*, 'The *Gayatri mantra* is mentioned both in the *Rig Ved* and *Yajur Ved*; it encapsulates the essence of Vedic knowledge. It can be somewhat differently interpreted, essentially it's a prayer to the all illuminating force—you may infer The Sun—simply put it means: May the light that illuminates the three worlds inspire and liberate my mind such that I can receive the knowledge of

Brahman the supreme reality. Chanting the *Gayatri*, which is also symbolized as a goddess, enlightens the intellect, liberates the mind from the duality of 'mine' and 'thine' and makes us receptive to the truth.'

Luv looked at Dev admiringly, '*Brahman* the supreme reality is not Brahma the creator, right?'

Dev nodded, '*Brahman* as I understand is reality of creation and destruction and creation, the universal energy which transforms but doesn't perish.'

'You mentioned *rishi*, is there a difference between *Rishi* and *Brahmrishi*?' asked Luv.

'*Rishi* is sage, *Maharishi* would be a great sage and *Brahmrishi* would be a sage who has transcended ego. I think sage Vishwamitra was eventually *Brahmrishi*.'

'So the analogy could be star, superstar and megastar,' said Luv.

Dev smiled back. Luv was curious to know more, 'And what is the significance of chanting it 108 times as my mother does, in fact, 108 seems to have some deeper implication isn't it, we have 108 beads in a *mala* too?'

'Yes,' said Dev, '108 is significant not just in Hinduism but some other faiths also. The number represents creation and existence.'

'Creation and existence!' exclaimed Luv sitting up in the bed.

'In Mathematics 108 is referred to as the abundant number, scientifically the distance between the Sun to Earth is 108 times its diameter, the distance between Moon to Earth is also 108 times the Moon's diameter. Shiva had 108 *shivaganas* or attendants; likewise Krishna had 108 *gopikas* as his followers in Vrindavan. Penelope, the devoted and loyal wife of Odysseus in Homer's Odyssey, was said to have 108 suitors. Chanting the *Gayatri* 108 times is said to bring us in harmony with nature and the universe.'

Luv's eyes were unblinkingly transfixed on Dev, 'What do you mean harmony with nature and universe, can you illustrate that a little?'

'At one plane to be in harmony with nature means to be one with it, to detach the mind from our body and observe ourselves too just as we observe fellow human beings and our surroundings. At quite another level, have you ever experienced that when you are feeling lonely or disappointed and there is merriment in the environment, you only feel sadder. A lonely person is in harmony with a poignant environment, and vice-versa.'

Luv was listening to every word that Dev was saying; he enquired further, 'How does 108 represent creation and existence?'

Dev recited a verse of Neeraj in response to Luv's question:

'Brahm roop hei ank nau, prakati roop hei aath,
Ek satya hei shoonya mei, simti srishti viraat!'

Loosely translated in English:

Creation is represented by nine, nature is symbolized by eight,
The universe is a grand-zero, that is the one truth straight!

'So Eklavya, 1 plus 0 plus 8, the three digits of 108, is 9. As Neeraj's verse so beautifully sums it up, number 9 represents the universal energy or *Brahman*, which can neither be created nor destroyed. Thus 9 times 3 is 27, 2 plus 7 is 9, 9 times 4 is 36, 3 plus 6 is 9. So 9 never changes, the supreme truth or universal force always remains perpetual. Humankind or human *atma* is symbolized by 8 which is ever diminishing till it meets the universal energy. Thus 8 times 2 is 16, 1 plus 6 is 7, 8 times 3 is 24, 2 plus 4 is 6, 8 times 4 is 32, 3 plus 2 is 5. But when 8 meets 9, 8 times 9 is 72 and 7 plus 2 becomes 9 again. So eventually, as our existence, simply put our age diminishes, human energy or *atma* subsumes itself in universal energy and becomes complete again. In this vast nothingness, in this massive zero, this is the one single truth, encapsulated in these four numbers and 108 is an expression of this creation and existence.'

Luv looked at Dev mesmerizingly, 'This is absolutely fascinating, Dev. But for someone who is not religious, how do you know all this?'

'Depends what you describe as religion, Eklavya,' said Dev.

'And how do you describe it?' questioned Luv.

'Self-reflection,' said Dev.

'One final question on the *Gayatri*...' continued Luv, 'my mother calls it *Sarvdevata Gayatri*. Why is that?'

Dev smiled ever so slightly, 'That's because every single syllable of the *Gayatri Mantra*, represents a god.'

'Dev, I don't know whether or not you are religious, but I marvel at your understanding of Hinduism,' said Luv.

'Hinduism and *Sanatana Dharma* from where it emanates, is a way of life, a scientific enquiry into nature and man's relationship with nature. You can be an atheist or an agnostic or a believer or an idol worshipper or an *Arya Samaji*, you are still a Hindu. It is completely pluralistic and liberal. No single founder, no compulsory belief, no organised place or method of worship, no single sacred book,' said Dev.

'Are you sure you can be an atheist and still be a Hindu?' asked Luv.

Dev nodded.

'Then, apart from being born a Hindu, are there any other distinguishing principles?' asked Luv who had been sitting upright in bed for quite a while now.

'I think, Eklavya, a belief in spirit or *atma* that is eternal and time being cyclical and not linear, are the main distinguishing principles,' replied Dev.

'Tell me, Dev, Sandeep mentioned that you once told him Hinduism and modern science and Neeraj's poetry all have a convergence, just explain this to me.'

'I find a clear convergence between *sanatana* principles, modern science and Neeraj's poetry. The *shrutis* that is Vedas and Upanishads are the spiritual heart of Hinduism, since spirituality by itself can be abstract and prosaic; we have the *smritis* like *Mahabharata* and *Ramayana* which make the spirituality vibrant. Likewise, Neeraj writes spiritual poetry laced with romance, his body of work is not only profound and classy but also popular. I have heard him say a few times in his concerts that "he who you are looking at is not Neeraj, Neeraj is someone else", so he distinguishes between essence and form. Hinduism too focuses on the spirit or *atma* distinct from the mere physicality. Similarly modern quantum physics describes nature at the atomic and subatomic level, unlike the traditional mechanical physics which studies objects and their motion,' explained Dev.

It was past 1 am but Luv was in no mood to sleep. He was too engrossed in Dev's eclectic elucidation. 'Another cup of coffee?' he asked Dev.

'Don't you have office tomorrow morning?' said Dev.

'I told you most of my colleagues reach by 11 am only.'

Dev softly laughed, 'Sure, my first meeting is also at 11:30.'

Luv prepared two cups of coffee, 'Continue Dev, this is too interesting!' he said handing over one cup to his friend.

Dev continued, 'Hinduism's belief in time being cyclical, and not linear from minus infinity to plus infinity, is consistent with the Big Bang theory according to which creation started after the big 'explosion' when space and time started expanding. Similarly, Vishnu's *dashavtar*, the ten incarnations, mirror Darwin's theory of human evolution.'

'So Dev, you are saying that what modern scientists discovered, the Indian sages too had discovered?' asked Luv.

'Yes, the sages reflected inwards for answers while the scientists analysed the external environment.'

'And they arrived at the same answers?' asked Luv.

'They did. That's why the essence of Hinduism and modern science are not in conflict with each other, they converge.'

'This is spellbinding!' said Luv, and then somewhat changing the topic he asked, 'Dev is there any right way to live?'

Dev had a somewhat lost look in his eyes, 'I suppose living without harming anyone physically or emotionally,' said he.

'That's all?' replied Luv. 'So nothing is good or bad, right or wrong?'

'Definition of right or wrong keeps changing with times Eklavya, what is morally wrong today will become socially acceptable tomorrow and law of the land day after. We are all products of the times we live in, and time is never still, so right and wrong cannot be cast in stone.'

'So, right wrong good bad are machinations of the mind,' remarked Luv.

'That's well put,' replied Dev sipping his second cup of coffee.

'That makes so much sense to me. Yesterday I was hearing a sports commentator say that Gavaskar played when India was in socialist times and there used to be rationing and so his batting was cautious and studied, while Tendulkar lives in a free market India largely devoid of shortages and where stock market is booming and that reflects in his batting which is bolder.'

Dev smiled. 'Four-five hundred years ago when the Bhakti movement was sweeping India, the literature and poetry was devotional—Kabir, Guru Nanak, Tulsidas, Meera—would have both influenced and been inspired by those times, while in the current century literature and poetry has been relatively more humanistic and iconoclastic. So time changes thinking and expression and values, that's why it is futile and unfounded to hold rigid opinions.'

By about 3 am, Dev couldn't keep his eyes open anymore.

'Dev, one last question and then we'll sleep. Our *Sanatana* principles are based on scientific enquiry and you say one can be a Hindu while being an atheist. So why were temples made, I for one love the energy in temples.'

Dev responded, 'Temples were meant to connect us to the cosmic dimension, just as our radios and TVs catch electromagnetic waves, temples are meant to help us experience the divine energy. That's why the deities are energized, you have heard of the term *pran-pratistha*?'

Luv nodded.

Dev continued, '*Pran-pratistha* means to infuse deities with energy, there is subtle difference between instilling life and infusing energy, but a temple can be established only after the *pran-pratistha puja*, that's why it belongs to the deity. And that's why we sense energy in temples, we feel connected to the divine power, we feel positive and some people can't hold their tears as the energy overwhelms them. So temples are the gateways to the universal force, the source from which humankind is created. Indeed there is science in temples too. In addition, of course, several temples are repository of art and culture, they reflect history of their time.'

Dev was getting up from his chair; his eyelids were heavy with sleep. 'Dev,' said Luv, even as Dev got up from his chair to go to his bedroom, 'this has been an evening to remember.'

Dev gently smiled at Luv and touched him on his shoulder, 'Goodnight.'

'By the way, how long will your 11.30 meeting last for?' checked Luv.

'2 hours.'

'And you would be in the Chowringhee area?'

'Yes.'

'So let's meet for lunch at Saturday Club at half past one, I will call Poulomi also,' suggested Luv.

'Sounds wonderful!' said Dev after thinking for a split second.

***

Dev had started hiring people for the Eastern Zone. The GM of Roqsanto Torsh Chemicals Ltd. had allotted a space in their office for Hindustan Roqsanto Ltd to use. 25 Torsh dealers in Calcutta, Durgapur and Siliguri, had been chosen for the initial launch of Roqsanto branded adhesives, resins and cleaning polishing products. 2nd September 1995 was decided as the official date for launch in Eastern Zone. Billboards were to start going up in the three Bengal cities from mid-August and a press conference planned for last week of August. Karan Varma, Adam Wouters and Dev were to address the press and announce entry of Roqsanto in Eastern India. Dev's meeting at 11:30 am with the GM of Torsh was to discuss details of these issues. He met a couple of candidates who had applied for sales jobs, discussed the Dealer Contract with the GM and local Sales Manager of Torsh, checked on the progress of sales tax registration and met the Ad firm representatives to finalise locations of hoardings. By 1:30 pm he left for Saturday Club to have lunch with Luv and Poulomi.

Poulomi was a lovely young lady, very cultured and smart and articulate. The moment Dev met her he sensed that Luv and she would make a charming couple. They chatted about the enchanting old clubs of Calcutta which Poulomi described as the 'mainstay of *khandani* Calcuttans'. When Dev enquired about members of these exclusive clubs she said, 'There are corporate members and also, in Bengal and Calcutta clubs particularly, the *bonedi* families.' She explained later that *bonedi* were the old and aristocratic families of Calcutta. The three of them chatted about life in the four metros and compared the culture of Bengal and Tamil Nadu with north India.

Luv put his arm around Poulomi and said, 'Polly, this man sitting across us, deducts marks for cultural stereotyping.'

Poulomi smiled at Dev who gently said, 'You know Eklavya better than I do.'

Poulomi shared her experience of Delhi, 'Bengal and Tamil Nadu are undoubtedly culturally very rich while Delhi is heterogeneous, but unlike in Calcutta and also Madras, where amongst the highly educated classes there is a touch of intellectual arrogance, in Delhi I never sensed such a sense of intellectual superiority amongst the well-placed people.'

'Delhi is about power Polly,' said Luv, 'money and contacts, not intellectual arrogance but material display.'

'And what has your experience been like?' Poulomi asked Dev.

Dev replied in a studied manner, 'I love the colourful energy of Delhi, the sea-side serenity of Madras and the unhurried simplicity of Calcutta.'

'You speak poetry, Devavratt,' observed Poulomi.

As they were driving back home in the evening and talking about the day, and Dev was telling Luv how much he enjoyed meeting and speaking with Poulomi, they saw some devotees of the ISKCON society chanting '*Hare Rama, Hare Krishna*'.

'Dev, I have sometimes wondered why they chant both Ram and Krishna, when it is international society for Krishna consciousness!' remarked Luv.

'I can tell you what I understood about *Hare Rama Hare Krishna* listening to Neeraj,' said Dev.

'I must start listening to Neeraj myself,' said Luv more as a reminder to himself, 'do tell me what you understood.'

'Ram is *Maryada Purushottam*, the upholder of *maryada* or honour; whereas Krishna is *Leela Purushottam*, the ultimate conjuror, *leela* meaning play or spectacle. Krishna is the *karmyogi* who honours responsibilities while moving societal norms forward. Ram represents the sole element of the universe, the universal energy; while Krishna—from the root *krsh* comes the word *aakarshan* or attraction—is ruler of the senses. When we see something nice our eyes get attracted, when we hear something melodic our ears get attracted, so Krishna helps us to experience Ram. For without our senses, we would not be able to feel the source of creation. Thus, life is complete with both Ram and Krishna, awareness of the universal force and awareness of self, hence the chant "*Hare Rama Hare Krishna*."'

'Marvellous, Dev, absolutely *marvellous*!'

Luv and Dev had another engaging conversation that evening mainly around options for Luv should he leave EHL after marriage with Poulomi. Luv was also keen to hear Dev's views on 'mythology versus history' to which Dev said, 'Ram and Krishna are great historical characters, terming history as mythology is almost conspiratorial.'

The next day Luv took Dev to Tollygunge Club for lunch, and in the evening Luv's neighbour Asha invited them over for coffee. Dev flew back to Delhi by the Thursday late-morning flight.

In late August, the MD of HRL Karan Singh Varma and the Sales and Marketing Head Adam Wouters landed in Calcutta for the press conference and also to review the preparedness for the launch of Roqsanto in Eastern Zone. 'Do you foresee any hitches with the launch and subsequent operations?' enquired Karan.

'Logistics is an issue here Karan,' said Dev, 'it took almost two weeks for the first set of lorries to reach Calcutta from the India Rasayanik plant in Pune. We cannot afford stock-out situations, definitely not at the start nor later. Then of course, there are regional differences in terms of infrastructure, industrial technology, price sensitivity and approach to business, and law and order in some places, which we have to address.'

Karan heard Dev carefully and then said, 'You have started well, let's keep the operation low cost. We have identified a candidate to be the Zonal Sales Manager for East, but he joins only by end October. So you need to manage the zone till then and perhaps a few weeks later for the hand-over and parallel run.'

'Is my posting decided?' enquired Dev.

Karan looked at Adam who said, 'Not yet, but as indicated earlier it would be either the North or West or Southern Zone—Delhi or Bombay or Madras, perhaps by year end or early next year. Any preference?'

'I am fine with any zone, just need a permanent posting so my wife and I can feel a bit settled,' said Dev.

Karan and Adam acknowledged Dev's position with a nod. 'Well done, keep going!' Karan gave a pat on Dev's back.

Two days before the launch, with all preparations done and about a dozen hoardings up in Calcutta and half a dozen in Durgapur and Siliguri, Dev woke up in his hotel room feeling under the weather. He took a paracetamol and tried to sleep. At about 10 am he got a call from one of the newly recruited sales executives saying that there appeared to be a problem with the dealers.

'What kind of problem?' asked Dev.

'They are indicating that they will not go ahead with the launch!' said the sales executive.

'What? Why?' Dev was taken aback.

'They are all in the Torsh office, all 25 of them, I think you should meet them Dev.'

Dev was feeling quite unwell and not quite in a position to step out. But if the dealers were refusing to launch it would be disastrous and almost signal the end of his job with Roqsanto. 'Ok, I will be there by 12:30 pm,' he told the sales executive.

When he entered the conference room in the Torsh office he saw all the 25 dealers: 23 middle aged men and two ladies including the smart Mrs Dhupar who used to run the dealership in Alipore in Calcutta. Dev sat down at the head of the table, 'Good afternoon, I hear all is not well.'

'Sir, we cannot proceed with the launch...*hobe na, hobe na*...you are discriminating,' said one of the middle-aged dealers who appeared to be the leader or nominated spokesman.

Dev had a puzzled look on his face. 'Which action of ours are you in disagreement with?' asked Dev feeling quite unwell.

'Sir, we are 160 Torsh dealers in Eastern Zone, and you have selected only 25, this is most unfair to our brothers and sisters, *hobe na*.'

Dev was stupefied, 'We have to start somewhere, we don't have the product or people to launch at all 160 simultaneously, as we expand we will offer distributorship to some and dealerships to most of the Torsh dealer community in East, it's after all the same parent company now.'

'No no, Sir, this is *bhery* wrong step, how our brothers are feeling you have any idea! *Hobe na*, Mr Rajvansh.'

Dev tried to reason with the dealers for about 15-20 minutes but his logical assurance was met with '*hobe na*,' meaning 'not happening'. Finally Dev said, 'I have been trying to tell you that we will cover all dealers in phases, but it seems there is something in my face that you are not taking me seriously.'

Hearing this Mrs Dhupar was the first to burst out laughing, followed by smiles and amused looks on the countenance of 24 others. 'Souvik da, let's accept what Mr Rajvansh is saying,' she said looking at the dealer who had been leading the discussions.

That day Dev realised how important humour is in management and leadership situations. As the meeting ended one by one the dealers came upto Dev and said, 'Dada, we have to show this protest; you please don't worry, we are committed to the launch.'

The launch in Bengal was successful. As the weeks rolled on Dev hired more staff and established stockists in Bhubaneswar, Jamshedpur and Patna as well. The Roqsanto products were successfully launched in all these markets. In Bhubaneswar, Dev had a wonderful evening with Sudhir, who by now had moved to Raipur in Madhya Pradesh and was visiting Bhubaneswar for a meeting. Sudhir's personality was similar to Dev's, he was thoughtful and devoted to his work. However, as Luv had observed, '75% of Kapoor's mind is focused only on his family and work, but that remaining 25% contains wackiness'. Sudhir used to feel absolutely free with Dev and they would laugh non-stop at each other's humour and wit when together. Sudhir used to love singing Hindi film songs but as Dev noted, 'Sudhir loves singing only flop songs!' Dev carried an audio cassette for Sudhir, it was a collection of Neeraj's film songs and the cassette was titled 'The People's Poet'. 'Something that has both literary class and lyrical melody', said Dev handing over the cassette to Sudhir.

During the Bihar launch, Dev and two of his colleagues boarded an overnight train from Jamshedpur to Patna scheduled to take seven hours. At Jamshedpur station the enquiry room was unmanned: Dev found his colleague Nirbhay Jha, who was local to the region, speaking into a solitary mike placed inside the enquiry room to check the arrival time of the train. From somewhere a voice came: 'Purnia Express is running 20 minutes late today'.

Nirbhay Jha explained to Dev, 'Earlier the enquiry room was manned, but on a few occasions the poor attendant was bashed up by miscreants when he informed them the train was running late! So now it's unmanned.'

The train Dev and his colleagues had boarded kept stopping every 15 minutes. Nirbhay Jha described what was going on, 'It is being flagged down at every village. Sir, we are travelling 2nd AC but in the second sitting class—in one or two trains, not necessarily this one—the window railings in the compartments are broken, villagers flag the train down and then to 'reserve' their seat throw their kid onto the berth from the window!'

That day it took the Roqsanto executives 17 hours to reach Patna!

Adam Wouters called a Zonal Sales Managers meeting in Delhi a week before Christmas. During lunch time he called Dev into his cabin and extended his hand, 'Congratulations, ZSM South!'

Dev took a minute to register, then thanked him and thought to himself, 'Madras again!' He was happy. He immediately called Meher and informed her. Before the meeting ended in the evening Wouters announced Dev's new appointment, the next day a memo was issued to this effect within the organisation.

Dev did a farewell trip to Calcutta. The dealers and staff were very sad to see him go. The Alipore dealer Mrs Dhupar remarked, 'I will always remember how you rose to the occasion in that difficult August meeting.' One of the dealers who Dev had appointed a stockist was misty eyed as he shook Dev's hand for the last time. Dev spent his last evening in Calcutta with Luv who told him he had formally proposed to Poulomi and that they would marry in the February of 1996.

Dev and Meher found a lovely flat on Sterling Road in Madras to rent. It was not very far from Spurtank Students Hall where eight years ago Dev had spent two unforgettable months. He was also just 10-minutes' drive from Nungambakkam High Road where Roqsanto's regional office had already been set up. Dev felt he had a deeper connection with Madras.

He had hardly been in Madras for a week when he got a call from Muthuraman who was a summer trainee in 1987 and Dev's classmate Jigsaw's room partner in Spurtank Students Hall all those years back. 'Dev da, I too am in Madras!'

That evening Muthuraman and his wife Shaila visited Dev and Meher. They had a two-year-old son who they had left at home with Shaila's mother. Meher and Shaila discovered a common interest in astrology. 'We have a family astrologer,' she said to Meher, 'he works in a post office in Anna Nagar, very simple man, but brilliant in astrology. Would you like to meet him?'

The following week while Dev was at office, finding his feet in a new business and work environment, Shaila picked up Meher and took her to the elderly slender looking expressionless astrologer.

He studied Dev's horoscope and also Meher's and then said to her, 'What would you like to know Madam?'

'Anything that you find striking?' said Meher.

'Madam, Sir has a polarized horoscope.'

'What exactly does that mean?' enquired Meher.

'He will have unexpected success and unexpected setback in his life,' said the astrologer.

'His health and job?'

'He will do very well in his job. Your horoscope adds strength to his professional achievement.'

Both the ladies smiled a bit. 'Longevity?'

'Madam, I don't like to comment on that,' he said.

'He should outlive me that is all I want.'

'You will not be left crying when Sir departs,' said the simple looking astrologer without any expression on his face.

New Perspectives

The 1990s in India was a decade of momentous change and hope for my generation. It was also a period of scandals and deep anguish. I mentioned earlier the mayhem in Kashmir in 1990 and how that poetry of natural beauty was shred to shrieks, the assassination of former PM Rajiv Gandhi in 1991 and the Bombay bomb blasts of 1993 were likewise gruesome. While there were these horrific events in the early part of the decade, there was also a new economic dawn with the 1991 industrial liberalisation and boom in employment opportunities. The economic optimism got somewhat scarred by the Harshad Mehta securities scandal—if 'kickbacks' was the new word we learnt during the Bofors controversy and 'RDX' the new acronym due to growing terrorism, the new addition to our lexicon during the stock market scandal was 'scam'.

The 1990s belonged unquestionably to Sachin Tendulkar, having made his international debut in 1989 he stamped his class as the world's greatest batsman during the last decade of the century. Such was his phenomenon that when Sachin scored big runs the stock markets would go up! He brought happiness to the heart of every Indian, every time he came out to bat chants of 'Sachin, Sachin' reverberated in the stadium and spectators would hold up placards reading 'Cricket is my religion, Sachin is my God'. The growth of TV and progress of Sachin complemented each other: big money came into cricket as captive audiences sat enamoured in front of the TV! Socialising was incomplete without reference to certain other TV programmes and channels too, like MTV, Zee TV, Star Plus, *Bold and Beautiful, Baywatch, Aap ki Adalat* etc.

Indian women started finding expression to their potential making significant contribution in all walks of society. Young Indian ladies began winning international beauty pageants, Sushmita Sen and Aishwarya Rai being most notable. Freedom and equal opportunity for each human being to work and live as they like, irrespective of all nature bestowed and man created differences, subject to well-considered democratic civil laws, is the bedrock of global peace.

Cine stars like Juhi Chawla, Madhuri Dixit, Aamir Khan and Salman Khan, who had announced their arrival in late-1980s started ascending the popularity charts in the 1990's. Madhuri Dixit set the silver screen ablaze with racy songs like '*Dhak dhak karne laga*' and '*Choli ke peeche kya hei*'; however it was the new film pair of Govinda and Karishma Kapoor that had the nation shaking a leg with them.

As more and more multinationals started entering India, and young men and women began earning more than their parents, advertising too blossomed like never before. Some of the ads on TV became more popular than the programmes they were being aired with! 'I am a Complan boy, I am a Complan girl', 'I love you Rasna' and 'Whirlpool, Whirlpool' are fresh in memory. Pepsi and Coke were using film stars and cricketers to fiercely compete with each other and painting advertising media blue and red respectively. But despite these manifestations of commercial modernity, on a fateful day in 1995 the country held its breath as people called each other to mention that 'Lord Ganesh was drinking milk'.

The latter half of 1990s in India was also marked with political instability and coalition alliances. Between 1996 to 1999 the union government fell and was formed again as many as five times. Caste factor continued to linger in politics. Despite the political flux, India self-assuredly pulled off nuclear tests in 1998. The multi-sectoral change that my generation has witnessed in their lifetime is mind rattling. In no sector has this change been more pronounced than telecommunications and information technology. Pagers had a short shelf-life for general communication, as our hands got hold of mobile phones, for the first time, in late-1990s. Internet, e-commerce, mobile phones and e-mail that are essential as oxygen and water today, came to be understood by the educated common man during mid to late-1990s.

India was beginning to flourish economically as internal industry and external trade barriers were being reduced. As India exposed her industry to competition and internationalization it put the nation on a higher growth trajectory.

Different dimensions of social competition too started becoming discernible in the 1990s. The upwardly mobile were doing up their apartments to the best of their pockets and taste. Builder flats, where old-type independent 200 square yard houses would be rebuilt into three or four modern flats, started coming up. In certain localities in Delhi, I could sense a competition between neighbours on who would construct a higher builder home! Exotic holidays, foreign brand cars and destination weddings gave the higher income group an opportunity to differentiate and distinguish themselves. Nowadays, of course, pictures of these style, fun and comfort statements are posted on social media, in the late-1990s social media had not quite hatched. The 45-year-old professionally qualified husband, having seen a smart woman at a party in a designer dress would gift the same to his wife on their anniversary and the 40-year-old wife, consciously climbing the social ladder, having seen her friend's husband play golf, would suggest to her husband 'why don't you also play!' 'Work Hard and Play Hard' became an oft-heard phrase and terms like B2B and B2C entered the corporate offices. 100 crore people of India were beginning to aspire and dream.

The tree of human progress stands in the soil rich with dreams. Dev's dreams, as he found himself back in Madras in early 1996, were around his family, a home, a child, growing in his profession and making a few foreign trips. Much as though Luv thought highly of Dev's professional capabilities and leadership qualities, he remarked to me after his recent meetings with Dev in Calcutta, 'Our friend is too righteous; it won't be easy for him in the corporate world'.

Dev settled in easily in his new job, he had inherited a good running operation. The zonal office was already established, he didn't need to hire too many new people nor set up stockists and dealer network from scratch or chase sales tax registration numbers. He was responsible for sales and marketing of Roqsanto branded adhesives, resins, cleaning and polishing products in the four southern states, manage the sales force and run the regional office. He was still reporting to Wouters who was the head of sales and marketing for the company. Dev let the operation of the Zone run with its previous momentum for a couple of months, getting to know all the team members and understanding the business dynamics in Tamil Nadu, Karnataka, Kerala and Andhra Pradesh. Slowly, he started effecting changes. He commissioned two new stockists, expanded the channel of distribution by appointing a few non-Torsh dealers as distributors, reconfigured the Zone into four areas as per the four states and assigned an Area Sales Manager for each, ran local marketing campaigns to create excitement around the brands, launched sales promotion schemes for the trade, established sales and management information processes, and fairly and generously recognized his team members for success including the office boy Joseph. Off the shelf ERP systems were still not prevalent in the mid-1990s, and local software companies would design specific computer-based accounting packages for companies. From those manual ledgers and hand-prepared trials balances and balance sheets in the 1980s to electronic stock and sales accounting system in mid-1990s seemed tremendous progress for us back in the day. HRL successfully trialled such a system in the Southern Zone.

Everything that Dev touched during his tenure as Zonal Sales Manager for south India turned to gold! Slowly the southern zone was being acknowledged by the senior management of the company as the best run zone, of course Dev's peers in the other zones didn't always think so! Whereas Dev was firm when it came to business deliverables, he enjoyed the company of his team members while maintaining professional distance. He nurtured his team without being prescriptive or patronizing and promoted the deserving ones even if at times he had to face resistance from HR.

Dev's cabin door was always open. He found very early on during his ZSM assignment that most of his team, with that gently shaking doll of the head, would agree with his views. 'Please disagree with me', he would say quite often in meetings, 'how else will we arrive at a considered decision.' Other than encouraging diverse opinions, whenever senior managers like Adam Wouters or Karan Varma visited the zone, Dev ensured that his team members got recognition for their achievements. Indeed, if on an occasion anything went turtle, Dev made certain that the blame stopped at his cabin. He always tried to be fair, gentle when a people situation so called for and tough when the business circumstances so demanded. People best rally around a leader when they find him or her to be fair, it doesn't matter as much if the leader is kind or firm, it is fairness and focus on team objectives that are hallmarks of good leadership.

On the personal side too, the Madras posting was memorable for Meher and Dev. They made friends with Shankar and Jaya in the neighbourhood, reacquainted with an old classmate of Dev from TMS who was now in Madras and married, and of course, Dev's summer training time friend Muthu and his wife Shaila lived not too far from their home in Sterling Road. Often they would all meet at each other's place for dinner. Usually the elders in the home of their friends would check with Dev if he had learnt any Tamil,

Dev's standard reply would be '*kuncham kuncham*' meaning 'little little', evoking gentle laughter on the serene faces of the elders followed by observation usually from the aged father '*nah nah*, it's not difficult'. Dev and Meher also joined aerobic classes, discovered the several delightful restaurants in Madras and the day was not over without a drive to Marina beach and either filter coffee at Saravana Bhawan or ice-cream on Pantheon Road on way back. Occasionally they would make a short weekend trip to places like Mahabalipuram, Bangalore, Tirupati, Pondicherry, Madurai and Cochin where the backwaters mesmerized Meher. They were both in love with the calmness and preserved culture in the South.

During their weekend getaway to Madurai, Dev had to step out of their hotel for an informal meeting with a colleague. When he returned Meher had already ordered lunch for both of them, Dev told her to cancel the order as he wanted to take her out to a local restaurant suggested by the colleague. The room service attendant however refused to cancel saying, 'Madam, KOT has been issued.'

Meher handed over the phone to Dev. 'Can you cancel the order please, we are going out for lunch', said Dev.

'No Sir, KOT has been issued Sir, cannot cancel,' said the attendant.

'Has the food been prepared?' enquired Dev.

'No Sir,' came the reply.

'In that case can you please cancel the order', Dev repeated his request.

'Cannot Sir, KOT issued Sir.' The call was ultimately transferred to the Manager who reiterated, 'Sir, the Kitchen Order Ticket has been issued, our systems don't allow us to cancel order.'

Dev smiled to himself as he was reminded of Luv's archetype: *the South is about systems and processes*. 'But the kitchen hasn't started preparing the food, has it?' Dev was puzzled.

The manager however expressed his helplessness. Then it struck Dev, 'Okay, can you please delay delivery of the food in that case?'

The Manager acceded, 'Sure Sir, when do you want it delivered?'

Dev said, 'After 8 hours please.'

After a few seconds of thoughtful silence, Dev heard the Manager say, 'Er, sorry Sir…?'

Dev repeated, 'Can you please delay our food order by 8 hours.'

The order was delivered at 9 pm! Dev and Meher were able to go out to the recommended restaurant for lunch.

Eklavya and Poulomi had got married earlier that year. Poulomi stayed on in Ellinson Hindustan Ltd. while Luv decided to leave as per company policy of not having both partners in employment. They had shifted to Bangalore where

EHL had a large office that Poulomi joined; Luv had just started his own business of organising group travel holidays and tours targeted towards large companies. EHL was his first client! It must have been late June of 1996 when Dev met his friends over coffee in Bangalore en route to the airport. He was flying back to Madras and didn't have much time.

'Do I need to tell you every time to stay with me?' said Luv to Dev. Poulomi too warmly repeated the invitation.

'This time both of you come over to Madras,' said Dev to them and shared the amusing Madurai incident.

'So Bhaisahab, did you think I was making up those cultural traits out of thin air, I have touched and felt all corners of my country!' remarked Luv as his friend and wife smiled.

Dev took their leave and following a half an hour flight back to Madras as he reached home, he saw a little paper sticker on his front door that read: *Hi Dad—I have arrived.*

It took some time for Dev to sink in that Meher was pregnant and he was going to become a father. 'Are you certain?' he asked his wife, still absorbing the upsurge of emotion within him.

'Shaila got the sample tested,' said Meher with a smile. She was due in January.

Over the next few months, Dev got even more protective of Meher. Like all first-time expectant parents, they both became 'half-obstetrician' themselves with scheduled visits to the gynaecologist, reading about childbirth and nutrition, and speaking with their parents. Little did they realise then how the child would become the focus of their lives in times to come.

'Motherhood is the most beautiful experience of life,' said Dev's uncle to Meher. A child is a tender dream on the eyelashes of her parents, the one flower that brightens an entire garden, the one melody that enlivens a gloomy evening, the rays of the rising sun and a marvel of nature.

'How would she or he look like!' wondered Meher. Perhaps, if it was a baby boy, he would go onto playing Test cricket, thought Dev, one of his unfulfilled ambitions! Perhaps someday they would find a home with a lovely garden where Dev could play with the child. A child gives so much meaning, so much depth to life.

Meanwhile, Dev was also keeping his focus on the performance of his Zone that continued to grow in strength. However, in the monthly national sales and marketing meetings he would hear an odd derisive comment from one of his peers like, 'South only sells low margin products,' indicating that while they were over-achieving volume targets they were doing so by selling the basic products and not the high-margin ones. Slowly even VP Adam Wouters started qualifying the success of South with 'the outstandings are on the higher side' or 'South's sales targets are relatively easy'.

Dev would feel his professional drive dampening a bit when he heard such comments. When any of his peers instead of discussing his function or zone would comment on South, Dev's initial reaction would be one of outrage. Soon he would remind himself that the 'bowler was trying to sledge and provoke' and he ought to be patient and 'keep his eyes on the ball', that his loyalty lay ultimately to his organisation that was paying him every month which allowed him to lead a life of dignity with his family, and his unwavering conviction in 'Satyamev Jayate'- truth will triumph.

On one of the weekends as 1996 drew to a close, Luv and Poulomi went visiting Dev and Meher. I too was travelling to Madras and we all stayed the weekend at Dev's. We called up Sudhir in Raipur from Dev's house, his marriage to Gayatri Vohra had been announced. Gayatri was a History lecturer in Delhi University and they were to marry in January 1997. After pulling Sudhir's leg, as men who have been friends since boyhood tend to do, we congratulated him and he expressed the hope that all of us would be able to make it to his wedding.

Later that evening, we walked down to a Chettinad cuisine restaurant on Harrington Road. As our *appams* and stew arrived on the table Luv said to Dev, 'Looking a bit preoccupied, all well, Dev?'

'Yes, yes, all fine,' said Dev with a smile.

'So long as wife and boss are happy with you, life should be cheerful! And I can see wife is glowing,' remarked Luv dipping his *appam* in the stew.

'Dev's targets for next year have been hugely increased,' said Meher with a little smile and some concern.

'So?' said Luv in a matter-of-fact way.

'So, nothing; how is your *appam*?' asked Dev.

'Targets will always be increased, have you ever heard of them being scaled down,' quipped Luv.

Dev looked at me and smiled. 'And if your performance has been good your targets will increase more, you will be a victim of your own success,' I said to Dev.

'The heavy investment in the new plant must be driving targets up steeply,' commented Luv, referring to Hindustan Roqsanto Ltd.'s multi-product plant coming up in Bellary in Karnataka, which was shortly to be commissioned.

'Office issues and organisational politics are everywhere, big company or small, multinational or local, private or government,' said Poulomi coming back to the topic, 'you should look forward to the happiest event about to happen in your life.' She looked at Meher and gave her a gentle hug.

'How is your work, Poulomi?' enquired Dev.

'Fine, Dev, I don't get targets the way you business guys get,' she replied with a smile.

'Polly, tell them about that chap in office who said Madam your dress is very nice,' said Luv to his wife. 'Ah, those sort of comments every working woman has to endure.'

'Really! Someone said that to you in office?' Meher was taken aback. Poulomi nodded ruefully.

'There was another male colleague who asked my company driver where all I go to,' said Poulomi.

'Gosh!' exclaimed Meher, 'in such a good multinational company!'

Poulomi continued, 'Majority of male colleagues are decent, but when I or any female colleague speak in a meeting they interrupt us. EHL is an equal opportunity organisation and my salary is on par with everyone at my grade level, but in some other companies a few of my girl friends tell me that for the same work they are paid less than the male colleagues. And this comment on looks and dress, if you are single, you've had it! My cousin sister works in an export firm in Delhi, she is single and at times she has come home and cried.'

Meher had a pensive look on her face, she asked, 'How will all this change?'

'We have historically been an equal society, isn't it?' I said looking at Dev, 'Women were always the fulcrum of Indian culture, wonder when and how this debasement crept in.'

Luv looked at me, 'Fulcrum?'

I shared whatever little I knew on the topic, 'I mean the Mother Goddess was always worshipped in India, we had the concept of *streedhan* a woman's inheritance rights, franchise rights were granted to all adult men and women after Independence, there were and still are matriarchal communities in India, that most famous spiritual debate on *gyan* versus *karma* a thousand years ago between Adi Shankara and Mandan Misra was judged by the latter's wife Ubhaya Bharati, and correct me if I am wrong, the horror of dowry is not an Indian practice.'

'Let's talk of the situation now Sandy,' said Meher, 'and this problem that working women face today.'

'Meher, this education needs to start from home,' I said.

'Sure, it needs to start from home Sandy,' said Poulomi, 'but that won't be enough. Stricter sexual harassment laws will need to be enacted.'

Dev looked at Poulomi in agreement. 'Real equality comes when this ceases to be an issue of serious discussion,' he said, 'but till such time education in homes, equal opportunity and diversity targets in organisations and stringent laws will be needed.'

Luv had finished his pudding too and said smilingly, 'Meher, Polly, can we chat about something lighter?'

Poulomi gently punched Luv on his shoulder, 'You are the one who started this!'

'You know,' said Meher concluding the discussion, 'families where women are respected always prosper. Woman represents *shakti*, strength.'

Dev added, 'Women and teachers, Meher—for communities and even nations to prosper women and teachers have to be respected—societies where women and teachers are not respected never do well.'

Next evening when Dev left to attend the wedding reception of his colleague, we all stayed back at his home. While having coffee Luv asked Meher, 'Whose reception has Dev gone for?'

Meher said, 'Joseph, their office boy.'

'Office boy!' Luv exclaimed and gave me a wide-eyed look and then smiled. 'Meher your husband doesn't talk openly with us about his stress, has he shared with you what's up in office?'

'He mentioned to me Luv that a couple of his peers, one in particular, has been mocking the accomplishment of Dev's zone in meetings and as a result his boss, who so far had been extremely supportive of Dev, is also now not all that complimentary despite Dev's good performance.'

Luv instantly remarked, 'Meher, in the corporate and business world, performance alone is not enough; alignment with the boss is as important, perhaps more!'

'You please explain all this to Dev,' said Meher.

'He must already know, and I can mention again, but your idealist husband will hear, smile but then carry on with what he believes is the right way.'

As the ladies got down to preparing dinner, Luv asked me to accompany him for a little walk, '*Khannae*, what did I tell you, Dev won't find it smooth sailing in corporate world. I am sure he would not even have expressed his disappointment to his boss against the attitude of whoever this politicking peer is. And you know, if you don't speak up and push-back against these tricksters they only get bolder.'

I nodded in agreement, 'Dev is too dignified to get down to the same level, Luv.'

'Then he will continue to brood. And Bhaisahab has gone for the office-boy's reception, what do we call it—goodness, faithfulness.'

'It's just genuineness Luv, I don't think Dev views human relations in terms of hierarchy of any kind.'

Eklavya looked at life in a far more practical way than Devavratt, he said, '*Khannae*, Dev is preoccupied because his boss is now a little fractious. We middle-class ones are always looking for endorsement—the world gives a damn for goodness or genuineness as you call it; people only look up to money and power. Sometimes you have to stand up for yourself and show a mirror to that selfish scheming get-ahead-at any cost fellow, what does Dev call him, ah peer!'

The retreating monsoon usually gets over by December in Madras, but on 30th January when Dev took Meher to the hospital for delivery it was drizzling. Sudhir was getting married the same day in Delhi and, of all people, Dev couldn't make it to his wedding.

At 3 pm, the medical attendant who was in the delivery room came out and said to Dev, '*Bye* Sir, *bye*.'

Dev looked at him attentively, 'Sorry?'

'Baby *bye*, Sir, congratulations!' Meher and Dev had had a baby boy!

'Mother and child both fine?'

'Both okay, Sir, both okay.'

After 15 minutes, a nurse brought the baby out wrapped in a little towel and showed him to Dev. 'Hi Vedant,' whispered Dev to the baby. 'My wife is well?'

'Absolutely well,' said the nurse, 'you want to hold baby, Sir?'

Dev was too anxious, he had never held a new born in his arms. 'I am not sure I will be able to,' he said to the nurse.

'Hold Sir, there is no problem.' Dev took Vedant in his arms! A little bundle of joy, the prince of their world, the inheritor of Dev's integrity and Meher's values, the destiny of his parents. Dev marvelled at Vedant's thick hair, prominent though tiny nose, and the almost shut harmless eyes which were oblivious of all organised religion, ideology or belief. He was holding love in his arms, pristine and tender. After four days Dev and Meher returned home with little Vedant. It was still drizzling.

Vedant was the loveliest baby if ever there was one. He had thick curly hair, large dreamy eyes, prominent family nose and even on his 15-day-old face, when I saw him, the hint of an innocent smile. As Dev would put him in his cradle that he had got made from a furniture store in Anna Nagar, his tiny hands and legs would flutter. When their neighbour Jaya came to see the new born, and as is customary, placed a little silver coin by his side, Vedant gave an acknowledging smile. Everyone laughed! 'Ah, he likes money!' said Meher and Jaya together and laughed. Dev and Meher had created a little lamp that would light up their entire home and illuminate their lives.

'Do you realise Dev, other than you, most people will call him Ved, the exact reverse of your short name!' I pointed out to my friend.

Dev laughed, 'I never thought of that, Sandeep.'

***

Roqsanto's multi-product plant at Bellary was to be commissioned in the April of 1997. It was to be inaugurated by Jerry Fraser the Marketing Director of Roqsanto Chemicals International Ltd., the parent company of Hindustan Roqsanto

Ltd. In March the MD of HRL Karan Singh Varma called Dev and told him that after the inauguration he was keen to show the Marketing Director one of the Zones. He suggested that Dev draw up a visit plan giving the senior visitor from London a 'cross-sectional view of the market, business issues and a little bit of local flavour'.

Meanwhile, Meher was keen to have Vedant's horoscope made and one Sunday morning, after the baby had gone to sleep, she along with Shaila went to the latter's family astrologer again. The slender looking expressionless astrologer recognized Meher and gave her Vedant's chart that he had already prepared.

'He will spend most of his life overseas, Madam.'

'Does that match with my husband's chart?' she asked the learned man.

The astrologer opened Dev's horoscope in his book, 'For sure, Madam. Sir is about to start the best *mahadasha* of his life, in all likelihood you will get transferred abroad.'

Meher had heard Dev refer to Roqsanto's operations in Dubai and recently started office in Singapore. 'Places like Dubai or Singapore?' she checked.

'No Madam, it will be further away, either Europe or America.'

'Thank you for your time. Anything else that you see?' Meher asked before taking leave.

'Madam, I must have told you last time also, Sir has a polarized horoscope, there will be unexpected success but also some sudden setbacks.'

Jerry Fraser's visit went wonderfully well. Dev met him and Karan in Bangalore and after making a short presentation to the senior managers about Southern Zone, took them to their largest adhesives and resins distributor in Bangalore. Later they visited the best management school in the garden city. That evening, they all flew to Madras. The next day Dev introduced his entire office and field team to the Marketing Director RCIL and MD of Hindustan Roqsanto Ltd. Howard Sadler, the head of Business Development for India had also flown in from Delhi for the day. Fraser addressed the regional team and told them how Roqsanto International had become one of the fastest growing chemicals manufacturing and marketing companies in the world through a 'combination of portfolio plays and organic growth.'

After the staff meeting, Dev took the visitors to see an industrial customer; they then lunched with the purchase manager of a large construction company who was buying adhesives and polishes from Roqsanto, as well as the director of a pharmaceutical and cosmetics company who was getting their solvents from HRL. Later in the afternoon they visited the workshop of a large automobile company, an OEM which was using Roqsanto resins. Dev had organised dinner in another hotel where Karan had invited some senior bureaucrats and company CEOs. The next morning, the last day of the eventful visit, Dev picked up Karan, Fraser and Howard and they drove to Mahabalipuram for a late breakfast.

Just before the visitors were about to depart for the airport, and Fraser and Howard had gone to use the facilities, Karan said to Dev, 'Well done, Dev! I have discussed your case with Jerry and he is happy to consider expatriation for you.'

'Thank you, Karan,' said Dev.

The MD continued, 'Expatriation is a bit of a process, will take some time to clear with HR and business etc. Make sure that your performance remains high during this time.'

Dev nodded and then asked Karan, 'If it does go ahead, what will be the likely location?'

'London,' said Karan Varma in a matter-of-fact way.

London sounded better than the best Dev could have imagined! Roqsanto Chemicals International Ltd. had two main international offices—London was the marketing headquarters and Hamburg in Germany was the manufacturing or works headquarters, referred to as MHQ and WHQ respectively. Karan's words—'make sure your performance remains high during this time'—were uppermost in Dev's mind. But Dev's targets were daunting and he was falling behind them. The Southern Zone was growing significantly over the previous year yet it was short of the current year's target. In an effort to motivate his entire distributor network and sales team Dev decided to organise their visit to the new Bellary plant in the first week of July. The plant visit was yet another 'new initiative' emerging from the Southern Zone and both Adam Wouters and Karan Varma cleared it.

Majority of the 40 distributors came for the plant visit, the entire sales team and selected office-based staff were also there. The two-day trip and the sales incentive scheme that the Zonal Manager announced at the plant were very well received. Dev felt good, he had done his best to achieve growth for the company in his Zone. Be it sales management or marketing, people or logistics, cash management or communication or work processes, he had covered all the bases. The distributors thanked him for a terrific trip even as Dev complimented all the plant-based team for organising the visit. Early morning on the third day, after the visit was over, Dev got into a newly launched SUV along with Raj Subramaniam, Suresh Fernandez and Prasad Shivaram the Regional Accounts and MI manager, the ASM Karnataka and Regional Marketing Manager respectively. They were planning to drive from Bellary to Bangalore, almost a six-hour drive, drop Suresh Fernandez in Bangalore by noon time and then take a late afternoon flight to Madras.

Less than an hour from Bangalore on the highway, in Chikkaballapur amidst the Nandi hills, their car driver tried to overtake a bus from the wrong side—from left. He was driving at about 60 kilometres/hour and as he came next to the bus, the bus turned left and the car with four Roqsanto managers was trapped! The driver of the car swerved sharply to the left to avoid a collision and next they knew the SUV had gone off the road, broken the concrete barrier on the left and was in a free fall! In that split second Dev and his colleagues didn't know how much they were falling: 10 feet or 100 feet or more. All of them instantly screamed as the thought of Vedant flashed through Dev's mind. Their car fell 20 feet and landed in the moat-like rocky ditch with a brutal thud, it then somersaulted!

Dev was sitting on the rear seat on the left. As they landed, Dev realised he was conscious; he then felt his person and seemed to be more or less fine. Then he saw his clothes—they were drenched in blood. He crawled out of the car and found it difficult to stand up; he had excruciating pain in his lower back. Suresh Fernandez and Prasad Shivaram also crawled out; they appeared to be bleeding from their heads. Their blood was on Dev's clothes. Raj Subramaniam, who was seated in the front, seemed trapped under the SUV. Prasad tied a handkerchief on his head and tried to lift the SUV just a bit so that Raj could slide out: character of a man is so evidently seen in moments of distress. He was successful! In no time traffic stopped on the highway and Dev could see a few people gingerly walking down the rocky incline to help them. He just couldn't stand up and put his arm around Suresh Fernandez so that he could walk a few steps to the edge of the ditch near the road. A couple of people lifted him from his thighs and two people pulled him up on the level of the road. They did the same with Raj Subramaniam, Suresh Fernandez and Prasad Shivaram. Dev saw the driver of their car also coming up the incline onto the road, he seemed to be in agony.

Somehow the four colleagues were put in a taxi which took them to a local hospital that gave them first aid and Dev heard a nurse say to a doctor, 'Seems like a back injury, Sir.'

The doctor replied, 'X-ray.'

After about two hours the doctor came to Dev who lay on a stretcher, 'You seem to have fractured a few lower vertebrae.'

The news of their accident reached Karan Varma and Adam Wouters and others in the management team who were all in a meeting in Bombay. The meeting was instantly concluded and the HR head of the company Zubin Tarachand took the next flight to Bangalore. He informed the Bangalore office of Torsh which was still operational. While the business tie-up with India Rasayanik Ltd had been ended after commissioning of the new plant, Zubin Tarachand informed their Bangalore office as well. Both offices immediately sent their local administration staff to Chikkaballapur in order to remove Dev and his colleagues from the local hospital there to the Regus Hill Hospital in Bangalore. That evening all four of them were brought in two ambulances to Regus Hill Hospital in Bangalore. Dev and Raj Subramaniam were sent for x-ray again before being moved into their rooms next to each other and divided by a wooden partition. Dev's aunt and uncle in Delhi were also informed of the serious accident as was Meher who, along with little Vedant, had flown the previous week to Delhi to spend some time with her parents.

The next morning Dev opened his eyes to see Zubin Tarachand along with a smart looking doctor.

'Hello, Dev,' said Zubin, 'This is Dr Sharad Ranganathan, the senior orthopaedic surgeon here.' Dr Sharad confirmed that Dev had fractured four of his lower back vertebrae and would need to be on four weeks complete bed rest, only after which could he stand up on his feet.

'Will I be able to walk again doctor?' asked Dev.

'You should be able to,' said the doctor.

'Are you certain Doctor? I will be able to walk again?' Dev pensively enquired again.

'As I just said, you should be able to walk and lead a normal life again.'

'How are Raj and Suresh and Prasad?' Dev checked with Zubin.

'Raj has had a pelvic fracture, four weeks bed rest like you, he is in the adjacent cabin. You can in fact speak to him as this partition is not soundproof,' smiled the HR head, 'Suresh and Prasad had cuts on the head, nothing serious, they have been stitched up and will be released today. We informed your father, your uncle that is, and I spoke to Meher as well. Your aunt will be flying in tomorrow.'

'Thank you, Zubin, its very kind of you,' said Dev still in pain.

'You will be just fine; you've had a providential escape,' Zubin gently touched Dev's shoulder, 'let me just look up our Accounts and MI Manager next door.'

Dev's back muscles had gone in spasms as a reaction to the severe injury he sustained. After the nurse had given him a muscle relaxant, a pain killer and a sleeping tablet and before Dev fell asleep, he thought of Meher and Vedant. All he wanted was to be able to walk on his legs again! Nothing, nothing else—sales targets, collections, expatriation, nothing mattered to him at that instant. He just wanted to be on his feet again, with Meher and Vedant. He just wanted to take care of his wife and their new born son. What would have become of them had he not survived; Dev wiped his moist eyes. Being a human being is not in the best interest of a human being! Man sowed seeds of chequered history the day, millions of years ago, he straightened his spine and from four limbs started to walk on two.

I heard of Dev's accident three days after the mishap when his uncle called me. None of us still had mobile phones and we communicated mainly through landlines. I immediately called Meher, she sounded very shaken. 'I don't have Eklavya's telephone number. Can you please ask him to look up Dev?' she requested me.

I came to know from Poulomi's office that Eklavya had taken a group of distributors and stockists on a company trip to Singapore and Malaysia, after which Poulomi and he were to be on two weeks leave overseas.

'Chikkaballapur! Of all places, Chikkaballapur!' I thought to myself. I remembered my late grandmother's story that God of Death arrives at the door of the person whose time is up. But seeing Dev's narrow brush with obliteration in that little-known town in Nandi Hills made me realise that it is man who reaches the home of God of Death when time is up, and not the other way around.

Dev's aunt reached Bangalore two days after his accident to be with him. He felt reassured to have a family member besides him. She contacted a distant cousin of hers, Nalini Jadeja, who lived in Bangalore and who Dev had met only once many years ago. For the next three and half weeks, every single day Nalini Aunty got home cooked lunch for Dev! S Jaikishan, the General Manager Finance of India Rasayanik Ltd. happened to be in Bangalore on annual leave and heard of Dev's accident. Dev and he had met a couple of times during meetings and that too when Roqsantc was just starting in India. For the two weeks that Jaikishan was in Bangalore, every single morning he came to look up Dev and carried some *idli* and filter coffee for him! It has never ceased to amaze me, in our difficult times, who all so unexpectedly step up to lend a helping hand. India Rasayanik's business tie-up with Hindustan Roqsanto Ltd. may have ended, yet Jaikishan was with Dev every single morning. Man's struggles of existence on this planet are so cushioned by the presence of such divine human beings like Nalini Aunty and S Jaikishan. And mankind shall continue to survive so long as man reaches out to fellow human beings trumping organisations, caste, gender, race, religion or nationality.

A few days later when Dr Sharad Ranganathan came to look up his patient, Dev asked him, 'Doctor, I hope you don't mind my asking again, will I be able to walk again?'

'I don't mind you asking me any number of times, my answer every time will be yes, you *will* be able to walk again,' replied Dr Sharad.

'Thank you, Sir. Twice last time you said—you *should* be able to walk again—I feel better since this time you said I *will* be able to walk!'

The faintest of smile came on Dr Sharad's lips, he said nothing to Dev, just instructed the nurse to continue with medicines and after three weeks get a lumbar belt.

Dev and his colleague Raj Subramaniam's only daily recreation was to chat with each other through the wooden partition. It was during these conversations that the Accounts and MI manager shared some remarkable facts with Dev—Ravan was the father of Carnatic music and Bappa Rawal the *Maharana* of Mewar not only defeated the first Arab invader of India, Mohammad Bin Qasim in 8th century AD, but thereafter established Rajput posts after every 150 kilometres from the Iran-Afghanistan area to present day north India; posts that fended off numerous invasions over the next 300 years. Rawalpindi in Pakistan is named after the great *Maharana*!

Luv and Poulomi returned to Bangalore after three weeks and drove straight to Regus Hill hospital. 'Couldn't you have waited to have this accident when I was in Bangalore!' said Luv in his usual mischievous manner.

Dev laughed a little, 'Don't make me laugh, my back hurts.'

That afternoon Dr Sharad visited Dev and showed him how to turn on his side and take support of his elbow to get up from bed. It had been over three weeks and Dev felt jubilant to just sit up on bed. Then the doctor taught him how to tie the lumbar belt and made Dev stand up on his legs and just walk to the door of the room and back.

'Any pain?' he asked Dev.

'Just a little,' said Dev, feeling euphoric within.

'Don't worry, it will settle down. Your muscles however will remain in spasms for some time to come, after you are discharged take some physiotherapy and do back strengthening exercises.'

An hour after the doctor left, Dev got up from bed again and walked to the telephone on his floor and called Meher.

'Walked a few steps today,' he told his wife.

'Nothing will ever happen to you; I have full faith in my God,' she replied.

'How is Vedant?'

'He is fine. Here, talk to him. Talk to Dad, say Hi Dad,' said Meher with Vedant in her arms.

'Hi Vedant, how are you *bachcha*?' said Dev into the phone mouthpiece. He heard Vedant's gurgling sound from the other end.

'Say we love you Dad, come home soon.'

Again Dev heard a little mumble!

'Is the date of discharge known?' asked Meher.

'Sometime next week.'

Dev was discharged a few days before Raj Subramaniam. Hindustan Roqsanto Ltd. had been a wonderfully caring employer, not only did they pick up all the costs of hospitalization but even flew Dev's aunt from and to Delhi. They supported Dev for the next month as he recovered in his Bapa Nagar home. It was only in early October that Dev, with Meher and Vedant and Meher's mother, returned to Madras. Dev was welcomed back very warmly in the Zonal office; none was as happy as Joseph even though he couldn't articulate his joy to see Dev back.

'I will get coffee for you, Sir,' said Joseph and ran to the pantry to make Dev's favourite filter coffee. Dev met Raj Subramaniam and Prasad Shivaram who had survived the car accident with him. It is only then that he learnt that the driver of their car that fateful morning had succumbed to his injuries!

The southern zone, under Dev's command, had grown the business by about 35% over a very successful previous year, yet had fallen well short of their target. Sometime between Christmas and New Year's in December 1997 Dev's office phone rang and the secretary said, 'Dev, Karan on line.'

It was not very often that the MD called directly. 'Hi Dev, how are you? Fully recovered from the injury?'

Dev mentioned that he was almost back to normal, though his back muscles were still in spasms and he would need to be very careful while lifting anything heavy or playing sport.

'Well Dev, congratulations, you have been accepted for the expatriation!'

It took a few extra seconds for Dev to respond, 'Thank you very much, Karan; and the posting?'

'London—the Marketing Headquarters!' said Karan, 'You will start getting all the details about work permit and joining date but I would expect all that to be sorted in a few weeks, time. You will be our first expatriate to the head office!'

Dev thanked Karan again and asked if he knew what role he would be doing in London.

'I think they are assigning you to the New Business Prospecting group. Roqsanto is evaluating opportunities in several new markets and people who have actually set up green field and brown field operations are needed to take those learnings into the countries we are not still present in or have a small presence. They have selected one person from Roqsanto China and yourself to join the current team.'

Dev was delighted, 'Would you know the duration of the assignment Karan?'

'I think three years. Well done, Dev, most people I know will give their right arm for a job like this in MHQ!'

On the 27th of February 1998, after Dev handed over the keys of his Sterling Road flat to the caretaker, he had tears in his eyes—perhaps for the first and last time in his life while leaving a place of posting. Madras had given him so much! He had had the most memorable time in the southern coastal city both professionally and personally. His southern zone colleagues gave him a touching farewell that evening and gifted him a grey coloured summer jacket. The next morning, he, Meher and Vedant flew to Delhi. On Monday the week after next, Dev found himself in a business class seat of the British Airways flight to London's Heathrow airport. A posting to London, particularly in the late-1990s, was as coveted as could get. In just over a year Dev had experienced so many different emotions and witnessed such new perspectives of life, including one of near death!

***

I have intended this book to be a narrative of India, as I have seen it since 1970s to present day, and will therefore skip the details of Devavratt's fascinating experiences in England and his travels around the world. That would be story for another day and subject matter of a separate book. I shall only and briefly mention the three distinct phases of Dev's overseas years in the remainder of this and following two chapters: the initial time of settling down in England, his global travels and discovery of the world and finally his meteoric rise as a professional.

Howard Sadler happened to be in London at the time and received Dev at Heathrow. He showed him the Roqsanto International office on The Strand, where Dev would be working, and which was referred to as MHQ. It overlooked the Thames with the enchanting South Bank across the river and the famous Trafalgar Square and Big Ben to the right when entering the imposing 20 storey grey coloured building.

Howard then dropped Dev at his hotel which was just off Victoria Street. 'Wish you a wonderful and memorable time in London Dev; none deserved this assignment as much.'

Dev thanked his colleague and invited him for a cup of tea.

'I would have stayed for a cuppa-tea but I need to meet an old friend on my way back, and you have had a long flight too,' said Howards shaking Dev's hand.

'Hiya,' said the young lady at the hotel reception, where are you coming from today?'

'New Delhi,' said Dev with a smile.

'Ah India! I have always wanted to go there. What's the weather like now in New Delhi?' she enquired while trying to find Dev's booking.

'It's getting warm now but still reasonably pleasant about 30 degrees.'

'Oh, how lovely! It's been miserable here this weekend, cold and rainy. Ah, here we are.'

After changing, Dev immediately went down to 'touch and feel' London. As he walked on Victoria Street admiring the sidewalks and pedestrian crossing, where as soon as a pedestrian set foot the traffic would stop, he saw the striking red-coloured telephone booths and stepped inside one of them to call Meher. A three-minute call to India cost Dev £5; that was almost Rs. 350! In the telephone booth he also saw stickers aplenty with tantalizing pictures of girls and their telephone numbers and an enticing message. He thought of mentioning this to Luv!

The next morning Dev woke up at 4 am, feeling as though he had over-slept. That was the first time he realised what jet-lag meant! He reported to Roqsanto MHQ at 9 am after his first journey in the London underground; Dev was wonderstruck with the fully signposted stations, how clean they were, how the gates opened when ticket was inserted, the escalators and the clear announcement to 'mind the gap'.

He met the expat department who told him about company accommodation, remuneration and other entitlements, opening of bank account and registering with National Insurance. He was then shown the New Business Prospects office in the imposing building. The NBP department boss was Alan Mantell while Dev's immediate boss was Peter Van de Ven, Head Commercial. Dev was to be the Commercial Strategy Manager—New Prospects. The four groups within the department were Commercial, Fresh to Portfolio, Finance-Legal and Technical. Dev made the acquaintance of Beth Wilson, one of the three secretaries who helped the team with administration matters. 'Your English is very good,' she remarked showing Dev his work station and office facilities. Dev certainly used to speak well but he thought to himself that a lot of his friends and colleagues in India spoke more or less like him. Beth's remark stayed in Dev's mind.

That afternoon Dev lunched with Axel Mercier who was originally from France and in the Finance-Legal team. Axel took Dev to the cafeteria downstairs where every day about 2000 employees used to have lunch. 'There must be people from about 50 different countries in the MHQ,' said Axel.

When Dev asked him about accommodation he said, 'There are beautiful fully furnished Roqsanto houses in Surrey which is about an hour by top train. But if you are first time in England you should stay in London and enjoy the city, it is so, err...how do you say it in English...such a fascinating city!'

Dev checked with Axel about house help, someone to clean and cook. Axel was a little surprised and said, 'Well, I hoover my flat myself. Most houses will have hoovers, otherwise just pick one up for 50 quid. Usually furnished houses going on rent have hoover, washing machine and iron. I iron my five office shirts on the weekend itself. And Claudette and I cook ourselves during the working week. You will find many curry restaurants and takeaways in London though.'

Dev was in a completely different world and work environment. Soon he realised that London and for that matter most of Europe, indeed the industrialized world, were DIY societies: Do It Yourself.

Indian food was referred to as 'curry' in UK, and chicken tikka masala pronounced *chicken teeka musala* was one of the most popular 'curry' dishes! In those initial days Dev would often hear his simple queries posed to colleagues around 'grocery stores', 'hairstyling salons' and 'reasonable place to buy clothes' answered with what he found quaint phrases like 'it's cheap and cheerful' and 'you get what you pay for'!

Peter Van de Ven was a pleasant and forthright person. In a few days Dev also met Alan Mantell who had a remarkable global perspective and explained to Dev how the services of their department were utilized by Roqsanto. 'Whenever the line heads of various geographies or the Global Strategy Vice President want to evaluate a new market anywhere in the world for investment they assign that project to our team. Also, moving into new marketing businesses in established geographies or plant expansions come to us for appraisal. So we are like an internal consulting team.'

Dev found a beautiful, fully-furnished and plush apartment in Notting Hill Gate in Central London and in a week after his renting it Meher and Vedant joined him. Meher was always cheerful and contented wherever they were, be it Kanpur or Madras. However, seeing the lovely flat and the posh neighbourhood she was absolutely delighted. Vedant had been standing up holding a chair or bed for a few weeks but that first evening in their apartment in Notting Hill Gate he stood up in front of the fireplace without any support and marvelled at his physiological change! Dev instantly took a photograph of his little son.

Dev began discovering completely new business language and ways of working at office. There was frequent reference to 'hurdle rate'; business meetings were garnished with pleasant humour and the turn of phrases were charming as was the gentle way of requesting work be completed by deadlines.

'Dev you will be able to turn this around by early next week, won't you?' said Alan—'We can discuss this till the cows get home,' said Peter in some context—'They have bowled a googly at us,' remarked Alan during a discussion. Often double negatives were used to compliment a person, thus the Fresh to Portfolio head who wanted to co-opt Dev for an India project said, 'Given Dev's utter lack of understanding of the Indian market, I thought it would not be a bad idea if he can spend some time on this project.' No week ended without all colleagues wishing each other 'have a nice weekend' and no week started without colleagues checking with each other 'how was your weekend'! No meeting started without reference to the weather and occasionally sports. Slowly it became part of Dev too to mention the weather.

As the summer set in, and Dev finally understood what those school English literature lessons written by English authors meant, when they started with 'once upon a time on a lovely summer day'—for in Delhi a cloudy day was a lovely day. He said to Beth Wilson, 'Its glorious today Beth!'

She smiled back at Dev and quipped, 'It won't last long, Dev.'

Two days later when it got cold and started drizzling, she walked past Dev's work station and said to him looking outside the window, 'Normal service is restored!'

Public transportation in London was so good that Dev didn't initially feel the need for a car. Meher bought a beautiful push-chair for Vedant from Mothercare store and every summer weekend the three of them would set-off visiting the countless tourist delights of London. A friend of Dev's uncle had told Dev 'London is an expensive city but you shouldn't keep multiplying prices of everything by 70, that way you won't be able to buy anything and enjoy yourself.'

While it was early days, and their posting was for three years, Meher and Dev started making casual enquiries about primary schools. They learnt that when the time comes, Vedant would get admission in a good primary school in their vicinity and that the public school education was free in UK. Earlier in the year, they had registered with the local Surgery that is the general physician doctors. The National Health Service surgeries and hospitals were likewise free of charge. To see the workings of a different and mature democratic welfare state was a fascinating learning for Dev and Meher. All public services worked smoothly and whether it was the Electricity or Council office someone always answered the telephone and politely said, 'How can I help?' The street sidewalks gently tapered down after every few metres for convenience of wheelchair and pushchair users and every time Meher was in the tube with Vedant, someone would get up as a courtesy for the mother with a small child!

Dev and Meher tried three Indian restaurants in the two mile radius around their house. While all had typical Indian names, they were operated by restaurateurs from Bangladesh and the food suitable for the Western palate. Dev and Meher found the north-Indian dishes in particular not to their taste. Over time they discovered some Indian restaurants run by Indians and while the food there was a little more to their taste, Dev always missed the freshness and fragrance and variety and spices of Indian food in India!

He was most keen to see a cricket match at Lord's and also experience the English countryside. Both exceeded his expectations. If watching the final day of an England vs. West Indies Test match that summer was memorable, Dev's rail journey with Meher and Vedant to Bournemouth and Oxford seeing the classic English countryside was captivating and fulfilling. The countryside was lush-green and gently undulating. The grazing cattle, the little brooks, the quaint country homes, the village high street—all added to the charm of the countryside making it as pretty as a picture postcard. Dev felt the need for a car then, in which he could drive through with his family and discover more of the mesmerizing countryside.

My friend had an unfamiliar feeling when he went to office on the 15th of August. Never before had he not had a holiday on 15th August! He also sensed an unfamiliar attitude and pronunciation when he lunched with some colleagues of Indian origin who had grown up in England and were now working in MHQ. Rajandeep Ahluwalia was referred to as Raj Walia in the office email address list, Prasoon Dey introduced himself as *Prassy* and Shalini Batra as *Sh-leeni Baatra*, pronouncing the 't' in her second name as it sounds in 'bat'; Raj and Prasoon addressed her as *Shaals*!

'Nice idea to organise lunch on the National Day', said Raj Walia, even as Dev was somewhat thrown by his referring to Independence Day as National Day! After checking a little bit about Dev, when he arrived in MHQ and what was Roqsanto doing in India, Raj and Prassy and Shaals started talking amongst themselves pronouncing naughty as n*oo-tee* and sorted as *soo-ted*. They discussed an organisation reshuffle and Prassy's recent holiday in Spain.

Dev was feeling a bit out of place when Raj Walia asked him, 'So what's your plan? Will you return to India after completing your assignment or apply for another job here?' He pronounced 'plan' as *plaan*, rhyming with *naan*, the way perhaps our schoolmate Manohar Pal Billa would have said!

During course of the remaining conversation Dev sensed that the colleagues on his lunch table, though of Indian origin, appeared oblivious and somewhat disinterested as to how India had economically grown and modernized in recent years.

When Dev shared his impression of that day's office lunch with Meher she said, 'There is an Indian couple in our apartment building too. Namita Trehan is the lady's name,

I have met her twice while returning from Sainsbury's. She moved from Bombay to England after marriage.'

A few days later when Dev reached home, he found their neighbour having a cup of coffee with Meher.

'Hi, I am Nam*eeta,*' she said extending her hand to Dev, dragging the second syllable in her name and pronouncing the 't' once again as it sounds in 'bat'. She had been living in London for 15 years and mentioned they would go back to Bombay for a holiday once in two years and while, 'Harry is not comfortable there but Sara has a whale of a time.' Sara was their 10-year-old daughter who was quietly sipping orange juice sitting next to her mother.

When Dev enquired if her husband was from England she said, 'No, no, he is from India. Harvinder Trehan is the name, he is a second-generation immigrant, his parents moved here when he was just five.' She pronounced Harvinder Trehan as *Haarvinduh Tree-hunn.*

Namita told them how Sara loves reading Harry Potter. 'Don't you?' she looked at her daughter.

Sara nodded, 'I love Harry *Po-aah*'.

Then the little girl asked her mother, 'Mum, mum, what's for dinner?'

Namita told her, 'Lamb steak with boiled potatoes and bread and butter pudding.'

'*Chappa-ee*?' enquired Sara.

'*Chappa-ee* you get only at Nani's, darling!' said Namita laughingly.

A few weeks later when Meher rang Namita's door-bell the latter opened the door with a puzzled expression on her face, 'Oh Hi! I wasn't expecting you, its Sara's study time!'

Dev and Meher never went to anyone's home unannounced thereafter. Today, in big cities in India, nobody visits anyone's house without calling, but in the late 1990's, and while they were in Madras, they would often stop by unannounced at Shankar's or Muthu's during their post dinner drives!

As Dev and Meher discovered more of London and the nature of life there, they would often chat about the various price deals available in high street retail stores all of which were pulsating with variety. 'It's Philip Kotler in action and expression,' said Dev to me once on the phone, describing the supermarkets and departmental stores of London.

There is something enthralling in being a foreigner. In the freshness and discovery of a new place, new ways of working and of engaging with people, new culture and customs and mannerisms, new forms of food and clothing, new history and new geography, the newness in humour, and having moved from a tropical country to a temperate maritime country, Dev and Meher were also experiencing very new weather when during summers there was sunshine till 9 pm!

London, like Delhi, offered all four seasons with their distinctive appeal. The colour of the leaves on trees changed as the summer made way for the fall. If the summer had been glorious, Dev found the autumn weeks melodic and tranquil. And slowly, as winter approached, the sun started setting by 4 pm. While London never gets freezing cold due to the warm ocean currents, and everything from homes to trains to supermarkets are centrally heated, the mid to low single digit temperature necessitated Dev to buy thermal vest, woollen peak cap, gloves and a thick warm overcoat. Dev, Meher and Vedant spent most of their winter weekends at home as it could get quite chilly outdoors. By 5 pm it would be dark and very still outside. Dev and Meher had not made any friends as yet, and even though they were together, for the first time in his life, Dev sensed what loneliness meant.

The streets and stores in London soon wore a festive look as Christmas neared. The fairy lights on trees and buildings and across streets made the entire city come alive with merriment. Dev and Meher with little Vedant in the buggy would step out in the evenings just to see the beautiful fairy lights. Neither Dev nor Meher had had wine by then and supermarkets were full of varieties of white and red and pudding wines. Dev bought his first Chardonnay and once they got back home he poured a glass for himself and his wife and then lit the delightful fireplace. How much their life had changed, how much they had experienced in the last two years. Roqsanto Chemicals International's MHQ was gorgeously decorated for the festive season. Everyone in office was wishing each other 'Happy Christmas' and so many of Dev's colleagues were hoping for a 'white Christmas'! Unlike many of his colleagues, Dev was working through the Christmas and New Years' time. As he would step into the tube to return home, he would take a seat and then wonder what his future held.

As he would get home and ring the bell, Vedant would come running to the entrance door. 'Dad, Dad. Dad has come!' The combined happiness of all success Dev had had in life till then—academic and professional achievements, marrying the woman he loved, opportunity to express himself on the cricket field, appreciation of his colleagues and warmth of several good friends—could not match the joy of that moment when his lovely son would run into his arms. 'Dad, Dad,' Vedant would exclaim elatedly.

Dev would pick up Vedant in his arms and kiss him.

'I made a drawing for you,' Vedant would say, still in Dev's arms.

'Show me, show me quickly!'

Vedant would go running to the bedroom to fetch the drawing.

'How was your day?' Meher would smilingly ask him from the kitchen.

Dev would stretch himself, take off his shoes and overcoat and sit on the comfortable lounging sofa in the living room.

'Dad, Dad, see!' Vedant would come and sit on Dev's lap, as Meher would bring him a cup of tea.

Pride, Criticism And Responsibility

Men and women, as they travel from one country to another, inevitably keep comparing life in one place to the other. Whenever he would be back in Delhi for leave, Dev would stick pieces of paper on the windscreens of wrongly parked cars outside his uncle's home with the scribble: *Wrongly parked—kindly park in allotted place.*

Back in London he would repeatedly go to Southall in search of that authentic *tandoori roti, tadka daal* and chicken curry. Over time Dev realised a few things: Once freedom, justice and equality of opportunity is, more or less, assured for citizens in a nation, all its other aspects are cultural and historical differences to be cherished. Depending on the observer, every nation has its charming and not so alluring aspects. Instead of value judging these differences if a person experiences them with a learning mindset, travel and interaction with people from around the world is perhaps the most enchanting and delightful of human activities.

As the millennium was coming to an end, I too found myself in England on a cross-posting that my company had selected me for. Eklavya's business of organising professional tours for corporates had got well established and he was taking distributors and managers of various kinds of organisations not just to south-east Asia but also to Europe. Sanju had set up his own accounting and consulting firm a few years back, and he too would travel to USA and Europe in quest for clients and growth. Our other friend from TAPS, Ramkumar, was working for a large engineering company in Delhi. Sudhir was in Indore; he was Managing Director of a mid-size public sector company. A couple of Dev's friends from Augustus College were running their own business; others were in professional employment in India. Most of his TMS friends were also with large corporate houses or MNCs in senior middle-management positions in India and as the country's economy increasingly integrated with rest of the world they had started making business trips abroad. There had been no contact with my distant cousins Gautam and Geeta for years; neither Dev nor I ever talked about them with each other.

Dev started travelling all over the world for work from 1999 onwards. His first year of international travel took him to unique places like Azerbaijan, Turkmenistan and Uzbekistan in Central Asia; Oman and Lebanon in Middle East and West Asia, and Morocco and Algeria in North Africa. He considered himself very fortunate to be part of an organisation that was giving him an opportunity to discover the world, indeed for business, at its expense. Dev's learning through his travels gave him matchless perspective not just on how business happened in different countries but also into the socio-cultural dimensions of different nations and continents.

For many projects, Dev was paired with Paul Anderson, who had been with Roqsanto International for 20 years and had two expat postings to Russia and Brazil. He had recently joined the New Business Prospects' Commercial team. Paul was about 10 years older to Dev, about four inches taller and 15 kilograms heavier. He was originally from Manchester, was always ready to have a laugh and had something amiable to say to anyone he met. Paul had rich hands-on experience, he had not been to any business school and his learning had all been at work. Dev always admired people with practical common sense and those who were not 'machine-made'. In Dev, Paul saw an upright and bright person from a newly industrializing country trying to find his feet at the international level, and informally, took him under his wing.

The emerging learning for Dev in those early international travels was while societal norms and cultures might be very distinct in different places, deep down how similar people from all over the world were! All seeking the security of a livelihood, the warmth of a little home with a few loving souls in it, a sense of some accomplishment, something to smile and laugh about; a fire lit in the kitchen for a decent meal and the opportunity to travel a bit and meet different kinds of people! Whenever he would board the return flight to London, Dev would think about Swami Vivekananda's quote: 'Every nation has a message to deliver, ambition to fulfil and a destiny to reach'; and try and work out in his mind what was the most discerning philosophical bequest he was taking from that country. As he would reach home in Notting Hill Gate he would hear the running steps of Vedant, 'Dad, Dad, my Dad has come, Dad has come!' He would look at Vedant and be wonderstruck how much he had changed in the week that he was away! And then with Vedant in his arms and Meher asking him about his trip he would say, 'Different places around the world are so distinct in how people live, and yet people of the world are so similar, so very similar.'

Dev bought a Ford Mondeo sedan in his second year in London and felt that their quality of life substantially improved with it. Thereafter he started driving to office and feeling more settled in London. Meher, Vedant and he holidayed in Paris and Switzerland and Barcelona that summer and later in early winters went to both the USA coasts. In USA everything was on a massive scale. Meher said smilingly to Dev as they returned back to London from San Francisco, 'The roads seem so quaint here now after those massive motorways of America!'

While their home was very comfortable and getting around in London was easy, doing all the house work themselves with a little child was demanding. With some savings in pounds in the bank, Meher started calling a young girl once a week to help her clean and tidy the home. The smart young Polish girl, dressed in working jeans and t-shirt, would charge by the hour and generally spend two to three hours every week helping Meher with house cleaning. The other help Dev had to occasionally call was a plumber as their bathroom and kitchen drains would sometimes clog up. Joseph the *plummer* as he would refer to his profession was an elderly man, half French and half Korean. He would address Dev by his first name and, whenever he needed to speak to Meher, as came naturally to him, he would say, 'Can I get a cup of coffee, darling?' or, '*Plumming* help is needed in all flats of this building, darling.' Meher and Dev would talk about Joseph's professionalism and congeniality. Meher then thought aloud about the young Polish girl, 'Even she carries herself with so much poise.'

Dev was also discovering the cultural diversity and fine subtleties of people's interaction in a professional setting at his office. In the early part of year 2000 he was once coming down the lift from the 20th floor when, on the 19th floor Jerry Fraser, the Marketing Director of Roqsanto International, stepped into the lift along with another man. Roqsanto International had just got into the top 100 companies of the world and Jerry was widely tipped to become its next Chief Executive. Dev wished Jerry who smiled back at him.

'We met in Bangalore and Madras about three years back Jerry,' said Dev.

'Yes, we did, you are here now?' said Jerry.

'I am,' said Dev.

'Coping with the cold!' remarked the Marketing Director as Dev smiled at him.

Just then the other man in the lift looked at his watch and said in a trifle perturbed tone, 'Jerry, how do you expect me to get you to Heathrow in three quarters of an hour!'

Jerry Fraser calmly replied, 'I am sorry Carl, my meeting overran.'

Carl was Jerry's driver. Carl was doing his job as indeed Jerry was his. They were equal as individuals, just drawing different salaries!

'Good luck with your assignment,' said Jerry to Dev as they got to the ground floor.

No work in this world, done honestly, is big or small. Dignity of labour, well ingrained in Dev given his upbringing, got further entrenched in him as a virtue worth striving for in whatever he did and wherever he went.

Peter Van de Ven, Dev's boss, had decided to leave Roqsanto following completion of his assignment and divorce from his wife.

'Oh! I am sorry to hear that', said Dev.

'That's okay,' responded Peter, 'My children have grown up; I can enjoy more now, you know sailing and cycling. And maybe circulate amongst singles again to see if I can find another lady.'

We are fallible mortals with human frailties. The ability to talk about one's failures and weaknesses openly and with a smile, and not taking oneself too seriously, is a revitalising strength.

Dev's new boss was Susan Thorpe-Jones from Liverpool; she was returning after completing her Masters in European History. 'She is an out-and-out Scouser, terrific sense of humour', said Paul to Dev.

'You selected Susan despite her being an Everton supporter eh!' joked Paul when Alan Mantell walked past them.

'Ah, she supports Everton does she, I'll work on that!' laughed Alan who was known to be a Liverpool football club supporter.

Paul later explained to Dev, 'We develop football club associations in our childhood and usually stay with them throughout life. Alan is a Liverpool man, Susan is an Everton girl and I am Manchester United. And now that you are here Mr Rajvansh you better support my club!'

Dev beamed at his tall and burly colleague.

It didn't take Susan too long to develop trust in Dev. She started nominating him for work in mature markets and that year Dev spent time on different projects in Netherlands, Greece and Australia.

In Netherlands, having completed their meetings, Axel suggested that they enjoy the night life in Amsterdam. He asked Dev if he had seen the red-light district to which Dev replied in the negative and his facial expression betrayed discomfort. 'It's just tongue-in-cheek Dev, as you would say in English; have a walk around and then we shall go for rice *staffel*.' Rice *staffel* was a signature dish in Indonesian restaurants in Amsterdam.

Dev found a number of women tourists as well walking around the canal and looking smilingly at the windows behind which stood the ladies of the evening. It was indeed, as Axel had said, tongue-in-cheek. The more people are repressed with stringent laws around so called 'adult-services' the more enticing they become, when such services are legalized with caution most adults know how to deal with that freedom responsibly.

Later that year, when Dev landed in Melbourne, he just had to see the Melbourne Cricket Ground. As Dev took a guided tour of the MCG, spending considerable time in the museum, he remembered some famous Test matches whose highlights he had seen on TV in his home in Delhi.

'*Gidday* mate,' said the tour guide as Dev approached him after the tour was over.

'Can I go to the centre of the ground, to the wicket please?' asked Dev.

'We don't really encourage visitors near the pitch.'

Dev gently smiled, 'If you came all the way to Eden Gardens and couldn't go to the pitch wonder how you would feel!'

The tour guide looked at Dev, 'Righteyo mate, you win this one.'

Dev's Dutch and German colleagues were surprised when he returned after four hours. 'You spent three hours in an empty stadium!'

Travelling brings newness and discovery and mental stimulation, people who travel tend also to become more open to diversity. Dev's London assignment and his global travels enriched him as a professional and a person. Working with people from around the world was an incredible learning experience though at times emotionally demanding. He had already changed his habit of regularly checking progress of any work he had delegated to a junior colleague or secretary before the indicated completion time. His team members supported each other and his boss was both proficient and friendly. An uncomplicated and frank working relationship with his boss was intrinsically motivating for Dev who was beginning to be seen as a very dependable international resource by his company. But by 2001, as his assignment neared its end, he had to decide what to do next.

Dev had always valued the guidance of Karan Singh Varma, the MD of Hindustan Roqsanto Ltd. Karan would always make it a point to check on Dev whenever he visited MHQ for meetings. On one such visit in 2001 Dev asked Karan for advice. 'You will always have a job in Hindustan Roqsanto Dev, but if another international assignment comes your way you must take it. Broaden your experience; it will position you well for senior roles in the company.'

A week after his chat with Karan, Susan asked Dev one day in office, 'Free for a beer later today?'

Dev said, 'Certainly.'

'Smashing! I'll get Alan also to join in,' said his boss.

That evening Alan, Susan and Dev walked to the nearby pub called Rock & Turtle.

'Now do you support Everton or Liverpool—that will determine the outcome of this discussion!' said Susan as Alan laughed and Dev smiled.

Alan Mantell said to Dev after they had all got their beers and some nachos, 'Dev you have the option of returning to Hindustan Roqsanto, or early next year a wonderful global job is coming available in the Plastics business based in London: General Manager Planning—Plastics. Plastics as you know is not only new for Roqsanto, it's also relatively complex as compared to our other global businesses. For you to do the GM role, which incidentally will be a promotion, you will need some appreciation of types of manufacturing processes and also an understanding of strategic marketing of both thermoplastics and thermosets. So if you are open for this assignment, we will need to send you to Germany for six to nine months, where our plants use four to five different manufacturing processes. Your family can accompany you or continue staying in London.'

Dev accepted the offer after pondering over it with Meher. They decided to request a family elder to come down from New Delhi for a few months to London while Dev relocated to Hamburg for what turned out to be just over nine months. He returned back to MHQ in London in 2002 and was placed as General Manager Planning—Plastics. He had a global responsibility and in two months after taking over did a whirlwind tour to Calgary, Houston, Rio de Janeiro, Cape Town, Dubai, Singapore and Melbourne. As part of Dev's promotion his company gave him membership of their exclusive recreation club The Roquersbury in Putney. Located on the banks of Thames, The Roquersbury was a beautiful spread-out club with various sports facilities including a boathouse, large lawns and a conservatory, conference rooms, restaurants and over a hundred residential rooms. Several friends and relatives from India and USA had started visiting Dev and Meher, and Dev would make it a point to include an afternoon at The Roquersbury and a cruise on the

Thames in the little motor boat hired from the boathouse in their itinerary.

While I was still in London my meetings with Dev were not very frequent, however, in the September of that year we met quite a few times thanks to visits of Sanju and Luv. Sanju and his wife Divya were on a business-cum-leisure trip. They spent a week with her aunt and uncle in Birmingham and were with me in London for a few days. We visited Dev's home for lunch and later in the afternoon drove to The Roquersbury for a drink, crossing several pubs on the way. 'The pubs are the heart-centre of socialising here, aren't they?' asked Divya.

As we all settled down with our coffees and beers looking at the Thames a hundred metres into the distance Dev raised his beer glass and said, 'Lovely to meet after a long time, wish you could have stayed with us also for a few days.'

'Next time, Dev', said Sanju.

'How was Birmingham, Divya?' asked Meher.

'Do tell them about Mr Kesh please,' said Sanju looking at his wife. Divya smiled.

'My Aunt's 25-year-old son Keshav obviously doesn't know how much India has progressed; he had an argument with Sanjeev about life in India. But he is a very bright boy.'

Sanju quipped laughingly, 'The bright Mr Kesh kept referring to his father as the 'law-maker' and Divya's aunt as the "food-maker".'

'How do you manage your food here, Meher?' enquired Divya.

'I do the cooking at home, Indian pulses and groceries are available in the supermarkets including packaged food, and if anything is not in the supermarkets then Dev gets it from Southall or Wembley. He helps me a bit in the kitchen when he is not travelling,' she smiled at her husband, 'and sometimes we get takeaways.'

Divya looked admiringly at Meher, 'It's fabulous you manage the home and a little child and the food all by yourself, and wonderful that Dev lends a hand.'

What Dev said during this conversation has stayed with me ever since. 'Divya, I have learnt never ever to complain about food now. I realise how much effort goes into its preparation and whether we are in restaurants or at home, the fact that someone is making food and placing it hot and fresh in front of us is such a blessing.'

'Are you in touch with any of the other school friends?' Dev asked Sanju.

'Apart from Sandy, I only meet Goldie occasionally.'

Dev smiled as the antics of young Goldie flashed through his mind. 'Where is he these days?'

Sanju told us how Goldie had not managed to qualify for the Air Force and for a few years taken to alcohol. 'He then joined his father's white-goods dealership, later got married.

His marriage did him very good; he became serious about work and family and grew the business. They now have three large white-goods dealerships and Goldie also took a petrol pump.'

'That sounds like quite a journey', said Dev.

'His wife is very gentle and religious; while Goldie still has the zany side, he is quite a changed man.' Sanju then told us about another memorable character from school, 'Remember Manohar Pal Billa?'

Both Dev and I said together, 'Yes, of course!'

Sanju looked at us with a straight face and said, 'He is dead.'

Billa had actually realised his dream of becoming a mathematician. He obtained a Masters and later even Doctoral degree from USA. Billa had returned to India and was teaching mathematics in a school in Ahmedabad. He died in the massive Bhuj earthquake in January 2001. 'He willed whatever he had to an orphanage in Rohtak, presumably near his native village.'

In this journey of life we meet so many different people and make impressions of them. Sometimes our impressions go wrong and occasionally time changes human beings; who would have thought the untamed Billa of school would obtain a doctoral degree and teach children when he could have made big money with his qualifications, and then will his possessions to an orphanage! The river of life creates erosions and depositions that are not always predictable; all that is predictable is that the river will ultimately meet the sea.

Eklavya spent a week in London that September. He had organised a group tour to Paris and Amsterdam, after the group returned to India he decided to fly to London and spend a week with Dev and me. He stayed for a few days with both of us. '*Khannae*, what a fascinating city!' he said as I drove him around London. We had dinner in Leicester Square after which we went to a gentleman's strip club.

'Something more to end the evening on a happy note?' he said to me naughtily as we came out of the club having seen pole dancing for nearly two hours. Dev was returning from his travel the next day, and the day after I drove Luv to Dev's place.

After greeting Dev and Meher, Luv was just mesmerized with Vedant who had recently started primary school, 'Such a delightful kid!' Vedant too got comfortable with Luv in no time.

Dev chalked out the weekend programme, 'Let's drive to Cotswolds tomorrow, three of us; day after we'll all do Roquersbury and a cruise on the river.'

'So Bhaisahab, you have been travelling the world, must be so thrilling,' said Luv to Dev as the latter drove onto the M40. 'Had some interesting experiences or its just airport-hotel-office and back?' he continued with a puckish shine in his eyes.

Dev looked in the rear-view mirror and smiled at me and then said to Luv, 'Sir in front of your experiences ours will be bland, so we are all ears!'

Luv rested his eyes for a minute on Dev and then stated anachronously, 'Dev has become so much more elegant, a man of the world, yet deep down he is still the same!'

Our friend at the wheel smilingly responded, 'I thought you were going to embark on your adventures with bewitching beauties and not discuss prematurely greying men!'

We all laughed.

'Well,' said Luv, 'I have hell of a good time wherever I go!'

'Pray elaborate,' I said to our amusing friend.

'I find red lights or sporting masseuse in spas and partake in carnal pleasures!'

'Paid sex you mean?' I asked him.

'Absolutely paid sex—cleanest form of sex!'

Dev repeated my words, 'Pray elaborate.'

Luv said with a straight face, 'What is there to elaborate! There are no lies, no emotional play acting, it's a clean half an hour transaction.'

'Does Poulomi know about this?' Dev asked Luv while waiting for the traffic from right to pass at the roundabout.

'No way, *yaar*, I wouldn't be here if she did. But why do I sense surprise in your tone, most of my friends explore the night life wherever they go.' 'Not a good enough justification for what you are doing behind your wife's back,' said Dev.

'Dev, men are not meant to be monogamous. I think even women are not but I shouldn't say that conclusively. I know your next remark would be how would these friends or I feel if the wives did similar hanky-panky. I think I would be miffed. But you know what, I find it hard to resist! And my love for my wife doesn't reduce one bit.'

Dev smiled at Luv, 'Okay, okay, who are we to make judgements!'

Luv then said with a pause, 'But one thing is sure, sex with someone known is most pleasurable!'

I commented from the back seat, 'So, Mr Luv has had an affair too, is it?'

'*Yaar* I am being honest and you are making me feel guilty,' said Luv with cheerless eyes.

'Stolen kisses and forbidden sex are always sweeter, of course, social repercussions have to be evaluated.' Luv also told us about phone sex which he had been 'trying' with one of his former neighbours.

Both Dev and I laughed loudly.

While late September was the end of English summer, that afternoon in Cotswolds at Bourton-on-the-Water was warm and splendid. We walked up and down the one single road: Luv was captivated by the beauty of the small village and the little brook on either side of which sat people with their picnic baskets.

'So, so pretty, Dev,' said Luv.

'Let's have something to eat,' suggested Dev after we had strolled for an hour.

As we found a little restaurant besides the rivulet, Luv was in a reflective mood. He started a discussion that went on till next day.

'What is the relationship between economic prosperity and cultural pride and nationalism?'

Both Dev and I gave him a mystified look. 'How come from paid sex and phone sex to this serious topic?' asked Dev munching a burger.

'*Yaar* this is my first trip to UK, but whenever I travel in Europe, I find people quite unperturbed, I sense a lack of ego and they talk about both the good aspects of their country and what they are not too proud of very frankly. They laugh at themselves unhesitatingly; achievement seems to dispel complexes. So it's made me wonder how cultural pride and nationalism relate to economic prosperity.'

'Cultural pride certainly creates a sense of nationalism. I suppose the correlation between nationalism and economic development is not as strong,' I said.

Dev was nodding, 'Yeah, I agree, cultural pride would lead to nationalism and that would fire the desire to build a prosperous nation but economic prosperity depends on how well human and natural resources are harnessed through proper governance.'

'Is nationalism a virtue Dev?' asked Luv still having his fish and chips.

'At the higher mankind level, nationalism is divisive. Rousseau said something to the effect that the first man who drew a line on earth stating 'this is mine' was like an impostor, and that the finest condition of man was the 'state of nature' somewhere between the beastly age and the current modern society. But can we return to that blissful 'state of nature'? Don't we all love our homes and want to make them more comfortable? So what's wrong in loving our land and nation? Of course, when that pride becomes overzealous and we stop objectively evaluating ourselves and our nation, and as you were saying, Eklavya, when we stop laughing at ourselves, that's when the expression becomes unpleasant. Otherwise, nationalism is a virtue.'

'Also, political boundaries remain imperative to protect people and property, there is no feasible alternative for self-governance other than the current nation states and elected sovereign governments,' I added.

Luv was still curious. 'You know Dev, when I am in Delhi and north India, and I see the straightforward person being referred to as *bechara* or poor fellow; and the guy who can swindle is called the 'smart guy', I wonder who our role models are. She or he who tries something new gets pulled down by mediocre people; jumping traffic lights, littering streets, making lame excuses, makes me think whether cultural pride in the past is more important or a sense of collective guilt of the present is essential to drive improvement and progress.'

As Dev began paying the bill, I looked at my watch, it was getting late and so I said, 'Luv let's continue this discussion tomorrow at Roquersbury.'

As we started our drive back to London we got into our boys' chat again. 'Still an ass-man Luv or any change in the kinky preference?' I poked him.

Luv chuckled, 'Becoming more and more of a bum-man *Khannae* with each passing escapade! All because of Purnima, my elder sister's friend!'

We laughed our way through most of the return drive.

The next day when we met at Roquersbury, we first went to the boathouse where Dev hired a motor boat in which he took Meher, Vedant, Luv and me on a memorable cruise on the Thames.

'I wish I had the money to buy one of these riverside homes,' said Luv seeing the beautiful houses on the banks of the river with their back lawns bowing into the water, 'This entire setting is so serene and spellbinding.'

After we returned Meher went to drop Vedant in the kids playing area, as the three of us settled in the conservatory. 'So where were we yesterday?' I said looking at Luv.

'Don't know where we were yesterday *yaar*, but right now I am in heaven!' quipped Luv sipping the red wine.

'I think you were saying a critical analysis of the present, sense of collective guilt as you put it, is more important than cultural pride to drive economic prosperity,' I reminded Luv.

'Clichéd wisdom sucks *Khannae* and Dev, what's the point that yoga was introduced in India 5000 years ago if a vast majority of people in India are physically unfit today, we achieved excellence in science and architecture yet today we accept mediocrity easily, we take shortcuts instead of establishing and following proper process. So my point was, fine I accept nationalism is a virtue, but instead of propagating cultural pride shouldn't we be focusing on work ethics, public manners, hygiene and relentlessly pursuing economic growth and giving all people a life of dignity.'

Meher joined us just as Luv was completing his staid postulate. 'Having a serious chat, it seems,' she said smilingly. Luv pulled out a chair for her.

Dev had a sober expression on his face. 'Eklavya, who can deny that there is no substitute for economic growth, not just for dignity of citizens but also world peace.'

Luv looked enquiringly at Dev, 'World peace?'

Dev continued, 'What I mean is that the world respects power, economic and military power, and hence every country has to strive for that strength. World peace depends on this balance of power.' Luv nodded as Dev further shared his thinking, 'For a nation it is important that her citizens are aware of its rich cultural heritage but also its current areas of development. Too much pride in the historical heights a nation had achieved without realization of existing limitations creates hollow pomposity, but no knowledge of past richness and only seeing current problems creates cynicism and morosity. That's why good writers show a mirror to the society, they both commend and censure; that's why freedom of speech is such an integral part of modern nation states which democracy nurtures.'

Luv was listening absorbedly to Dev, 'So Dev you are saying cultural pride and a sense of collective remorse in the present limitations—both go hand in hand?'

'Cultural pride, critical well-reasoned appraisal of present state of affairs, democracy and hard work, all four go hand in hand in bringing prosperity for any nation' replied Dev.

'So many ingredients?' said Luv enquiringly.

'Even at an individual level,' said Meher, 'ability to laugh at oneself without losing self-respect, to make friends with people from around the world without prejudice, to love completely without expected return and ability to stand one's ground on rational fact-based convictions, all four go hand in hand in making a well-rounded individual.'

Luv bowed a little in front of Meher. 'That made most sense to me, brilliant!' he said clinking his glass of wine with Meher's cup of cappuccino.

'So Bhaisahab, tell me how should a nation work on human values and work ethics at an individual level?' said Luv.

'Eklavya, nations have to work not just on GDP growth and human development index but also on the softer side—this is where family and school, public education, cultural heritage and honest writers and journalists play a part. They build the soul of the nation.'

With a studied look on his face, Luv asked Dev, 'You keep referring to 'nations' Dev, illustrate cultural heritage to me specifically with an India perspective.'

Dev had an intense look on his face. 'See you were speaking of people not respecting queues and making lame excuses, if you feel this is part of India so are the ancient achievements in science and statecraft, as is the vibrant democracy, the entrepreneurship, the fortitude and tolerance of people. Proper dissemination of all this will help—the old language, scriptures, *sanatana* principles, history—but if these go into cold storage then we will be taking one of the key anchors and source of pride away, potentially causing indiscipline and corruption.'

Luv still had energy left to discuss the topic, 'Dev, awareness of the past creates pride but only if there is inner sense of character, isn't it? And if you had to choose between pride versus criticism, which side will you tilt?'

Dev smiled at Luv, 'I would err on the side of pride, only err. But there is no substitute for economic growth, no substitute for dignity of life and dignity in death.'

'You mentioned democracy and freedom of speech more than once. So they are so absolutely integral to economic growth and happiness?'

Dev patiently responded, 'Absolutely integral, Eklavya, in the current state of political evolution of the world. Even totalitarian states can drive GDP growth, but democracy protects and nurtures freedom of speech, it allows different viewpoints to be placed in public. Food, clothing, shelter and freedom of expression and movement are necessary conditions for human happiness. Freedom of speech and sense of humour are ingredients for and expressions of a healthy society, of course there have to be understandable qualifications to freedom of speech in the interest of public order and national honour.'

After staying quite for a while Luv said, 'Always so wonderful to be with you Dev, I think you need to learn how to enjoy life from me and I need to learn everything else from you!'

Dev laughed, 'Life is so short, if you have learnt how to enjoy you've learnt all that there is to it.'

Luv smiled. 'Dev, summarise all this discussion we have been having in one line.'

Dev said thoughtfully, 'Have more pride, be less critical and be more responsible.'

Luv repeated Dev's statement, 'So I should have more cultural pride, be less critical, meaning be constructively critical of the environment, and be more responsible at an individual level.'

Dev gently nodded.

'And what can a common person do individually?'

'At the very least, each one of us can treat the people around us with dignity, we can all support each other in our limited way, and we can all respect public decorum better. Almost entirely in our hands to do this bit!'

Before that year ended, I met Dev one more time.

In the middle of December, I received a surprise phone call. It was from my distant cousin Gautam! It took me a while to register. 'Hearing your voice after a decade and a half! Where are you calling from?'

Those were pre-social media days when long lost friends and acquaintances could not be tracked at the click of a few buttons. Gautam was in London, en route to Calgary. He had been in Calgary all these years except for a few years when he was in Montreal University. He had flown in from Delhi where he had gone to sell off their old house, and got my phone number from my father. He was in a hotel near Heathrow and his connecting flight was next afternoon.

'All these years, Gautam, just didn't get any news from you or Geeta!'

Gautam was working in the Systems department of an upstream oil company; he had married a Canadian girl and Geeta had married an Indian settled in Calgary whose family was known to Gautam and Geeta's parents. Geeta had a four-year-old son while Gautam's wife was expecting.

'The years have flown past, Sandeep, I travelled to India just twice in the last 15 odd years,' said Gautam. I invited him home and after we had chatted for an hour, I asked him if he remembered Dev.

'Of course, of course, who can forget Dev!'

When I told him Dev was also in London he instantly said, 'Can we meet him even if it's for a very short while?'

There was a little silence at Dev's end when I called him and mentioned that Gautam was at my place, just for the evening, and keen to meet him in case he was free for an hour or even less. 'Sure Sandeep, I am home, do come over.'

Gautam met Dev very warmly and the hour-long planned get-together lasted for nearly three hours. 'Whenever you are in Calgary next you must spare an evening for me Dev, would be so nice to get to have a meal with you,' said Gautam. On his return home, Gautam sent an email to Dev sharing his immense joy at having re-acquainted with him and at the opportunity to meet Meher and Vedant.

The Global Head

'Use one kind word in every sentence, please.' Dev stood outside Vedant's primary school one Friday and could overhear the teacher since Vedant's classroom was close to the school gate.

'What are the three kind words we learnt today?' said the teacher.

'Please, thank you and sorry,' said the entire class together.

'Well done! Have a lovely weekend all of you!' she said.

'You too, Miss Jones,' said the whole class loudly and cheerfully.

Dev saw Vedant walk towards the gate; his smile widened seeing his father. There was a little girl a step behind Vedant.

'Go on, Lady,' said Vedant to her, side-stepping and letting his classmate exit from the gate first.

'Bye-bye Ved, see you on Monday', she said.

Dev hugged Vedant and they started walking towards their home. 'Had a nice day darling?'

'I did, Dad, Miss Jones gave me a smiley sticker for the sentences I made.'

Dev lovingly tousled his son's hair. 'How come you were referring to such a small girl as "lady"?'

Vedant looked curiously at Dev, 'That's her name, Dad!'

'Her name is Lady?' asked Dev a little surprised.

'Her full name is Lady-Bethany, we call her Lady for short. Just as my name is Vedant, but my friends call me Ved.'

Dev looked at his son affectionately. Man often doesn't realise how happy he is, it takes unhappy times to make him realise it.

It was still only a few years into the new decade but much had happened in the world in those early years of 2000s. The internet had spread rapidly and email had become the most popular form of communication. Free webmail services like Hotmail and Yahoo were available to everyone and no business card was presented without an email address on it. In his early years in Roqsanto International having teleconference meetings was a novel experience for Dev, but a few years into the new millennium it was videoconferencing that was the fresh business aid. SMS or text messaging using mobile phones was getting quite prevalent as well. The dot.com bubble had burst after an initial but brief promise though Amazon.com, the online retailer, was fast becoming a household name. Climate change concerns were growing around the globe and epidemics like foot-and-mouth disease and SARS had raised alarms in more than one country. The big news in the business world with implications for international politics was the rise of China and India. A series of meetings in Roqsanto focused on China and India and how the company could expand its footprint in these geographies. The acronym 'Chindia' soon expanded to BRICS to refer to the vast growth opportunity in Brazil Russia India China and South Africa. The economic and monetary union of Europe had been concluded and the Euro launched. However, the biggest, most devastating and tragic event that occurred in those early years was the blowing up of World Trade Centre buildings in New York in 2001. Terrorism came to be recognized as a massive global challenge after 9-11, as the New York attack came to be known as. It shook the world, heightened security concerns in most parts on the planet and changed the nature of air travel forever.

Dev was almost on the high table of his company and travelling worldwide especially to main business cities in all continents. While security checks at all airports had become stringent, they were particularly tight at several cities in the USA. Once Dev landed at Houston to find the immigration and security queue virtually starting at the exit door of the aircraft on the aerobridge! As in all countries around the world, Dev found his colleagues in Houston office using distinctive words:

they referred to distributors as 'jobbers', toilet as 'restroom', fizzy drink as 'soda' and foreigners as 'aliens'. However, what Dev loved was the straightforward approach to work. If he suggested three actions to the local Plastics strategy and planning team they would typically revert with 'understood the first two, say more about the third point.' If they felt the third could not be completed in the suggested time, they would be candid in stating 'first two will be done in a month's time, the third will need six weeks', and at the end of the committed time all actions would be accomplished! As always, on his flight back to London, Dev was trying to work out in his mind how his colleagues, from the leading industrialized nation of the world, followed instructions almost with military discipline!

Back in MHQ, Dev was frequently asked to join workshops that focused on India strategy. In the spring of 2004, he was invited for a meeting by his former team New Business Prospects. The same day Dev's sister-in-law Meghna, Meher's sister, was coming to London. Meghna was five years younger to Meher and was working for a big law firm in Delhi. She had spent a week in Frankfurt for their firm's client on an international arbitration case; and was going to be with Meher and Dev for a few days on holiday.

'Think of India as Europe,' said Dev in the workshop, 'just as there are 28 countries in EU which are very diverse, likewise India. The 28 Indian states have different languages and cultures and some states are economically much more developed.'

The good-humoured Paul had started affectionately referring to Dev as 'The Master'. 'We humble mortals gratefully accept the wisdom handed down by The Master!' said Paul as everyone in the meeting laughed. Dev had a self-effacing smile on his clean-shaven face.

Dev could hear Meghna and Meher laughing as he reached his home.

'Hi Bhaiya,' said Meghna giving Dev a bear hug. Meghna doted on her brother-in-law and Dev too treated her like his little sister.

'I am so sorry I couldn't get out of the meeting and receive you at the airport,' apologized Dev.

'You will be forgiven, Bhaiya, if you take me for a nice long drive around London tomorrow!' she said. Meghna was a charming, vivacious and intelligent young lady who never unduly bothered about commonplace things like bonus or promotions at work. Like Meher, she would instantly light up any gathering with her cheerful deportment.

Post-dinner, after Ved fell asleep, Dev lit the gas-fired fireplace as the three of them settled down for a chat over coffee. Meghna told Meher and Dev about their German client and its owners.

Meher looked at Dev and said, 'Meghna was telling me before you came about the palatial house the owners of this company have.'

Dev gently smiled. Meghna continued, 'Bhaiya, the Managing Director invited my senior and me for dinner to their place. The Chairman is her elder brother. She and her husband are so unassuming, which made that grand house even more royal. They have a centrally-heated swimming pool and tennis court in the house, and the Chairman also owns this yacht which stays moored on the river. Hans Schmidt, the Chairman, carries himself so modestly. And you know what?' Meghna paused a bit to sip her coffee, 'He spends four months every year in Rishikesh!'

'Rishikesh?' said Meher inquisitively.

Meghna nodded, 'He works in an *ashram* in Rishikesh, when he told me I enquired what took him to Rishikesh every year. You know what he said—"after establishing a successful business and buying this big house I realised something was missing; when I travelled first time to Rishikesh I found people there had very little belongings but they were still always smiling". He has now been going to Rishikesh every year for the last 15 years!'

'Spiritual places attract many prosperous people,' said Dev thoughtfully.

'What's the relationship, Bhaiya, between spirituality and materialism and happiness?' asked Meghna after a contemplative pause.

Dev reflected, 'Meghna, *dharma*, *arth*, *kama*, and *moksha* is the purpose of a happy life. So righteousness, fulfilling material and physical desires and, for want of a better word, spirituality; a balance between the material and the spiritual leads to contentment.'

Meghna delved further, 'Bhaiya, what exactly is materialism and spirituality, and how come those ascetics who have nothing appear happy?'

Dev again tried to find an answer, 'Materialism I reckon is tangible sources of pleasure—house, bank balance, family—while spirituality is internalization of the universal truth, an awareness of the ephemeral nature of life. Since material is temporary, materialism will lead to unhappiness with that which one doesn't have, especially without the anchor of spirituality or what we may call *dharma*. Having said this, I am yet to come across a person who is 100% materialistic without any concept, right or wrong, of the universal truth.'

Meghna tried to play back her understanding, 'So Bhaiya, you are saying that on the continuum of materialism and spirituality a totally materialistic person—not that you have ever come across any—will not be happy, but a totally spiritual person may well be content and blissful?'

Dev again smiled at Meghna and said, 'Something like that! In the earlier days a lot of people in India would voluntarily become *bhikshuk*, they would wander in search of truth and seek alms for survival. Such people were not unhappy. Mind you, being spiritual doesn't mean impoverishment. As I just said it only means being aware of this vast nothingness and transcending materialism even while living a material life. I am sure you have come across Maslow's need hierarchy: people move from physiological needs to social needs to ultimately self-fulfilment. Self-fulfilment might come through creating a successful organisation or philanthropy or owning a yacht or seeking truth. But spirituality in its sublime sense must mean negating the self that is going even beyond self-fulfilment. In that state of realization happiness and sorrow become two sides of the same coin, and man sees himself as part of nature and not distinct from it.'

Meghna concluded the chat, 'So a balance is needed between materialism and spirituality for dignity and happiness, the twain should meet!'

There were some big organisational announcements in Dev's company in the working week including news of Howard Sadler taking over as Vice President Strategy, Roqsanto Chemicals International Ltd. and Wang-Yong Huang, presently GM Plastics Roqsanto Canada, taking over as Vice President Plastics.

Dev was happy to hear that Howard was returning to MHQ but was sad to know that his boss Craig Hughes was leaving the company. Both Craig and his predecessor had rated Dev very highly and when Dev met Craig after the announcement he said, 'Time to return home my friend, but the work you are doing Dev is making significant difference to the business. Take it to its logical end; I will let Wang-Yong know in the handover that you should be retained in this role till next year end at least.'

Dev met Howard Sadler a few days after he had taken over and learnt that his wife Laura had been detected with cancer. 'It's in an early stage, Dev, so doctors are confident she will be fine.'

Dev had a concerned look on his face. Howard changed the topic of discussion, 'You tell me, how has this time been in London for you?'

'It's been terrific Howard,' said Dev. 'I have heard such wonderful things about you. They don't keep you in MHQ for long unless you are exceptional,' remarked Howard. Dev smiled a little.

'And have you and the good lady and the young one enjoyed London?' 'Absolutely wonderful Howard, fantastic place!'

'I remember you loved Madras as well.'

Dev nodded.

'You know what Dev; I have had the best time of my life in Delhi!'

Dev's annual trips to various global business hubs were coming up and he was starting with Calgary. He sent an email to Gautam, remembering their cordial meeting a few months earlier. Gautam instantly responded copying Geeta in the email: 'Dev so excited to know you are travelling to Calgary, please keep either the Monday or Tuesday evening free, Geeta and I would love to meet you over dinner'.

Dev felt a bit nonplussed. After all these years, he had Geeta's email ID! But the 1980s were long gone, those years when he held onto one picture of Geeta and a thousand thoughts were history. Dev was now in a marriage, in a beautiful marriage, and he wondered if it would be appropriate for him to have dinner with Gautam and Geeta! It was not in him to conceal anything from Meher.

'Of course you should meet them,' said Meher, 'come on, that was entirely in your mind, for all you know Gautam's sister never got to know what you felt. And who doesn't go through these early youth crushes? Just meet them as friends.'

Meher's advice was a very matured one, thought Dev. Yet in his mind there was unease and that one big question—did Geeta ever get that letter? Dev was unable to cast off the unease. Righteousness was integral to Dev, unlike Luv for whom morality was just a fashion that changed with time and place and net worth of an individual! Indeed, morality is a ring pushed onto the finger of middle-class hands, which the abjectly poor and awfully rich dispensed with long ago.

Notwithstanding the moral unease, there was a simmering keenness in Dev to meet Geeta if at all for one more time. As Nita Rajagopalan would say 'any romantic association, a one-way crush or a deep love affair, requires closure for both to move ahead without baggage'. Dev's self-knitted dreams of love in those early years—I have no reason to believe it was anything but one sided—had not yet had closure. I suspect somewhere he wanted to meet Geeta to compare the image he had of her with the real person, and somewhere there lay an unconscious call for 'closure'.

It was a pleasant Sunday evening when Dev landed in Calgary; he was to meet Gautam and Geeta on Monday evening for dinner in a downtown restaurant at 6:30 pm.

'So wonderful to see such a marvellous man in our city!' said Gautam. Dev gently smiled. 'Geeta should be here by 6:45, she finishes work by 6:30,' he continued.

'Where does she work?' enquired Dev.

'She is employed with a pharma company…there she is!'

Dev had for long thought he would never meet Geeta again. He looked in the direction of the entrance door to see a young lady in black trousers walking towards them with a soft smile. He realised he was very self-conscious. She rested her eyes on Dev who extended his hand, 'Hi, Geeta.'

Geeta warmly shook Dev's hand, 'Hi Dev, such a long time.'

Dev was nearing 40, Geeta was in her late 30s and she looked pleasant and elegant, but wasn't the 16-year-old whose picture Dev had kept for many years! As they got talking Dev realised even Geeta was a little self-conscious, but then his impression of her was of a reserved girl. Did her inhibited manner suggest that she had got that letter, wondered Dev.

'How are Meher and Vedant?' she asked politely.

'They are well, thank you. And how is your son, what is his name?' Dev could somehow not get himself to check about her husband!

'He is Devesh; quite a handful,' said Geeta once again with a very slight smile.

They ordered drinks and starters and as they got comfortable in each other's presence Gautam checked with Dev, 'So Dev, prior to this one how many trips to Calgary?'

Dev thought for a moment and said, 'This is my fourth trip.'

'And you never thought of checking if we were still here!' remarked Gautam half seriously, half in jest.

'Well, he had clearly forgotten us,' quipped Geeta, a comment which Dev didn't know how to respond to.

'Dev, you will need to excuse me just for 20 minutes, I can't resist seeing the last period of a hockey match and the restaurant has televisions only in those two corners, you chat with Geeta till then,' said Gautam getting up from his chair, and then looking at his sister, 'just order that steak which I always have for my main course, medium rare please.'

'The Flames playing today?' Geeta asked her brother.

'You bet!'

As Gautam excused himself, Dev once again felt a bit flushed and he sensed shyness even on Geeta's face. Dev and Geeta talked about their respective work and she asked him about his hectic travelling schedule. They ordered another round of drinks and the main course; after about 15 minutes, Dev asked Geeta with a withdrawn smile, 'So you are very well settled in Canada now, must have been quite a journey these last 20 years.'

Geeta didn't respond to Dev's remark, she slowly lifted her face a bit and looked into Dev's eyes. She looked into his eyes for that split second more. The contrast of her eyes was completely unlike what he had so far seen. Some stories and thoughts cannot be told in a 400-page book or a three-hour long film, some are conveyed in five seconds! Geeta had received that letter written 15 years ago! She didn't say so in words, her eyes did. She owed nothing to Dev, but that look seemed to acknowledge, if not reciprocate, the heartbeat of Dev from those long years of 1980s. It was the way an honourable woman speaks.

As his flight took off from Calgary, Dev settled in his business class seat playing back in his mind the meeting with Geeta. He realised that the young married woman he met a couple of days back was different from the image he had been carrying of a teenage girl, he also subconsciously knew that there had been no 'closure' and somewhere he wanted to meet her again. He felt uncomfortable with this thought and forced his attention back on his work and family.

'How was your dinner with your old friends?' asked Meher after Dev had rested for a bit back home.

'It was nice Meher, though different from what I had imagined.'

She smiled at her husband and said, 'It always is. Meeting childhood friends after a long gap is never the same, you have all grown up differently.'

Dev's new boss was different from his previous two bosses. Wang-Yong Huang didn't smile easily nor did he seem to trust most people including Dev. Informal team get-togethers became infrequent, on a rare occasion when their entire team met in the pub and were chatting about goings-on in the world, Wang-Yong said looking at Dev, 'What I worry about most is the population explosion in India, that's a bomb waiting to go off.'

Dev was surprised at the comment and responded with a wry smile, 'Well, India is the second most populous country in the world; India and China both have over a billion people and have to manage their growing population urgently but carefully.' Wang-Yong ignored Dev's response and looked elsewhere.

Roqsanto International used to have an annual training programme for all middle management staff who had been with the company for three years or less. Global heads of businesses and functions would make presentations to the new joiners in that high-profile, week-long programme. As Wang-Yong was travelling, he nominated Dev to be the presenter for Plastics. Dev was aware that all other businesses would be represented by speakers senior to him. He knew he had to raise his game—knowledge and presentation skills—to make an impact.

A man or woman grows only when he or she comes out of their comfort zone. This effort of going beyond the comfort zone may result in worldly success or failure but it always results in evolution. Dev reminded himself the need to step up as he drove to The Roquersbury in Putney where the training programme was being held. He started by introducing the big picture of the Plastics business and then discussed the operational issues including customer buying behaviour and plastics waste management, he showed best practice photographs and key performance numbers and had an engaging question and answer session with attendees laced with a bit of humour. In the end he summarized the main issues for the business and way forward. Dev's session was rated as the best by the trainees. It was then that Dev first discovered the public speaker in himself. On his return, hearing about the feedback, Wang-Yong rather grudgingly complimented Dev, 'It must be your training in the New Business Prospects that helped you make a good presentation.' Dev remained expressionless.

Towards the end of 2004 as Dev sat down with his boss for annual appraisal, the latter said to his subordinate, 'So what are you planning to do next?'

Dev was thrown by this loaded question. 'My impression is a year more in this job and then I look for my next role,' he said.

'When do you complete three years in this job?' asked Dev's boss.

'In a few months' time.'

Wang-Yong stoutly said, 'March end will be a good time for you to move to a new role. Let me know if you need any help.'

Dev got an average appraisal rating that year. More stressfully, he had about three months to look for a new role.

Dev drew his strength from a sense of spiritual detachment and Meher's caring support. The stress of finding a new job at his level of seniority within three months was lessened when Meher said to him, 'If not here then somewhere else, if not somewhere else then, anywhere else.'

In the January of 2005, two jobs at Dev's seniority level were advertised within the company: General Manager Plastics Middle East based in Dubai and General Manager Agrichemicals Far East based in Singapore. Dev applied for both.

On the last weekend of January, as Dev waited for the result of his applications, he sat in his living room looking at the gas-lit fireplace and the souvenirs on the mantelpiece. He saw the little glass *inuksuk* he had bought in Calgary and remembered it was Geeta's birthday in early February. He had exchanged two emails with her, one after his return from Calgary and the other on New Year's. Once again, with some self-doubt, Dev emailed Geeta asking her if he could call on 3rd February and wish her. Geeta seemed touched and replied, 'That's so sweet of you Dev, of course, call anytime!

It was late evening London time when, before leaving for home, Dev dialled Geeta's number. 'Hi Geeta, it's my great joy to be able to wish you today!'

'Hi,' said Geeta with not as much excitement.

'Happy birthday!'

'Thank you, it's nice of you to remember after so many years', she said.

'Hope you have a lovely year ahead. How have you been?'

'Thank you, all well with me.'

Dev wasn't sensing much verve in Geeta's tone, he nonetheless continued, 'Got something nice planned for today?'

'Look I am a little preoccupied right now and won't be able to talk for long,' said Geeta.

Dev was confounded by Geeta's inflection. He felt speechless for he had expected a different expression. 'Sorry I think I got you in the middle of something—have a wonderful birthday,' said Dev, sensing that he ought to keep the phone down.

'That's fine; thank you for calling, I appreciate it.'

Dev reclined in his office chair and looked out at the Thames and the evening lights from Waterloo Bridge to his left to Westminster Bridge to his right. He rued making that call to Geeta! Geeta had said nothing wrong, nor was my friend Devavratt at any fault. But thrown by her matter-of-fact tone, Dev concluded at that moment that it was futile to re-introduce the memories of a tender past to the austere realities of the present; it was best they stayed buried where they were and any further effort might only lead to corrosion of that softness. Dev never called up or met Geeta after that; it was what Nita Rajagopalan would describe as 'closure'.

A few days later Dev received an email titled 'General Manager Agrichemicals Far East—Update' which stated that his candidature for the position had not been successful. Dev's closest friend and confidante in office was Paul Anderson, he called him on the internal phone line and wondered if he was free for lunch.

'How is the great Master?' said Paul, giving Dev a hug who was waiting outside the staff cafeteria. 'That's a lovely little tie,' remarked Paul admiring Dev's red necktie.

'Something to brighten up an otherwise dull personality!' quipped Dev as Paul widened his eyes acknowledging the repartee. They chatted about Indian food, their respective families, Manchester United and their company's strategic moves over lunch. Dev clarified to Paul that in India there was no dish called 'curry' and this term to describe Indian food he had heard only after moving to England! Dev then shared with Paul his job issue.

'Hmm,' contemplated Paul, 'Tell you what Dev, let's take a little stroll outside, we can chat about this in fresh air!'

The two of them crossed the Hungerford foot bridge over the Thames and walked along the charming South Bank towards the London Eye. 'Have you spoken to Johan the Human Resources VP?' enquired Paul.

Dev shook his head, 'I know Johan reasonably well, very upfront and genuine.'

'Have a word with him,' continued Paul, 'Howard Sadler, isn't he your mate from India days, he is a senior VP.'

Dev looked at Paul and nodded.

'And you know Susan so well; she has just become head of NBP and always has a nice word to say about you, that's a door you can unhesitatingly knock on!'

Dev absorbed Paul's suggestions.

'So you see, Master, while this googly has been bowled at you it's not all doom and gloom,' said Paul smilingly.

'A cricket analogy from a Manchester United fan!' remarked Dev cheerfully.

'What about you Paul, aren't you looking for a change?' asked Dev.

'I am actually; it's been a long stint in NBP though I have been in my current Fresh to Portfolio role for under two years. They have advertised a terrific job just day before, Vice President Agrichemicals, global P&L accountability; superb line role covering the entire value-chain. I will apply for it,' said Paul.

Dev and Paul had struck a delightful and enduring friendship! They would enquire of and share with each other the social and cultural distinctiveness of India and Britain respectively. While Dev was not an introvert anymore, Paul was a total extrovert. They could both laugh at themselves and occasionally make light-hearted observations of the places they had grown up in.

As they turned around after reaching the Westminster Bridge, Paul asked Dev looking to his right on the South Bank, 'Can I entice you for a little coffee in one of these charming little cafes?'

Dev smiled, 'You certainly can!' Dev then remarked, 'I love your use of the word "little", Paul.'

Paul smilingly replied, 'It's a very affectionate term, isn't it?'

'It's most endearing, makes the remark understated, and understatements make people more receptive to them,' observed Dev smilingly.

'Ah! The art of the understatement—it's a fine art Master!' Paul then comically illustrated the art of understating things, 'My neighbour Mark stabbed my brother, so I am a *bit* upset with him these days!'

Dev burst out laughing again.

Dev paid for the cappuccinos and when they were just 100 metres from the office Paul said, 'Let me know Dev how the job search goes.'

'I will, and hope your application for the Agrichemicals role is successful,' replied Dev.

'Are you aware of CDE?' asked Paul.

'Have heard about it but don't quite know what it involves,' said Dev.

'It stands for *Compass-Delta-Entaxei*, nobody gets appointed as VP without clearing the CDE. Candidates whose applications are shortlisted for VP level job have to spend half a day with three very senior Roqsanto executives one of whom has to be from the Compass group—the highest grade level in the company! There is personality profiling and a case study discussion and formal interview followed by a drink in the evening. Only when the CDE signs off that you get to a VP level position.'

'Sounds very professional and thorough Paul,' remarked Dev.

'In some ways the most crucial half a day of your career if you are seeking a senior role,' concluded Paul.

'What exactly does the word *entaxei* mean?' asked Dev.

'Comes from the company's Greek origins, perhaps means approval or clearance' replied Paul.

'Interesting,' said Dev with a gentle smile.

'The Master!' said Paul opening his arms to give Dev a hug, 'always so wonderful to meet you!'

Dev met Johan and apprised him of his situation. 'I think there are only two jobs in India at your level and both are all taken, and the Hindustan Roqsanto MD is two grade levels above you and Karan still has a few years to go,' said Johan understanding Dev's predicament. 'Well, leave it with me Devavratt, there are a few roles coming up, let me find out from some of the senior VP's what they are looking for and if there would be a skill-profile match with you.' Dev also tried to reach Howard Sadler but learnt he was on leave attending to his wife whose health had deteriorated.

Dev and Meher always had more house guests than any of my other friends. 'It's a blessed home where lots of guests visit,' Meher would say to Dev. After they moved to London the house guests only increased. I reckon most stopped by because Meher and Dev would not only affectionately invite but warmly and graciously host everyone, a few I daresay because there was a nice apartment in Central London available! Most reciprocated genially as well.

Dev and Meher had also formed a wonderful circle of friends in London, and their plush apartment had become the popular party home for seven-eight Indian families! The shy Dev from school time had become the nucleus of these get-togethers, he would often include a fun quiz in the parties or suggest drives to touristy places around London and occasionally celebrate Diwali and Holi together. 'Dev is our leader for the next 50 years,' said one of their friends in the Indian group light-heartedly but not frivolously. As I wrote earlier, man often doesn't realise how happy he is, it takes unhappy times to make him comprehend it.

Shankar and Jaya, their friends from Madras, had twice spent a week with Dev and Meher in Notting Hill Gate. In February 2005 though, Shankar was travelling alone. 'Dev looks very preoccupied,' he said to Meher, who gently responded, 'Some work pressures.'

A day later Meher comforted Dev again, 'Something will work out; have faith in your organisation and in Krishna.'

Dev smiled back at his wife. He mentioned to her that he had already floated his CV to a couple of head hunters both in London and in India. He just wanted to give the best to his wife and his child.

It was towards end of February that Dev received a call from the VP Human Resources. 'Any progress my friend?' he checked.

'Nothing so far Johan, have that one iron in the fire though—the Plastics job in Dubai.'

'Right Mr Rajvansh, the VP Agrichemicals job has been on the company website for 15 days now, sexy job, global P&L accountability with supply chain through to sales and marketing all reporting into the VP, MHQ based line role; so far 17 applicants! The top guys aren't too excited with the current applications, they want to see a few more CVs, go for it!'

Dev mentioned to Johan that his application for a lower grade role in the Agrichemicals line of business had been rejected, so how could he expect to find a job in the same business and that too as head of business.

'For the Singapore job they wanted a local candidate Devavratt, this is a global assignment and your track record in international assignments is, how will they say it here in an understated manner, rather acceptable!'

Dev responded decorously, 'Johan, I think my close friend Paul Anderson would be an applicant for this job too.'

'And?'

'It would not be appropriate for me to apply for a job for which my friend is also an applicant.'

After a long silence Johan said, 'Let me find out if Paul is being shortlisted for the CDE.'

'Thanks Johan you have been so helpful!'

'We can't afford to lose you,' said Johan in a bright tone.

At 3:30 pm the same day, Johan called Dev again, 'Okay Devavratt, you are third on the preference list for the Dubai job, chances of getting it rather slim. Paul Anderson has not been shortlisted for the CDE for VP Agrichemicals. Today is last day for applying, send in your application now.'

Dev immediately called Paul on his mobile and told him of his discussion with Johan.

'Dev, if I am not getting the job, I couldn't wish it for a better person than you! Thank you for being so transparent,' said Paul in his usual manner.

Dev earnestly prepared for the *Compass-Delta-Entaxei*. At the end of the assessment, he was called in to where the three senior executives were seated, one of them said beamingly, 'So you want to know the damage?'

Dev smiled back.

'Congratulations Devavratt, you are one of the two applicants selected for VP level assignment!' They had assessed the candidates on seven leadership capabilities and the senior executive addressing Dev added, 'Your profile is so strong, you can virtually choose the job you want to do in Roqsanto.' A one-page feedback was given to Dev with the information, 'This and a detailed report on your leadership profile with one or two areas of development will be sent to your line and HR.'

Dev had become one of the youngest global head of a business in Roqsanto International!

Dev drove home and immediately hugged Meher, Vedant came running and he took him in his arms.

'Dad is smiling after so many days,' said Vedant looking at his mother.

Meher stepped back and giving Dev a salute, said, 'Well done, Sire!'

Instantly Vedant did the same and repeated after his mother, 'Well done, Sire!'

That evening as Dev and Meher sat down with a glass of wine she said to her husband, 'See, Dev, you were being unsure about Roqsanto. The company has been so wonderful to you!'

A few days later an official email announced that Dev would be taking over as VP Agrichemicals from 1st April 2005. He was very much on the high table of his company now. When Dev got a quiet moment, he reflected on the past few weeks. It was incredible how his applications for two lower-grade jobs were rejected and instead he was offered a higher-grade job and that too with global line responsibility! There must be some providential force behind this he thought. 'Effort versus Fate' is a dilemma that crosses most human minds. In Dev's mind there was little doubt that between hard work and that unexplained X-factor the former always won. However, the latter still existed! We all have to walk on the road sign-posted 'Hard Work' to reach a destination, sometimes 'Lady Luck' gives us a lift in her car; that car ride might cover 10% of the distance for some and 90% for others. But unless we step out on this road there is no chance of meeting Lady Luck—she runs her car service only on the long road sign-posted 'Hard Work'!

Vedant was growing up and while their Notting Hill Gate apartment was spacious it was still a flat with no garden. Dev's housing allowance had gone up with his promotion and both Meher and he felt they should move into a bigger house with a garden. Dev remembered that the previous year while driving to Kew Gardens they had lost their way in Chiswick area, about 4 miles from Notting Hill Gate, and found themselves on a beautiful wide road called Staveley Road that was lined with charming trees and lovely large villas on either side. 'What a marvellous area!' Meher had then remarked to Dev. Dev sounded off a couple of estate agents and on the weekend the three of them set off to view a few houses. The second house they saw captivated both Dev and Meher, it was a semi-detached fully furnished scintillatingly striking villa on Staveley Road, with space for two cars in the front yard and the most mesmerizing back garden they had ever seen! The landlord of the house mentioned that he had organised a garden party the previous summer with over 60 guests! Dev had always wished to have a house with a garden; after Vedant arrived, he had dreamt of playing cricket with his son in a house with a garden. Sometimes man's present reality far exceeds his sweetest and wildest dreams. As Dev and Meher checked with the landlord about the rent and details of the neighbourhood, Dev could sense his dreams realizing and something magnificent unfolding for his family.

Three days before Dev was to start the new role, he heard about the demise of Howard Sadler's wife. She had succumbed to cancer, leaving behind a nine-year-old son. Dev took over as VP Agrichemicals on the morning of 1st April, he softly chanted the *Gayatri mantra* as he took the chair in his new cabin; later that day he went to Teddington to attend the service of Howard's wife. Life and death, happiness and sorrow, day and night, success and failure, inexorably come and go in this world.

Later that year on a business trip, Dev decided to stop by in Madras, now Chennai, to look up his old office which he had so sincerely nurtured. He intended to spend an hour there but left in 20 minutes when he realised his old colleagues, who still had regard for him, didn't have the time! They were busy; they had learnt to live without him. The past is irretrievably frozen in time. This was the second occasion, the first being his February telephone conversation with Geeta, when this stark reality stared Dev in the face. At that moment Dev decided never to visit offices or homes from his past.

Part IV

World Is Rocked

The world is so fixated with power: money and muscle power, economic and military power of the State, power of love, power of solitude, power of chanting. In its simplest meaning, and at an individual level, anyone who can help or harm others is powerful. For all the hankering for power no civilization or nation remains prosperous and powerful forever—they rise and they fall. And for all the power that they may wield, not a single man or woman has had the brawn to walk on his or her legs to their own cremation or graveyard! When a man or woman gets power of any kind, real or imagined, he or she tends to become more self-confident and also, more rash, less patient and less sensitive with fellow human beings. It requires emotional maturity to cope with power with sagacity. For all his spiritual detachment and awareness of the transient nature of life and its temptations, and to paraphrase Eklavya, Dev didn't remain entirely untouched with the trappings of his heady success.

I had relocated back to India by then and bought an apartment in a high-rise condominium in Nirvana in Gurgaon on the outskirts of Delhi. Luv and Sudhir were in Bangalore and Raipur respectively. So Dev scanned and emailed some pictures of his new house to the three of us. Seeing the pictures, Luv wrote to Dev, copying Sudhir and me in: 'Awesome! Wish someone would invite poor me and Mrs Malhotra to stay in such a beautiful villa for a week this summer. Yours in expectation.'

Dev responded back on the same email: 'Dear "Poor Me", consider this email as an invitation for you and Mrs Malhotra for two weeks this summer in London. Yours in anticipation.' Luv and Poulomi spent about 10 days at Dev's in London in August that year. Their return flight was via Delhi and so I suggested that they spend a couple of days with me before flying to Bangalore.

Both Luv and Poulomi really liked my condominium and Gurgaon in general. '*Khannae*, there is sense of space here,' said Luv. 'The developments in India are now getting perceptible. You remember, in late 80's we would come up to 32nd Milestone for a beer and dinner; we thought no civilization existed beyond 32nd Milestone at that time! And see now, amazing!'

'Lovely apartments and villas and landscaping,' said Poulomi, 'reminds me of Dev's London neighbourhood!'

'But don't you find a bit of plasticity here?' remarked Luv in reference to the somewhat similar nature of high-rise apartment blocks, 'I wonder if this too will become a status-conscious place, like our beloved city 20 kilometres down the road!'

Most of the two days that they were with me though, we were chatting about their London trip. '*Khannae*, what a lovely house Dev has, with that stunning garden where Bhaisahab did a fantastic barbeque party for us! They had invited all their Indian friends too,' said Luv over a glass of beer on the first evening they were with me, and then after a pause, with a soft laugh, he added, 'except two.'

I looked at him enquiringly, seeing my expression he laughed louder.

'Except two?' I asked Luv.

'It's nothing, Sandy,' said Poulomi, 'this guy just likes to tittle-tattle!'

Luv continued despite his wife's rebuke, 'You know the first Saturday we were there, Dev had organised a picnic cricket match for friends and family at this lovely ground very close to Staveley Road. There were these seven-eight couples and their children, who I think you know, but there were also two more couples whose acquaintance they have made only recently. Both the guys work in IT companies, both moved to UK a year ago and the wives of both are now pregnant!' Luv continued to snicker as he narrated the incident, while Poulomi shook her head in disapproval. 'It was such a wonderful summer day and after the match we were all enjoying the picnic food and chatting when the discussion shifted to life in India versus life in the West. That's when one of these IT guys and the wife of the other started saying very critical things about India, I mean it bordered on detestation. Dev bhaisahab's face could barely hide his exasperation with them.'

'Then?' by now I had got curious as to where this discussion led to.

'Dev didn't say much except all places have their good and difficult aspects to living, and that most of them had grown up and received education and employment in India.'

'So typically Dev,' said I.

Luv carried on, 'The next morning Dev, Meher, Polly and I were having breakfast in the garden of Dev's home, Vedant was sleeping.'

'Oh, how is little Ved?' I checked.

'He is such a darling, such a lovely child, Meher is bringing him up so wonderfully,' said Poulomi smilingly.

Luv continued, 'So Dev and Meher were planning the week for us including this barbeque party the following Saturday. Meher said they would invite all the people we had met the previous day at the cricket-picnic; that's when Dev said rather emphatically 'except two'. Meher gave him a perplexed look and Dev repeated with a touch of arrogance, "I am not having those two couples in *my* house". I had never seen such a stern look on his face before *Khannae*!'

Poulomi tried to temper Luv's narration, 'Dev never said, "I am not having them in my house;" he said, "I would feel better not having those two couples in *our* house." Also, he has never been arrogant, he was just abrupt. And he explained himself Sandy, he said people who don't respect their homeland will never respect any place and they are just opportunists.'

'Then?' I was inquisitive to know where this ended.

Luv completed his narration, 'Then Meher told him that one of those chaps and the wife of the other guy had been critical of India, but they had not said anything against Dev or his family. She also reminded him that on occasions he too had been critical of India.'

I was looking intently at both Luv and Poulomi, 'Then?'

'Dev asked Meher if she had ever known him to show abhorrence for India, critically evaluating certain aspects of life is one thing, he said, and that's because we want the land where we grew up, found our family and received education and employment, to achieve its potential and attain its rightful place in the world, Dev added, but showing revulsion is another, and these people were showing revulsion and he just didn't want them at his home!'

After we had finished dinner, I took Luv and Poulomi for an evening drive where we continued our chat on Dev and Meher and their London trip.

'Our friend looks too dapper in his office suit!' said Luv, '*Khannae* Roqsanto International must be grooming him to become the MD of Hindustan Roqsanto?'

'At the very least, Luv,' I deduced, 'he is head of a global business at 40, so most definitely being developed for senior roles in the organisation.'

Poulomi then added, 'Dev said something else too Luv; tell Sandy his exact words.'

Luv thought for a moment and said, 'Ah yes, he said he had consistently got much more than what he deserved in terms of assignments and salary and perks, both with Torsh and Roqsanto!'

I smiled quite expecting a remark like this from Dev.

'So don't you call him arrogant, this is anything but arrogance,' said Poulomi quite firmly to her husband.

'Let's put it this way that Bhaisahab is not entirely untouched by his recent exceptional success,' replied Luv and then with his hands folded and a little bow of his head he said to his wife, 'Okay Madam?'

Luv then narrated another incident when they were all to go and see theatre in Leicester Square, but Dev got late in office. He called Meher and told her to come with both of us to Leicester Square and he would meet us there directly; when Meher said it would be better if he came home first, he said something like 'if I could I would have' and kept the phone down. 'So there is a touch of impatience and abruptness in our friend now,' concluded Luv.

Poulomi again shook her head, 'He is just very busy, in a high responsibility job.'

The next evening, I invited two of my school friends who were also now living in Nirvana. Dhiraj was in a villa in Calmwood Grove with his family, while Ira was in villa in Daffodil Clouds with her husband and daughter. I thought it would be nice to have them home for dinner and introduce them to Luv and Poulomi. The get-together didn't quite turn out pleasant though!

'*Khannae,* why is it that we like western names for our housing complexes and pet dogs, and give traditional Indian names to our kids,' said Luv laughingly. Later that evening when we realised that Ira's daughter was called Darshini and their dog was Daisy, I saw Luv giving me a fleeting wink! India had witnessed rapid progress in almost all fields from mid-1990s onwards; some of the best global automobile brands were also making their mark in the Indian car market. Indeed, both Dhiraj and Ira, with their respective spouses, had driven to my apartment in their Mercedes and Honda cars even though they were walking distance from my place.

Dhiraj's kids were studying in Pivotop World School, a new international school offering International Baccalaureate curriculum. It was located at the far end of Gurgaon about

5 kilometres from Nirvana. Ira's daughter was in The Aspen Millenium School, a new age school in Gurgaon that followed the ICSE curriculum. I was surprised to learn that not only their classrooms but also the school buses were fully air-conditioned! On learning that Luv and Poulomi had just returning from London, Dhiraj and Ira enquired about Dev; when Luv checked with them if they had been travelling to London as well Dhiraj's wife snootily said, 'Dhiraj travels to London as though he is going to Connaught Place.'

She was carrying a Christian Dior handbag, which Poulomi told me later may have been more than $1000! Obviously, both Dhiraj and Ira were moneyed people. When I asked them what they would like to drink, Ira's husband said, 'I only drink single malt Scotch;' while Dhiraj's wife said, 'If you have red wine, I could have that. In a red wine glass, please.'

Meanwhile, Ira's husband was narrating his travel experiences especially from the time they were based in Singapore. His focus was on psychology of non-resident Indians and attitude of 'people of the world' towards Indian professionals and traders. 'An NRI will never buy a $10,000 car unless he has at least $50,000 in his bank account,' he said with an omniscient tone.

Extrapolating one's own experiences of a lifetime to mean universal truth is a fantastic fallacy of the human mind. I could sense that Luv had already lost interest in the dinner get-together what with the subtle display of wealth, he was hardly conversing with Ira's husband or Dhiraj's wife, and once when Ira said 'Nope' to a question he asked her, and Dhiraj said 'Yup' to another conversational opener he almost totally quietened down.

What a paradoxical element money is—it brings freedom from hunger and subordination, it brings dignity and luxury; and then silently it becomes the great captivity! So long as *dharma* and *arth* remain equal partners money brings security and warmth, but the moment *arth* becomes too forceful, when money becomes its own reward, it then becomes the grand incarceration. It becomes the big O in the small word ego! Poulomi said very little after my dinner guests left, though I distinctly remember Luv saying to me, '*Khannae*, what is this 'Yup' and 'Nope' *yaar*! Sounds so damn unsmart! Why can't they simply say Yes and No!'

I heard only twice from Dev over the next several months, first time an email that he sent when he was travelling to Rio de Janeiro: 'The most beautiful city I have seen, the blue Atlantic waters and Copacabana beach, Sugarloaf mountain and the cable car, that tropical rainforest-like drive up to the Corcovado, an interesting sugarcane drink *caipirinha* and above all, the friendliest of people. Incidentally, it will be impossible to take Eklavya away from the Copacabana beach where ravishing girls with a prominent reverse wear dental-floss bikinis!' And second time was on 1st January 2006, using a £5 calling card, as he always did, a phone call with New Year greetings.

In the April of 2006, an event occurred which was to apparently change the course of Dev's life forever! Dev's sister-in-law Meghna had suddenly fainted during a family function in Delhi. She regained consciousness in no time but couldn't see from one eye! The initial medical examinations reported a condition called myxoma—a tumour of the heart! The doctors advised a surgery within 10 days, with only a 50% chance of success. The second opinion confirmed the first. The surgery was to take place in Delhi in the last week of April.

Meher was shattered, Dev too was gloomy. But he had absorbed a few shocks in his life. As Meher asked Dev to immediately book their tickets for Delhi, Dev was caught in a perplexing dilemma. Every two years Roqsanto International organised a two-day off-site meeting where the top brass of the company, all VPs and above, congregated to evaluate current state of the company and decide its future direction. All departments and sub-organisations within Roqsanto drew their objectives from this top leadership meeting that established the strategic course for Roqsanto International. The Zurich meeting was going to be Dev's first and he was scheduled to present not just the performance of Agrichemicals but also lead the discussion on 'trends in new markets'. It was an opportunity for Dev to not only meet the entire top management but also reinforce his position as a senior global executive. Roqsanto Chemicals International Ltd. was a caring organisation and had he requested he would have been excused from the meeting, but Dev thought other than moral support he wouldn't have been able to do much during his sister-in-law's surgery. He therefore suggested to Meher that she flies to Delhi and that he and Vedant would join her after Dev's meeting, which was three days after the surgery. I suppose Meher was astounded with Dev's priority!

'I will ask Sandeep to be there for any help,' he said to Meher, 'and either I will take Vedant with me to Zurich or check if he could stay with one of our friends here.' Meher had been numb since she heard 'only 50% chance of success' and Dev's subsequent decision would have only made her more distraught.

Meghna's surgery was not successful! While the tumour was removed the doctor regretfully said, in my presence, that Meghna had got paralyzed and for the foreseeable future would have to be on the wheelchair. Dev reached Delhi a few days after the surgery and couldn't believe the condition of his sister-in-law: once so vivacious, she was now expressionless, in almost a lifeless state on the wheelchair. It takes not a wink for Time to strike down its own creation, when it so whims. Time was to also deal a devastating blow to Dev in the near future.

In the summer of 2006, I mentioned to Dev that I was planning to take a vacation and visit London. I expected the usual large-hearted, open-arms enthusiastic invitation from Dev and was therefore a little surprised when he didn't show much exuberance and instead checked with me, 'What dates are you looking at?' Of course he did say later during the course of that conversation, 'I should be in London at this time, you are most welcome Sandeep.'

Dev's home exceeded the impression I had of it from the pictures he had sent electronically and Luv's description of it. However, perhaps for the first time since I had known her, Meher looked very solemn. Dev too was not the lively person he had grown into in recent times. I could see flashes of the old Dev in him—preoccupied and withdrawn—and like in those old days his smile was not reaching his eyes.

Whoever met Dev after that only used a stronger than earlier adjective to describe him: pondering, bothered, worried and poignant. For someone as phlegmatic as him to betray such despair on his face and in his manner suggested to me that he was carrying intense anguish within. Meher was making a trip to Delhi every six weeks to be with Meghna and her parents. And during her visit in March 2007, she called Dev and told him that she intended not to return back! It is not for me to state anything more, not that Dev shared much more with me in any case. Meher had decided to separate from Dev!

Over the years Dev had become closer to Sudhir. Perhaps only he knew what had happened, perhaps even he didn't. I learnt only from Sudhir about Dev's separation. Surely it was temporary I thought, as most marriages go through turbulent periods; however, Dev's unspoken words and his distressed manner suggested it wasn't temporary! Dev's world was rocked.

Dev was too proud to tell me much about his personal life, and whatever little he shared it is not for me to mention anything more. I shall focus only on how Dev coped with his new status of a single parent. Indeed, the 10-year-old Vedant was to be with Dev. Devavratt Pratap Rajvansh was just starting his sternest test of life—he had to raise Ved and do his job and manage his home, he had to go out and earn for Ved and himself and yet had to give his maximum time to his only child. He had to be not just a father but also a mother, not just a friend but also a brother for his son, of course like all of us, he also had to be an employee—a boss and a subordinate and a colleague. He was a devastated and defeated man, yet he had to be strong and happy for Ved.

Truth tends to travel on the back of a tortoise, while gossip runs and jumps like a hare. Dev had to immediately confide in his boss what had happened, he had to of course share with parents and he mentioned to Sudhir who he knew would let Luv and me know. However, before he realised this news had spread amongst Dev's other friends and relatives, colleagues and acquaintances. While a few of them called up to check 'what happened' and 'can we help', almost half of Dev's friends in London, amongst the seven or eight families, seemed to instantly make themselves less available! Dev's boss advised him to take a fortnight off just to 'get to grips with the situation', and his aunt flew in from Delhi to be with Dev and Vedant for a few weeks.

During that fortnight when he was working from home, Dev decided to go to office once and meet Paul Anderson and Howard Sadler. 'This is so distressing to hear Dev, but time is also the great healer,' said Paul over a cup of coffee, 'In a few years' time this pain will lessen and you will find a different equilibrium in life.'

Howard closed the cabin door of his office as he saw Dev in. 'So your situation is now the same as mine, my friend,' remarked Howard, who like Dev was a single male parent. 'How is the son?'

'Don't know what to say, Howard. He has been remarkably calm though twice in the last week he developed fever and day before I was called by his school saying he appeared very disturbed.'

Howard thought for a moment and then said, 'Wonder what's going on in his tender mind, though I must say little kids can be quite strong at times. What's the plan now?'

Dev shrugged his shoulders, 'Not sure, Howard.'

'You've grown up in Delhi, haven't you, Dev?' Dev nodded.

'Some family there?'

'Yes, my parents are still there, also some cousins and extended family,' replied Dev.

'If I were you, I would relocate to Delhi. If family is there, Dev, not just the lad but even you are going to need that support. And the surroundings would be familiar, notwithstanding your fondness for cold London and hot Chennai!'

Dev greatly respected Howard's opinions, and said, 'Howard, we are so well settled here: Vedant at his school, I in my job, am able to afford such a nice comfortable house, good social life; for Vedant in particular this is his home now.'

Howard gently shook his head, 'Dev, who will take care of Vedant when you need to travel? Who will fetch him from school and help with homework? What if you fall sick? Jobs come and go, money comes and goes, but a son is forever. If you could have family support here, I would never advise you to relocate, give yourself some time and you might come to the same conclusion. And once he comes of age you can always come back, someone with your capability will always have a job.'

Around this time, contrary to his nature, Dev started speaking with astrologers! He reached out to that old Chennai astrologer and Dev's uncle also asked him to speak with an astrologer in Delhi who he had made the acquaintance of. A helpless, answer-deprived man becomes susceptible to the supernatural and what the ultra-rational might describe as superstitious. Dev was desperately looking for answers; he couldn't understand what was happening in his life and why it was happening to him.

'Sir, you are running the Moon *mahadasha*,' said the Chennai astrologer, 'and on top of that the seven and a half year Saturn transit. While I don't see a separation in Madam's chart, in your chart there is a very high risk of it. You are dead in the middle of the seven and a half year Saturn transit which is a very difficult time, please visit a *Shani* temple in London Sir and offer prayers there.'

When Dev enquired what the future might hold for him the astrologer said, 'I think Madam and you will get back together Sir, also in all likelihood you will relocate to India. When your Moon *mahadasha* gets over in 2014 and the Mars *mahadasha* starts you will move again, *mangal* will again take you out of India.'

The astrologer in Delhi was a retired Army officer who explained both the science of astrology and placement of the planets in his horoscope to Dev, 'Devavratt, there are people who don't even know the ABC of astrology and still dismiss it as a hoax. With respect to life and creation, you can either think of us as a biological and chemical accident or believe that there is some reason behind creation. If it's the former belief then whether it is the universal force or God or astrology you can be dismissive of all, however if there is some rationale in Creation then I would think of astrology as God's way of macro-managing His creation. As in companies where micro-management is disapproved, so too God doesn't micro-manage; however, through planets and stars and how they influence us God macro-manages the Universe and life within.' An areligious Dev, who had always been sceptical of the supernatural, listened carefully to every word that the wise retired Army officer was saying.

'Yes, you are running the Moon period,' said the Delhi astrologer, 'and also the seven-and-a-half year Saturn *sadhe-satti*. This will be the most difficult time in life for you. What happens during the Moon *mahadasha* is that your natal Moon gets activated; moon as you know wanes and waxes and so the 10-year Moon period is very unpredictable. The Moon rules the emotions, you will tend to feel elated and then suddenly depressed, happy and then soon sad during this *mahadasha*. Saturn is 'lord of *karma*'—he is a strict though just judge of your actions—so having Saturn transit combined with Moon *mahadasha* is a double whammy! Do two things please: immerse raw pulses in running water twice or thrice a week and chant the *Maha-mrityunjaya mantra* every day, it is the *mantra* of Shiva. Hopefully you will come out of this difficult period with relatively few wounds.'

'If Saturn is a judge, then it means I would have done some very bad *karma* to go through all this,' said Dev on the phone.

The retired officer replied in his soft voice, 'Devavratt, *Shani* or Saturn is indeed the judge; he metes out karmic justice. *Karma* or actions not just of this lifetime but good and bad deeds we accumulate from previous lifetimes too! That is why we find straightforward and honest people in current lifetime also suffering, and many sly cunning people doing so well in current lifetime. We pay for our *karma*s not just of this lifetime but for good and bad *karma*s of previous lifetime too.'

A vulnerable Dev did everything he was told. Vedant would also go along with Dev as he prayed in the *Shani* temple. It was a new activity for little Ved who would keep looking at his father as he knew something unfortunate had happened with them. With pain in his heart Dev would gently smile at his son whose innocence would momentarily moisten Dev's eyes. He would instantly collect himself, he had to remain strong and cheerful for his child.

'I am saddened to hear Dev,' said Karan Varma when Dev met him in MHQ a few days later during the former's London visit. 'So what do you want to do now?'

'At a crossroad Karan; discussed with Howard, he strongly suggested I relocate back to Delhi.'

Karan thought for a moment, 'How old is your son?'

'Ten.'

'He is very small, you are going to need family support Dev, I would agree with Howard; don't think this is really a crossroad, I would imagine Delhi might be the only option.'

Dev checked with Karan what job opportunities might be available with Hindustan Roqsanto Ltd.

'You will have a job with Hindustan Roqsanto, it's still your parent company and it would be unwise not to use your vast international experience. However, what job I can't say right now. You are aware how much the company has changed; as of now Plastics, Paints, Adhesives and Resins and Industrial Construction all have business heads, but over the next six months opportunities will come up.' As Dev got up to take Karan's leave the latter gently patted Dev's back, 'Build your life around your son, Dev.'

Sudhir and I tried to be in regular touch with Dev particularly during this time. When Dev told Sudhir that his aunt needed to get back to Delhi he asked Dev, 'So how will you manage now? Who will pick up Vedant from school?'

'I have thought of keeping a nanny, Sudhir, but just can't get myself to reconcile with the idea. For the next couple of weeks, I have permission of my boss to work half day at office and late afternoons from home.'

'Let me see if I can get some time off from my office and come over to London for a few days,' said Sudhir. Dev told me on two separate occasions at least that Sudhir was the sincerest person he had come across—'If I could be even 50% as sincere as Sudhir' were his exact words. Sudhir flew all the way from Raipur to London in end June that year to be with Dev for a few days.

On his return, Sudhir was to land late night and his connecting flight to Raipur was early next morning. My flat in Gurgaon was just a twenty-minute drive from Delhi's international airport and given the very short layover we decided that Sudhir would spend the night at my place and next morning I would drop him at the domestic airport.

'How was the trip?' I asked him as we got into my car after I had received him.

Sudhir was always very measured while talking about serious subjects; he wasn't given to any exaggeration. 'I hope Dev survives the current time,' was his reply.

'He is trying to put up a brave front but seems like a man who is losing confidence,' said Sudhir about Dev. 'He keeps laughing and joking with Ved, but his eyes are totally cheerless. You know, two days after I reached, Vedant came down with fever. As I was retiring for the night, I saw Dev half-reclining in bed besides Ved, putting cold packs on his forehead. I sat in the bedroom for 15 minutes and tried to chat with Dev. He was telling me that two families—amongst their friends circle in London—were in touch with him; three or four had simply withdrawn! Then, a cousin and a friend had called him earlier that day, and both the cousin and the friend's wife who came on line later started their conversation with: "I don't want to pry, but what's really happened?" Anyhow we took Ved's fever and it had come down to 100, so I told Dev to get some sleep as well. I woke up around 4:30 am to go to the loo and saw Dev still half sitting in bed with his right hand caressing Ved's forehead. I tried to speak softly so as not to wake up Vedant and held Dev by his left hand, Sandeep his hand was ice cold! Day before in the morning I saw Dev half-reclining in bed at 5 am though his eyes were shut, once again his hand was colder than ice!'

I looked at Sudhir not knowing what to say.

'His house with that garden is so beautiful, but to what avail. Even when we were playing cricket in the garden with Ved, Dev seemed elsewhere; he shares his logistical challenges but doesn't say much about how he is feeling from within.'

'Has he kept a nanny for Vedant?' I asked Sudhir.

'Yes, there is a Polish lady, but Dev says he can't get himself to accept the nanny picking up Ved from school and giving him a snack on return. He wants to do everything himself, doesn't want to leave Ved even for a moment.'

I shared my thought with Sudhir, 'He will need to be practical, doesn't really have an option. Anyway, what is Dev planning now?'

Sudhir replied, 'Ved's school will close by end of third week July, Dev will take a call then but all indications are that he will relocate back to Delhi.'

As I was driving Sudhir to the domestic airport the next morning he shared another little incident. 'At the immigration yesterday, I met one of our batchmate from TMS, Tapan Walia; don't think you know him?'

I shook my head.

'Tapan Walia was returning from Dubai, he and his wife know Dev and Meher quite well; you know what he said to me when I mentioned I had flown back from London where I was with Dev? He said: "Rajvansh must have done something inappropriate; my wife feels he travels all over the world so he must be womanizing". This is social morality.'

Once again I didn't know how to react.

As I drove back on NH8 Sudhir's words kept ringing in my ears: *this is social morality.* The social order and the definition of right and wrong, keeps changing from one generation to another; in our lifetime alone social norms have changed several times: it reflects in changes in dressing, speech, human relationships, family values and eventually laws. Yet who can stop a Tapan Walia and his sharp-tongued wife from muttering claptrap from their big-mouth! Smaller the man, pettier is the comment.

Two days after Sudhir left for Raipur, Luv called me and checked about his trip and Dev's wellbeing. I mentioned to him whatever Sudhir had shared and also that Dev had pretty much decided to relocate to India.

'What!' exclaimed Luv, 'he is going to leave that terrific global job and that beautiful home and London!'

'He is, doesn't have very many options,' said I.

'Let's do a three-way phone call with him, *Khannae*, he is probably not thinking clearly these days.'

What was meant to be a conversation to let Dev know that we were with him as he navigated through unprecedented turbulence in life, turned out to be very different with Eklavya sharing some stark, almost brutal facts with him.

'Dev, I guess it's a bit futile to ask how *you* are doing, but how is Ved?' asked Luv when we started our chat.

'We are both surviving, Eklavya,' said Dev soberly, 'living one day at a time.'

'I hear you have almost decided to return to Delhi.'

Dev replied in the affirmative and briefly said, 'Family support and some cousins, extended family and all of you'.

'Dev, such a marvellous job, heading global operations, such a beautiful home, Vedant growing up in a wonderful environment, you are going to let go off all this!' said Luv.

Once again Dev's reply was very laconic, 'I cannot do my global job with all the travel and take care of Ved and manage the home. So I am thinking of taking an assignment with Hindustan Roqsanto. Have spoken to our MD already.'

For the next half an hour it was mainly Luv who spoke.

'Dev, my younger sister who now lives in Bombay got divorced four years back. I am still in touch with my former brother-in-law, so what I am telling you is with near first-hand experience. When you say family support, I presume you mean your parents, they are getting on in age, what are you expecting from them? They are now in Malviya Nagar right, next to the crowded main road.'

Dev's uncle had, post retirement, built a small 200 square, yard house in Malviya Nagar in South Delhi, much against Dev's suggestion. It was next to the crowded main road.

'From that luxurious home on the grand Staveley Road to a small house in Malviya Nagar, do think this through. Think how Vedant will struggle to adjust; even if you implore yourself to. Get a nanny for Ved, he will settle down much faster in a place he has spent 10 years in. When you say "all of you", I presume you mean friends. You don't build a life around friends, I am not saying you are intending to, but look at all those you called your friends over there, I believe half of them have disappeared! Of course, Sandeep and Sudhir and I, and I am sure a few others, will be there for you, just as you have always been there for us; but you are going to be a single parent, a single male parent at that, believe me most of your friends will change. The change will be subtle. You can't throw parties now, even if you settled down and bought yourself a flat in Gurgaon, the wives of your friends will have no company in your living room; people socialize as couples after a certain age. They will come twice or thrice, make sure you offer good chicken and beer, but barely one in five will reciprocate! That's because your position is weakened now, of what use are you, and most will exploit it. How long will you invite guests without any reciprocation? You know my brother-in-law is such a simple and lovely guy, as is my sister, and their separation was for such frivolous reasons, yet every second person who knows him and me seems to insinuate that it was his fault, he must be having an affair, or being emotionally cruel, he must be somehow in the wrong! It is as difficult being a single man as it is being a single woman, even in this day and age.'

Dev listened very carefully, as he always did, and said, 'I have to live my fate, Eklavya.'

Luv wasn't done and continued, 'You know, people will want to know what went wrong, they will appear concerned and preface their inquisitiveness with an "I don't want to pry", basically you will become their drawing room conversation topic! And this "extended family and some cousins" you talk of, come on Dev, when will you stop betting on the goodness of human beings! This so-called extended family is the first to distance themselves in such situations; you are of little use for them. You won't even have a house in London to offer if you relocate. And I'll tell you what you will hear from them: "you are not the first person with whom this has happened" and "you should also move on" and "nobody can help you in this situation" all to be read as: "deal with your situation yourself don't bother us!"'

I felt the need to temper Luv down a bit and said, 'Luv you are painting too harsh a picture.'

Eklavya said calmly on the phone, 'I am merely stating what I have seen, and Sandeep I think our friend is realistic enough, though I feel you bet far too much on goodness of human nature, Dev.'

'Anyhow Dev, take this decision with eyes wide open is all I wanted to emphasize,' said Luv again sounding serious. 'Sorry if I was too harsh or insensitive. I am sure you very well appreciate that Hindustan Roqsanto and Roqsanto International are also commercial organisations. You will need to earn your salary everywhere. Your colleagues will be your competitors for senior positions which only get fewer as you go up. Some might even feel threatened by you and jealous of the success you have had thus far. You won't be able to give your 100% to your company now, and even if your 70% is better than 100% of several others, the 'perception' will be that your attention to work is not undivided. Karan Varma will leave someday, your senior colleagues in London who have been so supportive of you will leave or move onto different jobs within Roqsanto; consider yourself lucky if you can survive for a few years. And just my final two pence on extended family and friends, if in five years' time you can count those who stood by you on more than one hand then I will start believing in the goodness of human character as much as you do.'

Very Few Options

Dev had very few options left. He officially communicated to his line manager and HR focal point in Roqsanto International his intention to return to India to Hindustan Roqsanto, simultaneously he also let Karan Varma know of his plan. There was no job at Dev's level of seniority at that time in Hindustan Roqsanto, however Dev wanted to move soon so that he could get Vedant started off in the new school academic session in Delhi. Dev's boss was understanding of the situation and suggested that if Dev so desired he could remotely work out of Delhi for 50% of his time and be in London for remaining 50%, and once he found a job with his parent company he could repatriate to Hindustan Roqsanto. Of course, the London-Delhi-London travels would have to be for Dev's personal account.

Vedant was misty-eyed as he and Dev locked their house on Staveley Road in early August of 2007 to board a flight to Delhi. However, he quickly hid his emotion and started telling his father how his friends and teacher in school had bid him goodbye! They took one of the rooms in Dev's uncle's small Malviya Nagar house in Delhi, which Dev tried to make as comfortable for Ved as possible: he installed a window air-conditioner, bought a new flat-screen TV and connected Ved's PlayStation with it and set up a small study table in the corner of that room. Dev's uncle had been scouting some of international schools in Delhi and surrounding areas since Dev told him to look for IB curriculum schools so that Ved's transition from his primary school in London to the new school in Delhi could, he hoped, happen with relatively less difficulty. Going forward as well, Dev thought, studying in an international school would make it easier for Ved to get admission in a good foreign university. The three shortlisted schools were The British School in Lutyens' Delhi, Pivotop World School just beyond Gurgaon and The Apricus International School in the Qutub institutional area which was quite close to Malviya Nagar.

Apricus was closest to their home and with Dev's time for returning back still unclear, his uncle reckoned that it would be far more practical to go with Apricus. Apricus International School admitted Vedant, Dev found it 'good enough' at best and not as impressive as Pivotop or British School, however he was in such a disturbed state of mind with so many difficult tasks to do that safely re-settling Vedant, even if not as well as he would have desired, meant that he could now focus on finding a job back in India and closing down his house lease and other personal matters in London.

Dev felt utterly helpless at the way events were turning out. As if the drastic change from a happily married person with a beautiful family to a single parent with broken marriage was not traumatic enough, the further adjustment from his spacious Staveley Road house in London to one room in Malviya Nagar was going to be an onerous if not impossible one. The exasperation in fighting for space for even parking a small car in front of his uncle's house and the heavy congestion on the road and incessant blaring of horns barely 25 metres from the gate of their residence made him feel almost suffocated.

The night before Dev was to leave for London, Vedant hugged his father like he had never done before and slept. He didn't say 'Dad, don't go' in words, but he said so in every other possible way. Ved was a brave little boy, but he was still a little boy. He still needed lots of love and care, and Devavratt was trying to be simultaneously a strong father and loving mother. He also had to be an employee and so, till he found a job in Delhi, had to shuttle between London and Delhi.

Dev went up and down between London and Delhi for eight months, alternately spending 15 days in Delhi and 15 in London, flying economy class at his personal expense. On his flights during this time, he always had the same thoughts: if something happened to him who would take care of Vedant, how would he raise Ved and do his job and give his son a normal childhood, what if Roqsanto couldn't give him a job in India. And then his mind would go back to that school cricket match when he batted with the last batsman, who couldn't even hold the bat properly because of a congenital deformity in his arm, and they scored 90 odd runs together and won the game! Dev remembered how they had won against all odds, by just not giving up, playing ball after ball after ball, taking singles on the fifth or sixth ball of the over to shield his less able partner, but never giving up just never giving up! All that he could do now too, thought Dev, was just take the 'right actions', he could pray for good result, but that alas was never going to be in his control. Krishna's wisdom through The *Gita* remains eternal.

There was enough happening at the airports and in flights to distract Dev, if not amuse him, from the difficulties he was grappling with. He would see 'middle-income' women at Delhi international airport wearing *salwar-kameez* with trainer shoes; he could understand the functionality but not ignore the oddness. The husband, pot-bellied and balding, and also in trainers, would be trying not to show his curiosity with the surrounding sights and occasionally telling his wife to be careful of her purse that had their passports. Then there would be the smarter woman in black trousers with her kids, presumably visiting her parents in Delhi, her MNC executive husband not with the family on this trip, talking loudly to her kids in a put-on accent, making sure everyone in the queue heard her and understood that she actually was 'settled in the West'; or the real foreigner in a Stetson hat looking half in amazement half in derision at the scenes around him and speaking assertively with airport attendants. Then a set of six young men in their 30s, with unkempt stubble, ill-fitting trousers and a laptop bag on their shoulders talking about their 'on-site posting' with one of them, presumably their boss, wearing a black suit with no tie and looking all important. Amidst all this Dev would admire the new world-class Delhi International Airport.

It was in the March of 2008, after Dev had just landed back in London and reached his empty home, that he saw an email from his HR focal point in Roqsanto International titled 'Opportunity in India'. The email stated that Dev get in touch with the HR focal point when he was in the London office next.

When Dev opened his private Yahoo email account, he found an email from one of his London 'friend' who had since, along with his wife, distanced himself from Dev. This email came out of the blue, without any contextual discussion or provocation, and he reminded Dev how, three years back, when all the friends with families were planning a weekend outing in London, Dev had ridden roughshod over his suggestion and eventually got everyone to agree to his proposal. *What you are going through is God's way to humble you; may God humble you forever*—wrote Dev's London 'friend'. Dev was taken aback at this senseless outburst via email; he just closed in on himself and never met this family again.

From what I knew of Dev, and not too many knew him better, he had always been self-effacing but first Luv's somewhat offhand insinuation of Dev's 'arrogance' and later when I heard about this 'God's way to humble you', it jarred me no end. A day before Dev had left for London in March 2008 he had called up his college friend Ajay Jaiswal, who was successfully running his soft furnishings business, to wish him on his birthday. Jaiswal told him that he and his wife Juhi were also travelling to London a day after Dev was to leave. 'Most welcome to come over to my house Ajay, I am going to be in London for the next fortnight, of course I am there by myself now.'

Jaiswal replied, 'Thanks Dev, but we are staying with another family friend, they are very close to both I and Juhi and very hospitable.'

Dev repeated a watered-down invitation, 'Okay, come over for a meal whenever you get time in the next two weeks,' to which his college friend said, 'We'll try but it's unlikely since Juhi is going to be with me, perhaps we'll see you on your next Delhi trip, give us a call when in town next.'

Dev kept the phone down: Jaiswal's statements indicated that Dev was neither as 'close' nor as 'hospitable' as his other friend was, and since they were a 'couple' visiting a single man, never mind if he was a childhood friend, it wasn't too alluring a prospect. The final reference to himself as 'us' instead of 'me' suggested to Dev that his old friend now placed himself on a distant if not rather high pedestal!

Dev was in the midst of a season of losing friends. As it is with age number of friends decline, and while friendships mature with time, to go flat, one terrible moment is enough. Dev had just experienced two such moments in the space of two days!

The very next day Dev met his HR focal point in MHQ. After they had exchanged pleasantries, he said, 'Dev after all that happened with Enron, and the legislation of SOX compliances, large companies world-wide are strengthening their controls. We intend having a Business Efficiency Manager for Hindustan Roqsanto as well, the job will cut across all businesses in India, it will require the incumbent to not just implement controls, but identify areas where there is flab and also where a synergy is possible within businesses and perhaps regionally over a larger geography by doing things differently.'

Dev at once knew he was not quite cut out for this role. His strength was business management, business strategy and people. A job that cut across verticals and functions would need clever and sometimes shrewd manoeuvring which wasn't his strength. He also saw this position as career limiting if not career ending.

Dev had very few options, Roqsanto International was at least offering him a position based in Delhi and allowing him to keep his grade level. He also had the comfort of Howard, with whom he had such a good personal rapport being the top boss for all business efficiency teams worldwide. Karan had always meant well for Dev and was still the MD of Hindustan Roqsanto. The job may not have been to his liking, it would also to an extent impact his career, but he would live to fight another day. His main focus, or as he later reflected, his only purpose to live, was Vedant.

As soon as his appointment as Business Efficiency Manager for HRL was announced, Dev confirmed to the landlord the date he would be vacating his rented London home. A few days before 30th April 2008, when he was to leave his lovely Staveley Road house, the cousin of a London friend of Dev's came to his residence to buy his Ford car. 'How much are you expecting for this?' he asked Dev.

'What are you happy to give?' replied Dev.

'The cars manual indicates £1600 for a used Ford of this vintage in good condition. Would that be fine?'

Dev looked at the young man in his late twenties and said, '£1000 will be more than fine.'

The young man was radiant with the much lower than anticipated price, he readily made a cheque out and collected the car and relevant papers and left. The car in which Dev, Meher and Ved had happily travelled all over England was no longer his! Dev smiled to himself—at a time when most of his life was coming apart, he at least secured the goodwill of a young man by foregoing £600.

The Inventory Clerk reached Dev's home on 30th April to do the inventory check after which Dev shut his home and stood at the gate looking at it for one last time. He had, though ever so briefly, realised his dream of a home with a garden where he could play with his son and relax with his family. That dream lay shattered now. Man begins to truly understand life only after all his dreams are broken.

The India to which Dev was returning was very different from the one he had left 10 years ago. Hindustan Roqsanto's Delhi office had also moved to Qutub Institutional Area in a swanky building—underground parking with auto-lifting beams, elevators announcing floor level, office door entry through fob cards, cafes and restaurants at ground level, marble flooring and well sign-posted fire exits, open seating workplace with coffee machines and conference rooms large and small—all made for a modern, plush and cheerful office. Vedant's school was just 10 minutes away from Dev's office with fully air-conditioned classrooms. From year IX onwards all students were expected to have their own laptops; even school buses were air-conditioned but Vedant wasn't using one since Dev would first drop Ved to school in his car and then carry on to his office. Dev had hired with my help Kundan Pal Singh, a *pahadi* driver; 'people from the hills are honest and loyal' was one of Dev's impressions. Sometimes Dev would take half an hour off from work and pick up Ved from school in the afternoon and drop him home and return to work: despite all that he had seen in his short tender life till then, Ved would always have a smile on his face as he saw his father at the gate of his school. In all the years that I have known Vedant not once have I heard him complain of anything in life!

The world was going through its most serious financial crisis in living memory in 2008; Dev would hear his colleagues in Delhi office talk of risks and opportunities in stock market. His bank in Delhi had assigned him a Relationship Manager who was professional and persuasive and would discuss online stock trading, large caps and midcaps, FMPs and EMIs and would tell Dev, 'Sir this is the best time to invest in mutual funds, in FDs you don't even cover inflation.' While the chaotic traffic and 'me first' driving culture perturbed Dev the most on his permanent return to Delhi, he was enthralled by the impact that technology including IT, retailing and shopping malls, global brands and customer service, media and modern housing were having on urban Indian society and day-to-day life in cities!

Dev had been seeing global brands of cars on Indian roads in recent times and he himself was given an air-conditioned, high-end automatic gear shift car by his company! Premium differentiated fuels were now available in petrol stations and on a few occasions when Kundan Pal Singh was on leave, Dev hopped into the Delhi Metro and was awestruck by its quality and efficiency. He would often take Ved to the Ansal Plaza Mall, soon several other upscale malls like the Select City Walk mall in Saket and DLF Promenade Mall in Vasant Kunj opened up. These malls were as good as any in world and all popular international clothes and accessory brands had stores in them; the malls also housed multiplex cinema screens and ornate restaurants. Traditional Indian *mithai* and snacks vendors like Haldiram's and Bikanerwala had become ever so trendy, their success made a case for allowing multi-brand international retailers in India. Foreign branded flat screen TVs with dish and set-top boxes had widely entered homes in urban India, media was so vibrant that every evening any government action or lack of it would be fiercely debated on numerous TV news channels, and *Kaun Banega Crorepati* was a superhit TV show featuring Amitabh Bachchan whose popularity had grown further still. Not only online banking but even online dating and marriage portals were being widely used, renewable forms of energy were being talked about and Dev would often hear clever new-age terms like 'thought leadership', 'domain expertise', 'thanks for reaching out' and 'thanks for doing heavy lifting' in office conversations!

These emblems of development helped Dev in only fleetingly diverting his mind away from his emotional turmoil, simmering financial insecurity, and social and professional challenges. From Vice President, he was now a Business Efficiency Manager having to deal with business heads within Hindustan Roqsanto and a hard-nosed boss Liam Wouters based in Dubai. He had no official authority over the four main business verticals or support functions but had to deliver 'efficiency' related changes. R Harish, the Plastics head based in Mumbai, was an intelligent and articulate manager; he was also thin-skinned and ready-to-get-offended extemporaneously, often tactically! The last thing Dev wanted to hear was an announcement that Howard Sadler was leaving Roqsanto at the end of March 2009; when Dev spoke with him over phone Howard mentioned that he felt stretched beyond his maximum energy levels doing a high pressure-job and taking care of his son. A week later there was another announcement that Howard was being replaced by Wang-Yong Huang who would be relocating to Hamburg to the Works Headquarters and managing the business efficiency teams out of WHQ. In all his years with Roqsanto, Dev had had the most strained working relationship with Wang-Yong. He felt fate thwarting him at every step of his life at that time!

No sooner had this high-level change taken place that Dev started getting pointers that he 'needs to do more' and 'show stronger leadership'. Liam Wouters told him,

'Harish feels that some of the proposals you are suggesting will harm his business; you need to work on managing stakeholders better.'

Some of the old-timers like Suresh Fernandez and Nirbhay Jha and Raj Subramaniam who were still in the system and were looking for new assignments contacted Dev; he tried to help each one of them by either finding a role in his small team or requesting the heads of various businesses in HRL to consider their candidature. On more than one occasion Dev's hiring recommendation was met with Wouters' raised eyebrows or the HR focal point saying, 'Let's look at a few more CVs'.

If at office Dev was beginning to sense push-back, if not disapproval, Ved was struggling at school. The previous year Dev had received a call from one of Ved's teachers complaining, 'Mr Rajvansh we gave three questions in the IT test to the class, your son is saying he doesn't like the third question and so is not attempting it.'

Dev was a bit amused, in Ved's school in London if a child was finding any exercise or question difficult, he or she would say to the teacher, 'I don't like this question'. The teacher would then check with the child what he or she would like to do and encourage them to work in their chosen area. Ved was still in that mould! When Dev met this teacher a few days later she told him, 'Mr Rajvansh, we have counselled your son, please don't scold him, he is very sweet.'

Dev thought to himself—I feel like scolding you, why would I ever scold my child! At Apricus International it seemed that while the school was following the International Baccalaureate system, the teachers came from the old ROTE method of learning and their focus was marks, marks and only marks! A week later Dev received a call at 10:20 pm from Ved's class teacher requesting him to be in school the next day at 2:30 pm. Dev took time off from his office and reached Ved's school, he was promptly accosted by the French teacher who told him, 'Mr Rajvansh, Vedant has got just 16 marks in French test.'

'And the test was out of how many marks?' asked Dev,

'Twenty-five, Sir.'

Dev was perplexed, he had been called at 10:20 pm the previous evening only to be told that Ved had scored 16 marks out of 25! 'That's first division marks!' said Dev incredulously.

'Sir other students have all scored over 20.'

Dev looked at her and said, 'I am very happy with the 16 Vedant has got.'

The teacher didn't know how to respond. For the first time, it appeared, a parent was telling her that he was happy his son had not got higher marks! 'Sir, marks determine status in society.'

Dev looked at her in the eye and retorted, 'I neither seek such status nor need such society.'

Dev was feeling perturbed with the push-back he was getting in office, his poor networking skills not helping his cause; and he was gravely disturbed with the constant 'he needs to improve a lot' comments from Ved's teachers. He got to the end of his tether when one day Vedant's Physics teacher called Dev and said, 'Mr Rajvansh, Vedant is not showing improvement in Physics, we know there are some problems at home, but you will need to do something urgently for Vedant to show better results.'

The insolence of that teacher—she actually had the cheek to say 'we know there are some problems at home'. Dev decided that once the academic session was over, he would pull Ved out of Apricus International. Things came to a head when, a few months before end of the academic session, Vedant was asked to write an essay in the English class on 'A picnic with my parents'. Vedant must have recalled his father telling him, while taking him to a cricket match at Ferozeshah Kotla sometime ago, 'Vedant we will have an enjoyable picnic at the cricket.'

Ved vividly described the scene in the stadium in his essay. The English teacher all but struck out the essay with the remark 'This is not a picnic' and gave Ved 2 marks out of 10. Dev was incensed with the grading! He decided to approach the school principal, showed her the essay and grading and told her, 'You need to decide whether your focus is academics in this school or education!'

The principal to her credit showed understanding and assured Dev that she will give a serious thought to what he had said and change Ved's section. Dev's mind however was totally made up by then, 'I realise being a school teacher would not be easy, I am also sure this method of teaching and emphasis on marks would work for several students, but it's not working for my son or me.'

There is a saying that one plus one equals eleven. As a single parent, Dev carrying all the weight of responsibility by himself must have felt like the load of eleven people. Further, and more acutely, Ved's tough toil at school and the demands of his exacting job accentuated by evident dissatisfaction of his manager and a few other stakeholders, not to mention the social unease and a house which wasn't comfortable, all made for such a strenuous situation that it started showing on Dev's person. He was greying fairly quickly and extra inches began accumulating on his waist. His eyes had gone listless again, like those sunken eyes of his early years.

During a family get-together at festival time, his cousin remarked apathetically, 'You are not the first person going through this, you must move on.' Once at a gathering of college friends, Anshuman Pant told him, 'Dev nobody can help you in this situation.' Dev's position had become so weak that once Tank, who I knew from TMS days, said to me, 'I don't even wish it for my worst enemy.'

Amidst all this torment, Dev would find energy to somehow grind on when he looked at Ved's innocent face. He had to live for his son, only and only for his son, he had to give little Ved the foundation so that he could make a life for himself.

Both Dev and Vedant found recreation in Akshay Kumar's cheerful movies. If in the 1990s Hindi film industry was making slick romantic comedies shot in European locales, in late 2000s it was biopics and historical dramas being produced with realism and grandiose respectively. Also on display were 'twist in the tale' kind of polished films like *Race* and *Dhoom* with excellent camerawork and editing.

Cricket remained their main common interest. India had won the inaugural 2007 Twenty-20 World Cup, and while the Indian Premier League T-20 tournament with franchise teams format launched in 2008 was becoming extremely popular, in Dev's mind, nothing could compare with the sublime and riveting nature of Test match cricket. Yet, when it was on TV, Dev and Ved would snugly settle in their bed, half-reclining on their pillows, and enjoy the T20 IPL match and the commercial dazzle that came along with. Even as a 12-year-old Vedant was beginning to appreciate why his father so loved Test match cricket and described T20s as 'amusement cricket'.

By mid-2009 Dev had started actively looking for a flat in Gurgaon, he had to somehow and somewhere improve his and Ved's life. He had been to my apartment a couple of times earlier and really liked the Nirvana Township. I told him to come over and spend a weekend with me so that I could drive him around Gurgaon and introduce him to a couple of real estate agents; Dev would very seldom stay at anyone's home and after his separation he had become even more circumspect, but he agreed on that occasion to come over for the weekend. Eklavya had a couple of meetings scheduled in Gurgaon the following week and when I told him that Dev will be with me on Saturday and Sunday he said, 'Let me also try and come *Khannae*, if Polly doesn't mind too much.'

I decided to do a dinner at my house on Saturday evening, and invited Sanju and his wife Divya and also Ramkumar. I also felt obliged to invite Dhiraj and Ira with their spouses, despite that evening five years ago when Luv and Poulomi didn't quite enjoy their company, since they were my neighbours in Nirvana and I had availed their hospitality twice.

Luv hugged Dev when the latter was dropped at my place by Kundan Pal Singh on that Saturday morning. 'So happy to see you Dev, the greyness gives you a distinguished look; though I can see you need a health club membership!' Dev enquired about Poulomi and how Luv's business was going and after a cup of coffee we got into my car.

'*Yaar*, I am not the typical businessman,' said Luv. While no work in this world is in any way lesser than the other, the nature of a person's profession tends to impact his or her outlook and personality. 'Business guys, for all their enterprise, view most things in terms of money and opportunities, and don't hesitate in making last minute changes to programmes if a business opportunity springs up, even if it inconveniences those involved in their programme!'

Dev smiled at Luv, and the latter himself said, 'I know, I know, I still love generalisations!'

'Bhaisahab, you find India changed?' Luv asked Dev.

'Absolutely, and most of the change appears to be for the better,' said Dev from the front seat.

We all spoke about the development in Gurgaon itself—the wonderful apartment condominiums, 24 hours power and water supply, round the clock security, intercoms in the buildings, power efficient ACs, LED bulbs, cafes galore, wine shops, restaurant flyers being distributed in housing societies and people ordering food on the phone, excellent private universities and international schools offering IB curriculum coming up.

Then Luv added with his usual mischievous expression, 'I have also discovered spas in some big hotels in three cities in India where cross gender massage has started!'

'You want to say more?' I poked him.

'I have made friends with the masseuses now; they give me extra service!'

Dev and I both laughed. 'Whatever happened to Purnima, your sister's friend?' I enquired while remaining on the topic of Luv's escapades.

'*Yaar* I lost touch with her ages back, and the last two times I met her I got the impression that she didn't want me to feel her bum now that I'm married!' replied Luv rather remorsefully.

'Oh that's not fair,' said Dev, play-acting with a serious look. I couldn't control my laughter and almost lost control of the car steering.

'She stood with her back so adjacent to the wall that I couldn't give her a hug nor reach her amazing ass.'

Both Dev and I chuckled softly. 'And what about your lady neighbour and with whom you were having phone sex?' I probed.

'*Khannae*, you remember everything, *haan*!' said Luv. 'With her too there isn't much contact; she kept talking about her acidity problems whenever I called her in recent times and began signing off emails with "regards"!' said Luv ruefully.

'This is a wonderful road,' said Dev as I turned right from Golf Course Road onto the Sunset Boulevard Road which has an undulating hilly touch to it. At the intersection we saw a new development called Meliora Heights.

'Buy a flat here, Dev,' said Luv instantly.

'Looks really beautiful from outside,' agreed Dev.

'Let me call Chawla ji, he is a good broker and will know if flats are available in this development,' I reckoned.

All my dinner guests arrived around 8 pm. Sanju hugged Dev, while Ramkumar formally shook hands though with a smile. Ramu was always correct but reserved. Dev gave a half-hug to Divya, while Ira gave him a bear hug. All the three ladies greeted each other with a hug and peck on the cheek. Dhiraj and Sanju greeted each other's wives and Ira with a peck on the cheek. Everyone was casually though smartly dressed; all the ladies were either in skirts or trousers. My mind for a fleeting moment went back to how my father would greet my mother's friends in the 1980s, always with folded hands. The saree and *salwar-kameez* was now only occasionally seen in get-togethers of my friends, and in shopping courtyards and in malls in Gurgaon and Delhi. After everyone had warmly exchanged updates with Dev, and he had congratulated Sanju for growing his accounting firm beyond Indian shores, the discussion veered towards the social change in India and how boys and girls could be freely seen holding hands in public places and sometimes even kissing especially in BPO campuses!

Ira and Dhiraj's wife knew each other really well, then started talking about a common friend of theirs, Natasha, who they were referring to as Naughty. 'Naughty keeps two boyfriends at a time, not more!' said Dhiraj's wife as Ira laughed and the others either smiled or heard curiously.

As I learnt during the chat, Natasha was in her early forties, always been single, and was a senior executive in a five star hotel in Gurgaon.

'How many has she had so far?' asked Ira.

'Who knows, seven, maybe eight, she is just enjoying herself, while we have been dancing with the same man for nearly 20 years!'

Once again both laughed while Sanju playfully nodded his head and said, 'Hmm, would be nice to meet this oversexed babe.'

'She is exactly that, Sanju,' said Ira, 'but also a very intelligent girl.'

'Deadly combination,' quipped Dhiraj in jest.

'You come across a lot of *bindaas* girls these days,' said Dhiraj's wife, 'but Naughty actually lives life as she pleases,' and then she added softly leaning towards Ira, 'she doesn't give a fuck to the world!' Divya and Dev were gracefully silent during this conversation.

I couldn't help thinking, despite all the positive economic and social change that we had been discussing, despite Bharat being a land where men and women had evidently always been equal especially in medieval times, and in spite of women having become more assertive in 21st century as compared to our growing up years, gender biases still existed. There is no difference between men and women in intellect or capability or for that matter enjoying their sexuality. Yet a man seeking multiple sex partners is a 'stud', while Natasha was discussed as though she had 'easy virtue'; and through our 'harmless' party time banter most of us were, including two of the three ladies present at the gathering, perpetuating this gender prejudice.

As we served dinner Dev realised that Dhiraj's children were at Pivotop World School and that both Dhiraj and his wife were delighted with the day-boarding Pivotop with a sprawling 30 acre campus offering IB curriculum.

'Are they obsessed with marks?' asked Dev.

'They strike a good balance between academics, sports and life skills,' replied Dhiraj's wife, 'I can introduce you to their admissions head in case you are interested.'

We then discussed how the cut-off percentage for Delhi University college admissions had soared. 'Unless you get over 97% marks today, you won't get a sought after course like Economics or B.Com Honours or Physics in a top DU college now!' said Ira.

Dev pursed his lips, gently nodding and looking at me.

Once all my guests had left, Luv wanted to know how Dev had been getting along since he relocated to India. 'Are you in touch with Meher?'

Dev was uncomfortable responding to that question. Nonetheless, he said, 'Vedant meets her occasionally.'

Luv quickly changed the topic and enquired how his relocation to Delhi had been.

Once again Dev didn't directly answer Luv's question, instead he said, 'India's soul is vast and all inclusive Eklavya, for centuries it has assimilated people from all over the world, different religions, languages and diverse cultures.'

Luv looked at Dev intently and remarked, 'And will you say the same for the section of society with which you, in your situation, are interacting?'

Dev remained quiet. A dry smile momentarily came to his face, he said nothing though.

Before 2009 was over, Dev finalized Ved's admission in Pivotop World School and purchased a three bedroom flat in Meliora Heights on the intersection of Sunset Boulevard Road and Golf Course Road in Gurgaon. On his first visit to Pivotop itself his mind was made up, and on his next trip he took Vedant with him who also loved the school, its layout and the courtesy and friendliness of the admissions head and director. After a short test, Ved's admission was confirmed.

Dev's official international travel had become almost non-existent. He would only occasionally travel to Dubai to meet Liam Wouters. In early 2010 when he boarded the Delhi-Dubai flight, he scarcely realised that that trip would have an impact on his future life in more ways than one. In his annual performance appraisal discussion with his boss,

Dev was considerably marked down! Some of the 'opportunity to improve' feedback was such that he had never heard earlier in his over 20 years of work life. Dev had learnt it is somewhat futile to argue against an appraisal and took the feedback on his chin, though deep down he was intensely disturbed. As he boarded the return flight and took an aisle seat in the front row he wondered where his employment was headed towards and how would he take care of Ved should anything untoward happen. Just then he saw a well-dressed Indian lady walk into the plane with a little girl, presumably her daughter. She took the two seats also in the same front row though across the aisle.

Dev would hardly ever converse with his co-passengers and he very gently smiled at the lady across the aisle and she gracefully said, 'Hello.'

Dev couldn't help thinking how elegant she was. The stewardess announced that the flight was delayed by about half an hour, hearing which Dev closed his eyes and reclined in the seat. He opened his eyes when he heard a second announcement that the flight was further delayed. He checked with the lady across the aisle, 'Did they say why the take-off is delayed?'

She replied, 'The stewardess told me they are waiting for a passenger,' and then pointing to the vacant seat next to Dev she added, 'Likely to take that seat.'

Dev then introduced himself, 'I am Devavratt Rajvansh.'

'Bhavini Narang,' she said, and as Dev looked at the little girl besides her, she added, 'My daughter.'

A very familiar looking gentleman then entered the plane who the stewardess showed to the seat next to Dev. It was Anosh Munsherji, the famous industrialist, who headed one of the largest Indian business groups Khodayji Dinshaji Traders Ltd, which had also become one of the largest trading companies in the world. Munsherji gently bowed both to Bhavini Narang and to Dev, 'I am very sorry for causing this delay.'

A snag had developed in Anosh Munsherji's private jet and so he had to shift to a normal commercial airline. While lack of networking skills was Dev's weakness, one of his strengths, developed over time, was the ease with which he could engage with the seniormost and eminent people as well as those in blue collars. He had a brief conversation with Anosh Munsherji complimenting him for growth of his conglomerate and also for their strong business principles.

'What do you do Devavratt?' enquired the tycoon.

'I work for a company called Roqsanto, Mr Munsherji', said Dev, 'was in London with Roqsanto International till last year, managing a global business, now I am with the Indian subsidiary Hindustan Roqsanto based in Delhi.'

Anosh Munsherji smiled, 'A company called—it's a top 100 organisation of the world, and so well admired! Do give my best to Karan Varma.'

Dev nodded. 'You know we have often thought of getting into energy and chemicals trading, but our portfolio of other commodities has shown sustained growth so we've not had the push to establish a team dedicated to energy and chemicals.'

'It's also a fairly specialized activity', said Dev.

'It certainly is,' replied Munsherji. Dev didn't want to show excessive eagerness in conversing with such a senior industrialist, and so even though he would have liked to chat more, he also wanted to allow Munsherji his space. He therefore quietened down as he saw the industrialist look into his Blackberry.

'Mama, will *Nanu-Nani* be at the airport?' said the little girl to her mother.

Dev smiled at his co-passenger, 'Visiting your parents?'

'Yes,' replied Bhavini, 'and I couldn't help hearing that you are based in Delhi.'

'I am, currently staying in Malviya Nagar.'

'Oh, my parents are in Panchsheel,' she said.

'That's next door. You presumably live in Dubai,' reckoned Dev.

'We do,' said Bhavini.

Dev would not have carried on the conversation further, but there are moments in our lives when we do things out of character. 'Are you working in Dubai or a homemaker?'

Bhavini replied with poise and a smile, 'I am a journalist, but have the option of working from home. So am a bit of both!'

Dev smiled back.

It was after a couple of minutes that his lady co-passenger then said, 'I heard you say you were in London?'

Dev nodded, 'Till last year.'

Bhavini then checked, 'Hope you wouldn't mind my asking if you were in London for a long time.'

Dev instantly responded, 'About 10 years.'

Bhavini gave Dev an intent look for the first time, 'You know I am doing a series of articles on Indian diaspora titled "The Peripatetic Indian", I have interviewed Indian friends and acquaintances from Singapore, USA, Canada and of course, Dubai, if you wouldn't mind sparing an hour it would be nice to have the perspective of someone from UK.'

Dev thought for a moment and then replied, 'Certainly.' He then handed Bhavini his business card.

'When is it convenient for you to speak?' she enquired.

'Late morning on either Saturday or Sunday.'

'Thank you,' said Bhavini Narang.

Eklavya Was 75% Right

In late January 2010, a few days before Vedant's 13th birthday, Sudhir who was in Philadelphia for an official visit sent us a picture on e-mail. The picture showed him seated in the Museum of American Revolution in Philadelphia holding a small placard which read 'I am a fan of Life, Liberty & the pursuit of Happiness'. The quest for joy and bliss is the most legitimate entitlement of every living creature. Yet every pleasure is so transient, every meeting ends in separation, every birth matures towards death and every river eventually falls in the sea. Life seems to be an ocean of sorrow in which boats of happiness set sail: we all get into these boats, some for short others for longer time, but the ocean remains one of grief, pain, separation and death.

Dev too was trying his best to keep Ved and himself on one such boat. His new apartment, where interior work was going on, and Ved's new school where he was to start by midyear gave him hope. He had stopped celebrating his own birthday, so the only annual function he would do was Vedant's birthday. On Ved's birthday in 2008 almost everyone invited had come. In 2010, only 50% of Dev's friends and extended family whom he invited made it convenient to attend. Some didn't even bother to inform him that they would not be able to make it. Dev felt let down since he was expecting a much larger crowd.

About a month later, Dev was to visit Chennai for office work. A few days before his flight he decided to call Shankar and Jaya, his close friends who were still in the coastal town. 'Hope all well with you and Jaya and the little one, Shankar,' Dev warmly greeted his friend.

'Hi Dev, nice to hear from you, yes we are all good.'

Dev then told Shankar that he was planning to be in Chennai a few days later.

'Give us a call when you are here, we could meet for a coffee,' replied Shankar.

Dev hung up after a courteous 'hope to see you soon'. He was not intending to stay with Shankar and Jaya in any case, he was booked in a hotel; but it hit him when Shankar didn't even invite him for a meal let alone ask him for stay over while he was in Chennai. He was seeing an aspect of the world he had till recent times not quite experienced. That old adage had only slowly been sinking into Dev in the last couple of years: 'You laugh and the world laughs with you, you cry and you cry alone'...all alone!

However, his contact with Bhavini Narang had become quite regular since their chance meeting a couple of months earlier. Bhavini had thought of including Dev's experiences as a 'peripatetic Indian' in her series of articles, but presumably after hearing his story she decided otherwise. They had started emailing and more than occasionally calling each other. Even an apparently phlegmatic man like Dev, who could drown in his own sorrow and draw a strange inspiration from it, needed a woman to talk to! On her part, Bhavini must have been at that stage in her journey, mid to late 30s about 10 years into a marriage, where a woman feels at an emotional low-ebb and is grappling with existential questions and the need for something extra from life. She must have found in Dev a decent and intelligent man who was fighting against odds. It would be fair to say that both Dev and Bhavini had started seeing 'a friend' in each other.

Sudhir was the one friend Dev was in frequent touch. He and Ved had in the previous year, at long last, met Sudhir's wife Gayatri and their daughters when they were all travelling to Delhi. Gayatri was as sincere and bright as Sudhir, and as a History professor at University she and Dev had many interesting topics on Indian history to discuss. It was in 2010 just before Dev and Ved were to move into their new apartment, that both of them went to Raipur to spend a long weekend with Sudhir and Gayatri. Sudhir had asked Dev to speak at the

Dharamadhikari State Training Institute on 'Project Appraisal' to the state civil servants and then enjoy the weekend at their home. In due course he put Dev in touch with the National Training Academy in Dehradun where young central government officers would be trained and Dev became a guest speaker both at the Raipur and Dehradun training institutes, in fact he became a very popular and sought after guest speaker on management and public administration related topics at both places! Over the next few years Dev and Ved would make at least two trips a year to Raipur, Dev would speak at the State Training Institute and then they would spend the weekend with Sudhir and Gayatri and their lovely daughters. Sudhir and Dev would frequently use statements and remarks made during their time in 1980s at TMS in their conversations and then laugh thinking about those old incidents. Sudhir would quip with an admiring nod of the head, 'I think we'll grant it to her,' whenever Gayatri made a pertinent point, or Dev would say, '*Bhery* much possible,' when Sudhir would wonder if a particular situation in office context was possible! Dev and Vedant found the warmest of family atmosphere with Sudhir and Gayatri and the daughters.

Dev's uncle had a sad and worried look on his face when Dev decided to move with Ved, to their flat in Gurgaon in the April of 2010. He was stressed as to how Dev would manage the home and food, his job and Ved's studies and their health all by himself; however he was also much attached to his Malviya Nagar home and so felt helpless about the situation. Dev set up his apartment elegantly, he would keep thinking how he and Meher had set up various homes during their time together; now that he was finally decorating and furnishing his first owned home he had no partner with him to advise on colour of upholstery or brand of TV or size and shape of dining table!

Whenever he spoke with Bhavini he would ask her on living room lights and design of curtain and what kind of microwave to buy. He would always check with Vedant too, whose usual response would be, 'It's nice, Dad; whatever you choose is fine.' Ultimately, Dev's apartment reflected his personality: there was warmth in the home without any clutter, the furniture and fixtures were elegant and comfortable without being loud, all the white goods were established brands and functional without being over the top. Dev made his apartment really snug for Ved who began to love the flat and his little room; there were three large gardens within the Meliora Heights complex, two grocery stores, swimming pool and a clubhouse and round the clock security, Dev didn't have to worry when Ved would go down to the garden to play or to buy a chocolate from the grocery shop. He also managed to find a male cook, again a pleasant *pahadi* guy named Dharamveer in his early 30s, who would come every evening and hum songs as he cooked food for Devavratt and Vedant.

In the June of 2010, Ved got into the Pivotop school bus which would stop right outside Meliora Heights, the first time he was using a school bus in his little life; he took a window seat and waved placidly to his father. Dev waved back with a subdued smile as he saw another chapter of life unfolding. Both Vedant's muted wave and Dev's restrained smile carried a message of 'incompleteness'. Something was missing in their lives. Something is missing in every human being's life; something is missing in nature's creation.

Ved adjusted in Pivotop fairly quickly. The school ambience was relaxed and conducive for creative learning. The teachers didn't appear overly concerned if a student's performance was average for some time; 'he will catch up at his own speed' was the encouraging approach; the school also actively supported students trying different life skills, crafts and sports. The setting was liberating, it was a day boarding and Ved would have his lunch in Pivotop canteen and return by 4:30 pm by the school bus. Dev would occasionally go to the school in the afternoon to pick up Ved, whenever he finished office early or was working from home; he would make it a point to meet the principal and admissions head and sometimes even the director and have a friendly chat with them. He found the teachers and senior management of the school very understanding and there was a matching of wavelength between them and Dev. He could sense that Vedant would do very well at Pivotop World School.

To give his son that extra academic input, which Dev hoped will also help build his confidence, he thought about engaging a Maths tutor at home. It was an interesting action replay of life when Dev discovered that Mohan Raj Midha, who taught Dev way back in 1982, and wrote 'Do you want 90+Δ?' in his notebook, was still around and giving private Maths tuitions. Mr Midha gladly agreed to help Ved; however he couldn't drive to Gurgaon. And thus for the coming four years, till Ved completed his school, Dev and Ved's schedule was to spend Sunday night till Friday evening in Meliora Heights in Gurgaon and then drive to Malviya Nagar on Friday evenings and spend the weekend there. Not only could Mr Midha drive easily to Malviya Nagar to teach Ved on weekends, but our school friend Ramkumar had generously offered to help little Ved with physics and chemistry so long as he was studying these subjects. So Dev and Vedant's weekends started with Mr Midha's visit to their Malviya Nagar home, followed by a trip to Chirag Enclave in late afternoon to Ramkumar's home, who Ved addressed as Ramu Uncle, and a movie in Select City Walk Mall Saket or a dinner in a South Delhi restaurant.

Week after week and month after month, Dev would wake up at 6 am, make a quick breakfast for Ved and himself, get Ved ready for school and give him a small box of sandwiches just in case the school lunch was not to his liking. As Ved would board the school bus by 7:30 am, Dev would drive to his office in Qutub Institutional Area. He would work till almost 4 pm, then drive back to Meliora Heights to receive Ved by 4:30 pm, give him a snack and go over his tests and assignments or finish pending office teleconferences. While Ved would be downstairs in the gardens playing, Dev would settle the home and await Dharamveer the cook. Before dinner father and son would complete school homework and assignments, and post dinner they would watch a bit of TV with episodes of *The Big Bang Theory* being their favourite. After Ved would go to bed, Dev would ensure that his school uniform for next day was ready, and then for the next hour or so he would immerse himself in Neeraj's poetry. The soulful depth and melody of Neeraj's rendition, the song of sorrow and of human love, of changing social norms and of spiritual consciousness, would soothe Dev's own agony. He never took to alcohol because Neeraj's poetry was so intoxicating and so cathartic. Dev's eyes would slowly close; he had to wake up by 6 am again the next morning! All his inexorable labour, all his physical fatigue and all his mental stress were tolerable as Ved began doing well in school again!

However, Dev's position in office remained anything but strong. Even though a few of his 'business efficiency' ideas had been successfully implemented neither Liam Wouters nor Wang-Yong Huang appeared positively disposed towards him. In fact, Liam Wouters pointed out that his leaving office by 4 pm daily wasn't exactly exemplary! Dev mentioned that as a single parent he had to get back home to his son and that he was getting into office early, he was the first person in office every day! Further, he was doing other meetings via teleconferencing in the evenings. Wouters didn't react, he went onto point out that Dev needed to be more hands-on, and that he was expected to not delegate as much. As Kundan Pal Singh would drive Dev from Qutub Institutional Area to Meliora Heights, Dev would look out of the car window and wonder whether his management style and work approach which propelled him to becoming one of the youngest VP's in Roqsanto had turned outdated or was his effort really falling short of what was expected, whether his discomfort in a role cutting across verticals and his lack of shrewdness in managing stakeholders creating a negative impression or had his managers just formed a negative perception of him due to reasons unknown to Dev. Be that as it may Devavratt Pratap Rajvansh exhorted himself into remaining softly enthusiastic about his ongoing assignment and quietly optimistic about his future professional career.

Dev's self-contrived enthusiasm and optimism suffered a big blow when he learnt in October that year that 31st

December 2010 was to be Karan Singh Varma's last day with Roqsanto, and that he was retiring. Further, Liam Wouters would, for the time being, be double-hatting from Dubai as Managing Director of Hindustan Roqsanto Ltd.! Mid-40s to mid-50s is a dicey age for privately employed working professionals, their costs are high given house mortgages and children's education, and if they sense they are not going to 'make it' and if their circumstances are as fragile as Dev's were, then it becomes a triple strenuous whammy!

Dev was marked down yet again in the annual performance appraisal, second year in succession. While this time he mentioned his achievements and well considered approach to his assignment, his boss looked at him expressionlessly and said, 'Let's focus on the areas of development we identified today.'

Dev couldn't help thinking of the *Compass-Delta-Entaxei* evaluation in 2005 where one of the comments in feedback was: 'Strong leadership profile with potential to successfully deliver in the very challenging and senior most roles in the organisation'. Two successive years of mediocre performance was ominous for Dev.

Devavratt had informed Bhavini that he was to be in Dubai for his appraisal; she had sounded truly elated on the phone. They dined together on both the days he was there. 'My mother is over these days so she is pampering her granddaughter, my husband is as usual travelling on work.' Bhavini could sense Dev's morale was very low; she earnestly and unconditionally supported him and suggested he actively starts contacting head hunters and looking at options in the wider employment market.

I will do whatever best I can, and leave the rest to Nature, thought Dev with a feeling of exhausted surrender, as he and Ved prepared to enjoy the World Cup Cricket to be played in India through March that year with the final scheduled for 2nd April 2011. When on the 2nd of April Mahendra Singh Dhoni lifted the ball over long-on for a six and twirled the bat in his hand signalling India's world cup triumph after 28 years, a billion prayers had been realised and the nation erupted with joy! From Chepauk to Ferozeshah Kotla and from Eden Gardens to Wankhede Stadium there were celebrations galore. Dev and Ved had been watching the world cup finals on a large screen in the lawns of The Palms club near HUDA City Centre in Gurgaon with a few of Dev's colleagues and their spouses and children. While everyone was dancing and hugging each other, Dev's mind was preoccupied with 30th June 2011, the day his ongoing work assignment was to end.

Dev had not succeeded in finding his next job with Roqsanto, his marked-down appraisals seemingly stood in the way! He started actively sending his CV to the well-known head-hunters in India only to repeatedly hear: 'Your domain expertise is petrochemicals, we will get back to you if a suitable assignment comes up in the sector'. Dev tried to unsuccessfully reason with them that his 'domain expertise' was business strategy and marketing and managing large businesses and people. Crestrail Consultants who had been chasing Dev when he was in London, and had told him with his profile he could get jobs at the Rs. 3 crore annual salary level, also gave him the 'domain expertise' response now and further added that his business efficiency role and location constraint of being in Delhi were also a hindrance.

In early June, Dev got a call from the head of HR in Hindustan Roqsanto Ltd. asking him how he was getting along on Roqsanto Roles, the in-house jobs portal of the company where all vacancies across the world were posted. Dev mentioned that he had applied for three jobs which had been advertised as 'virtual' however he had received a regret for all.

'Okay Devavratt, Liam Wouters will call you and discuss options,' said the HR head.

Two days later Wouters called Dev and told him, 'Rajvansh the Industrial-Construction business head job might come available in a few months, time, you could apply if interested.'

'Would the incumbent need to be necessarily based in Chennai, or can it be done from Delhi?' checked Dev.

'Chennai, absolutely Chennai,' said the stand-in Managing Director.

'As you know Liam, I can't leave Delhi-Gurgaon till my son completes school which is mid 2014,' submitted Dev.

'Sure, in which case keep looking on Roqsanto Roles. Your current assignment ends on 30th June but you have been with us for long, and given your situation, I am authorizing six extra months so you have enough time to find your next role; will put you on a business development project in the meanwhile.'

Dev wasn't exactly sure how to respond, he knew his marked down appraisals would hinder him tremendously, he thanked his boss nonetheless and checked, 'And what happens if I am unable to find a role by December end, given that I have not had very good ratings last two years?'

Liam Wouters replied instantly, 'In that case you could opt for voluntary severance.'

After 30th June, Dev was not really required to attend office regularly, he was told to hotdesk whenever he needed to use office. He was expected to focus on finding his next job, and he had been given a liberal six months for it. Dev kept applying for jobs within Roqsanto; he kept getting rejected. Even in the external market his 'domain expertise' and seniority and location constraint and an ongoing 'non-business role' impeded him! All these years he had somehow tried to balance Ved's needs with his job, now he shifted his attention almost entirely to his son's requirements. This was an important year for Vedant, he was to appear for class Xth examination in mid-2012, known as the IGCSE exam.

Dev ensured that it was not just Vedant's academic needs that he concentrated on—he would keep inviting friends and at times colleagues and extended family members to his home for dinner get-togethers, every summer he and Ved would go to London for holiday and stay at the enchanting Roquersbury Club for a fortnight and he would also keep taking Ved for excursions to touristy spots around Delhi and request a couple of friends and their families to join in the outing.

On one such excursion, I was with Dev and Vedant when we went to Agra to see the Taj Mahal. We booked ourselves in a five-star hotel for the evening; the mid-sized coffee shop in the hotel where a la carte breakfast was being served the next morning was quite full when the manager courteously showed us to our table.

In a few minutes one of the waiters politely asked us for our breakfast order. 'Sir, it will be about 10 to 15 minutes,' said the waiter respectfully.

Dev smiled at him and replied, 'That's fine, please take your time.'

The breakfast arrived in about 15 minutes and it was splendid. As we were enjoying our first meal of the day, we heard a lady from the adjacent table ask a waiter loudly, 'We ordered breakfast 10 minutes back, when will you get it?'

A minute later a man seated on another table scolded a waiter sarcastically, 'We asked for warm milk for the child, will you get it tomorrow!'

The waiters were constantly on the run and graciously telling the guests that their order was on the way. Dev was feeling disturbed at the way these well-to-do people were speaking to the waiters; he was disapprovingly shaking his head. Then we heard another man take off boorishly, 'Is this a 5 star hotel! The service is pathetic; where is our corn flakes and omelette!'

Dev could not take it any further. He asked the young man waiting on our table to call the Manager and also all the waiters.

'What happened, Sir?' checked the surprised waiter circumspectly.

'I just wish to speak with the Manager please and also all your colleagues if you don't mind,' said Dev getting up from his chair.

The Manager hurriedly approached our table with five or six waiters. Dev spoke to the Manager, alternately looking at the waiters, and loudly enough for the entire restaurant to hear, 'You are providing such good service here, it is as good as anywhere in the world; you are well within your rights to tell the guests to be patient! Please don't let anyone bully you or shout at you, okay.'

The Manager and waiters were pleasantly astonished. They expected yet another reprimand. They looked at Dev and then each other in bewilderment. I glanced around the coffee shop, especially at those people for whom Dev's message was meant; I found them all looking elsewhere, none towards us!

'Thank you, Sir,' said the Manager gently, 'thank you very much.'

While I knew Dev had a strong sense of fairness and steadfastness to dignity of labour, I had hardly seen this side of Dev earlier. As he settled back on the table to finish his breakfast he said to me, 'Sandeep, I find the customer service in hotels and airlines in India, and in retail stores and banks here so good, that to find people speaking curtly to these boys and girls is totally unacceptable.'

When we asked for the bill as we finished our breakfast, we found the Manager approaching our table with two three waiters besides him. Dev looked up at him and repeated, 'Can we have the bill please?'

The Manager looked at Dev, 'No Sir.'

Dev gave him a puzzled look, 'Sorry…?'

The Manager again said, 'No bill for you Sir.'

Dev got up from his chair and smiled at all of them. 'Please,' he urged, 'please do give us the bill.'

'No, Sir,' said almost all of them, and the Manager again said, 'No bill for you Sir. It is our privilege to have you as a guest, Sir. Please accept this breakfast for you and your family from our side, Sir.'

On several occasions I have seen this dichotomy in India: the lesser educated, the so-called blue collar workers, the less privileged and people of very modest means show a much larger heart and finer human values than the rich elites. We eventually paid the bill but not before the coffee shop gave all of us packed snacks and soft drinks, for our drive back to Delhi after visiting the Taj Mahal, with their compliments.

In mid-December, Dev again received a call from the HR Head enquiring about his progress in finding the next role. 'What did Liam Wouters indicate?' checked the HR Head.

'That I would have the option of a voluntary severance in case I failed to get a job by December end.'

'For that we will need to put you on a three months' notice. Shall we issue that in early January?' said the HR Head more as a statement than question.

Dev had no job left in Roqsanto!

In the six plus three months that he got, he ensured that all his team members got placed in their next assignments. In the last week of March 2012, Dev was in the Qutub Institutional Area office almost every day fulfilling the final departing formalities. Most of his office colleagues had no idea that Dev was serving his last few days with the company, where he had spent nearly a quarter century if his time with Torsh Chemicals was also counted. There had been no announcement that 30th March would be Dev's last day. Around lunch time on Friday the 30th of March when Dev was returning office laptop and phone and signing employment ending documents, word got out that that he was leaving Roqsanto.

His admin assistant who had known Dev since his first day in early-1990s rushed to him with tears in her eyes, 'Dev! Dev, you are leaving?' she exclaimed.

'I am,' smiled Dev.

'Nobody knew; there has been no announcement!' she looked disturbed.

Dev shrugged his shoulders.

Just then three of four of the office colleagues gathered around Dev, though none of his old team members were to be seen around. 'Dev you were going to walk out just like that!' said one of them. They hurriedly organised a send-off that afternoon with some cake and flowers and after a few nice words from a handful of colleagues, Dev walked out from the office of Roqsanto for the last time. He had given the best years of his life to the organisation, which had for the most part justly rewarded him. Devavratt had got to see the world several times over thanks to Roqsanto, he had made friends from many countries and got to understand different cultures and ways of working in different parts of the globe. He had been paid well, 'more than he deserved', to use his own expression.

Yet, at the prime of his youth when he should have been at the peak of his professional career, Dev was now unemployed!

Eklavya called me after he learnt of the latest development in Dev's life. '*Khannae*, Dev could have handled these last few years very differently with much better outcomes. Where does he go from here now?'

I didn't really have an answer for Luv. While he wasn't saying much, I could see Dev besieged with social, emotional, logistics and now professional and financial challenges. He was putting on more weight, greying much more rapidly, he would always smile when we met but his face was showing stress and his eyes were sunken, as they used to be in school days. He dropped the idea of looking for a full-time job till Ved completed school which was going to be in 2014. From where he had slipped to, Ved did fairly well in IGCSE examination securing B and B+ grades in most subjects and a couple of A grades as well. He decided to take Economics, Psychology and Mathematics as his higher level subjects for the forthcoming two IB years.

As Vedant started year XI at school, Dev had to keep himself professionally occupied. He may have had the financial resources for surviving the immediate future, but Ved's university education lay ahead as did much of their lives. He had been speaking at Dharamadhikari State Training Institute in Raipur and National Training Academy in Dehradun, and so when one of our old TMS professors Dr Rajeshwar Desai who was now the Dean of a new business school, Capexx Institute of Management, invited him to become an adjunct faculty Dev readily agreed. Dr Desai asked Dev to teach Competitive Strategy; with his easy conversation style, full of anecdotes and illustrations related to the topic and simple elucidation of the subject, Dev became an instant hit with the students at Capexx. He was hardly going to be earning anything but he would keep himself in circulation.

The weeks started rolling into months, Dev's routine focused entirely on Vedant's education and growing-up needs. They would still be in Malviya Nagar over weekends with Mr Midha coming over to teach Ved and they would spend the weekdays, when school term was on, in Meliora Heights. Kundan Pal Singh was still driving them and Dharamveer was still cooking for them. Dev kept taking Ved to London for a fortnight every summer for vacation, they would spend a few days every year in Raipur with Sudhir and Gayatri and their daughters, and Dev would frequently invite friends and now his ex-colleagues with families over to his apartment in Gurgaon for dinner get-togethers; occasionally, some extended family member too. Ved did very well in his class XI school examination in 2013, and was confidently set for his last year in Pivotop, with the final International Baccalaureate examination scheduled for April of 2014.

I got to learn so much more about the travails of a single male parent in a conversation we had in the November of 2013. That was the first time I also heard about Bhavini. Sudhir was over in Delhi for a ministry meeting and was spending the Saturday at Meliora Heights. Dev asked me to join them for the evening.

'Has Ved decided what to study at University?' checked Sudhir as we settled down with a beer each.

'Economics in all likelihood with some credits in Psychology perhaps.'

'India or England?' I enquired.

'It will be in England, Sandeep,' said Dev, 'this summer we visited a few Universities in England, and Vedant loved the Weymingham University. It's a lovely university spread well over 350 acres.'

'So what will you do Dev?' I wondered.

'I would like to be around Vedant while he is at University, but unless I manage a job back in UK that won't be possible.'

Sudhir and I both gave him a quizzical look. Dev gently smiled, 'Renting even a small flat and living in England is expensive, as of now I can put Vedant though University, but without an income it won't be possible for me to also live there.'

'And have you started looking for a job in England?' I asked.

'I will start early next year.'

Sudhir got up to get himself another beer from the fridge, 'You should have put in more effort in looking for a proper job here itself, after you finished with Roqsanto. And I have been telling him for years, Sandy, to have a female companion too.'

I looked intently at Sudhir, 'Female companion! He has become ultra-careful in having just a normal social conversation with a woman now.'

Sudhir then added with a shake of his head, 'This morning I learnt that even the little working girl who mops and cleans this flat comes only when Ved is at home, and not when Dev is alone!'

Dev was expressionless as he listened to both of us take up his case. My mind went back to a conversation Eklavya and I had had with Dev on the phone some five years ago, when Luv had exhorted Dev not to give up his job in London since his life neither in UK nor in India would be any easier.

'Thank you for your concern boys, but don't you find me conversing as normal with Gayatri or Poulomi or Divya for that matter?'

'You know what we mean Dev,' remarked Sudhir.

'I do,' replied Dev, 'but for that, you need to have something still here,' he said pointing to his heart.

Once again Sudhir and I exchanged a glance. 'You need a woman to talk to Dev, a single woman we mean, with whom you can discuss matters you can't easily with a male friend.'

That's when Dev shared with us that our school and TMS friend Nita Rajagopalan had got divorced and was in San Francisco, she would occasionally email Dev. 'And whenever I need a woman's opinion, I speak with Bhavini, you don't know her, will introduce her to you when she is in Delhi next.'

Once again Sudhir and I were disappointed to know that Bhavini was a married lady. As Dev put it, 'Over the last three odd years, she has been the most sincere friend to me.'

It was sometime later that I learnt that Nita had actually proposed to Dev on the email, and my friend had courteously, typical of him, declined saying that he did not have it in him to reciprocate any soft feelings anymore and it would be unfair on the woman for him to indicate otherwise.

Luv's words from that conversation five years back were coming back to my mind, 'Dev how are your cousins and other relatives?'

Dev gave me a confused look, 'Should be fine. Why?'

I tried explaining myself better, 'I mean are they in touch with you?'

'One or two are.'

I tried not to sound too inquisitive, 'If you don't mind my asking, did any of your extended family members, cousins or relatives, ever call you in these last five or six years and check how you are getting along raising a child all by yourself?'

Dev gave me a long intense look, he lowered his eyelids and then raised them again, and then he gently shook his head. He then said sounding reflective, 'Sandeep, I too haven't called anyone to check how they are doing!'

'Is that because you are a single parent?' asked Sudhir.

This time Dev gave Sudhir a deep look, 'Yes. Given our social order, I think its best that those who are leading normal family lives call me whenever they feel like, rather than the other way around.'

'Why?' I wondered, 'Lest they feel you are calling to seek any help?'

Dev simply looked at me without saying anything.

'Everyone who knows you even slightly would be aware that unless it's a dire situation you will never ask for anything,' I added.

'I feel better this way, Sandeep.'

'What about friends and colleagues?' enquired Sudhir.

'What about them?' said Dev.

'I mean you keep having these dinner get-togethers at home, sometimes in club and restaurants, do they also invite you to their homes? Do they call and check how you and Ved are doing?'

Dev smiled at Sudhir, a smile that combined sadness, resignation and detachment all at the same time, yet somewhere his eyes showed a resolve to carry on with whatever life was throwing at him. 'Three of us are in regular touch aren't we? Then of course Eklavya and Vikrant, Sanjeev and Ramkumar and Nita, Gulshandeep and Rohit Sahni—in touch with different friends in different ways. And yes with friends like Sanjeev and Ramkumar, I go to their homes quite regularly. With ex-colleagues after you leave an organisation very few stay in touch, so I am in touch with two or three former colleagues only.'

'While you were still working were your colleagues in touch with you socially, would they reciprocate your invitations?' quizzed Sudhir.

'I would say a third did occasionally, but it's not something that I ever gave a second thought to.'

'Dev, you remember that chat Luv, you and I had on the phone when you were still in London and contemplating to return, when he was urging you not to give up your job and relocate?' I jogged Dev's memory.

He nodded. 'I would say Eklavya was 75% right!' remarked Dev with a little brightness in his sunken eyes.

As we finished our dinner Dev took a pill from the leaf of tablets lying on the side trolley. Sudhir twirled his left hand wondering what the medicine was for.

'Blood pressure,' said Devavratt.

When pain becomes excessive it brings its own solace with it. Inspirational words sound meaningless and motivational speakers seem manipulative particularly then, those one-liners like 'darker the night, brighter the dawn' ring so hollow. Dev was facing the cruel reality of life, many would resign to nemesis after so many setbacks while a few might fight against their ill-fortune. Who is to say what is good or bad, right or wrong, brave or weak: man's journey is half-truth and half-imagined. Sorrow is a perennial river, if not the deep lonely sea, happiness is a seasonal pond. Sometimes Dev seemed to me like a semi-dead person going through life, other times he appeared to be living a death, day after day. His fairy-tale life was long over, but life wasn't over as yet.

Networking skills was not even remotely an area of strength for Dev, and he had given up on head-hunters to help him find a job in India. He didn't know whether it will serve any purpose trying the same route for a job back in UK. In January of 2014, Dev called up his former colleague and friend Paul Anderson. Paul had recently finished his time with Roqsanto as well. He indicated to Dev that some of their previous Roqsanto colleagues were now working with other organisations, and he would check with them if they needed an experienced resource like Dev. 'I have never had the need to approach head-hunters in UK, Dev, but you don't lose anything contacting one or two,' said Paul on the phone. By end February Dev was getting anxious, he wanted to be close to Ved when he was at University, for which Dev dearly needed a job. He had had no breakthrough at all.

On the first weekend of March, Dev decided to take Vedant to Vaishno Devi. Sanju, Divya and their son, and I too joined Dev and Ved for the trip to the shrine. On our way back we booked ourselves for one night in a hotel in Jammu, since our flight back to Delhi was next morning. I went to Ved and Dev's room around 8 pm that evening to check how they were after our 26 kilometres walk up and down to the shrine. Vedant had become almost as tall as Dev by then, the cut of his face and smile very similar to his father's.

'Come in, Sandy Uncle,' he said, opening the door.

I saw Dev reclining in the bed seeing TV news. 'How are the old bones?' I smilingly asked him.

'A sweet ache in the shins,' he replied. Dev had a very simple heart, but I couldn't somehow say the same about his mind, due to his occasionally complicated thinking. He was non-religious, religion for him meant self-reflection, but he was quite spiritual. It took me a while to understand this. Yet he would visit temples, whenever he did, with utmost reverence. 'It's always a surreal experience to be at Vaishno Devi,' he said.

'Anything interesting in the news?' I checked, pointing to the TV and taking the single sofa chair in the room.

Just then the famous industrialist Anosh Munsherji appeared on the screen, he was being interviewed on recent performance of his company Khodayji Dinshaji Traders Ltd. 'I met him about four years ago,' said Dev sitting up a little upright in the bed. Munsherji briefly mentioned the successful performance of some of their verticals. Talking about the new initiatives of his company Munsherji mentioned that only last year they had got into Energy and Chemicals trading; when asked by the interviewer where the new business was based he said that energy trading hubs were Houston, London and Singapore and apart from establishing small outfits in Mumbai, Delhi and Singapore their main trading office for energy and chemicals was in London.

'Dev, why don't you apply to him?' I suggested.

Dev said after a thoughtful pause, 'I met him four years back and we barely said hello as co-passengers!'

'Never mind, nothing to lose,' I added.

On return to Delhi, Dev found out Anosh Munsherji's email ID from the internet and sent him a mail introducing himself, attaching his CV and stating that having worked in Roqsanto, an organisation where business principles were sacrosanct, the first company that came to his mind, now that he was seeking new employment, where integrity and fairness were likewise unswerving was Khodayji Dinshaji Traders Ltd. whose recent energy and chemicals trading venture may wish to utilize his service. Dev didn't really expect a response to his cold email from such a senior business leader.

Greetings, forwarding to HR for favourable consideration—Anosh Munsherji replied in two days' time! Dev was delighted. He pinched himself and read the email again! Two further days later Dev received a phone call from the HR head of Khodayji Dinshaji Traders Ltd. inviting him to Mumbai for a discussion on what job he could do based in London!

The HR lady offered a position to Dev in the newly established Energy and Chemicals trading vertical and made him join a teleconference with Bhavesh Kumar, the head of the vertical also based in London, who welcomed him by saying that they would benefit a great deal from his rich experience. Dev almost couldn't believe how swiftly and effortlessly the job came his way. At about 5 pm, a lady walked to where Dev was sitting and said, 'Mr Munsherji will meet you now, Sir,' and she showed Dev into the office of the CEO.

'Nice to meet you again Devavratt, thank you for thinking of us for employment prospects, and welcome to your new company.'

Dev was overwhelmed by the man's humility. Famous people might reach the top due to various reasons, but they get to successfully distinguish themselves in that position only with humbleness and grace. In the five minutes that

Anosh Munsherji spent with Dev, he did put in a gentle word of caution though, 'Our team in London is new, they are all bright young traders but don't know much about the energy and chemicals industry, that's where your expertise will come in. I can see both in your CV and person that you are fairly distinguished, it may require a little effort to adjust to the new work environment.'

Dev went straight to Pivotop World School from the airport the next day. Vedant had not seen so much relaxation on his father's face for ages! Dev shared the wonderful news with his son and back home that evening they ordered a nice Chinese meal from outside and enjoyed it while watching *The Big Bang Theory* on TV.

Ved did well in his final IB exams and qualified for admission to the Weymingham University in England. And, Dev was set for the second time in his life to fly away to London for an employment assignment. Yet how different it was from the first time when he was so much more excited and so much happier.

'I salute you son,' said Dev's uncle as he took his aunt and uncle's blessings while bidding them goodbye. 'I salute you for all that you have stood for and done despite all the difficulties.'

It's taken me better part of 27 chapters to flashback to my association with Devavratt Pratap Rajvansh and our several friends and acquaintances, and share some images of India in her eventful voyage from the 1970s to 2014. Let me now devote the last three chapters to communicate what became of Dev and the exceptional Vedant in the years that followed, Eklavya and our many other friends, and above all the continuing journey of the land so fondly, and constitutionally called Bharat.

No Reason To Die

As the cab driver drove out of the apartment complex I heard Dev call out to me holding the entrance door of the block of building where he had rented a flat. We went up a flight of stairs and into Dev's small one-bedroom home. The flat, though tidy, reflected Dev's state of mind and it couldn't have been more different from both his swanky Notting Hill Gate apartment and his palatial Staveley Road villa! While the flat was in a lovely location, all the furniture and appliances looked a little tired and the walls carried whispers of loneliness. The teak-finish cupboards had Dev's clothes and personal effects yet reverberated with emptiness. It was clear that Dev was going through the motions of life somewhat indifferently.

After I had settled down, I asked him about Vedant and how he was getting on at University.

'Weymingham is a beautiful university; Vedant is loving it there. He has made many friends and is participating in several societies.'

I was very happy to hear, 'So wonderful to know that Dev, has he become more outgoing?'

Dev nodded. 'Not introverted now!' he said smilingly.

'And how is your new company and new job?'

'It's okay, they are a decent group with good work-life balance; with better soft skills they could be even more successful,' said Dev.

'Soft skills?' I wondered.

'Teamwork, communication, leadership at upper-middle management; massive productivity gains can come with improvement in these areas at least in this new vertical.'

I asked further, 'And how about your boss?'

Dev thought for a moment and then replied, 'He is a good eight-ten years younger to me, intelligent person but is very keen to show every time that *he* is the boss! Doesn't know much about energy and chemicals industry though understands his company in and out. He didn't like when in a meeting I once pointed out, contrary to his understanding, that oil price remains more or less similar across the world at given point in time though natural gas prices can be different from one supply envelope to another.'

I knew exactly what Dev meant. Some people from our neck of the woods can be too thin-skinned, waiting to get offended. 'So Dev, you have a job in a very good company, you have a steady and decent income, you have a pleasant little flat in a superb neighbourhood, Ved is happy at university, you own a fine apartment in Gurgaon—some issues here and there but it's a fairly happy situation.'

Dev replied after a pause, 'Yes, fairly happy!'

That evening, as Dev went into the kitchen to cook for both of us, I sat with my laptop on the dining table about six feet from where my friend was, since Dev didn't need any help with the *daal-chawal*, asparagus and *aloo-matar* he was preparing.

'Isn't Google incredible, Dev; you can look for anything and anyone!'

Dev nodded.

'And these social networking sites, you can connect with just about everyone you wish to be in touch with!'

Dev didn't respond to my statement on social networking sites and so I said, 'Presume you are not on any, Dev?'

Dev shook his head, 'I tried briefly a while ago, found it intrusive and so now I am only on WhatsApp. What about you?'

'I am registered on a professional networking site; not the social sites where pictures are posted and friend requests sent!'

Dev smiled, 'Let me guess, Eklavya will be on all!'

I laughed and responded with a vehement 'Yes.'

Everyone seems so joyful on these social media portals! People post snaps of their fun events, their travels and new cars and even food they are eating! Their connected friends, in turn inevitably compare their unhappy and travel-excitement-lacking lives with those pictures, and still respond with 'all of you are looking wonderful'!

Two of our female classmates had posted their pictures with their growing-up daughters, and their girl-friends had responded with 'Muaah' and 'Awww' and 'Oh my cuties'; their male friends' general response was 'looking like sisters' in an effort to acceptably flirt with their female friend, clearly conscious of the fact that her husband and *jeejaji* will also be reading such comments. Such men on their social network page would post pictures of themselves either indulging in adventure tourism or with their high-end cars, the last labelled 'my new toy'. Their male friends' typical response would be: 'When do I get a ride in it?'

On the professional networking sites, everyone appears so damn successful posting their 'excitement with the new challenge' in an understated yet public announcement of their promotion and landing a heavy-duty job title! In the March of 2015, however, at least Dev and I still understood the word 'viral' to mean an ailment causing fever.

As the pressure cooker whistle sounded, it struck me to ask my friend, 'When did you learn cooking Dev?'

He smiled, 'Only after returning back to London. Bhavini sends me recipes and whenever I get confused or the dish doesn't come out well, I ask her!'

Dev had introduced me to Bhavini the previous year, and clearly there was a deep bond between them; she was a very well-spoken young lady who carried herself with poise. I couldn't help thinking of Nita and how she had proposed to Dev. I recalled Divya telling me that one of her single lady friend had once met Dev at their party and was keen to contemplate a future with him, however when Divya checked with Dev, he had very politely expressed his own helplessness to even think on those lines. Over the years, Dev had come to expect almost nothing from anyone. I suppose that when a man needs nothing from others, almost nothing, he appears that much more attractive.

I remained fairly busy during my two week trip to London with professional engagements. Whenever I returned home I found the old box style TV always on! Once I asked Dev how come he always had the TV on! 'Makes me feel there is someone else at home,' was Dev's response.

I realised this was how lonely people lived. Living alone may bring strength, yet as Dev himself put it, 'It's not something I would recommend to anyone'. On the weekend while I was there, Ved came in from Weymingham to meet me. It was absolutely delightful to see him; he had become confident and certainly outgoing, he looked very smart and I could clearly sense how much he had matured in less than a year of being at university.

I don't think Dev felt settled in his new organisation, despite it being such a preferred employer due to its business growth, well acclaimed fairness and career opportunities. He felt under-utilized. He could not be put on a trading desk and his boss would occasionally consult him largely to understand the intricacies of chemicals businesses. In the December of 2015 when the HR lady from Mumbai was visiting London, Dev said to her that he would be better utilized as a soft-skills trainer since—at least in his vertical—he saw a clear training requirement for staff members. She nodded, but as Dev suspected, and I was certain, she didn't quite appreciate being told about 'training need' by a relative newcomer albeit senior, since that was her area of work in a way. Dev could be rather upfront in professional situations.

Two events occurred in 2016 which were to yet again change the course of Dev's life. In the March of 2016, when Dev was remotely working out of Delhi for a fortnight since he wanted to spend time with his uncle who had been keeping poor health, the latter had to be removed to the hospital and was admitted into the Intensive Care Unit. Dev's uncle was facing a multi-organ failure and was put on ventilator. Dev postponed his travel back to London, and when his uncle showed recovery in ICU, he asked the attending doctor if he was 'out of danger'.

'You have brought a dying man to hospital and you are asking me if he is out of danger!' the Doctor shot back.

Dev was taken aback. Dev brought his uncle back home and organised a full-time attendant for him. Once his cousin from Mumbai came to Delhi, Dev left for London. 'I am going to miss you very much son,' said his uncle as Dev hugged him goodbye. That was the last time Dev saw his uncle who had been very much his father! In less than a week after his return to London, Dev's cousin called him at 4 am UK time to inform that their father was no more. Dev got on the 10 am flight from Heathrow to Delhi.

Man has several debts to pay in life. The debt of the teacher was repaid as *gurudakshina* during *gurukul* times and nowadays in the form of tuition fees; the debt of the father is repaid by taking the family tree forward through progeny and by doing his last rites respectfully, the debt of the mother can only be repaid by becoming a good honest human being and one who stands by his or her family and friends in their time of need; and then there is debt of Mother Earth, death is the repayment of our debt to Earth. That's why the day death becomes optional, the day man conquers death as he has surmounted birth, may well be the end, not only of existing religions and philosophies, but also of humanity as we know it. Man is moving ever closer to that point. *Sanatana* principles envision time being circular and moving in four great *yugas* as a sine curve, while the better informed already believe that *Kaliyuga* has bottomed out, it is not inconceivable that man's fabled immortality will cause a bigger death, that of Earth and perhaps Universe. It is not implausible to imagine Earth collapsing upon itself with the unpaid debt burden. In addition to these debts, there is one more obligation we all have, I shall write about it in the last chapter.

Dev completed the last rites of his father, and after a fortnight of his cremation returned to London and to his work place. Dev's cousin in Mumbai, the only biological child of his uncle and aunt, mentioned that he would try and seek a transfer to Delhi to be closer to their mother but that would be possible only sometime in 2017. So every six to eight weeks Dev, who had the option of working remotely at times, would fly to Delhi to be with his mother for a week to ten days and operate remotely from the Malviya Nagar house.

Vedant successfully completed his second year at University, and was with Dev in their little Chiswick flat during his summer break in July and August of 2016. They both joined the local cricket club and played two matches together. Dev not only failed in both games but sprained his shoulder while bowling, and when he came into bat at number six he could scarcely believe the alarm in him as the ball went whizzing past. Dev's body was giving him a message; that was the last Dev played a proper cricket match. When he mentioned this to

Sudhir on the phone he suggested that Dev pick up golf. When a team member of Dev's from the local cricket club learnt that Dev was opting out of the team, he called him and said, 'You have so much passion for cricket, why don't you consider taking up umpiring?'

A few days later, when the local GP asked Dev to get an x-ray of the shoulder and ultra-sound of the abdomen and Dev mentioned this to Bhavini, she told him emphatically, 'Dev, you are struggling with cooking and doing every other household chore yourself, you already have BP, now this x-ray and ultra-sound, your mother is by herself in Delhi; once Ved finishes University you should come back. Stay with KDTL, they have global operations, ask them to give you a job in Delhi.'

Dev thought about all three suggestions: Sudhir's, his cricket team member's and Bhavini's. The first two he decided to immediately put into action, while he kept mulling over Bhavini's idea.

After Ved returned back to Weymingham for his final year, Dev made his regular trip to Delhi to look up his mother. It was during this trip that he decided to discuss with his boss the possibility of doing his current job out of Delhi. On his return to London, Dev asked his boss if the company would be open to considering the option of him doing his current job from Delhi. Following a quick chat with the HR Head, Dev's boss confirmed that he could move to Delhi by mid-2017 in his current job.

Dev greatly enjoyed the umpiring course conducted at Lord's in the second fortnight of November; he got 49 out of the 50 questions correct and qualified in the umpiring examination; he could now officiate as an umpire up to a certain level of competitive matches in England and also in India. When I mentioned this interesting accomplishment of Dev's to Sudhir and Luv, their delighted exclamation was identical, 'And what question could Dev have gotten wrong!'

Fiction can never be as strange as fact. Two days after Christmas, I was in my new apartment in Gurgaon which I had traded against my Nirvana flat, it was a cold and misty night typical of north India that can both be spectacularly tranquil and eerily gloomy depending on the state of one's mind. As I switched on the news channel I saw at the bottom of the TV screen a flash scrolling: *Famous industrialist Anosh Munsherji dies in a freak accident.*

I couldn't believe what I was reading and changed to a different channel where the news anchor was reporting that Anosh Munsherji had slipped on the staircase of his office, sustained a head injury and succumbed to it six hours after the accident! I immediately made a free WhatsApp call to Dev. He too had just learnt about the tragedy; he was saddened to hear but as usual undemonstrative.

'Why don't you all make a trip to London,' said Dev to me on a WhatsApp call in February 2017, 'I don't know how much longer I will be here for. I will post on the *Active Volcanoes* group as well.'

The world had moved into an age of instant pervasive communication and all old school or university mates, drinking or sports or travelling friends, ex-colleagues, apartment owners in a building society and those sharing a common avocation formed WhatsApp groups and gave themselves cute names like *Active Volcanoes, Jawani Diwani, Crazy Boys of TMS, Lovely Moms, Kautilya 1986, Cedar Tower 8 Residents* etc.

'May not be in London for long or with Khodayji Dinshaji for long?' asked Luv on the *Active Volcanoes* WhatsApp group which had Sudhir, Dev, Luv and myself.

'London for sure,' was Dev's reply followed with a winking icon. So Sudhir, Eklavya and I booked ourselves on a direct flight to London, for Saturday the 6th of May, to spend 10 days with Dev; we were all to stay in his small one-bedroom flat in Chiswick.

As the three of us completed security check at the elegant Delhi airport and walked towards our boarding gate, Sudhir suggested, '*Chalo* let's have a coffee.'

Luv quipped instantly, 'Learn modern day language, Bhaisahab, today's smart ladies and trendy men would say—"let's catch a coffee!" What, *Khannae*?'

I laughed and retorted, 'If you said this to Dev, you know how he will react?'

Before I could complete, Sudhir quipped, 'Dev would say—"I can only ever catch a cricket ball or a cold!"'

We all laughed. 'Sudhir and Devavratt are alike in so many respects,' observed Luv. 'Nowadays you not only "catch a coffee," but when modern city-dwellers wish to eat, they "grab a bite". "More power to you", "I was super busy", "This place is rocking", "LOL and AWOL"—learn this new lingo, Bhaisahab. And I wonder where this "good on you" and "stay blessed" has come from; on my birthday "stay blessed" is constantly flashing on my phone!'

Sudhir and I had a good laugh.

'One that disturbs me the most is "Rest In Peace" or RIP when people learn of someone's demise. *Arrey*, the Hindu belief is that the soul transitions and comes back in another form, we don't have a permanent heaven or hell! Why can't people say "*Sadgati*" or simply "*Om Shanti*"?'

Sudhir and I smiled at each other.

Dev had hired a car for our 10-day visit; he received us at Heathrow. Both Luv and Sudhir were meeting him after a while and were astonished at how much he had greyed. When Eklavya commented on that first evening, after Dev had wished us good-night and retired for the night, that, 'Dev has quietened down more and his eyes don't match his lips when he smiles.' I couldn't help thinking how Dev's personality had come a full circle.

Dev had planned our vacation wonderfully: drives to Central London and walks in the Westminster and Leicester Square area, a couple of theatre shows, part of an evening in a gentleman's night club specially for Eklavya, two trips to his old club Roquersbury and motor boat ride on the Thames, a day at Lord's to see a one-day match, a couple of dinners at two charming restaurants in Covent Garden where Paul Anderson and Howard Sadler, his old friends from Roqsanto joined us, a day out at Bourton-on-the-Water in Cotswolds and further to Stratford-upon-Avon, and finally a delightful country drive all the way up north to Weymingham University where we met Vedant who was just about completing his graduation! In between we would leisurely walk on the pleasant Chiswick High Street and enjoy the pub and several cafes there. It was however our many chats in that little bedroom of Dev's flat that I most remember.

'So nice to have all of you over,' said Dev with a warm smile, 'wish you had made it earlier.' Luv and Dev were both sitting on the carpeted floor next to the double bed, while Sudhir and I were half-reclining on the bed by its head-rest.

'What are your future plans Dev?' enquired Sudhir, 'you wrote on WhatsApp that you may not be in London for long.'

Dev gently nodded, 'I had checked with the company last year if I could do my current role out of Delhi, they had agreed in principle. But now I am getting feelers that it will be some other role.'

'So that's fine isn't it?' I asked.

Dev smiled wryly, 'It's a role lower than my current grade.'

'Oh!' said both Luv and I together.

'Then?' asked Sudhir.

'I either accept it or nothing!'

'And you can't just stay with your current role in London?' Luv wondered.

Dev shook his head, 'I need to relocate back Eklavya, the die has been cast.'

'Did the change in position happen after Munsherji's demise?' I asked.

Dev pursed his lips, shrugged his shoulders and waved his left hand, seemingly saying 'perhaps'.

'All will be well, Bhaisahab,' said Luv getting up from the floor to get himself more beer from the fridge in the kitchen, 'Where will they find a resource like you!'

As he came back into the bedroom, Luv asked all of us, '*Yaar* tell me, why are *Navaratra*s celebrated twice in a year?'

I gave him a blank look while Sudhir slowly said, 'There is *Chaitra Navratra* in April which marks the spring harvest and it's dedicated to the worship of goddess in her nine forms that is Kali, Durga, Parvati, Shakti and so on. And then there is *Ashwin Navratras* that coincides with season change again, onset of autumn.'

'So is it mainly to do with harvest or change of season?' Luv enquired further.

Sudhir was doubtful, 'Ma Durga symbolize Nature as well and of course feminine energy and *Navratras* does exemplify victory of good over evil; but I am not certain why it's observed twice a year.'

We all looked at our host, 'Dev bhaisahab, enlighten us,' said Luv.

Even Dev didn't look too sure, 'Well, I have a hunch but I too am not cent percent.'

'Your hunch on this subject will be better than the information of all of us put together,' smiled Luv.

Dev smiled back, 'I think the *Ashwin Navratras*, which fall just before Dussehra in September-October time started with Lord Ram. Long time back I read Nirala's famous poem "Ram Ki Shakti Puja" and my understanding is based on that *kavita*.'

We were all looking at Dev attentively.

'Ravan was proving to be a very powerful adversary, so one day, I think it was Jambavan who suggests to Ram that he pray to the Goddess for more strength. Nirala incidentally spent a lot of his time in Bengal where the Goddess is known as Shakti, hence "Ram Ki Shakti Puja". So as the poem goes, Ram sits in prayer to the Goddess, seeking more strength; and he keeps 108 lotus flowers as offering to Ma Shakti. Since he is engaged in battle he cannot wait till *chaitra* time to offer prayers to Goddess. On the ninth day of the reverence, as he is about to conclude his prayer and offer the 108th lotus, he discovers that the last lotus has disappeared! Ram cannot leave the invocation without completing the offering as the prayers will be ineffective, and so he draws an arrow and decides to pull out one of his eyes—as you know the eye has been compared to the lotus flower: *chakshukamal*. Just before he does that, Mother Goddess appears and pleased with his devotion, blesses him with all the strength, all the *shakti*! Ram defeats Ravan the next day, we know that day as *Vijaya Dashami* or Dussehra today, and the nine days preceding *Vijaya Dashami* are *Navratra*s. Hence *Navratra*s twice a year, Eklavya. Once again, I can't be absolutely sure and my understanding is based purely on Nirala's poem.'

We were all captivated by Dev's description; Luv stood up and with his head and stretched out arms bowed to Devavratt. It immediately came to my mind and so I asked, 'Where is *Shakti* vis-à-vis the trinity of Gods?'

Dev replied intently, 'In my understanding, Shaktism and Shaivism and Vaishnavism are the three main streams of Hinduism which in turn has emerged from *Sanatana* principles.'

Two days later, as we settled down in that little bedroom late in the evening, our discussion was that typical chat on life in London versus life in Delhi, cultural habits in England and India, and diversity in different regions of the world. '10 pounds congestion charge, 10 pounds for parking and 100 pounds for an Indian meal that was just about edible; London is too costly!' remarked Sudhir.

'Not if you are earning in pounds,' retorted Luv.

'Even if you are earning here, London is a costly city,' I added.

'London might be costly but see how clean and well organised it is!' observed Luv. He then carried on, 'Dev, Sudhir and I spent a couple of days with Sandeep in Delhi and Gurgaon before flying here. We went to Select City Walk Mall in Saket, there were two rich looking women behind us in the mall so I held the door for them. They walked past through the door without any thanks or a smile or acknowledgement, as though I was a doorman! At our boarding gate this bulky lady wearing *salwar-kameez* and sneakers with a teenage boy was ahead of me in the premium economy line, the attendant told her she needed to go to the economy queue, so she hurriedly and rather aggressively turned around and actually hit me with her elbow and bag but carried on without any 'sorry' or 'excuse me'. So London is costly and Indian food is not to our taste but this is what happened in Delhi. How do you win this one?'

Dev said with the slightest smile on his lips, 'It helps me to live knowing that death is down the road.'

We were all stupefied with Dev's response.

'That's a terrible statement, Dev,' said Luv.

'Correction,' continued Dev, 'it helps me to live reasonably happily knowing that death is somewhere down the road.'

Sudhir, Luv and I exchanged a quick glance and Luv repeated, 'That's still an awful thought, Dev! I am asking you if you had a choice, how would you decide where to live; there are trade-offs everywhere.'

'That's the answer, Eklavya, there are trade-offs everywhere, you have to just see the pleasant features wherever destiny takes you and enjoy those. London is costly, Indian food to our taste is not easy to find, if you are without family it can be lonely, but as you just said it is so well organised, the public services and supermarkets run effectively and smoothly, the roads are clean and traffic orderly and parks enchanting, the history of the city is well preserved and is fascinating, there is dignity of life and labour, the theatres and sports are accessible and pleasurable. Likewise, Delhi has colourful energy, notwithstanding the energetic woman who elbowed you, it has a never-say-give up manner to it, the food is incredible, malls are exquisite, house help and even home tuitions are readily available and affordable, you experience all seasons, there are people to talk to, banking system is more advanced than most parts of the world, housing is good and relatively inexpensive. So enjoy London and enjoy Delhi, and Bangalore and Raipur!'

We all laughed a bit.

'What the hell was that fatalistic comment all about! We are all walking towards death and that helps you live?' inquired Luv with a sceptical look.

Dev evaded the question by saying, 'Some other time.'

'Okay Bhaisahab, you have travelled all over the world many times, what are the one or two features that instantly come to mind when you think of different regions of the world?'

Luv asked Dev. Dev looked at Luv absorbedly, 'What exactly do you mean by regions?'

Luv tried to elaborate, 'I mean, what comes to your mind when you think of Asia or Europe or Africa?'

Dev thought a little, 'It would take a lifetime to accurately put a finger on what describes some individual countries, let alone regions or continents! But to attempt your favourite generalisation, Eklavya: in Asia, relationships are very important; relationships permeate business life as well.'

Sudhir interjected, 'Relationships are important everywhere Dev, isn't it?'

Dev nodded, 'They certainly are, the old boys associations play a significant role in Europe as well, but relationships are like a hygiene factor in several parts of the world; but in Asia, relationships are imperative. Hospitality is perhaps a corollary of relationships, I am sure you have sensed yourselves, great hospitality being a hallmark of several Asian countries. Then in much of Asia I have seen an undercurrent of a dilemma—whether to look towards the Western world for inspiration or to their own rich heritage and ancient culture.'

This time Sudhir nodded in agreement. Dev continued to think aloud and try and answer Luv's poser, 'As I said, in Europe the old boys associations are important, and another distinctive feature I discerned while running business operations in Europe is emphasis on first principles; so when I was running the Agrichemicals business for Roqsanto, if we were launching a new oil product for agriculture use, in our European team we would start by discussing 'why are we in the Agrichemicals business' before we started discussing the modus operandi of the new product launch. In North America, the business culture and nuances are distinctive. In terms of people management, I found America quite effortless and straightforward. The boss is important everywhere, more so in America. And then I would think the dollar value of all projects and activities needs to be fleshed out.'

Luv replayed back his understanding, 'So North America is "boss" and "dollars."'

'You know something Dev, you must write a book,' said I. 'On not just ways of working in different parts of the world but also on distinctive cultures and social norms as you experienced them in various countries.'

Sudhir added further, 'I couldn't agree more, write with an Indian context in the sense as Indian business organisations spread globally what socio-cultural practices of different countries should be borne in mind for success.'

'Bhaisahab, let Dev complete his response to my question first; let's discuss this book idea once he has succinctly described South America and Africa, please!' said Luv in his inimitable way.

We all smiled.

'Well, I have travelled to Brazil quite a few times but only once each to Argentina and Venezuela and Guatemala. In Africa, have been to South Africa thrice which is quite different from Kenya and Ghana, which again are very different from Morocco and Algeria where I have travelled to once for a few days only. So, describing all these fascinating countries in a couple of words, I would most certainly be off the mark!' Dev said self-effacingly.

'*Arrey yaar*, a few top-of-the-mind pointers,' urged Luv.

'Brazil is the friendliest place on Earth. They work hard, as they do in Argentina, but they enjoy their party and football to no end! For many African countries, they have had political instability and coups, and in all my global assignments we would keep our African operations simple, investment and product portfolio limited, and get our representatives there to follow basic organisational processes only.'

Luv stood up from the floor and clasped Dev's hand in appreciation, 'So Latin America—party and football; and Africa—the key words you used were "coup" and "simple" and "follow". Brilliant, Devavratt Pratap Rajvansh! A quick loo break for me and then book idea!'

We all laughed.

'*Haan bhai*, so we want Dev bhaisahab to write a book?' asked Luv more in a statement form as he sat down on the carpet in the corner of that small bedroom.

Dev had a gentle smile on his face which didn't match his sunken eyes.

'Sudhir and I meant the suggestion seriously,' I repeated what I had said earlier, 'You must, Dev! Coalesce all your experiences around the world into a story form and as Sudhir said, draw out practical tips for Indian industry and working executives which will help them succeed further.'

Sudhir went a step ahead, 'Perhaps also lessons that the world can learn from Indian civilization, *vasudhaiva kutumbakam*, unity in diversity, *atithi devo bhava* and so on.'

Luv hastily added, 'And also what we can learn from the world—being in queue, holding the door for those behind us, offering right of the way to the properly waiting car.'

Dev responded in a mellow manner, 'It is actually Sandeep who should be writing, he has such a good expression.'

Sudhir and Luv both had a cheery look on their face, the latter immediately said, 'Also a good idea! Both of you write a book each, whoever finishes first and gets it published and sells at least a thousand copies is the winner!'

Sudhir concluded our chat on book writing, 'Sandy, you write on India, a story on all the colours and beauty and ironies of India; and Dev, you write on your experiences around the world and what other countries can learn from Bharat and what we can imbibe from other nations. And yes, whoever finishes first and gets the book published and sells a thousand copies is the winner—all of us will have his picture in our living rooms for all time to come!'

We all laughed heartily.

The idea of this book of mine was conceived that evening in the May of 2017 in Dev's little flat in London. Sudhir and Luv made Dev and I shake hands in agreement of this literary endeavour!

I do also recall a saucy chat we had one evening, during that 10-day vacation, as Dev was driving us back home. As always Luv observed, '*Yaar*, while in the throes of excitement, nothing is better than the act of sex, but after climax I always feel all this was so futile and I want to run away to my solitary freedom after the volcano erupts. It's been the same for last 30 years!'

We all laughed as Sudhir nudged Luv, 'Poor you!'

We flew back to Delhi after a delightful 10 days with Dev. A month later, Dev told us that Vedant had completed his final year of university with a first division, which in England means above 70% and that overall he had secured a high 2-1 in graduation. Little Ved, not so little now, had not let his father down. It was overwhelming for me, and I wonder how sweetly overpowering it must be for Dev; from that desperate traumatic situation 10 years ago, step by step, pain by pain, all that hard work, all the sacrifice, all those social and professional and emotional and logistics challenges—through all that turmoil Vedant had finally blossomed! The icing on the cake was a week later when during a group WhatsApp call, Dev told us that Vedant had even landed himself a job. Sudhir, Luv and I all exclaimed when Dev mentioned the organisation with whom Vedant was to start as a Management Trainee that September: Meridian Promissory! The same top international bank with which Dev had done his summer training way back in 1987! Vedant was to be based out of London and work in the city. Dev was finally and truly a happy man that day.

However, his own batteries were pretty much depleted. He was burnt out. He had become tired of his corporate life. That endless and subtle pushing for deliverables by hierarchically senior managers: 'I think the presentation can be made sharper'...'You have been somewhat conservative in setting your targets'...'I am sure you will do better in the next quarter'—

those non-stop 'online trainings' with some colleagues actually displaying the computer generated certificates in their work area, the show of exuberance by the more crafty staff members at the 'old wine in new bottle' company policy so as to appear aligned with organisational direction, that sitting and listening to the boisterous 'motivational speaker' when the only motivation Dev had was to bring up Vedant and see him succeed in worldly terms too, that constant selling of oneself in different ways—Dev was very tired of these accessories of corporate life. HR people had started seeing him as 'experienced but a trifle cynical'—Dev would smile to himself when he picked up this feedback. He told Sudhir that he deletes 'motivational and inspiring' messages on WhatsApp without reading or seeing them and that he is, 'Happier in my de-motivated and uninspired state'. And so, in early December 2017, Dev tendered his resignation at Khodayji Dinshaji Traders Ltd.; it was readily accepted. He was set to return once again to India!

In the February of 2018, the India that Dev was returning to was a very confident and 'new India'—though due to frequent visits to Delhi during his previous four years—the change did not strike him as stark. 50 was the new 40 as far as fitness for many of our friends was concerned, while 50 was the new 60 as far as corporate employment went. Sense of entitlement was far less and people didn't seem to care whether or not the person they were doing business with was good at English or not, only skills mattered and of course, money mattered a lot! Destination weddings had become ever more popular amongst the super-rich with the locales being not just Goa and Jaipur but as far as Dubai and Bangkok, and as exotic as quaint towns in Italy and Greece. 'Destination weddings create better memories,' is how I heard the hosts of two such grand events describe them. The affluent business people, senior corporate executives and government officers had started referring to their house help as 'our staff'. Maslow's Need Hierarchy didn't seem to start from 'physiological needs' for urban millennials since their parents had already provided financial security for them—they could thus think and talk and write blogs on bigger world issues like 'community service' and 'sustainability'. Such millennials also appeared to form genderless friendships. Reading as a habit and interest had, however, significantly reduced with them. The society was changing rapidly. Women were clearly more assertive and it was unsurprising if a woman introduced a man accompanying her as 'my boyfriend'. There was much more openness and much more affluence and mental health issues were being talked about explicitly.

Bharat was becoming a password and username driven economy: there were mobile apps for everything, millions of users had Uber and Ola apps on their phones; likewise food delivery apps like Zomato and Swiggy were ever so prevalent;

Airbnb and Oyo were growing rapidly enabling good and affordable accommodation for travellers; online education, DRS in cricket, OTT platforms for TV entertainment, AI and Cloud—there was a digital revolution underway! Online banking was growing tremendously including mobile banking apps; online banking and digital transaction systems made payment of bills so convenient! Advertisements of soaps and detergents and suitings-shirtings had disappeared from media and instead, adverts of cars, mobile networks, digital products and 'mutual fund *sahi hei*' were being televised 24x7. The words 'tablet' and 'kindle' meant computerized communication gadgets and had nothing to do with medicine or hope. Several management schools had set up incubation centres to encourage entrepreneurship; there were start-ups galore most seeking to reach massive valuation of $1 billion that would classify them as 'unicorn'!

As Dev soaked in and even relished this enormous change, he slowly started pursuing all his passions. Passion is the closest synonym of life. Both in the summers of 2018 and later in 2019, he travelled back to London and umpired league cricket matches; he would stay in Vedant's studio apartment and cook for him while there. He would be back in India after two months of stay in London and during the winter months of north India, play golf at the charming courses in Delhi and Noida and Gurgaon and formed a good circle of golfing friends in the process. He became a very popular public speaker on management-related topics like Strategy and Leadership and other soft skills, speaking at business schools, corporates and when Sudhir would invite him, at a few government training institutes as well. I once attended his session in early 2019: he was rich in content yet made the topic simple and lively, peppered with illustrations and stories without losing focus on the subject he was invited to speak on. He was remarkably practical and would establish an instant connect with the audience. The master of any subject is able to explain it in story-form, those who cannot simplify a complex topic haven't really mastered it.

What struck me in that session was how an inherently quiet person came alive in front of the audience. I also distinctly remember Dev saying in response to a question that it is futile to criticize the government all the time for everything, and that two things that each one of us could do ourselves right away was to 'stand up for each other' and enhance the 'dignity of labour'. He would give the example of the hockey-based film *Chak De India* where the team's winning effectiveness improves once the two forwards start supporting and not out-smarting each other.

On dignity of labour, he would recall the 20-year-old incident in his London office where the Marketing Director of Roqsanto apologized to his driver for running late! 'Do we even know the name of the security guard who wishes us *Jai Hind* every day in our condominium? Do we even check on the well-being of the children of the lady who cleans and sweeps our homes?'

One of the participants in that session asked Dev about positive thinking; Dev instantly and with a smile, replied, 'I am not the right person to discuss positive thinking since I think negatively.'

The audience was stunned for a moment and then the questioner got up and said, 'Sir, I am so happy to hear this! Someone at least can speak honestly. I was really exhausted constantly hearing about positive thinking from other speakers!' He started clapping and then the entire audience gave Dev a standing applause.

It was Dev who asked me if I had started writing the book as discussed sometime back in London. I had been contemplating but not put pen to paper. I shook my head. 'What about you Dev?' I checked.

He nodded, 'Yes, I have completed first three chapters. Why don't you also start, Sandeep? Didn't Sudhir and Eklavya set up a contest between us!'

I smiled at him and promised, 'I will begin, today itself! And what are you writing on?' I further enquired.

'Exactly what we agreed,' replied Dev.

'Have you thought of a title for the book?'

Dev looked at me a little fixedly and said, '*With Bated Death*.'

'Why such a distressing title?' said Luv when over the phone I told him about my chat with Dev. 'Dev has no reason to die, *Khannae*. I wish I could have his lifestyle—guest lectures all over the country, cricket and golf, writing a book, not answerable to anyone, Ved has done so well, touch wood and Sudhir was saying he and Gayatri and kids are going for a Caribbean cruise in February next year and Dev may join them. What a life!'

Who knows what was going on in Dev's mind! He didn't come out openly, only ever so seldom a comment like, 'We are all walking towards death, some alone some with people;' and then once when he, Tank and I were playing golf at Qutub Golf Course on a scintillating sunny day in the January of 2020, he said in some context with a smile, 'I feel I am in the October of my life'. Clearly Dev's personal life, or lack of it, had left a lifelong scar and hurt, and while externally he found several enjoyable distractions, he could deep down not emerge from the shock of what had happened nearly 15 years ago.

While Tank, Dev and I would often discuss changes in the corporate and professional environment in India, most of them positive, a comment made by Tank stuck in my mind. He said, 'Eight out of ten people in the world achieve leadership positions not because of competence but lack of it—since their bosses don't feel threatened by them.' I would occasionally; think of Dev and a few other friends of mine who never reached the top of their organisations despite their potential, indeed there was some substance in Tank's point of view.

'It's not a good title,' said Eklavya to Dev over a phone call after our discussion about the proposed title of Dev's book. 'You are writing on the diversity in the world from an India perspective—how does *With Bated Death* resonate with it?'

Dev heard Luv; he didn't respond.

An Eternal Morning

The change my generation experienced has been dramatic and unprecedented. Much of the change that has happened in India from 1970s to now, that is mid-2020s, has been for the better; though in pursuit of modernity and iconoclasm within some limited sections of society, there has been a tinkering on the edges and some beautiful and harmless cultural customs discontinued as a consequence. An odd young bride refuses *kanyadaan* though she goes around the sacred fire seven times at marriage ceremony, and the irreligious middle-aged man takes pride in the fact that he cremated his father not on wooden logs but in an 'environmentally-friendly' way and did not immerse the ashes in Ganga but sprayed them in the garden soil! Of course, each has the right to live life in his or her own way.

I briefly mentioned in the last chapter about my chat with Vikrant and Dev on changing business landscape in India. New age Indian entrepreneurs are brilliant; their understanding of the business environment and their value proposition is superb. They are ambitious and whatever little I have seen they have their hearts in the right place. Indian IT industry is $220 billion and employs five million people and continues to contribute significantly to nation building. India has become a digital power in the world and the leader in digital payments, there are unicorns galore and the Jandhan bank accounts linked with Aadhar and Mobile, are delivering social benefits at an unparalleled scale. Rural India has more internet users than urban India today.

India is now the second largest food grain producer in the world—from 'ship to mouth' in the 1960s to 'Indian farms to worldwide plates' today! India emerged as pharmacy of the world especially during the 2020 and 2021 corona virus pandemic. The gender ratio in 2021 showed more women than men in India, an indicator of social development; population growth has slowed down which is both good for obvious reasons and not so good since it may reduce economically productive workforce. Life expectancy of Indians has significantly increased to 70 years while infant mortality rate has steeply fallen since 'freedom at midnight'.

Bharat has remained an enduring democracy and is today nearly a $4 trillion economy with a per capita income of $2000 per year, which was $60 at the time of Independence. Her foreign exchange reserves places India in the top five nations of the world. Just to put in perspective, if India has grown, so has the world economy which is $100 trillion now, and the growth of India's per capita income is matched by several economies. Further, whilst earlier 20 rupees could buy a US dollar, today nearly 80 rupees buys one dollar; and China, the traditional competitor, has pulled away from India in the last three decades and its GDP is touching $20 trillion now. Yet India's growth and success is to be celebrated, though poverty eradication and not just poverty alleviation, has to be the burning lamp raging in the heart of every right-thinking Indian. Bharat's journey is so well encapsulated in the slogans given by her leaders over the decades: in the mid-1960s it was *Jai Jawan, Jai Kisan* in reverence to the brave soldier and the indefatigable farmer, at the turn of millennium it was repositioned as *Jai Jawan, Jai Kisan, Jai Vigyan* in recognition of science and technology, and 20 years later the celebratory call is *Jai Jawan, Jai Kisan, Jai Vigyan, Jai Anusandhan* in acknowledgement of the importance of entrepreneurship, though the literal meaning of the last term is research.

Encouraged by Sudhir, Eklavya and Devavratt, I started writing this book in late 2019 just before Covid struck the world. It's taken me three years to get this far. So much has changed in the world since then!

The lexicon of the world changed during the devastating corona virus. Pandemic, quarantine, social distancing, lockdown, comorbidity, hand-sanitizer, face mask, hybrid working etc. became the vocabulary of the world throughout 2020 and 2021. I need not elaborate on the colossal impact on all walks of life that the Covid pandemic had, except that sitting at home and when not involved in webinars I began writing my book. Often Dev and I would check on the progress of our literary efforts and exchange thoughts and hearten each other.

Any prose or poetry or idiom that does not touch human consciousness is as futile as that corporate presentation made in head office which is detached from the market reality or that government scheme that remains on paper and never reaches the citizenry. Literature that doesn't enlighten or provoke thought or inspire or strip social hypocrisy, that does not evoke beauty or soothe pain or blossom dreams, such literature must go into the refuse bag and left outside the home for collection.

When writing is an outcome of sublime thought and compassion, it is almost a flower grown in God's garden. Such writing not only creates fragrance but it becomes the seed for transformation and a cornerstone of new pristine civilizations. Dev and I regularly discussed Valmiki, Ved Vyas, Chanakya, Vivekananda, Aurobindo, Gandhi, Bachchan, Neeraj, Premchand, Marx, Rousseau, Hegel, Hobbes, Adam Smith, Ayn Rand, Shakespeare, Conan Doyle, Dan Brown and so on, and wondered that if we could even 'become a single word' of their works, our literary effort would be most self-fulfilling.

As Dev and I raced each other in completing our respective books, we would have WhatsApp video chats, I found him getting more and more emotionally reclusive. He wasn't morose but clearly lonely. His loneliness seemed to compete only with his fatigue. He seemed to be helpless at the shut doors of his heart, someone who could never 'move-on', and very often I saw in him a dead man wandering around in a hurry to complete his time on Earth. Of course, during lock-downs and travel restrictions he couldn't meet Vedant, since he was in Malviya Nagar and Gurgaon, and Ved in London, which heightened his stress and sense of material detachment. While in 2018 and 2019 he led an enviable life pursuing his passions, I was thrown by his comment in 2021 when he once said to me impassively, 'I have lost trust in myself.' When a man stops trusting himself, he has either experienced big failure or betrayal or encountered stark truth in life.

'Why are you making me a central character in your book, Sandeep? I have led an average life,' he remarked.

'I have to mention that incident Dev—jack of all trades, master of business administration!'

We both laughed over the video call that day in the March of 2021.

Dev completed his book well before me and Sudhir put him in touch with a good publishing house. He presented me with a copy of *With Bated Death* in the September of 2021 with the handwritten autograph: *To half-century of indispensable friendship*. We hugged each other.

'We should do a book launch, Dev!'

'Sudhir's transfer to Delhi is due by end of this year. We can think of a launch once he too is here.'

He couriered a copy to Luv with a small message on first page: *Dear Eklavya and Poulomi—In endearing mischief and enduring grace respectively.*

A few days later, Luv sent a WhatsApp message to Dev that read: 'Congratulations to the finest man for a lovely book with a terrible title. Poulomi *gracefully* seconds this message!'

What struck me as I read through Dev's book was its simplicity. Dev had the simplest of heart though I wouldn't use the same description for his mind. Dev's book was Dev's heart. Simplicity brings longevity—people remember the simplest of poetic lines and phrases forever; even in human relationships and in romance, in lectures and customer value propositions and batsmanship, simplicity generates lasting impact. *With Bated Death* was a captivating book on different cultures around the world and without much value judgement it celebrated global diversity. Dev wrote a chapter on a 'utopian nation' that combined what to him were the best cultural values and democratic principles and economic arrangements from all places in the world he had visited. He adroitly weaved in what the world could learn from Bharat and also what India should emulate from different nations.

Dev wrote adoringly about Bharat: 'where river is mother, guest is God and the world is a family'. He covered democracy in great detail—a country of 1.3 billion people with a thriving democracy and freedom of expression is something to be proud of, given the diversity within India it makes the democracy even more vibrant. He did qualify democracy as a system where there is 'equality of opportunity' and not 'equality of resources and rewards' which are a function of capability and risk-taking, and that exercising franchise is only a small aspect of democracy. *With Bated Death* described 'freedom of speech' as the most cherished of human values, though given the increasing incidents of incendiary speech around the world one of the global challenges is how to balance the two. He stressed on the need for education ecosystem of all nations to teach literature and poetry and the correct history and 'rights and duties' to young people for nation building. Dev also took the liberty to veer a little in his book into what is success in life and secret of happiness. At a time when love for gadgets exceeds love for human beings and when 'data' is spoken of as a factor of production and profit winning, much as we would speak of land labour capital and enterprise in our economics lessons in the 1980s, Dev extolled human relationships and passion and immersing in the moment and ability to 'give to others' and dignity as measures of success and happiness.

Dev wrote considerably about the futility of strong beliefs because except death and love everything else in life and world is subject to constant change. All human beings have their own 'truths' and who is to judge whose 'truth' is correct and which is false. Acknowledging that our own understanding is limited and might be erroneous, and being adaptable to change, seems to be the starting point of wisdom. He justified the title by implying that it is not just human life that begins and ends and begins again, but also civilizations that rise and fall, and rise again.

Sudhir's transfer to the Centre came through with effect from 1st December 2021 and around this time I asked Dev if he was thinking of a formal book launch.

'The publishers tell me the book is not doing well, Sandeep,' he said a little dispiritedly, 'so they are not too enthused about a launch.'

'Really!' I was disheartened to hear, 'Why is it not doing well?'

Dev mentioned that the publishers had told him based on feedback from book stores that there was hardly any enquiry let alone sale. *With Bated Death* seemed to have failed.

It was in mid-January 2022 when Luv was visiting Delhi that we all met in Sudhir's just-allotted house in New Moti

Bagh. When we got down to discussing Dev's book Sudhir said, 'It's such an informative book and easy read, wonder why it's not doing well.'

'Change its title, Bhaisahab, I have told you all along that this is a terrible title.'

Dev's eyes lit up and for once, he took Eklavya very seriously. The next day he called up the publishers and they were open to reprinting the book with a different title. In a telephone chat that Dev had had with Bhavini, she told him, 'Use the word "eternal" in your title; just somehow use eternal!'

Dev re-titled the book *An Eternal Morning* and by February, the old book with a new title and new cover could be seen at quite a few bookstores in Delhi. He edited the older version at four places in order to validate the title, and implied that happiness of people was not just linked to material affluence but more to relationships and sense of forward movement or hope.

The world judges a book by its cover! The world still very much judges a book by its cover. *An Eternal Morning* started doing wonderfully well and in no time the publishers started getting orders by the thousands. Towards the end of May 2022, the publishers and Dev went in for a formal 'launch' of the book, the invite for which was sent out in Sudhir Kapoor's name.

'It's a bit late for a launch, isn't it, Dev,' I remarked to my friend.

'It's actually a celebratory function, Sandeep,' said Dev, 'the book has sold 20,000 copies. Nowadays books have a short life cycle so the function is also meant to extend the life cycle by getting some more publicity.'

An Eternal Morning had by then received positive media coverage albeit limited to two short write-ups and a five-minute report on a TV channel, and one of the objectives of the function was to get more media exposure.

So many of Dev's old friends and a few members of his extended family came for the book function which was organised in a club in Lutyens' Delhi. By then news had spread of *An Eternal Morning*'s success, and on our school and TMS WhatsApp group people had been writing rave reviews. Some of the friends and extended family members who came for the launch had no contact with Dev for years!

I was amazed to meet Tarun Mehra or Goldie after decades, our mischievous school friend who would describe himself in TAPS as 'beast-cum-barbarian'. Goldie had become a Krishna devotee and was a teetotaller and vegetarian now, both he and his wife were very gentle and pleasant to talk to. During our conversation he mentioned that life was like a feature film being projected on a screen. When the film finishes, we realise there is nothing but a blank screen, it was all an illusion.

I had been regularly meeting Sanjeev Agnihotri or Sanju and his wife Divya, they had always been a delightful couple and the former was still his usual easy-going good-humoured self despite the heady success he had achieved. Sanju's son had also become a chartered accountant and recently joined his father's firm which had become one of the largest in India.

Ramkumar had led the most disciplined life and stayed with the same engineering company for nearly quarter century. He was still living in Chirag Enclave in the same house and got married in his late 40s. Ramu was almost identical in demeanour to what he was in school, and his wife was a very composed lady who was a primary school science teacher. Dev momentarily put his hand on Ramu's shoulder and reminded Sudhir how selflessly our school friend had taught Vedant: 'People like Ramkumar come once in a generation.'

Nita Rajagopalan was in San Francisco and couldn't make it to Dev's function. Dev forwarded to me her WhatsApp message: 'Sorry Dev, won't be able to travel to Delhi at this time, though I would have loved to be there. Read the book twice—fascinating! It's so much you—simple and straightforward with some complex twists and turns! Hope to meet soon, all my love always.'

I ran into a few of Dev's Augustus College friends at the function and instantly recognized Gulshandeep and Ajay Jaiswal. Gullu was very much the happy-go-lucky person he always had been, he and his wife ran a Public Relations firm with head office in Gurgaon which had several international clients as well. Of course, I knew Vikrant or Tank as we called him from our MBA days and in recent times, he and Dev and I had been playing golf together. He was the CEO of Korean electronics company based in Delhi.

It was delightful to meet quite a few of Dev's batchmates from TMS, who were all a year senior to me and Luv at The Management School. There was never a dull moment with Rakesh Mutreja or Voltage and Jeet Tandon or Jigsaw around! Voltage had long since finished his corporate employment and was now running a venture capital business; he had recently become a grandfather. Jigsaw was a head-hunter based in Bangalore. Sudhir observed how gentlemanly Voltage had become, 'Half the excitement from our lives was lost the day Voltage sobered down!'

I met Pranav Chaturvedi or Pracha after ages. 'Oh *Praaji*,' he called out to me, 'I always thought Deva will become a writer someday.' Pracha had been in Hong Kong for years where, after finishing his time with various MNCs, he had started a restaurant—Gaon Ki Handi. He was still big and burly and bearded and he still had that earthy eastern UP accent.

Simrin Avasthi or Happiness still looked as she did in university and had a beaming smile on her face. She wasn't working anymore. Akash Samarth was as calm as he had always been; he was operating his own boutique finance firm based in Mumbai. He was always unruffled and at the gathering made light of his health issue with the expression, 'Oh, *koi na*'.

Dev's colleague and friend from his days at Torsh Chemicals Rohit Sahni came a bit late but it was nice to see him. He had retired from Sollater Agrogleam, a Canadian agri-products company as their Managing Director. 'I had been telling Dev for 20 years to write. Glad he finally did,' he said to me with a smile.

Our Professor at TMS Dr Dastur, who was Dev and Sudhir's dissertation guide, was also at the book function. He had long since retired from TMS and was one of the guests of honour at the occasion, the other three being Karan Varma, Howard Sadler and Inderpal Singh Sodhi all of whom had been Dev's senior colleagues at Roqsanto and Torsh Chemicals respectively and for whom Dev had very high regards. Howard joined from London over a video link as did Vedant who couldn't take leave to travel at that time.

Knowing how close Dev's friendship was with Bhavini I wasn't surprised to see her; she travelled all the way from Dubai. Dev had requested me to keep a front row seat for her and his mother who was well into her 80s and had a sense of pride in her eyes at her son's literary achievement. Two of Dev's cousins with their spouses and three of his golfing friends were also at the gathering.

Of course, Sudhir and Gayatri were the de facto hosts as not only had the invites gone out in the former's name but after the formal welcome by the lady anchor, a known TV personality, she handed over to Sudhir for his introductory remarks. Eklavya had flown in from Bangalore just for that one day since he had house guests. Dev was disappointed that Poulomi couldn't make it.

Self-praise is no praise, it's the worst form of delusion. Not once during the felicitation and discussion on the book did Dev come anywhere near it, though with childlike zeal he mentioned how he had put his best in the book and every word was from the heart. The function lasted just over an hour after which Dev signed a few books and later all the guests walked to the lounge downstairs where a high-tea had been organised. Sudhir's home in New Moti Bagh was just a 10-minute drive from the venue of the function and after all the guests had left, Gayatri asked Dev and me and Luv to come home for dinner. She repeated the invitation sensing a little dithering amongst us.

'Can I get Bhavini along as well?' Dev gently checked with Gayatri.

'Of course! Of course!' said Gayatri, putting her arm around Dev's lady friend.

'I will drop you back in Panchsheel,' said Dev to Bhavini.

***

'My picture?' exclaimed Dev to Sudhir opening both his hands and looking around the living room as we reached the latter's home, as if to say 'where is my picture as per our agreement?'

Sudhir and Gayatri both laughed. 'Why do you think Mrs Kapoor insisted you come home?' remarked Sudhir as Gayatri went inside the house and got a beautiful framed picture of Dev!

'Put it up with your own hands,' she said.

Dev looked at Sudhir and Gayatri visibly overcome with emotion. He closed his eyes so as not to show the tears swelling in them. He shook his head, opened his eyes and said softly with a gentle smile, 'No, no, I can't, also I didn't mean it seriously.'

'But I meant is seriously, go on put up the frame there,' said Sudhir pointing to a nail on the wall.

Dev again shook his head.

'*Yaar*, I will put it up,' said Eklavya in his usual bouncy way and placed the frame on the nail. 'By the way before you ask us, *Khannae*, lets show him,' said Luv, extending his smart phone towards Dev and making me do the same.

Once again Dev couldn't hold his tears as we showed him a picture each on our mobiles of Luv and I putting up his photo in our respective living rooms. 'I am very fortunate,' he said almost inaudibly and very emotionally.

Rest of the evening we were all chatting about the various guests at the gathering and some of the questions posed by the anchor to Dev. Post dinner and just before it was time to leave Luv asked Dev, 'So Bhaisahab, of all the roles you did in the past and are doing now, Sales Manager, Planning and Strategy Head, Global VP, public speaker and trainer, and now writer...'

I added, 'Cricket captain, umpire, golfer...'

Luv picked up what I said with a nod, 'Yes, cricketer, umpire, golfer etcetera...What has been most fulfilling?'

Dev looked at both of us and plainly responded, 'Being a mother.'

For the first and only time that I have known, Luv was totally speechless. Nor did Sudhir or Gayatri or Bhavini say anything.

The Loveliest Bend

Nature and society have a way of making human beings irrelevant in worldly terms as they lose their work value and vitality. The sooner a person accepts this reality the easier it becomes to live with irrelevance, though accepting irrelevance does not mean cessation of *karma*. I suppose that is what Dev meant when Simrin Avasthi admiringly but somewhat cryptically remarked at the book function, 'You are always the hero, Dev, you can win from any situation!'

And Dev responded with a gentle smile, 'When you are equally happy to get defeated, life is not so bad my dear.'

Dev wasn't a defeatist, he liked to win, but he had learnt to take failures in his stride. In recent years he was living an enviable life—with sports, public speaking, travelling and now with his successful book, above all having the freedom to devote his time as he liked—yet often spoke about death. I reckon the thought of death keeps a man tranquil when he is failing and humble when he is succeeding.

I had written about the debts of a human being in the chapter 'No reason to die'; there was one debt which I thought would be best mentioned in this the last chapter. In addition to debt to the teacher, parents and Mother Earth, every person owes one more debt: that is to oneself! By living life engrossed in activities that he enjoyed, Dev was, unknowingly perhaps, repaying that debt to himself.

While his friends had planted the idea of a book in his mind, he had said to me more than once, especially when I asked him how he would feel if the book didn't do well, 'I am writing the book as much for myself, Sandeep; it would be nice if a lot of people read and like it, otherwise I would still have the satisfaction of having left behind these thoughts; Vedant and this book will remain in the world after I am gone.'

Two days after the book event, Dev left for London to spend a few weeks with Vedant. He had not met Ved for over two years. In the course of his many discussions with his son, Dev said, 'I have some pounds in my bank here from the time I was working in London, take them from me Vedant whenever you want to do your Masters or decide to buy your first flat.'

Ved looked at his father, 'No Dad, you have done enough and more for me, let me try and pay for these myself.'

Dev smiled back, 'No father can ever do enough for their child, sweetheart.'

On his return to India, Dev fell into his normal routine of giving public lectures and conducting training programmes and playing golf usually with Sudhir and me and Tank. Of course, with the success of his book, he began getting some interesting commercial offers like one of the OTT platforms approaching him for script writing! Also, as he basked in his literary accomplishment, some of his relatives and friends who had not been in touch with Dev, or vice-versa, for reasons I needn't elaborate again, had been calling on him. Dev met and spoke with all his 'long-lost' acquaintances with courtesy but could never find that old warmth in himself!

Dev and I and our friends had all reached a stage of life where we would be discussing health issues. We had all become more accepting of idiosyncrasies of our kith and kin. We would all laugh more easily. We would speak of little pleasures of life as the secret of longevity: a game of golf, eating nutritious food in moderation, light exercise, an odd drink, enjoying the company of old friends and indeed, some sex. Dev did not, but all others discussed erectile dysfunction too and laughed at how life was impacting us almost similarly.

As the weeks rolled on, I found Dev getting more and more austere in his thinking. He never had religious beliefs in any case and seemed to have rid himself of any other strong opinions and ideological tenets and status-enhancing traps and sharp ambition or bitterness that he may have carried. He recognized the power of science and technology as almost providential but used only as much technology as was necessary for him to book a cab or order food at home or do email and online banking. At a time when people have almost become slaves to their mobile phones and when computers have started asking humans whether or not they are robots, and despite what he may have experienced personally, professionally and socially, he continued to believe in the goodness of human beings; not dogmatically but in terms of always giving benefit of doubt to people around him. He had nil, well almost nil, expectations of others. I had realised fairly early in my life that it was never the man with money and estates who was the king and my association with Dev reaffirmed the view that only he or she, who had no expectation from others, was truly wealthy!

The Covid times made death so cheap; fast-paced development and resultant social transformation have made divorce commonplace; and data revolution has made life so digital, if not robotic, that it's hard to define a 'winner' in this ecosystem. And those who carry pain for a lifetime are anything but 'winners'. Yet Dev never thought of himself as a 'loser' either. He never came to terms with the idea of 'moving on' yet did not describe himself as unhappy; negative thinking and alone indeed but never unhappy. He never understood the skill of 'networking' but always had quite a few friends from whom he expected almost nothing. He roughly ran away from 'motivational speakers' but told Sudhir he felt perfectly fine in his 'uninspired state'. He was becoming more and more like plain water! All he seemed to be left with was a beating heart and harmlessness. Yet he was passionate to live and zestful about whatever he was engaged in. At the cost of repeating myself, passion is the closest synonym of life and he or she who lives without passion is like a fire that burns without warmth or light.

Golf was our newest passion, as the weather got less hot in late September, our golf rounds increased. Sudhir, Tank, Dev and I would discuss numerous topics, serious and light-hearted, as we explored the several beautiful golf courses in Delhi-NCR. We were once discussing if ours was the last generation that cared as much for our parents as for the children. Sudhir, Tank and I were of the view that our children were unlikely to be as concerned about us as we were of our parents. Dev however had a different point of view, 'I find today's generation as conscientious, if not more, as we were. They have their heart in the right place. When the time comes, they will do the best for their elders; of course, social norms keep changing and for that we mustn't bemoan the new generation.'

We had a lovely eight to ten weeks of golf and so enjoyed our banter after the game was completed usually over coffee or a beer. With Covid travel restrictions eased, we were planning a golfing holiday to Thailand in the January of 2023. We were then in the December of 2022. How I wish that time had never come.

On Thursday the 29th of December, we decided to celebrate Sudhir's birthday by playing at the fantastic Qutub Golf Course teeing off at 11 am. Sudhir used to join us for golf on weekends only but as he was on leave for the last few days of the year, he, Tank, Dev and I looked forward to our game on a beautiful Delhi winter day with the charming golden sun shining benevolently! By 10:55 am, three of us were near the starter's shed and Tank remarked, 'So unlike Dev to not reach by this time.'

We waited 10 more minutes; it was very unlike Dev to neither reach at the appointed hour nor message. I tried calling him but his mobile kept ringing.

'What should we do?' I looked at Sudhir and Tank.

'Have never known Dev to not keep the time nor inform of delay!' said Sudhir, looking a bit concerned. 'Was he in Gurgaon yesterday or Malviya Nagar?' he asked me.

'I think he was in his Gurgaon flat where he had a meeting with some OTT producer this morning; that's why we didn't come together, that gentleman was going to drop Dev here. Let me try calling Aunty.'

Dev's mother who was usually in their Malviya Nagar home picked up her phone and confirmed the same, '*Beta*, Dev has been in Gurgaon for last two days; he is supposed to come here today afternoon. He asked me to send Kundan Pal to the golf course with his golf kit by 10:30 am. I spoke to Dev last night but he didn't pick up my call this morning.'

We all thought Dev had got busy with the OTT programme producer. Tank playfully remarked as the three of us decided to start the game without our fourth friend, 'Dev is now going to become a famous content creator in the glamour world, we better get used to him not keeping time with us!'

Sudhir gently shook his head, 'Very unlike Dev, hope all is well with him.'

All was not well with Dev! As we took a break after 9 holes, I saw 2 missed calls from Dev's mother. '*Beta*, I sent Kundan Pal to Meliora Heights and he kept ringing the bell of Dev's flat but he didn't open the door. Dev's car is in the parking and the security people at gate can't confirm if he went out by another car.' I mentioned to her that Dev was supposed to come to Qutub Golf Course with someone else and he must have got delayed in that meeting. 'I am getting worried, Sandeep, can you please try and check his whereabouts?' she said very anxiously.

I called up someone else I knew in Meliora Heights and took the front gate security number from him. After a few minutes of explaining the security supervisor gave me the number of that OTT producer who visited Dev at 9:15 am that morning. I called up the gentleman and he said, 'Sir, I kept pressing the doorbell of Mr Rajvansh's flat but nobody opened the door, I tried calling him twice but the bell kept ringing. After waiting for about 10 minutes, I left.'

I enquired further how he was allowed entry into the condominium since front gate usually calls up the flat occupant; he said that when he arrived and gave his name and the flat he was visiting, the guard allowed him in. 'I suppose Mr Rajvansh would have told them earlier of my visit.'

We stopped our game there and tried calling Dev again, his mobile and landline both kept ringing. I decided to go to Meliora Heights, Sudhir said he will look up The Homeland Centre in Lodi Road where Dev was a member and used to spend time, while Tank went to his mother's home. After an hour of explaining and much persuasion, the estate office agreed to break open Dev's apartment door. I found Dev on the bed in his bedroom, absolutely still, his right hand on his chest and his left hand extended on the bed towards the mobile phone.

I called out his name loudly and then shook him, there was no response! He seemed not to be breathing. I instantly called an ambulance while the two estate office people with me called for an in-house doctor. The in-house doctor arrived in five minutes, he examined Dev and then turning towards me, said to my extreme shock and horror, 'Sir, he is no more!'

The medical staff in the ambulance arrived sometime later and confirmed what the in-house doctor had said, 'He has been dead at least 12 hours, maybe more. Seems like a heart-attack.'

I don't even want to recall how the rest of 29th December 2022 went. An absolutely shaken Sudhir reached Meliora Heights and said something to the effect that he had sent an air-ticket to Ved and he would be on his way. Tank brought Dev's mother over; she was in an inconsolable state. Dev had died all alone, evidently in his sleep.

Vedant arrived in the early hours of 31st December; clearly, if I knew anyone who could be as stoic as Dev it was his son. Ved was expressionless, his face hiding immeasurable pain. Eklavya and Poulomi had reached the evening before. Luv was as inconsolable as Dev's mother. He had barely collected himself but as soon as he saw Sudhir, who had been out organising Dev's cremation, he hugged him and both broke down. Dev's cremation was at 2 pm on the last day of 2022 at Lodi Road crematorium.

There were very few people at Dev's cremation, not more than 20, though I think a newspaper announcement had been made and of course, the information posted on WhatsApp groups. I was surprised to see Bhavini there; I had not informed her and I wondered how she got to know. She was sobbing and covered her face with a scarf as we laid Dev's body on wooden logs.

Some people announce their arrival with the sheer aura of their personality, others with their position of fame and power and still others need styled clothes and fancy cars and gadgets to make an effort to be distinctive; wrapped in a white shroud though everyone looks similar. In the crematorium there are no biases or ideologies, no richness and no intellectualization—everyone is the same, starkly and completely same. I had never seen Sudhir and Luv so devastated. I could sense how grief-stricken Bhavini was. I felt terrible about Dev's old mother and was shattered at the thought of what was going on within young Ved as he lit Dev's funeral pyre.

After the pyre had subsided, Sudhir mentioned that he and Gayatri, and Eklavya and Poulomi were taking Dev's mother to her Malviya Nagar house and be with her for a while. I saw Bhavini walking away slowly, still sobbing in her scarf.

Two persons who seemed they didn't want to leave Dev even after he was consigned to the fire were Kundan Pal Singh and Dharamveer, his driver and cook respectively. They were neither crying nor saying anything, they were just very loyal to Dev and attached to Vedant.

Ved not only looked like Dev but also spoke as gently as him, 'Sandy Uncle, would you drop me at Mom's house in Defence Colony? She wants to do a prayer for Dad.'

I drove Vedant to Meher's Defence Colony house whose location I still vaguely remembered. I had not met Meher for over 15 years and wondered what she looked like after so much time. She wasn't outside her home and coming from the cremation ground, I didn't want to go in. So, I dropped Vedant outside and solemnly told him about the last rites we had to do over the coming few days.

'Yes, Uncle,' he said, his eyes had tears in them but he was not crying. Dev was gone but his appeal was so alive.

After we had immersed Dev's ashes in the Ganga and completed the *puja* by the river side, a little bare-bodied boy extended his arm towards Vedant seeking alms. Ved looked at him compassionately and he gazed at Ved expectantly. Ved then put his hands on the little boy's slender bare shoulders and ever so tenderly smiled at him. He said nothing. The boy said nothing either, he simply withdrew his extended arm and smilingly went running away. Dev was gone but his appeal was so alive!

There were a few more people when we organised Dev's final prayer meeting in an Arya Samaj *mandir*. Three of his cousins, some of our school friends with their spouses, Dev's college and TMS friends, Bhavini and her daughter, a couple of his former colleagues, a neighbour or two, some golfing friends and a few students who Dev had taught at various institutes in and around Delhi. I thought Dev had touched many more lives, but then the world is a busy place. And death is just a song of the evening. It is a mere bend in the caravan of life that the convoy makes not of its own volition.

Dev's mother told all of us to keep coming home; she said that would make Dev very happy in whichever world he was in. Two days later Sudhir and I went to Dev's Malviya Nagar home, we asked Ved to meet us there so we could work out the inheritance details. I saw a smiling picture of Dev on the living room wall next to his father's. Sudhir and I looked at each other, little did we know six months back when we put up Dev's picture in our living rooms as a celebration of his book, that that picture would come to have connotation of mortality. Every moment that is about to occur is so uncertain.

Three weeks later, I met Sudhir and Gayatri for a coffee. When Sudhir stepped out of the restaurant to take a call, Gayatri said to me, 'I don't know if Sudhir will ever come to terms with Dev's departure, you know, Sandeep, what he said to me yesterday—he will never be able to celebrate his birthday again!'

A few days later, Luv called and gave me somewhat surprising news—Poulomi and he had decided to adopt a baby! They had completed all formalities and were going to an orphanage in Bangalore that weekend. They adopted a baby boy who was just about two years old. When I called Poulomi to congratulate her, she was so overwhelmed that she was hardly able to speak.

'What are you naming him?' I asked and all I could hear was muted sobbing.

Luv took the phone and told me Poulomi was overcome with emotion. I tried to understand her state of mind and asked Luv the same question, 'What are you going to name the child?'

In the most uncharacteristically sombre tone, Luv replied, 'Devavratt.'

Meanwhile at home, I tried to find that old picture of ours which was taken after we won that cricket final in school way back in 1980. I haven't been able to locate it yet though I know it is somewhere. In one of the trunks in the loft though my eyes fell on that stump that Dev had got for me and which I had forced him to sign. I held it in my hand and looked at it with a feeling which I find impossible to describe. Most of what was written on that wooden stump—*TAPS 1980 Cricket Winners* and *Devavratt Pratap Rajvansh*—had got smudged and was illegible. The only bit which was faintly visible was '1980' and 'Dev'! I have got that stump framed and put it up next to Dev's photo in my living room.

Dev experienced 100 years of living in his 57 years of life. As that old astrologer in Chennai had told Meher, he encountered unexpected success and unforeseen setback in life. He took both in his stride and kept adapting, kept living. He died an outwardly happy man; intrinsically, I sense, he was empty. He had let go off most beliefs and all ideology; he drew on no knowledge accumulated over his life to argue, he used it only to teach and consult; there was no ego left in him, no ecstasy or dismay, no burning desires, no expectations and no seasons. Most people remain in a state of 'becoming' till the very end, seeking some form of recognition till their last breath. Dev too remained involved in some form of professional work and passionately engrossed in his avocations till the end. However, mentally, he had moved beyond the state of 'becoming' or seeking recognition. He had gone beyond adjectives in his life and certainly in his death. He was just a silent river moving on, inevitably to meet the sea.

Dev came empty handed and departed empty handed from the world; he just left me with memories, many many memories. Through this book, I tried to relive some of them.

Main Characters

1. Devavratt Pratap Rajvansh (Dev): The protagonist
2. Eklavya Malhotra (Luv): Narrator's batchmate at MBA institute, friend of Dev and the narrator
3. Sandeep Khanna: Narrator of the story and school time friend of Dev
4. K.K. Ramkumar (Ramu), Sanjeev Agnihotri (Sanju), Tarun Mehra (Goldie), Manohar Pal Billa (Billa), Nita Rajagopalan: Dev's classmates and friends in school
5. Murari Lal Bhola, Bihari Lal Bhola, Mrs. Chopra, Miss Trehan, Shamsher Singh: Teachers in Dev and narrator's school
6. Gautam and Geeta: Children of narrator's father's cousin
7. Mohan Raj Midha (Mr Midha): Dev's maths tutor
8. Ajay Jaiswal (Jaiswal), Vikrant Rajput (Tank), Gulshandeep Singh Kohli (Gullu), Anshuman Pant (Anshu), Dhananjay Dayal (DD), Nita Rajagopalan: Dev's classmates and friends in college

9. Pranav Chaturvedi (Pracha), Rakesh Mutreja (Voltage), Jeet Tandon (Jigsaw), Simrin Avasthi (Happiness), Aakash Samarth, Sudhir Kapoor, Nita Rajagopalan, Vikrant Rajput (Tank): Dev's batchmates and friends at MBA institute
10. Dr Rajeshwar Desai, Dr Dastur, Dr Partho Lahiri, Dr Tarneja: MBA teachers at TMS
11. Muthuraman (Muthu) and Saritha: Summer trainees in Madras
12. Inderpal Singh Sodhi, Bhagatveer Bhatia, Debashish Biswas, Kamal Goswami: Senior Managers in Torsh Chemicals
13. Rohit Sahni: Dev's senior colleague and friend in Torsh Chemicals
14. Sushma Masi (and her son Kunal): Dev's Aunt's cousin sister in Lucknow
15. Arup Sanyal, Meghraj Singh, Raghunandan *ji*: Sales team members in UP in Torsh Chemicals
16. Karan Singh Varma, Howard Sadler, Adam Wouters, Zubin Tarachand: Senior managers in Hindustan Roqsanto Ltd.
17. Poulomi Sen, Gayatri Vohra and Divya: Wives of Luv, Sudhir and Sanju respectively
18. Muthuraman (Muthu) and Shaila, Shankar and Jaya: Dev's family friends in Madras

19. Raj Subramaniam, Srinivas Rangarajan, Suresh Fernandez, Prasad Shivaram, Joseph: Dev's team members in Roqsanto in southern India
20. Jerry Fraser: Director of Roqsanto Chemicals International Ltd. (RCIL)
21. Alan Mantell, Peter Van de Ven, Susan Thorpe-Jones, Craig Hughes, Wang-Yong Huang, Howard Sadler, Liam Wouters: Senior managers in RCIL and Dev's bosses at some point
22. Axel Mercier, Paul Anderson (also Dev's friend): Dev's colleagues in RCIL
23. Bhavini Narang: Dev's friend in Dubai
24. Anosh Munsherji: Head of Khodayji Dinshaji Traders Ltd.
25. Kundal Pal Singh and Dharamveer: Dev's driver and cook respectively